THE PHOENIX PROJECT

Book I: Flight

Katherine Macdonald

CHAPTER I

My name was Eve.

It was assigned to me at birth, when I was christened "the first success". Shortly after, they made a boy, Adam. Go figure.

I was fond of it to begin with. I was the first. The best. The original. I lorded myself over the other experiments, flaunting my specialness. I was such a snob, but I didn't know better, and for a long time, I didn't have anything else to cling to. My name was all I had until the others squirmed into my heart and made me who I really was.

When we escaped, I chose a new name. Ashe. It was the first real choice I'd ever had in thirteen years.

They didn't give the others names. Perhaps they had too many to name. Perhaps they only named us after a sense of pride. We were the first born. The leaders. I was the leader of the Alpha team. Adam the leader of Beta. They only brought us together to test us. To fight.

My nursery was a rectangular room with four concrete walls and no windows. Artificial light filtered from the ceiling. The room housed six beds, a trunk at the bottom of each for regulation clothing, and nothing else. The beds weren't always full, but for as long as I can remember, I shared that room with two other people. They were the only constants. Others came and left, but the three of us were always together. We made a perfect team. Eve and Alpha-2a and Alpha-2b. They were brothers, so identical that the scientists used to have to use their brands to identify them... at least at first. I always knew the difference between them, mainly because I could feel the presence of one of them inside my mind, all the time. It was stronger than a feeling, but less than a voice. It is difficult to explain; it was so much a part of me. I only knew the true weight of it when it was gone.

I didn't think there was anything unusual about it at the time. I thought it was the way we'd been designed. It was a very bad day for us when our keepers realised the connection between me and "Alpha-2a". Gabriel. Gabe. *My Gabe.*

I cannot remember how old I was when I realised that they had numbers, rather than names, or when I knew that that wasn't right. I think I asked the kind scientist about it. There was one, just for a few years. I don't remember anything about her, other than her soft voice and the fact she always said sorry when she poked us with needles.

"Why do I have a name and the others don't?"

She smiled at me, a slight laugh dancing in the corner of her mouth. I didn't know what amused her at the time. "You're special," she said, drawing back her syringe.

"They're special too."

"But you were the first."

"Adam got a name. He wasn't the first."

"Do you think they would like names?"

"I like having one."

A few days after, she gave me a book to read while she was running some tests. There were two angels in it, called Gabriel and Michael. That night, when I went back to the dormitory, I gave them their names. When we escaped, and I shredded mine, the others kept theirs. "You gave us ours," Michael said, and that was the end of the matter.

We named the others that shared our cell, as well. Archer, Forrest, Moona, Abigail, Ben. Archer died in a training accident. Forrest got sick. Moona was labelled "defective". It made me love the others more, and hate my captors. I can't remember ever wanting to be there. My training was eclipsed by a singular goal: I was getting out one day, I was taking the others with me, and I was burning our prison to the ground.

It wasn't until the accident that Gabe and I started to plan our escape. We knew we might not have much time. We were afraid of what they would do to his brother if we couldn't get out. It took weeks of careful strategising before a window of opportunity presented itself. We woke the others. We left our cell. We got to the van. The gate was open by the time the alarm sounded.

We did not burn the place to the ground. We did not all get out. Five of us left that room, and only four made it to the city.

We were on the move for twenty-four hours. At the end of that time, our captors were closing in on us. Gabe caused a distraction. I heard the gun, but I felt it too; that piece of me that was tied to him, the little part of me that I could not name, shattered in an instant. It was like being thrown into a void. I knew silence for the first time.

I led the other three to Luca, to the slum-city that skirted its borders. We knew so little of the outside world. We had been told it was a dark and dangerous place, riddled with famine and disease. They were not wrong, but it was an easy price to pay for freedom. Even in those early days, we never regretted leaving, never let ourselves for one minute pretend we were better off in a cage.

Gabe would have killed us if we had, and his memory kept us going when it would have been easier to stop.

I still think about the ones that we left, the ones that didn't escape with us, the ones that would be born afterwards. I remember a handful of others spitting off into the darkness, seizing their moment for freedom. I don't know who they were, or where they went. I know Adam wasn't among them. I remember his face as we passed his room, shaking in dismay and disappointment. He called out to me. Not to let him go, but to come back.

We never did see eye to eye.

Sometimes, I lie awake at night and think about who he fights now, and what they must do to him. Did their experiments grow with their creations? What fresh tortures did they invent? I run my fingers over the tiny pinpricks of the binary brand on my wrist, the one scar that never fades. The proof of my birth. The notion of my ownership. Mine should read something "one". What number are they at now?

I try not to think about it. It's not my fault they were left behind. It's not my fault they exist in the first place. It's somebody else's problem.

"Well, a girl's got to eat! Please don't try to do anything heroic. You're cute, I admit, but I will knock you out. And someone's gotta get your buddy out of here before those guards get up. Stay safe!"

I wish I could see his face as I bolt away from the scene, carrying a box two men struggled to carry, leaping up onto a roof, over a wall and off into the night.

Today was a good day. Nobody died, and I am unstoppable.

CHAPTER 3

I slow down a few streets later, and stop to catch my breath. The punch to the side smarts, and carrying the cargo isn't doing me any favours. Luckily, the drop-off point isn't far away. I decide to soldier through it.

Abe pays me promptly and has me load it into a van for one of his boys to take to a warehouse near the border wall into Luca. I don't ask what's inside, or why this package in particular is so popular. Partly because there's no point, and also because I'm anxious to get home and it's still quite the walk. We live at the top of this deserted building right on the outskirts of Luca's Terminal City, so far out you can see the ruins of the woodlands spilling into the concrete. It's part city, part jungle. Surrounded by rubble from some long-ago war and sitting right next to the scrap heap, it's hardly paradise, but it's a scrap of freedom we've moulded into a castle.

It takes me a long time to get home, and it feels even longer, climbing the stairs in the dark, with only the occasional flickering light to guide me. The price you pay for living so far out. But we needed the space. We needed to be close to the wilderness in case we needed to run, and despite my method of dispatching guards, we try not to draw too much attention to the whole super-powered thing. It's best to be as quiet as possible, most of the time.

Our apartment has one big open space, a bathroom, and three bedrooms. There was a hole in the roof when we first moved in, so we just slept in the big one together. We always had, after all. But when we started fixing up the place, we became a little more daring. Abi really wanted her own space and since she was the only one that had any concept of style, we let her have it. Mi was still adapting to his blindness at the time; he took one of the others so that he could have a space with nothing to bump into. Plus, he was the lightest sleeper. He needed somewhere as quiet as possible. Ben and I shared for a couple of years. He liked it that way. Didn't like being alone.

Then he grew up and wanted his own space too. Mi came up with the idea of putting a curtain across this little alcove we only really used for storage. We installed a bed there with a chest for clothes and plenty of boxes for his homemade toys. Then we all had our own space. Mine was pretty bland – especially compared to the rainbow explosion that was Abi's domain– but I enjoyed having a place of my own, four walls I could do anything with. Not that I really did. Our main room was full of paintings that Abi had rescued or created, but mine only had a handful of drawings that Ben had done at school. My favourite was the one of all four of us, labelled "my family" in his juvenile handwriting. Abi had added in a fifth figure later. I almost shed a tear when I saw it.

Throwing open the door, I dump my jacket in Abi's skilfully painted basket, and am greeted immediately by the smell of something utterly delicious. Beef stew, thick with carrots and onions, and freshly-baked bread.

Abi is sitting cross-legged on the rug by the fire, sketching away, winding her spare fingers through her great mass of wiry black curls. Back at the institute, she used to look like a ghost, a slim whisper of a thing that could blow away in the wind. Something about that place dulled her, sucked the colour from her skin, made her dark eyes hollow. But she has blossomed in this land of dirt and chaos, and the vibrant colour of her soul now spills out into everything she touches. Abi was built to be a thinker, a human computer, capable of working out every probability in an instant. Her rebellion was becoming an artist, filling her world with ideas rather than absolutes.

Mi and Ben are sitting on the mismatched sofas, a chess-board propped on a crate-table. Mi is tall and slim, as light as a feather in every touch and action. His hair is white gold, soft as a child's, and although his eyes are colourless now, I still remember them as they were before the accident, somewhere between green and gold, and almost indistinguishable from his brother's. No wonder I named them after angels.

Ben is the only one of our little family that remotely looks like me, with his tangled mop of brown hair, but his eyes are as dark as peat while mine are described as "cat like" by those trying to be nice and "snake-like" by those who are maybe a little more on the mark. They're likely a by-product of the cocktail of genes I've got sloshing about inside me. You want cat-like agility? Fine! But you may wind up with a few feline characteristics.

Mind you, I was one of the lucky ones. There were others far worse. I would not have been called a success if I'd had any other features.

Mi tuts loudly. "Where did you move?" he asks. He must know I'm standing there, but either he's thinking too hard or he doesn't want to break concentration.

"Um," Ben glances down at the board, "knight to D5?"

"Hmm. Good move." Mi stops for a minute. "You're not cheating, are you?"

"No!"

"Good, because cheating against a blind guy–"

"How could I cheat? You remember every move!"

"Aha! So you've at least *thought* about cheating–"

"Are we celebrating?" I ask Mi, the very aroma of the beef making my mouth salivate.

Mi turns his face towards me, at the same time that Ben leaps off the sofa and charges at my middle.

"Ashe!" he screams, launching his arms around me.

"Hey, bud. What's up?"

"Mi is teaching me how to play chess."

"The kid's a natural."

"We're *all* naturals," I argue. "It's a strategy game."

"True. You'll notice I didn't put him against madame, however."

"Good point." I sit down on the old, moth-eaten sofa. "What's with the beef?" I ask again, as Ben scurries back to his game. We don't often get beef here. Beef is expensive, usually only used for trading to those more elite clientele. We're more rat, hedgehog, pigeon people.

"Baz had a big order for Luca. Had a few offcuts that weren't quite good enough. Said we could have them as a treat."

"A treat? What for?"

"Apparently, it's been five years today since I became his apprentice."

Baz is the local butcher, and we owe him more than I like to admit. I made myself useful to him when we first arrived in the city, selling him whatever we caught and couldn't eat. The relationship could have ended there, but Baz has got a bit of a soft spot for kids, and he gave us more than we gave him, in those early days. Apparently, I'm the best hunter he's had in years and he was just "hedging his bets" but he didn't have to give us oil or bread. He didn't have to help us find the attic. He definitely didn't need to take the risk of hiring a blind twelve-year-old to be his apprentice.

"We've been here *five years?*" says Ben incredulously. "That's forever!"

We all smile at his definition of forever, but Abi's eyes rise across her sketchpad and lock onto mine, just for a moment. The look on Mi's face is telling, too.

Five years since we lost Gabe.

"Speaking of forever," says Abi, swiftly changing the subject, "is that stew done yet?"

Mi laughs, and bounds into the kitchen. "Give me five and lay the table."

The food is barely cooled by the time the table is laid, and is still practically scolding when we guzzle it down. There's not a scrap left for tomorrow, but Abe's payment should take care of meals for a while now. I might even be able to get us some new clothes, fix that leak, stock up on some grain for the winter, top-up our energy stores...

I look around at my family, eating dinner out of chipped bowls, laughing, not caring about their threadbare clothes or the slight leak in the ceiling. I didn't know the word "family" until we came here. I must have heard it, somewhere, when they were teaching us to read and write, but I never questioned its meaning. I didn't know what it meant.

The second I heard it, I knew what we were. It kept me sane, even when a part of that family was missing.

It was worth it, right? I ask the voice in my head, the one that isn't really there any more. *This is what you wanted, isn't it?*

It's close, Gabe. It's so close.

CHAPTER 4

Ben asks me to put him to bed. He's at this awkward stage where half the time he insists he's too old for this, and then the other half of the time he's running after me begging for a tuck in. I'm exhausted, there's a hot, dull pain in my side, and I could really do with a bath. But I say yes; I don't know how much more time I have left with him like this.

Ben is eight; he was only three when we escaped from the Institute. I carried him most of the way to Luca on my back. He has some memories from back then, some nightmares from time to time, but he's the most normal of the four of us. He doesn't have the same training, mental or physical. Together, we've taught him how to control his abilities, so as not to draw attention to himself, and how to fight, just in case we ever have to run again. But otherwise he's just like all the other kids at the local school. He tells people I'm his sister, and that our parents died when we were young. Orphans are not uncommon here, and no one questions it.

Tucking him in tonight, I remember when he came to us. We woke up in the middle of the night to the scientists wheeling in a little plastic box. We ignored it at first. We'd been taught to be wary of new things; it was invariably some kind of test. But then the box started to cry.

I looked across at Gabe in the dark, his eyes wide. He shook his head.

Don't.

The crying intensified.

We knew what babies were. We'd seen them in the wards,

on gurneys, in the labs. But the nearest we'd been to touching one was when Abi arrived several three years ago. But by then, she was already a toddler.

I don't know how long it was before I left my bunk and crept over to the plastic box. I don't think it was long. I stopped caring if it was some kind of test, if what was inside could hurt me, if it was a trick or puzzle. I had to comfort whatever sad little thing was there.

I lifted the lid. Inside was a small, round, wiggling bundle, with tufts of dark hair and even darker eyes. He looked up at me, and, for a second, his cries subsided. In that moment, something changed in me that I cannot explain, even to this day.

I brought him to my chest as the cries intensified. I had no idea how to hold him properly. He was so fidgety and floppy and loose.

"Don't cry," I whispered. "You're all right. I've got you. There there."

I do not know where these words of comfort came from, but I took him to my bed, wrapped him in my blankets (he had none) and just held him. I didn't know you were supposed to rock babies back then... I'd never seen it done before.

He fell asleep in my arms, which is where he slept almost every day for the next three years, until our escape. I cannot quite explain the terror of being his person, of worrying why they had given him to us, if they would take him away. I was absolutely sure he was some kind of test, but perhaps I passed it. Perhaps my reward was keeping him.

I'm not sure what I would have done if they had tried to pry him from my grasp. I'm fairly sure I would have killed them.

"Ashe?" Ben pulls at my sleeve. "What are you thinking about?"

I pull the blanket so far up it reaches his ears, and lean down to smush my nose against his. "Just how much I love you."

He pulls a face, and disappears under the covers. I get up and turn off the light. A little voice whispers "I love you" in the dark.

And this is why I have trouble killing people. That boy murders my stony heart.

I forget my bath for a moment, and head up to the roof. The glittering city of Luca towers in the distance, its lights stretching to the stars. It is a beautiful night, if you ignore the dogs fighting in the street below, the screeching of alley-cats, the distant jeers of some other people with some other problem. Once more, Gabe's face joins my thoughts. What would he have made of all this?

A little while later, Mi joins me on the roof, carrying a medical kit.

"You hurt?" he asks.

I half-sigh, half-laugh at him. "How do you *always* know?"

He shrugs. "Something in your voice, I guess. Broken ribs?"

"Bruised, I think."

"Can I take a look?"

"I don't know, Mi, *can you*?"

He makes a hollow, chuckling, tutting sound, his hands already moving towards my middle. He presses against them lightly, reading the slight tremor in my voice.

"Just bruised." He reaches into the kit beside him and begins smearing on a thick, cool paste. I am familiar with most of Mi's medicines by now, but this one smells different.

"New formula?" I ask.

"I'm experimenting with valerian root," he says, not that that means anything to me. Mi's herb garden is pretty much his baby, although Abi occasionally helps out if he can't identify a plant by colour or scent alone. "Let me know how it feels."

Bruised or even broken ribs never hold us up for long. I'm probably looking at about three days, and I won't even feel it after tomorrow. We're far from impervious to pain, but it doesn't seem to hold us back much, and Mi's medical skills are pretty solid. We all learned basic field skills back at the Institute, but once we got out, Mi realised we couldn't rely on any one else if we were ever seriously hurt. We wouldn't be able to afford a real doctor, and we couldn't afford the questions it would bring. Someone with real medical training was bound to notice how different we were.

So, Mi started studying, eating up whatever he could get his hands on. He practised stitches on the dead pigs Baz purchased, in the early hours of the morning, before carving them up. Real doctors were hard to come by in the slums, but apothecaries were fairly common. I'd run errands for them to bring him back fresh cuts of medicinal plants.

I was his only live patient. He's saved my life on more than one occasion.

The first time, I was about fourteen. I'd taken on a big job. Out of my league, really. Too big for one person. Mi was running support for me, of course, but I would have needed at least three people in the field to pull this off. Long story short, I didn't. I escaped the compound with a bullet to the gut. I was bleeding badly, but I couldn't afford to stop running until I lost them. I ended up in an alley, rapidly losing consciousness, the stones underneath me slick with blood.

That's when the others found me.

"We've got to get her out of here!" Abi was screaming.

"We can't move her. She'll bleed to death before we get her anywhere."

Mi's voice sounded solid and calm, but there was the slightest waver in it. I had never been able to read Mi's mind, but I felt I could then. *You can't die, do you hear me?*

Dying sounded easy at that point. Simple. Like sleep. Just a few more minutes, please...

"Ben, grab her legs. Prop them up."

I was aware of being moved, of falling further backwards. Hands, hands all around me. The pain was dulling.

How could he bring Ben here? How dare he let Ben see me like this–

I think then, that that was the moment I realised how truly terrified Mi was. I looked up at him, and, for a second, his face was crystal clear. Only it wasn't his face. It was Gabe's.

Perhaps I wanted to join him. Perhaps he was there to yell at me not to. But suddenly it was Mi's face again, then Abi's and Ben's. I was not going to leave them like he did. I was going to live.

I screamed out loud when Mi pulled the bullet from my abdomen, clutching my baby's hands. I screamed, and I knew that if I could make that much noise, I had enough fight left in me.

I was up and running again within a week. Well, maybe not running. I'm not completely superhuman, after all.

"You're thinking about him, aren't you?"

I give a little nod, before remembering that's wildly unhelpful for him, and make a short sound instead. It's all I can manage.

"The first thing I thought when Baz told me that it had been five years was, *it has been five years since I have been with my brother.* The second thought I had was how could I have forgotten the date?"

"Time moves quickly out here," I say.

"It sure feels that way, doesn't it?" He leans back against the railings. "It also feels like forever ago, doesn't it? Another lifetime."

"Almost." Gabe was not another lifetime. Gabe was this one.

"I'm never going to stop missing him," Mi continues. "But... I think... I think he'd be happy, if he knew where we were now. I think he'd be proud of us."

I think so, too.

"Do you think the others miss him?"

"Abi must. She idolised him."

"She never says anything."

"When do we?"

Gabe is an unspoken thing between Mi and myself. I think

we both still talk to him. There will be a moment when something happens that reminds us of him, and I'll look to Mi, and he will smile or stiffen, and I know he's thinking of him. Mi's never been able to read my mind in the way Gabe did, but he comes very close.

We still talk about the Institute though. Jokes, mostly. If Ben says, "This food sucks," we will always retort with, "Better than the slop they used to serve at the Institute!" We'll talk about our training (sometimes thankful for it). We'll laugh at something they never taught us.

We don't talk about the other things. The tests. The experiments. The things they made us do. We don't talk about the nightmares, other than to let Ben know we have them too, and it's OK.

Abi doesn't talk about any of it. She never speaks of it. I wonder if she likes to pretend that that was another life. I wonder if that's why she doesn't speak of Gabe.

"Do you ever wonder what would–"

"Don't," says Mi shortly.

"What?"

"Don't wonder the what ifs. You can lose yourself in those questions. Life only moves forward."

Abi's probabilities usually support one outcome. Usually. But there are always variables, and my mind always wants to calculate them.

What would have happened if Gabe survived?

I wonder what questions Mi loses himself in.

CHAPTER 5

The next morning, I get up before any of the others, grab a leftover hunk of bread and a slightly wilted apple, and head off into the wilderness to see if there is anything to be salvaged. Baz has a good buyer lined up for any deer, if I can get it, but as usual it's slim pickings. We were all taught to hunt at the Institute, although it's a different thing out in the open, and often I can come back with nothing at all despite having been at it for hours. Thieving is easier; more reliable, more money. I don't ever want to have nothing. I've seen people dying of starvation in the slums, too old, too weak, too ill and too alone to find food. Most people here are good folk, but no one is choosing a stranger over their own family. I'd rather watch a stranger die than Ben.

The others are a bit more liberal. I've often caught them giving out "leftovers" and know we won't be eating well that night. Mi is softest, and will go without entirely if it means someone will go with. That's why he's so skinny. Of course, he's at no risk of starving. None of us would ever let it happen, and he's so well-liked he'll find the favours returned a thousand times before he's at any kind of risk. Not, of course, that I don't worry about him anyway. I worry about them all. Mi brings a bit into the family with his job at the butcher's, and Abi sometimes hawks his herbs, but they would struggle to get by without me.

Which is why I have to stay as safe as possible, and not get involved with anything too risky.

After a couple of hours in the wilds, I give up with only a

rabbit to show for it. I dump the thing at Baz's before heading to the market to see what I can get with my meagre offerings. As usual, it's awash with people. When we first arrived here, I was amazed by the sheer number of them. I'd had no idea so many people could even exist in one place. It is a haze of odours, few of them pleasant, and every sense is invaded with a veneer of grit and dirt. A thousand colours coated in green and brown and grey. There was only one thing about the market particularly interesting; a mural painted on the side of one of the warehouses. It's a phoenix, a fire bird, emerging from the flames. It's the emblem of the rebellion, the aptly named Phoenix Project, a rag-tag group of misfits attempting to steal from the rich and give to the needy. They tend to work in the shadows and don't reveal their affiliations publicly, but if they die in the line of duty, their names are added to one of the phoenix's feathers.

There are a lot more names now than when I first arrived.

I once thought about joining them, when we were new to the slums. They take in lots of orphans, and we needed food and a roof over our heads desperately. But they also do dumb stuff like blow up political buildings in Luca Proper, and I could do without the publicity. Plus, it's not like they keep any of the stuff they steal and... girl's got to make a living.

I don't spend too long staring at the mural. Prices are high today and I'm not in the mood for haggling, so I just I buy some supplies for dinner and decide to call it. I'm heading out when I see Doctor Herb at the door of his surgery, turning people away.

He's not a real doctor, of course. Those are gold dust here in the slums. But he's about as good as many people can get. I've never seen him turn people away again, and one man looks like he's about to get aggressive. His shoulders are winding for a punch.

"Everything OK, Doc?"

The man clearly recognises me, because he backs down immediately and shuffles off. A couple of other customers remain, brows furrowed in confusion.

"Hmm? Ah, yes, thank you." The Doc pushes his chipped specs back up his nose, fiddling with the cuffs of his threadbare sweater. "Just... just a little short on supplies today."

His disgruntled customers begin to disperse. He nips back into his surgery, pulling out a sign and a piece of chalk. He scrawls a note quickly: *no medicine, some treatment still available.*

Doc's going to have angry customers all day, wanting things he simply does not have. Guy must be desperate.

"I can check out our herb garden, if you like?" I suggest. Doc can't offer much in return for Mi's cuttings, but it never hurts to have someone owe you a favour.

"I need more than just plants, I'm afraid," he returns. His voice is barely more than a whisper. He looks tired and grey, in need of a doctor himself. "There's been another outbreak of the pax," he says, virtually inaudibly.

Even I tense at this. Thanks to the altered DNA flowing through me, myself and my little crew appear to be immune to this particular strain. Years ago, following the wars, when mankind was already struggling to survive, the pax reared its ugly head for the first time. The disease starts off with typical flu-like symptoms, but then a purplish rash appears. Your limbs harden, your lungs turn to iron, and your body basically calcifies over a period of a couple of weeks. You feel all of it, but you won't be able to scream.

Supposedly, the pax is the reason Luca has a wall and a terminal city in the first place. The slums were where they sent the sick to die. At least, that's how it started. Then it became the place they dumped their criminals, or those too sick to work, or those they simply didn't... like to see.

Baz came from Luca. He was one of their merchants, a chef. Then he lost his hand in an accident and was suddenly deemed "unfit to work" –a crime punishable by exile. It's the most Institute thing about the outside world: only the strong can live within the sacred walls. Only it's not the strong, it's the pretty.

Lucans hate anything that doesn't fit into their concept of beauty.

Theoretically, the pax should have wiped out the world by now. It's pretty darn contagious, but luckily, only after the rash begins to spread. That usually leaves everyone with enough time to sweep off the sufferer to a distant part of the slum, where they'll die in the street, or, if they're lucky, the old community hall set up as a quasi-hospital. It's mostly run by sufferers, but those early on in the throws of the disease. No one else will risk it, apart from maybe their loved ones. Mi wanted to volunteer, but I told him someone was bound to notice his immunity at some point. We couldn't risk that kind of exposure.

"Well, that bites," I say. "Let us know if you need anything?" I offer, really hoping he doesn't.

"I thank you, Ashe, but I'm hoping... I'm sure my supplies were merely delayed."

"You were expecting something?" Proper medicine is rare in these parts. I mean, super rare. I've never seen Doc have much more than herbs, bandages, and the occasional bottle of antibiotics, which will sell for a steal to the right buyer. I've fenced a few in my time.

"Yes, I have a, er, contact..." His eyes dart somewhere behind me, and then hurriedly at the floor. I don't need to follow his gaze; I know where he was looking. Doc's friends with the Phoenix crew. No surprise, really– how else would he stay in business?

I've always thought of the members as ragged orphans, little more than pickpockets, but it occurs to me that if they manage to bomb Luca every now and again, they're probably fairly well equipped. Equipped enough to have gear, and weapons...

It's got to be a coincidence, right? There's no way that box contained medicine– which is surely in abundance in the city? It couldn't be that I'd stolen the Doc's shipment?

I'm going to regret this. "Hey, Doc, this shipment you were expecting. How big was it?"

"Um, not too big," he says absent-mindedly, trying to tidy up his chalk scrawls. "But probably in one of those new heavy anti-theft containers. There's a new drug in there that's worth a small fortune."

"Right…" I say. My insides twist. Life would be so much easier if I could rid myself of any form of guilt whatsoever.

"Why do you ask? Do you think you've seen it?"

"I just… I'll keep my eye out for it. Next time I'm running an errand."

"Thanks, Ashe. I appreciate it."

"No problem, Doc." *It really isn't.*

He gives me a watery smile, and steps back inside. I stand in the street for a few moments longer, before slowly making my way back home.

CHAPTER 6

I mean, it's not really my fault. I didn't know what the package was for. And if I hadn't shown up those Phoenix guys would probably be dead, and Doc still wouldn't have his supplies. And if, by some miracle, they'd survived and escaped with the loot, the Doc indicated it was for pax patients. They're going to die anyway.

Slowly, and in pain.

Sometimes, for fragments of seconds, I wish I'd never escaped from the Institute. Eve wouldn't have felt guilty. Eve knew only the strong survived. Eve was fearless. Ashe was weak and stupid and–

Eve was also a weapon, and I prefer being human, even when it brings conundrums like this.

I am silent for the rest of the day, casting the occasional non-committal sound in Ben's direction when he chatters non-stop about school, grunting my approval at whatever Mi has rustled up for dinner. Abi puts Ben to bed tonight; she must be able to sense something is amiss. It is only when things fall silent that Mi turns to me and asks what happened, and I spill my guts.

He listens carefully, nods attentively, and only speaks after I've finished. "So," he says, "what are you going to do?"

"What *can* I do?" I reason, "I can't exactly steal them back–"

"Do you know where they've gone?"

"Abe's warehouse. I've dropped stuff off there before. But if

I take it back, he's gonna think for sure it's me, he knows my style by now. We need his jobs–"

"So, you do nothing, and people die because of it?"

"I mean, they were going to die anyway..."

Mi lowers his eyebrows. For a blind guy, he can really stare right through you. "Have you considered a third option?"

"No, but I'm all ears."

"What if you could get someone to steal it for you?"

"Are you offering?"

Mi glares even harder. "The two guys who tried to steal it to begin with. You think they're part of Phoenix?"

"Makes the most sense, but they aren't exactly the easiest people to get hold of."

"Doc Herb knows how to find them."

I cringe guiltily. Going back to the Doc means probably admitting I was involved in the theft in the first place, and as much as I might pretend I don't care what people think about me... the Doc's an exception. I could kid myself and say it's because he's a useful ally, but at the end of the day... the Doc's a good person who thinks well of me. I don't have many of those in my life.

"Ashe?"

I get up and grab my boots before I can reconsider. "You win, Mr Conscience, you win."

Mi smiles. "Stay safe."

"Always do."

"No you don't."

Well, I always *try*. And I'm not planning on doing anything dangerous tonight, just delivering a message. They can do whatever they want with it after that point, and I won't have to be responsible.

The light is still on at the surgery when I arrive. I can see the Doc through the window. There's a net curtain for privacy but my eyes are pretty good at seeing through it. The Doc's cleaning up for the day, sterilising his instruments and... bandaging his own arm. Guess even doctors can be clumsy. I rap lightly on the door. He jumps up and scuttles towards it.

"Ashe?" he frowns. He must be used to the occasional late night visitor, in desperate need of his help. But it's never been me before. We don't get sick. He unbolts the door hurriedly. "Is everything all right?"

"Fine," I say shortly. "Do you mind if I come in?"

"Now isn't the best..." His eyes dart back to the desk. What is he hiding?

"It's about the supplies."

"Ah," he softens slightly, "Very well. Come in then."

He moves aside, and I slip in. His surgery is nothing like the ones I grew up with. Everything is worn, from the stuffing in his chair to the cracks in the plaster, and it's full of books and towels and jars of herbs. Our labs were pristine and clinical. I can tell you which one I'd prefer to be poked in, however.

"I think I know where your supplies are," I say quickly.

I wait for him to ask how, but he does not. "I see," he says. "Where?"

"A warehouse near the wall. I doubt they'll be there for much longer. I need to let your contacts know where they are, as soon as possible."

"I can pass the message on," he insists, "if you draw me a map–"

"They should probably go tonight."

"Ashe," he says softly, "I want that shipment. I really do. But I cannot give you their names, or their whereabouts."

"Then they're as good as lost."

The Doc sighs. The clock on his mantelpiece ticks loudly. "I tell you what," he starts, "there's a chance they may be by in about an hour. They said they were going to try and find me something to offer my patients. If you wait in the alley at the back... then I can say I've kept my word, but you can tell them all you know."

This is probably the best that I can hope for, although I don't relish the idea of chilling out on a rooftop for an hour, especially with no guarantees. But for some stupid reason, my conscience won't excuse me, and before I know it I'm secreted at the top of a rickety old fire escape composed almost entirely of rust.

The things I do for this city.

Years of training and biological programming have made it so I can stay focused for long periods of time, and I don't feel the effects of the cold as much as others might. Boredom, however, is an innately human quality that I haven't been able to shake, and even super-humans will get a sore butt after sitting on it for an hour with nothing to do except write out the address of Abe's warehouse.

Even at night, there's no such thing as quiet in the slums. There's always something happening, somewhere. A siren far-off, a Lucan raid. Drunken labourers stumbling about, local women of the night peddling their wares. A couple argue in the next street over. She thinks he's cheating on her. I can hear every word, if I want to. I can hear nothing, too. I have complete control of my senses. I'd go mad, otherwise. Some of the others did.

Finally, blissfully, I see two men approach the Doc's door. They look perfectly ordinary. Bundled up against the cold, but casually dressed. Not like the guys last night–

Except, they *are* the guys last night. A little harder to identify without their gear, but definitely the same two. Nick and... Pilot, was it? Great. I wonder if they'll believe my sudden change of heart?

I watch as they pass a small bundle of rags to the Doc. He looks very grateful, but I can tell by the way the package is held that not much is there. Probably just bandages, maybe some pills if he's lucky. He mutters a quick thanks, they apologise for not having much more, and the Doc's eyes glance upwards as if searching for me. Now there goes a man who can't keep a secret, but the other two don't seem to notice. They say goodbye and turn around.

I drop down several stories and land neatly in front of them. Pilot shrieks and stumbles back.

"Glad to see you back on your feet," I tease.

"You!" he hisses.

Nick is trying very hard not to grin as he pulls his comrade to his feet. "Smooth, bro."

"It's her!"

"I've got eyes."

I joked last night about him being cute, but it's more noticeable now in the lamp light, and when he's trying not to smile. He's got tousled, dark blond hair, high cheekbones and a certain... *glint* in his eye that is hard to easily define.

"Look," I interrupt, "I'm gonna level with you. I'm sorry I stole what you were trying to steal. Your need was clearly greater than mine. But I think I know where it's being kept, if you want to try and commandeer it again."

"How do we know this isn't a trap?" Pilot narrows his eyes.

"Guess you don't. But there's not really anything in it for me. And if you need the supplies so badly, you'll risk it anyway."

"Why don't you just steal it back?"

"I don't want my contact getting suspicious. It needs to be someone very clearly not me."

"And who are you, exactly?"

It's Nick this time, his head slightly tilted, staring at me like I'm some great cosmic puzzle. I can't work out if I like it or not. He's not scared of me, he's not repulsed by me. He's not creepily undressing me with his eyes. He's just... intrigued?

I've never been that fabulous at reading emotions. This was something I was tested on, at great length. I get the basics right. Motivations though, more subtle things... they allude me like smoke on water.

"I'm... just a concerned citizen, trying to get by." I reach into my jacket pocket and retrieve the folded piece of paper with the address on. I hold it out. "This is the place. Take it or leave it."

Nick reaches to take it, but Pilot grabs his arm. "I don't buy it. We should get out of here."

"Probably," Nick agrees, "but we do need those supplies. Thanks for the intel." He takes my scrap, holding my gaze as he does so. "We'll take it from here."

"You should go tonight," I advise. "My contact never keeps hot stuff around for long. Too risky."

"We'll evaluate all our options," Nick assures me. "Thank you."

I nod, not sure what else to say, and leap back onto the fire escape. I'm on the roof by the time they start to move, and quickly too. They race around the corner to an old van.

"We're going *now*?" Pilot whispers.

"You heard her. We need to act quickly. We'll radio for back-up."

"Nick, this is not how we do things!"

"I won't do anything risky."

"Like I believe that."

I didn't tell them that Abe's warehouse would be guarded by Lucans. I didn't tell them that they'd be better armed and better equipped than the first place I took them from. Unless their van was stocked with gear, they'd be going in utterly defenceless. They could be killed.

The van starts to speed off into the night, and despite my better judgement, I'm already leaping onto the next roof, following them.

CHAPTER 7

I lose track of the van at one point, once we get out of the windier streets and the roads get straighter. I'm fast –I can clock forty mile an hour at my top speed– but not for long periods and a van can top that anyway. Luckily, I know where they're heading, and no one has stormed anything by the time I show up.

Wisely, they park their van a few streets away and walk the rest of the distance. The warehouse backs onto Luca's wall. I strongly suspect it has direct access through a sewer or vent or some other backwards channel, because a lot goes in that never seems to come out, and there are a lot more guards than there should be for a mere smuggling operation. If Lucans are involved, it's about keeping us separated, and them rich.

As I anticipated, it's closely guarded. There are two at the door, and another above on a walkway, dressed in black and trying to blend in. They don't want anyone to know there's anything too important inside, but my eyes catch a couple of flashlights darting about through the windows. That's at least five, probably more. What will our interlopers' tactic be?

Their tactic appears to be to wait for back-up, another smart move. Within a few minutes, a girl arrives on a motor-bike. She's dressed like a typical lady of the night, in tight dress with fishnet stockings, but she carries herself more like a soldier. She looks a little uncomfortable in the heels. They converse quietly below me, but I can hear every word. They're wondering if they should wait for any others, but the girl –I think they call her Scarlet– says no one is close by, and time is of the essence. Nick looks at her sheepishly, glancing at her outfit.

"Plan 7?"

She sighs, but nods, and totters out of the alleyway on her ridiculous heels, a great beaming smile plastered across her face. Nick and his companion dart off in different directions.

Scarlet catches the eyes of the guards. One immediately goes for his gun, pointing it in her direction and yelling. The other holds up his arm and moves towards her, grinning. He's still telling her she needs to move away, but he doesn't see her as a threat.

This is his mistake.

Pilot kicks over a nearby bin. The guards immediately turn towards him, giving Nick enough time to sneak up behind the one with a gun and Scarlet enough time to disarm her, ahem, admirer. He's utterly bewildered when she turns the weapon on him and smashes his face with it.

Unfortunately, none of them notice the guard on the walkway until he starts shooting.

All three immediately flatten themselves against the wall. The guard rains down a hail of bullets, but there's no way he can reach them at this angle. It doesn't matter; in a matter of seconds, others will storm through the main entrance. They will be standing right in their line of fire, no more than fish in a barrel.

They are going to die, and I only have a few split seconds to alter this possibility.

Don't do it, Ashe, says the grounded, rational, cold part of me. *It's too dangerous. They should have been more careful. It's on them, it's on them...*

But they wouldn't be here if not because of me, I argue back, *and does it really matter? Will you sleep easy tonight knowing you could have saved them?*

I sigh, mentally kicking myself, and move back a few paces to give myself a running jump.

The guard is still shooting blindly, but he jerks around

when he registers my presence and fires in my direction. Bullets streak the air beside me. One catches my side, but I can't stop. My grip fastens around the muzzle of his rifle, pushing it to the ground. My other fist circles to his face. He hits the decking, and a second later I swing his weapon into his temple and down him.

Three pairs of eyes stare up at me.

Guess I'm involved now.

The shooting has alerted the other guards. There's shouting inside. Two are heading up the stairs to meet me on the walkways. More are heading for the doors. Crap. I clutch my side; at least I'm not bleeding badly, but I'll have to sweep the area for blood before I leave. This is one of the reasons I avoid dealing with Lucans; they have an actual police force. They have labs and scientists and resources. If my blood winds up on a crime scene, it's going to show some abnormalities. I don't know who that would get passed on to. I was never able to work out if the Institute was government-funded, or privately owned. I'm not sure where their links lie, and I never want to find out.

But there's no time to check for blood now. I pull a handkerchief out of my pocket and stuff it under my jacket. A temporary measure.

Two more guards burst onto the walkway. They only manage a few shots before I disarm them both. I throw their weapons down to the others. Usually I avoid guns, but this is an us-or-them situation. Scarlet didn't seem to be sporting a weapon at all, and this is turning into a bloodbath.

I duck into the warehouse.

Assuming that the walkway is probably safe from intruders, most of the guards have congregated around the entrance. It would be easy, very easy, to go back outside, grab the first guard's weapon, and finish them all in a haze of bullets. But I came here to save lives, not to end them. I don't want any blood on *my* hands tonight, even if they might be on the hands of the others. Still, I'd be a fool to drop down into the pit of guards as is. I can certainly handle four of them, but not when they're trigger-happy and I'm already injured. It's too risky.

What are my options?

I need something to distract them. Or blind them. Preferably the latter. I can't risk them opening fire. I don't have anything on me, but then it occurs to me *I am in a warehouse.*

It's a large room, with huge industrial shelves stacked to the ceiling. Crates and boxes in abundance. Somehow, I doubt they all contain medical supplies.

I leap across to the nearest shelf and tear open the first container. Some kind of tech. Useless without the skills. The next one contains assault rifles– not what I'm looking for. The explosives in the next crate might not be totally useless –although potentially lethal if I'm not careful– but the fourth is perfect.

Smoke grenades.

Not wasting any more time, I unpin one, hurl it to the ground, and watch the guards disappear under the haze. One of them lets off a string of bullets. There's a scream and one rolls out of the smoke, clutching his leg. What idiots.

I drop down into the mass and wrench a weapon out of somebody's hands. I cannot see through the smoke. I'm as blind as they are. But I can feel their presence, their movements. I've sparred with Mi many times since we escaped from the Institute. It was only fair to do it blindfolded.

Everyone is downed by the time the smoke clears and I swing open the doors. The guards outside are all out, too. Only one looks definitely dead. Nick looks across at me and smiles as he runs across the lot.

"I thought you didn't want your contact getting suspicious?"

"Trust me, this is not my style, *at all.*" I gesture to the piles of unconscious bodies. "I take it you remember what you're looking for?"

"Where are you going?"

"Checking for cameras."

There was definitely one on the walkway, and one by the door. I can easily wrench them off the walls, but by that point the feed's invariably been sent to a back-up server. I need to make sure my face isn't on anything. This isn't just about Abe figuring me out. This is about something getting back to the Institute.

A small station overhangs in a corner of the warehouse, filled with bluish light, like the sort you get from monitors. I leave Nick and the others to search for the goods and race towards the steps. A few leaps and I am up. As anticipated, it's a room full of monitors, each of them showing a different part of the base... and several are playing back my face.

There is one single, solitary guard in the room, unarmed and trembling.

"Look," I say, "you've seen me in action. Can we just cut out the part where I threaten you and remind you what you've got to live for, and you just wipe everything?"

I should probably kill him. Five years ago, I would have. He's clearly seen my face, seen my skills, and could identify me to Abe. But I'm hoping the fact I arrived with a group will throw him off if he tries to describe me, and Abe doesn't know about my abilities. As long as he doesn't see my eyes too clearly, we should be fine. I'm fairly ordinary-looking otherwise.

The guard reaches out tentatively towards the key pad. I watch him carefully, making sure he deletes everything.

"Smart man," I say approvingly.

There's a voice from outside. "We've got it!"

"If I were you, I'd let us get away before calling for back-up," I warn.

The man gulps. I take that to be a yes, and turn back to the door. I've barely stepped over the threshold before there's a hard, cold pain at the back of my head. I grab the railing, but it slips out of reach, and suddenly I'm launching towards the concrete floor below.

CHAPTER 8

"Is she still bleeding?"

"Um... no."

"Why are you saying it like that?"

"Because... there's no wound."

"No wound? She fell like thirty feet!"

"I'm telling you, there's no wound!"

I bolt upwards, cracking my head on a low metal ceiling before crashing back down. I'm in van, hurtling along a road. Panic splits through me before logic takes over. I'm not strapped down. I'm not in a cage. I'm not going back to the Institute.

"Hey, it's all right." Nick is by my side, hands up, palms facing me. He approaches me like one would an injured animal. "You're safe."

"What... what happened?"

"A guard hit you over the head with a fire extinguisher and you fell," says Scarlet.

"A fire extinguisher?" I cringe. "Oh, that's embarrassing."

"I don't know. You fell thirty feet and escaped apparently unscathed. That's pretty impressive." She pauses, as though waiting for me to chime in. "How did you manage that, exactly?"

"I'm made of diamonds and rubber," I explain. "I neither break nor bruise."

"You've been unconscious for twenty minutes."

"I was installing updates."

Twenty minutes. It's a good thing they dragged me out.

Who knows where I would be now if they hadn't?

I bet Mi is worried.

"Where are we going?"

"Back to base. We wanted to have a proper doc check you out."

"Well, that's great, but I think I'm fine. If you could just pull over–"

"You might have a concussion," says Nick. "Or internal bleeding."

"Both doubtful."

"Um... head injuries like those should take days, even weeks to recover from," says Scarlet pointedly. "You... you should not be this lucid. At all."

"Like I said, diamonds and rubber."

"And why is that, exactly?" The corner of Nick's mouth is twitching, as if he knows exactly why, or is halfway to it.

"Hmm, what d'you think, Nick?" asks Scarlet. "Mutant? Alien? Bitten by a radioactive spider?"

Nick grins at her, as if sharing some kind of private joke. "I'm thinking more *chimera*," he says.

My blood chills. Chimera. In mythology, it's a fire-breathing hybrid creature made up of multiple animals. In science, it's a single organism with more than one set of DNA. Technically, I *am* a chimera. They didn't often call us that, but the name was on all the documents. It was the Institute's full name. The Chimera Institute.

He knows. Somehow, he knows what I am.

Nick must see something in my eyes, because his grin immediately drops. "Hey, it's all right. I didn't mean anything by it–"

"Let me out," I say forcefully, "let me out *right now!*"

The van jolts to a halt. I'd barely registered we were slowing down. Pilot hisses into the back. "Well, you can get out, but you're not going anywhere, Little Miss Super-freak. You're entering a classified area."

Nick slides open the van doors. He holds out his hand. "It's not as scary as Pilot makes out." He smiles. "Promise."

I hardly need Nick's help getting out of the van, but for some reason, I take it anyway. I am lifted out into a gargantuan underground hanger. There are at least ten vehicles parked and ready, vans, trucks, range rovers, plus numerous motorcycles. Others line the walls at the side, propped up, engines exposed, being fixed and refitted and improved. There are people everywhere, moving with the same busyness and purpose as market-goers. The air is thick with fuel and engine grease, and the sounds of welding and bolting.

Scarlet grins at the look on my face. "You ain't seen nothing yet, Supergirl," she says, unloading supplies. "Come on, we'll give you the tour."

"Are we sure that's wise?" Pilot interjects. "We still have no idea who she is."

"We know she saved our asses tonight," Nick says quickly, his eyes still tight on me.

"Could be a trap. She could be a Lucan spy."

"She went to disable the cameras. Would a spy do that?"

"A clever one would, if she were trying to throw us off the scent."

"I got knocked out by a fire extinguisher," I say incredulously. "I think that counts as 'not clever'. Also, I told you to let me out. Make up your mind."

Pilot mutters something under his breath and then goes silent. Nick gestures towards a set of large, mechanical doors at the end of the hanger. "Shall we?"

I nod, and follow him into another room. It is just as large as the first, but divided into a series of pods and platforms. The light feels more natural here, and it's cleaner, but all around is steel and glass. Huge pipes and vents criss-cross the ceiling. There is a constant whir of machinery, of a thousand voices speaking at once. How big is this Phoenix Project? I'd always thought it was a bit of a rag-tag group, a few dozen, a hundred at most. This place is like a city, a mechanical warren.

"Welcome to the Phoenix Project," Nick announces. "The

dorms are that way, the mess hall's down there, engineering is at the bottom... but I think the medical bay is our first port of call."

Scarlet and Pilot follow after us, dragging the heavy supply crate. "Don't suppose Miss Super-freak would like to do the honours?" Pilot huffs.

I smirk at him, taking it from them with ease and lifting it onto my shoulder. "Where to?"

Nick laughs, mostly at Pilot, and says he'll take it from here. He pouts before heading off.

"See you around, Supergirl." Scarlet gives me a casual salute which I almost return.

"This way."

Nick takes me to the medical bay. I'm expecting something like the Institute, something dark, cold, clinical. There's a little of that; the place is mainly white and glass and metal, and stocked with the usual medical supplies, but everything is somehow... softer, as if the room itself is at ease. There're a couple of patients with minor injuries being seen to, and they're laughing and joking as they're getting stitched up. There are kids' drawings taped to one of the cupboards, books and a potted plant. I won't deny the fact that my spine clenches when I see a tray of needles, but I'm able to calm myself down. This place doesn't feel very threatening.

Nick walks me into a study off the main area, and points at a place for the crate. There's a woman sitting at the desk there, dressed in a white coat. She's pretty, brown-haired and bespectacled, a few lines of silver in her messy bun. She's slim as a rake, but there's a softness to her, especially when she turns around and sees Nick. Her face erupts into a smile.

"Oh, thank the lord," she breathes, getting up from her seat, "I was getting worried. Where have you been?"

She looks like she wants to hug him, but then she sees me standing there and stops.

"Hi, Julia," Nick says. "This is... actually, I don't know your name."

"Ashe," I tell him.

Julia stands dumbfounded. "Ashe," she repeats.

"Yeah, she helped us get the supplies back. Turns out she's incredibly handy in a fight."

Julia crosses the room, and peers at me closely. Her eyes seep into mine. "You don't say."

"She got hit on the head pretty hard, I thought we should have her checked out. Her side's cut too, but it doesn't seem to be bleeding any more."

"Hmm? Yes. Quite right."

Julia gestures towards a bed in the corner, which I hop onto without being told. The sooner I get this over with, the sooner I can go home. Julia runs a light over my eyes, and finds nothing untoward. She examines the graze at my side, cleans away the dried blood, and finds the spot almost healed. It still smarts a bit, but there's nothing she can do but slap on a bandage. Even that feels pointless to me.

"You say she got hit on the head?" she asks Nick, moving apart my hair to check.

Nick nods.

"There's no injury."

"Yeah," I tell her, "I'm pretty strong."

"But you did lose consciousness?"

"I'm not completely invulnerable," I add, a little crossly. I'm just so tired. "Shall we throw a fire extinguisher at your head, Doc, and see how you manage?"

Julia looks flabbergasted.

"She's joking," says Nick.

"How would you know?"

"I'm hopeful." He smiles at me, and then he looks back to Julia. "So, Jules, what do you think?"

Julia can barely take her eyes off me. "Where are you from, Ashe? You're... you're not from Luca, are you?"

I shake my head. "Please," I start quietly, "don't... don't tell anyone about me. I don't know what you know, but–"

"You're a chimera," Julia says promptly. "A genetically engineered superhuman, born and raised in a lab and bred to be the perfect soldier."

"How... how do you know that?"

"There have been rumours," Nick chips in, "but about five years ago, we found someone who confirmed it. A girl, a lot like you. Said she escaped from this place called the Institute, she and a couple of others."

Five years ago. So we weren't the only ones that escaped. Others did too. I wonder who?

"Did she have a name?"

Julia shakes her head. "Way I hear it, they didn't give you names."

"Not all of us," I say quietly.

This is unreal. There are more of us out there. More of us who made it out, made lives for ourselves. I feel a strange kinship with his unknown girl. I want to find her, or at least find out what happened to her.

"Were you given a name?" Julia asks.

"Yes," I tell her, "but I got rid of it once I was free of that place."

Julia nods, as if she can understand perfectly why I did that.

"Well, needless to say, I give you a clean bill of health, Ashe," she concludes. "And... don't worry. We won't tell anyone about you."

There is an almost painful earnestness to her voice. Trust is a luxury I can barely afford, but I believe her. Or I want to, which is almost as good.

"Thank you."

Nick claps his hands. "Right, well, I'll give you a lift back then."

"You can just let me go–"

"Policy, I'm afraid. Shouldn't really let non-members see where we are."

I could probably work it out even if he blindfolded me, listening to what we pass, feeling every turn and bump in the road. But there's no need to tell him this. "All right," I agree. "Thanks again, Doc."

"Just Julia, please. And... any time. If you ever need any-thing–"

"I'm pretty good at taking care of myself, but I appreciate the offer. Shall we?"

Nick leads the way back through the corridors to the hanger, and stops in front of the van we arrived in. He slides the back open. "You... you need to ride in here," he explains. "Not allowed to–"

"I get it," I snap, although I don't relish the thought of being inside a small, enclosed space.

"I promise I'm just going to–"

"Please don't make me regret helping you."

I leap into the back and slam the door shut myself. Nick exhales, almost inaudibly, and climbs into the front. The van hums into life. There's a whir and a click of the big doors open-ing, and we slide out onto a road. It's gravelly, and I catch the scent of pine. We must be near the edge of the slums.

"So," Nick sounds into the back, "whereabouts do you live?"

"Near the old wire gate, by the wildlands."

"That's far out."

"We like our privacy."

"We?"

Shoot. "I have a family, of sorts," I admit.

"Like you?"

"More or less."

All falls quiet for a moment. We hurtle along the roads, turning right at one point. Gravel turns to proper road. We're back in the city.

"I'm sorry for putting you on the spot about the chimera thing," Nick says eventually. "I didn't mean to spook you."

"I wasn't spooked," I snap.

"Unsettled then. Annoyed. Whatever. I was just... excited. You're like a real life superhero."

I chuckle hollowly. "I'm only one of those things."

"What if you could be more?"

"What?"

"What if you could be a real life, genuine superhero? Even more of a crime-fighting badass than you are now?"

"It doesn't pay the bills," I say simply.

"There's more to life than money."

"Not if we end up starving because we don't have it."

"You've seen HQ. Do any of us look starving to you? We look out for one another."

"So do we," I return. I bite my lip. "Look, you guys have got a good thing going, can't deny, and I won't get in your way. But you saw me tonight, with the cameras. I... I can't afford anything that might get me noticed. Because worse than starving would be going back *there*."

I'd die before I let them take any one of us, but I might not have that option. I might be forced to watch while they 'scrap' Mi. I'd see them dragging Abi away, turning her back into a computer. I'd watch them turn Ben into a weapon, when I had fought so hard for him to be anything but.

And what would they do to me? How much of me would survive what re-programming they certainly had in store?

"I'm sorry," says Nick eventually. His voice is tight, almost like he's seeing what I'm imagining. "I didn't think of that."

"It's all right," I tell him truthfully. "I try not to think of it either."

The rest of the ride continues in stony silence. It's uncomfortable, but something in me is a little bit fearful when it draws to a close. I did not want longer of *this*, but I am not keen to say goodbye. That's new.

Nick slows the van and turns off the engine. He leaps out and opens the back. "Is this close enough for you?"

My building towers nearby. He couldn't get much closer. The inky black sky seems voluminous tonight. I feel like I'm being swallowed.

I nod. "Thanks for the ride."

"Do you want me to walk you to your door?"

I think I'm going to miss that grin, silly and stupid though it sounds.

"Somehow," I reply, "I think I'll be fine."

He offers out his hand. "I'm Nick, by the way. I'm not sure I–"

"I know. Your buddy Pilot has a big mouth."

"That he does. It... it was nice to meet you, Ashe."

I take his hand. "It wasn't entirely horrible to be met, for a change." I pull my hand away, whisper goodbye, and don't even wait for him to climb into the van before heading inside. I'm aware that his eyes are on me, and I don't care.

I don't think I've ever made so many mistakes in a single night.

I make one more going into the flat. It's completely dark, so I naturally assume everyone is asleep, and I don't think to scan for anything out of the ordinary, to listen to where my sleeping family are, for example. I march straight into my room, pull off my jacket, and switch on the light.

Mi is sitting on my bed.

"Jesus Christ, *Michael!*" I hiss, narrowly stopping myself from screaming. "Don't sit in the dark! It's terrifying!"

"*Terrifying?*" Mi seethes. "I've been terrified for hours! Where on Earth have you been?"

I quickly fill him in on the night's escapades. He chastises me for being reckless for a while, double-checks me for injuries, and then finally calms down.

"They asked you to join?" he asks eventually.

"Yup. Guess they saw my potential."

"Well, who wouldn't? But you said no?"

"Of course I did. We can't risk that kind of exposure."

"Right. Of course. Sensible."

"Mi?"

"It's just... don't you ever wish you could do more?"

"What do you mean?"

"Is it enough, just to live out our lives like this? Don't you

49

ever wish things could be better?"

"I guess, but–" It's better than the Institute. Yes, we're often cold, and food can be a struggle, and the city is full of crime and disease, which isn't pleasant to watch even when you're immune to it. But am I willing to risk our freedom on a dream? "It's too risky."

"I know. I know it is. But I just... I wish we could do something."

"You can always join them. Be their court herbalist."

Mi sighs. "You and I both know there's a limit to what I can do."

"Mi–" I hate it when he talks like that. It's rare that he ever reminds us of his disability; it's rare that he ever shows it affecting him. He's not limited in my eyes, because there's no limit to how much I love my brother.

"But you... you've always been pretty much limitless."

I cannot think of much to say to that, so I mumble something about riskiness and tell him I'm tired.

"Just... think about it, Ashe," he says as he leaves the room. "What if these people could help us too?"

"What do you mean?"

"You always said you wanted to burn the Institute down. I hear they're pretty fond of fire."

CHAPTER 9

When we were about nine, Gabe and I discovered a small vent in our room. It was not wide enough for a person to get through, but if we tampered with the cover, angling it a certain way, we could sometimes hear our masters talking in a connected meeting room nearby.

It became a form of entertainment for us, and another one of our little secrets that we kept from the others. After lights out, we'd creep out of our beds, press our ears against it, and listen as they compared our scores from the latest tests, talked about new plans, new experiments or new developments. They compared us to other units, other individuals. Summed us up in numbers.

It wasn't always entertaining. Sometimes, you'd hear what awful things they had in store for us next, and then had to creep back to bed and pretend you'd heard nothing. I remember them discussing whether or not to scrap Moona, and how each morning after, we wondered when they were going to do it. *If* they were going to do it.

One night, some weeks after Mi's accident, Gabe and I stayed up late listening to them.

"Alpha-1, AKA Eve, is still my preferred candidate," said one. "She outperforms the others in nearly every respect. She appears to have been accepted as a leader, and she has a loyalty to the rest of her unit that is... commendable."

"It is possible, however, that she is too emotional. The recent incident with her comrade–"

"True, but paired with Adam–"

"I believe some tests are underway there, already. We have

samples from both of them?"

"Yes. I hear they are mixing well. The results look promising."

"Keep us informed. What do the psychologists say, regarding Eve? Is she loyal to us?"

"She follows orders, usually without question. There have been a few incidents; she does not like to kill. She has asked us before, '*why did you make us do that?*'"

"Was an answer given?"

"Yes. She was told that he was weak and she was strong. That that was the natural order of things. She appeared to accept that, but later responses appeared to suggest that she was questioning that logic. She responded better when told that the targets were a threat, or bad people."

"A sense of morality. How very interesting."

"Or self-preservation. It is difficult to be sure."

"Let's review the other applicants... Alpha-2A is also very promising..."

I do not know what they were comparing us for, what mission they had in store. We never stayed long enough to discover it, and this was not what we were listening for. We were waiting for them to discuss Mi.

He was the final item on their agenda. An afterthought. They spoke about him as if discussing who would be cleaning the room after they left. It was so brief. No, he didn't seem to be healing as they hoped. Bionics weren't an option. Transplants were unlikely to work with his genetic make-up.

"Well," said the Director eventually, "we'll give it another week or so, just to be sure. If nothing improves, we'll have him scrapped. A pity, it was interesting having two of them. No matter. Now, shall we–"

Beside me, Gabe fell into an utterly silent, almost invisible, dark, cold rage. He would have crushed anything in his hands to death.

We started planning our escape that night.

We didn't tell the others at first. Ben was too young to

understand, to keep a secret. Mi, we feared, might tell us not to try. That he wasn't worth it. Abi figured out what we were doing. We should have told her from the beginning, but we were scared. Perhaps she would turn us in. Perhaps the odds wouldn't support it. But she never told us those odds, and we could not have done it without her.

If we'd had more time, perhaps we could have done it better. Perhaps I could have saved everyone. Maybe Gabe wouldn't be dead.

Mi is right. We never get to know 'what if', but I cannot stop myself from wondering.

CHAPTER 10

I'm not joining the Phoenix Project. I'm not putting my family in danger. It's not worth it, not worth it.

"Are you all right?" Abi asks, looking up from her painting. We are up on the roof, and I'm pummelling our make-shift punch bag with way too much energy for this early in the morning. It spins around hopelessly on its chain. "You seem a little tense."

"Fine," I hiss, and then punch the bag so hard that the seams split and the sand begins to spill over the floor. "Dammit!"

Abi tosses me a small sewing kit.

"Wow, are you still telling me you can't actually predict the future?"

"I calculated that there was approximately a 95% chance of you splitting the bag this morning."

I unclip it from its chain, scope up what I can of the sand and funnel it back in with my hands. "That's high."

"Given the fact that your strength increases rapidly with your fury, and coupled with the bag already being damaged from–"

"OK, OK, you don't need to explain it!" I stuff the bag with a bit of foam, fold the seams back, and begin to thread the needle. This proves tricky with my current lack of patience. Abi could probably give me the odds on me doing that successfully, too. I sigh. "I ran into the Phoenix Project last night and they asked me to join."

Abi just nods. "Makes sense."

"I'm sorry, what?"

"Well, the odds of running into them at some point, given your general activities, were fairly high. Slightly lower were the odds of you revealing your abilities to them, but they were still up there. I don't even need a calculator for a brain to tell you that the odds of them *not* asking you to join after that were pretty darn slim."

"Could you have warned me?"

"Would you have changed anything based on my prediction?"

She's got me there.

"You said no, I take it?"

My silence is all the answer she needs.

"Shame."

I groan. "Not you too."

"Mi agrees with me? That's nice. I wasn't sure on that front."

"It's too risky, Abs."

"Yes, for us."

"What do you mean?"

"There are approximately eight thousand people living in the slums," she explains. "Eight thousand people living and dying in the dirt, in this city alone. Luca isn't alone in the world. Think about how many people we could help, if we put our minds to it."

"We?"

"Well, I wouldn't let you do it alone."

"It's... we'd... we'd never help that many!"

"We'd help more than four, which is all we are. That's almost a certainty."

I swallow uncomfortably.

"I know you think we're the most important things in the world, because we are, to you. But everyone else feels the same about their people."

"I know that."

"When we escaped from the Institute, there were sixty-four other children that didn't," Abi continues. "They're our people too."

I don't want to think about them. I don't want to think about the rest of Luca. I don't want to open the door to the big moral, philosophical question: *what are our lives worth?* Because I know it's selfish not to fight, and in some ways I know it's selfish to want to protect Mi, Abi and Ben, especially when two of them so clearly want to help others themselves. But I lost Gabe, *I* lost him, and there would be nothing, nothing left of me if one of them was ripped from me too.

I abandon our punch bag.

"Whatever," I tell her. "I'm going to the market. These needles are wrecked. Anything else I should pick up there?"

"You should call in on the Doc. Check he has what he needs."

I don't bother to thank her. I head down the fire escape, grab my jacket, and then spring down the outside of the building. It's still early. There's a damp mist clinging to every concrete surface, amplifying the greyness and the grime. The market is the wrong place to be going. I should head out into the woods, away from people, away from swirling thoughts of responsibility and danger. I should go and shoot something. That would make me feel better.

But sometimes I'm not even in the mood for following my own advice, so I head to the market instead.

The sharp edges of the city are sharper this morning, and everything is harder to ignore. My mind is stabbed repeatedly with a thousand images of gaunt children, the hollow eyes of starving men, the dark circles of women who have gone too long without food to feed their babies. There is a haunting eeriness to the old abandoned play park, the final solitary swing screeching in the breeze. By the side of the road sit a dozen deserted cars, picked at like carcasses. There's a whisper of another murder last night, a theft gone wrong, of course. Two kids left orphans in the process. The thief's or the victim's? Does it matter?

I tell myself this place is better than the Institute, mainly because I can leave it any time I like. Go somewhere else, just as awful, or try and make it in the woods. We could, of course. We could survive the harshness of winter. We can defend ourselves from anything out there, and we can hunt. We wouldn't starve.

These people would. These people have no choice.

It is almost a relief to get the market. It's barely open yet, but that's all right. I decide to follow Abi's advice and call in on Doc.

The Doc is actually heading out. He's loading up his bike with his medical bag, which seems a little fuller than usual... are those clothes sticking out of it? His wife is standing at the threshold, quietly sobbing. Why doesn't he go to her?

I have a terrible, sinking feeling, especially when he stops packing, and turns around to look at her. His fingers twitch. He wants to reach out and hold her... but he can't. He doesn't dare.

"Oh, Doc..." My voice slips out.

When he turns around and faces me, I see the glimmer of a rash on his neck. "Ashe," he says softly. "Thanks for the supplies, by the way. We got them this morning, but by then..." He gestures to the marks on his neck.

"This is my fault."

"You couldn't have done anything to prevent this," he says. "This was inevitable. But it's all right. I've still got a bit of time. I can help out at the infirmary before... before. And Millie here will take over the business."

In all the time I've known the Doc, I've never really spoken to his wife. I didn't know her name was Millie. I'm not even sure I know what *his* real name is.

"I... I'm sorry." What else can I say?

"It's all right, Ashe," he repeats, mounting his bicycle. His words are for himself rather than me. "It's all right..."

"It... it doesn't feel all right," I reply blankly, trying not to look his wife in the eyes. "What... what can I do?"

He smiles weakly. "In this world?" He shrugs. "Just do a little bit of good, wherever you can. That's what I've tried to do."

His wife immediately begins to wail, and her cries crawl into my bones. Suddenly, I am running. I have to get away from this *noise*, this all-consuming sound that infiltrates my very being. I try to filter it out, like they taught me back at the Institute. I focus on the beating of my heart instead, but my pulse is racing and presses against my eardrums like water in the lungs of the dying.

Doctor Herb may be right when he says I couldn't prevent this. But he could be wrong. *Don't wonder the what ifs.* I cannot save him. I cannot know if I could have saved him if I'd done something long ago, but what I can do is move forward, and try to do something good for the next person.

This doesn't sound like me, but it doesn't sound like Eve, either.

I am on top of the rooftops, heading out of the city, flying through the air and half-wishing I could just splatter on the concrete and stop feeling everything that I am feeling. But every time it rushes up to greet me, I roll against it, springing up and over and going on.

There are only a few points in the city where gravel meets road, and only two on the western side. Only one includes a right turn. I drop down the final building and sprint out of the slums, into the undergrowth, up the gravel path. It's well-maintained for a road outside of the city, or even in it. Of course, it would have to be.

I do not know how long I run for, but eventually, I see it: an abandoned railway tunnel. The entrance has been supposedly boarded up, but a quick inspection reveals the facade; a metal door underneath wooden boards.

Knocking isn't going to do the trick, but it occurs to me that an operation like theirs probably has cameras. Sure enough, I spot one squeezed in between the bricks, carefully concealed but visible to anyone with super-sight. They probably aren't going to respond to a stranger unless I do something to grab their attention. I could write "take me to your leader" in the stones, but that could be seen as a threat. Only

Nick –or possibly Scarlet or Julia– would let me in.

I pick up a stick and begin to part the gravel. The doors click open not long after I finish my message.

Get Nick.

He stands in the dark arch of the hanger, trying not to look too smug. "You really have a way of getting my attention," he says.

CHAPTER 11

"I have a few provisos," I tell Nick, as he escorts me back inside.

"Shoot."

"Anything happens to me, you protect my family."

"Standard. What else?"

The next one is a much, much bigger ask. If I was the sort to tremble, or choke, I probably would. "If... if there's ever a chance to destroy the place that made me," I start, "I want your help to do it."

Nick stops moving and stares at me.

"Only if it's safe enough," I continue, "I don't want to put anyone in unnecessary danger, but the Institute needs to go down. I don't know entirely what their long term game plan is, but I can't imagine it'll align with yours, and you'll probably end up with several superpowered allies in the process, so it's a win-win for us all."

He nods shortly, and continues moving. "All right."

"That's it?"

"Well, Rudy will have to sign off on it, but he already knows about the Chimera Institute, and it's been a target of his for years."

"Right... who's Rudy?"

"Our noble leader. Come on."

He leads me off a walkway and through the mess hall. Scarlet and Pilot are having breakfast at one of the tables.

"Hey, it's Supergirl!" Scarlet grins, looking much more comfortable in a tank to[and cargo pants. "Good to see you again."

"I have a name," I say pointedly. "It's Ashe."

"Yeah, we know. Nick won't stop talking about you."

Nick's cheeks redden. "It's been like, ten hours! I've mentioned her maybe like, twice. In passing."

"You were talking about her after she first stole the package," Pilot spits, his mouth full of porridge. "It was a bit weird, actually."

"Yeah, well... please shut up." He scratches the back of his neck, avoiding my gaze, and points to a corridor a little further on. I try to hide my smile. "It's this way."

We come to a study, a proper one, lined with books and filled with maps and papers. There's a lot of tech around too, which jars slightly with the smell of dust and paper. A huge table dominates most of the room, loaded with a full-scale hologram of Luca. This is expensive tech– I've not seen anything like it since I left the Institute.

Standing in front of the hologram is a man so large, so impressive, that my immediate thought is that he would stand a good chance in a fight against me. He is the human version of a tank; solid, muscular, heavy. He's dark, with close-cropped curls, and a prosthetic arm that far from being an exploitable weakness, looks more like he has a weapon attached to his shoulder. It's metal and completely flexible. Where on earth did he get it?

He glances up sharply as we enter and switches off the hologram. "Nick?" he says shortly.

"Bought you a new recruit, Captain. This is Ashe." He looks at me, as if asking for permission to share my history. I was expecting this, and I nod. "She's a chimera."

Rudy straightens up, coming forward to inspect me. He folds his arms. "Are you, now?" His voice is cool and measured, and gives nothing away. "I've only met one chimera before, and she didn't stay long enough for me to ask many questions. She wasn't too keen on sticking around. You are?"

"I've been here for five years," I say. "Haven't been scared off so far."

He smirks, but there's no warmth there. "Haven't come forward so far, either. What's changed?"

"My outlook."

"Is that so?" Rudy surveys me carefully. His gaze is like stone.

"She won't be staying with us," Nick adds. "She has a family."

"A family, you say? More like you?"

"Yes."

"Do they not share your change in outlook?"

"They encouraged me," I say, "but they're... a little young or otherwise... unable."

I don't like describing Mi that way, but I don't want to explain him in any more detail right now. Having one of us exposed is enough.

"Unable?" Rudy tilts his head. "Never met anyone unable before."

I glance across at Nick, hoping he will say something. "So... what would you like me to do with her?" he offers.

Rudy shrugs. "Take her to Harris. Give her an ID. Level one, of course. Then have Julia assess her. Let's find out what she can really do."

Nick looks back at me, just as perplexed. "OK," he says, "we'll get on that."

We head out, Nick quietly closing the door behind us.

"That was..." he starts.

"Intense?"

"Incredibly. He can be like that at times. His job is to distrust everyone until proven otherwise. I should have warned you."

"I'm naturally distrustful myself. I get it." I shrug, trying to loosen the weight of Rudy's glare from my shoulders. "So... who's Harris?"

CHAPTER 12

Harris is the resident tech expert. He lives in his lab in a corner of the compound– actually lives there. He has a bed set up at one end and a kitchenette in the corner. That part of the room is dotted with stale coffee cups and breadcrumbs, and the rest is a mess of wires, screens, wheels, motherboards, motors and bits of metal. The only thing that's spotless is the floor, likely because Harris is in a wheelchair and wouldn't be able to move if his messiness erupted onto the floor as well.

Harris reminds me of electricity. He speaks rapidly, his blond hair sticks out at all angles, and his fingers are constantly moving. His legs are twig-like, but his arms are trunks, covered with scorch marks and scratches. Unlike Rudy, he's incredibly excited to meet me, at least... I think he is. He gets through about twelve sentences before my ears adjust to his speed.

"So, level one?" he repeats.

"I'm sorry, what now?"

He grins. "Level one access. Standard for newcomers. Will get you in at the gates and communal areas. You'll need someone above you to get anywhere else."

"Sure."

He whizzes over to a computer and starts punching stuff in. "What's the name?"

"Ashe. With an E."

"Gotta surname that goes along with that?"

"Um..."

Here in the slums, surnames are not essential. Everything is so informal and undocumented that I've never really been asked for one. The one name has always suited me just fine.

"Not really, no."

"Another orphan, eh? Don't worry, we get a lot. Do you want to pick one?"

"I don't know. Surprise me."

He finishes inputting information into the computer and attaches something it; the card-maker, I assume. Then he pulls it out and comes racing back to my side. I'm not paying much attention; there's so much in this room to look at. Is that a mechanical arm on the table over there? One of Rudy's?

"Hold out your arm."

I hold it out, expecting him to hand me a card. Instead, I feel a sharp pain in my wrist and glance down to see the thin shaft of a needle sitting in my flesh. Panic splits through me and my limbs go everywhere at once. Things clatter to the floor. Harris skids to the back of his lab.

"Hey, hey!" Harris' eyes are wide. "I'm sorry, I didn't mean to–"

Nick stands between the two of us, but hovers closer to me. "Ashe has a thing about needles," he explains. "I'm sorry. I should have warned you–"

I stare down at my arm. There's nothing there now, not even a mark, but for a second I was back in the Institute, being pinned down, poked and prodded again and again. My breath uncoils in my chest.

"I'm all right," I tell Nick, waving his hand away. I don't want to look at Harris. I chew my next words. "Sorry for pushing you."

"Yeah," he says, his eyes still wide, "I probably should warn people before I stick 'em with needles. Lesson learned."

"I thought you were giving me an ID card."

"Those get lost," he says. "That won't. ID chip."

Like the ones they have in Luca, I realise. To get anywhere in the city, you need an ID chip. They're worth a small fortune on the black market. Something tells me this one couldn't take me in through the gate, not that I have any desire to go to that mechanical metropolis.

There's a knock at the door, and Julia arrives with a steaming mug. "Delivery!" she announces, beaming at Harris. Her eyes then fall to me. "Ashe."

"Hey. I'm back. Think I might have broken your technician though."

"Who? Harris? He's still mostly upright."

"Thanks, Jules." He wheels forward and takes the mug from her hands, then glides to the back of his lab to hide all the other cups, not particularly successfully. "You've already met our newest recruit then?"

"We met yesterday."

"Did she almost attack you, too?"

"That is my speciality." I turn to Julia. "Rudy says I'm to come to you for assessment. You can take my blood pressure, listen to my heart, ask me any questions you like, even x-ray me if you want, but you are *not* to stick any needles in me, are we clear? I've had enough of that."

Julia nods. "That's more than fair. Would you come back to the clinic?"

I'm only too happy at the moment to get away from Harris, ashamed of how I reacted. I mumble a goodbye and follow Julia out.

Back in the lab, she completes all the usual tests. She is most pleased. She asks me how fast I can run, how much weight I can carry, how long I can hold my breath underwater, what my senses are like, what my range is for each.

Nick, who has not yet found anything else to do, is very impressed. "Really? You can hear everything in a market-place?"

"More or less, if I concentrate."

"How do you not go insane?"

"I'm pretty resilient."

The truth is, we had to learn, because if we hadn't... well, the end result was a bullet, not insanity. That's what happened to Moona.

"And you can jump several stories without breaking anything?"

"Yup."

"How long would it take for a broken bone to heal?"

I haven't broken anything for years because I'm fairly indestructible, but I do know the answer. They used to test us. "Depends on the bone," I tell him. "Fingers or toes, about twenty-four hours. Femurs or bigger breaks maybe a week until we're fully up and running again."

Julia pales, perhaps realising just how I would know this. "Are your family like you?" she asks. "Do they have any additional abilities?"

"Abi is a human computer," I tell her. "And she's not as strong or fast as the rest of us. Mi is synaesthetic. Ben doesn't have anything unusual about him that we know of, but he was three when he got out and hasn't been fully tested."

"I see," Julia swallows. "It's just the four of you?"

Gabe's face flashes before me, but I manage a nod. "So... are we good here?" I ask her. "All cleared for duty?"

"Yes, quite!" She pushes her glasses up her nose and turns back to her computer. "It was good to see you again."

I look at Nick. "What now?"

"I guess I walk you to the exit," he says, "and then we'll call you when we've got a mission."

"How will you contact me?"

He reaches into his pocket and tosses a small communication device in my direction. I've used more advanced ones in training, and I know the Phoenix tech is better than this, but I guess they don't want to flaunt it to outsiders. Ones like this aren't uncommon in the slums.

"Keep it on you at all times," he suggests. "Come. I'll take you to the exit."

We don't go to the hanger. Instead, we head to a different part of the compound, another series of tunnels that require Nick's no-doubt high-level access ID. How deep and how far does this place go?

"OK, your headquarters are a *little* impressive, I admit," I tell him, as we walk along the dimly-lit tunnel. "Can you come over to our place and fix the lift? Or give us hot water? I would *kill* for hot water."

Nick chuckles. "There's showers in the dorms if you ever want to use them."

"I'll be back tomorrow."

Nick mutters something so incomprehensible and so quiet that even my super hearing can't make it out. We walk on further into the dark.

"Can I ask you a question?" he asks.

"You haven't stopped so far."

"Why Ashe with an E?"

No one has ever asked me this before, and it's funny that of all the questions he could have picked, this is the one he chose. "What?" I say, half-dumbstruck.

"You chose your own name, right? Why spell it with an E?"

"Because no one could tell me not to," I explain. "My second act of rebellion. Plus, I liked it. Made it more mine... made me more me."

Nick smiles. "For the record, I like it. Not that it matters."

It shouldn't matter, but I like him liking it. I should probably tell him this, but by the time it occurs to me to thank him, the moment has slipped away.

"We're here," Nick gestures to a ladder above us. We emerge in the basement of an abandoned building, not far from the market. I can hear the sounds of it permeating the stone.

"Got a lot of these concealed entrances?"

"A few. I'll let you know about them one day."

I tap my device and smile at him. "Call me."

CHAPTER 13

"So, I've joined the Phoenix Project, told at least three people about our background, and placed all of our lives in jeopardy," I announce over the dinner table. "Are you all happy?"

Mi and Abi both start clapping. Ben needs reminding about what the Phoenix Project is, but then quickly follows suit.

"Ashe is going to be a superhero!" he squeals.

"Not quite, buddy."

"Are you going to help people?"

"That's the plan, but–"

"That's what heroes do!" He gets up off his seat and launches himself at me. "And you're already super, so–"

Oh, this boy. Just five little words from him and already I'm turning to goo. I clutch him to me, trying to stall time. If I hold him fiercely enough, he'll never grow up. He'll remain this sweet forever.

"You are adorable, child," I say, releasing him from my grip. "Don't ever change."

"I won't," Ben promises, completely unaware that he has absolutely no choice in the matter and that change is inevitable. He skips off to his room to get ready for bed. Abi and I clear the plates wordlessly, while Mi wipes down the table. The rest of the evening ticks by. Ben reads to me, Abi sketches, Mi goes up the roof to tend to his herbs. He doesn't come back down until the other two are in bed. He's been pulling on his hair; a nervous habit. He's not as still as he usually is when he sits down beside me.

"So, when do I sign up?" he asks.

"For what?"

"I want to join the Phoenix Project, of course."

"You?" Abi had expressed an interest, but I'd ignored it. She's too young to be putting her life on the line.

"You said they have a doctor," Mi continues, "a *real* doctor. I want to ask if she'll train me."

I have never, ever asked Mi what he really wanted to be, if he could be anything. We've never had much of a choice. But *of course* Mi wants to be a doctor. He'd be perfect.

Then I think about Rudy, asking if my family shared my outlook. Does that mean that he'd welcome them? He was clearly suspicious of me. Does it look worse, showing up on day two with new recruits?

"Mi..." I start carefully.

"Don't."

"Don't... what?"

"Whatever you're going to say about it not being safe, or someone needs to be here for the kids, or *whatever* excuse you're going to come up with. I don't want to hear it."

Mi's knuckles are white, his fingers pulled into fists. He does not sound like himself. He sounds... he sounds like Gabe, coiled up with rage.

"I wasn't–"

"You don't see it! You haven't seen it! But all this time we've been here, *all these years,* I've heard every cry and every scream of every person you told us we couldn't help! And I know you've had this sudden change of heart, which is great for you but not for me!"

"Mi–"

"I need to do something! I need to make up for..."

"For what? You haven't done a thing wrong in your life!"

"Not a thing wrong?" Mi laughs hollowly. "I killed my brother."

Not that, not this. Anything but this. How long has Mi felt this way? Why didn't he tell me? Is this why... is this why we never speak of him?

"No, oh no, Michael... it wasn't your fault. It wasn't *any-one's* fault."

"It doesn't matter. It was because of me, don't you see?"

"Or me," I whisper, my throat tight. "I could have been the one to cause the distraction. If I'd thought of it, like a leader—"

"We needed you more. Gabe knew that. But me... I was expendable."

I am not going to cry in front of him. I'm not. I manage to keep the tears back, but my fist is another matter. It hits Mi so fiercely that it knocks him straight to the floor. I stand over him, holding myself back.

"You are not expendable to *me*," I hiss. "I love you. We love you! You must know that?"

Mi sits up, clutching his jaw. "I know, of course I know that! And I love you too, to pieces. But not like you loved Gabe. You would have been happier, if he'd have lived, and I had died instead."

I don't know if I believe this. Life without Mi? Unthink-able. I've never lost myself in *that* "what if?" I think what he's trying to say is that I wouldn't be so closed-off, that I might be... less empty, had that particular piece of me not been torn away. But I don't want to imagine life without Mi.

"I'm not sure if that's true," I say quietly, "but I truly, hon-estly, genuinely believe... that this world is a better place for having *you* in it."

Gabe was too much like me. Too suspicious, distrustful, too quick to anger. The world does not need more of me.

I sink to the floor beside Mi, flexing my hand. He leans out to take it, massaging the fist that punched him mere moments ago.

"Then let me help it," Mi begs. "Let me make something worthwhile come of my brother's sacrifice."

"All right," I concede. "Just... just give me a few days to get a feel of the place first. The leader doesn't like me much."

Mi groans. "What did you do?"

"Nothing! For once!"

He does not look particularly convinced. "You aren't just trying to buy time are you? To find another excuse to keep me away?"

"No. I promise you. No more excuses."

"What... what changed your mind, in the end?" he asks.

He's smiling now, which makes my stomach clench. He's not heard the news. I had forgotten to mention it.

I take a deep breath, and tell him about Doctor Herb.

CHAPTER 14

Two days later, I decide to bite the bullet and go and see Abe for another job. I don't want him getting suspicious about the warehouse incident. My absence will speak louder than my presence.

As anticipated, Abe is in a terrible mood. He doesn't mention anything about the warehouse, but he snaps that he's got nothing going and to come back in a week. It's the longest time I've gone without a job from him in a while, but I'm relieved to be out of there. I head to the market to look at the notice board, to see if anyone's got an errand I could run. There's nothing that suits; plenty of stuff I could do, but too easily. I grudgingly leave those for someone who needs them more.

My feet take me in the direction of the phoenix mural. I didn't tell Nick, when he asked, the entire truth about my name. I chose it the day we first arrived in Luca. We were ragged, half-starved, exhausted, aching, and broken beyond measure. We were all so choked up with grief it's a wonder we could even breathe. I thought life would just slip out of me. Surely, without Gabe by my side, I couldn't live. He was the skin of my soul. He held all of me together.

And yet, air still filled my lungs. Blood still pumped around my body. It might have felt like I died with him, but I was still standing. Standing before an enormous fire bird, with the words emblazoned on the brick above it, "we will rise from the ashes".

I wanted to rise. I wanted to be reborn. Ashe rose from Eve.

I didn't want to credit the Phoenix Project with inspiring my name. It felt a bit too sappy. Nick might have said it was fate, and I hate that. Nobody is pushing me in any direction but me.

I'm still standing at the wall when a van screeches round the corner, crashing into one of the stalls. It's a sleek, pristine thing. Not one of Phoenix's, not one of any of ours.

Oh, oh no...

Soldiers pour out the front, dressed in protective gear and heavily armed. The back of the van is wrenched open, and three bedraggled people are yanked out. They are dishevelled, and covered in a blotchy, purple rash.

Late-stage pax patients.

I don't know how they managed to stay hidden for so long. I don't know what they were hoping to do, but I do know that something very, very bad is going to happen.

The patients lie there in the dirt, too fearful or too sick to move; it's impossible to tell. One of the soldiers decides this isn't good enough. He starts to shoot.

If he wanted them dead, they would be, but he fires deliberately at the ground, causing them to scatter like marbles.

The crowd goes wild.

Within seconds, absolute pandemonium has obliterated the morning. People are screaming, moving in every direction. Stalls are torn down. Bullets are firing. Bodies hit the floor. Blood explodes in the air. It worms its way into my nostrils.

This is not the first time something like this has happened, and I have already shot up a building to escape the madness. Usually when there's a raid, I just run. As long as Mi and Abi and Ben are safe, I don't stick around.

But not any more.

Do I try to take out the soldiers? There are five of them, keeping close together, all armed, geared up, and clearly well-trained. I would struggle to take out all of them without risking injury, and I'd have to kill them. I couldn't risk them reporting back. No, taking them out is too risky, especially as I'm alone–

But I'm *not* alone, am I? I snatch the device from my back pocket and press down the button. The radio hums into life.

"Hello?" says a voice on the other end.

"There's a raid at the market!" I rush. "Five heavily armed soldiers. One van. They've released three pax patients and are firing on the crowd–"

There is an eruption behind me. A building is on fire. An abandoned one, I think, but cinder and smoke stream out onto the pavement. Fire spits into the sky, towards the neighbouring building...

Oh God. The School. Abi. *Ben.*

I shove the device away and vault down the side of the building, rolling onto the ground below and sprinting towards the school. The roof is on fire. A corner of it has been struck by debris–

No, no, no–

Kids are pouring out of the building, most white-faced but unhurt, a few coughing and covered in soot. Several are screaming, sobbing, shrieking. None of those could be Abi or Ben, they're both too tough. I check the silent ones, seizing their faces and almost shoving them away. Some parents have already arrived. I pass them over, moving further and further towards the building.

"Mrs Brook!" I spot Ben's teacher. "Mrs Brook! Where's Ben?"

"He... he was right behind me..." Her face is white. "I swear he was–"

"Ashe!"

It's Abi. She's fine, not even dusted in ash. We clutch each other tightly, briefly.

"I can't find Ben–"

I nod, and we are both already moving into the building. We call his name. No reply. This should not shock us too much; Ben has never learnt to focus or filter out sounds as well as the rest of us. He probably just can't hear us over the screaming and the flames.

We split. I take the corridor closest to the chaos, towards the fire. Ben is small, Ben is smart. He knows what to do if he's stuck and can't get out. He's safe, he's safe, he has to be.

"Ben!" I call out. "*Ben!*"

I switch my filters on. It's hard to do when I'm so close to panicking. For a moment, all I can hear is my heart pounding in my ears. It might as well be a siren. I pluck it out and shelve it, I turn off every sound I can. There is no screaming, no crying, no crackling of fire. There is only the sound of breathing.

I follow it, still calling, and am rewarded when I hear a tiny voice.

"Ashe! I'm here!"

He's half under a wall, a huge metal beam crushed against his back. For a moment, I think he's trapped –why else would he be there?– but then I realise he's holding it up. I scream for Abi, hurtle forwards, and ram myself underneath it instead. Ben rolls away. I keep lifting, as hard and as quickly as I can, because I understand immediately what Ben was trying to do; he was trying to save the three kids trapped on the other side.

Abi appears, shouldering the weight with me. Together, we heave it upwards. Ben pulls out the other three from the debris. Some of them are bigger than him.

"Get them out!" I yell.

It's not just the metal beam we're holding at this point. It's practically the whole damn building.

I wait until the four of them are well clear before nodding at Abi. We drop it and race back to the entrance. Mercifully, the whole building doesn't collapse, but shrivels inwardly like a dying spider.

Outside, the three other kids are safely installed in the arms of their families, and I immediately haul Ben into mine. I want to scream at him for being so reckless, but I can't. It's all I can do to stop myself from sobbing. Abi hovers close by and I pull her down too, and then we hear another voice, calling all our names so quickly they seem to slide into one.

"Ashe, Ben, Abi!"

It's Mi, slithering through the crowd, hands outstretched, searching for us. We've barely had time to open our arms before he collides into them, and we crash to the ground, a huge mass of limbs and tears.

"Is anyone hurt?" he asks.

"I'm fine, Abi's fine," I rattle. "Ben?"

"My back's a bit sore."

"He was holding up a building, Mi," Abi gushes. "It was the bravest thing I've ever seen."

I ruffle his hair, wiping my nose on my sleeve. "It was the dumbest thing I've ever seen. Don't risk your life again, bud. Come and find me and I'll put mine on the line instead."

"Thanks for coming to get me."

"You know I always will."

The sounds of screaming have dissipated. I listen closely; there's no more gunfire, and the van is gone from the marketplace. I touch Mi's arm.

"Look after them," I tell him. "I have to go check on something."

I disentangle myself from Abi and Ben and head back to the square. It is a gutted thing. Not a single awning is still standing. Food is strewn across the floor. Fruit flesh lies in the gutter, sponging up the blood. There are several dead, more wounded. I spot Julia moving among them, helping them towards a not ill-equipped medical van. Millie comes out of her clinic, offering blankets and bandages. The people are being fixed, but there's little to be salvaged from the wasted food, the ruined wares. Lifelines.

Scarlet and Pilot move those who are beyond medical care to the side of the market. Already people are coming forward to claim them. A tiny child sits beside the body of one man. Please God, let her have a mother. Don't let her be alone in this world.

One body lies completely ignored in the centre of square; one of the pax victims. No one is fully sure how long it takes for an infected body to be safe to handle once deceased, and no one is keen to find out. Being immune, I could just pick him straight up, but I don't want people to panic. I yank a ruined tarp out and wrap it around his body before moving him to the side. No one will weep over him. No one will claim him. His family, if he had one, will never get to bury him.

Scarlet and I lock eyes. "One of the pax victims," I tell her, assuming by now everyone knows how this whole thing began. "There were two more–"

"One safely escorted to the infirmary, another in the wind," she tells me. "I imagine she's holed up somewhere, terrified. People are out searching now. Good people."

People who won't just gun her down.

Finally, I spot Nick. He's administering first aid to an old woman. He looks up before I'm at his side, as if he can sense me approaching.

"Ashe–" he stands up.

"Tell me we're going to do something," I demand, "Tell me there is a plan to get back at them for this, that we're not just going to let them–"

"There is," he says. "Or there will be."

"Let me be a part of it."

He nods, not even bothering to say he'll have to ask Rudy or anything like that. He must be able to feel the fury radiating from me.

"Are you all right?" he asks instead.

"They attacked the *school*," I hiss. "My kid was in there–"

"Your kid?"

"My... Ben. He's... he's not my baby, not really. He's just a kid and he's *mine.* Those bastards could have killed him today."

"Ashe is very protective," Mi materialises at my side. "You should have seen what she did to the guy who–"

"You're supposed to be looking after Ben and Abi!"

"They're fine, I gave Ben the once-over. Figured I could do more good here."

"Fine," I say through gritted teeth, "Nick, this is Michael. Mi. He's basically my brother. Mi, this is Nick."

Mi reaches out to shake his hand. "Nice to meet you. Is there a doctor here I can lend my services to?"

"Um, sure... do you need any help finding her?"

"Nah, just tell me what she looks like."

Nick blinks incredulously.

"He's joking, he does that," I explain. "He enjoys making people uncomfortable. She's at your three o'clock, Mi. Twenty feet."

Mi mutters his thanks and wanders off, leaving me alone with Nick. The devastation swells behind him. So much ruin.

"Why do they do things like this?" My voice is a lot softer than I'm used to, a lot more helpless.

Nick sighs. "To remind us that we're not really free. That they have more power. And to curb our population. Our numbers have been getting a bit high lately. They don't like it."

What had Abi said? That there were eight thousand people, living here? And Luca wasn't alone in the world. There were other glittering cities and their terminal city slums. We could get to another one, if we wanted, if we could steal the fuel or find a mode of transport that didn't need it. Another eight thousand a few miles away. An army, if we mobilised.

I wonder if any other cities got hit today.

"Ashe?" Nick reaches out, his fingers stretching towards me. He doesn't quite make contact. "What are you thinking about?"

I turn my thoughts back to the issues at hand. "I'm thinking there's a lot to be done," I tell him. "And this place isn't going to clear itself."

CHAPTER 15

I've never helped clean up after a raid. I stay wide clear of any affected area, as if it is infectious. I might run supplies for people who ask, but I've never helped move away the wreckage. I've never boarded up shop windows. I've never prepared a body for burial.

We do this first, digging the graves far out of town and transporting the bodies in the vans. No one will touch the pax victim but me. Even Nick seems cautious.

"You should be careful," he says, when he sees me heading towards him. "He might still be–"

"I'm immune," I say sharply.

Nick's brow furrows. "No one's immune to the pax."

"A happy by-product of my spliced genes," I explain. "Too much cat in me."

"Did... did anyone use you to engineer a cure?"

"No, funnily enough, in the thirteen years they had of cutting me open, they never thought of that!"

"Sorry," Nick says. "I just–"

"It's fine. I get the curiosity. Yes, they tried, but they could never create a vaccine, or a cure. We're only immune because of our genetic make-up, which is pretty darn hard to replicate."

Nick falls quiet, but he helps me unload the victim, very carefully. We place him next to the others in a mass grave. A few family members have brought down trinkets to be buried with them. Someone scatters them with petals. A priest of a kind arrives to say a few words.

I have never been to a funeral, and my immediate thought

is that I would be quite happy never to go to another. The grief in the air is palpable, a thick miasma of misery. It is far more catching than the pax. I did not know these people, but I mourn them. I stand by Nick's side as the dirt is piled, and I almost want to take his hand. It feels a little like I'm falling.

He, I think, has been to a few. There is a stalwartness in his shoulders, a tightness in his cheeks. He is someone who has learned how to look, how to behave, but his eyes brim nonetheless. His body betrays him, as does mine.

After the dead are taken care of, we return to the square and sort through the debris. A lot of young people, some children even, help to sort what can be salvaged. Someone from Phoenix tries to work out what belongs to who. The awnings are pulled out of the wreckage, at which point a flock of old folk appear out of nowhere, armed with needles and thread. They take them to the side, sit down for the long haul, and stitch what can be stitched.

I work tirelessly. Others come and go, but I do not stop. I don't need to. I board a dozen windows, fix a dozen stalls. I carry boxes, load vans, fetch and take supplies. As long as I work, I don't think. I'm less angry.

"Here," Nick pushes a hot bowl into my hand. "You should eat."

"I'm not hungry."

"You've not eaten all day."

"It's only–"

I stop. The skies are darkening. Daylight has almost faded entirely. I've worked away the entire day.Nick smiles wearily. "You've done all you can today. Sit down for a moment. Let me look at your hands."   "My hands?"

It takes me a minute to realise what he means, but they are red, raw and blistering. It'll heal quickly, of course, but they're still a mess now.

Nick directs me to upturned crate and I slurp a couple of mouthfuls of the lukewarm, flavourless broth, while he goes to fetch something. The food is unappetising, but welcome nonetheless. I hadn't realised how hungry I was. My stomach rumbles and unfurls.

"How can someone not realise they're hungry?" Nick chuckles, returning to my side. He pries one of my hands away from the bowl. "Or hurt?"

"I'm very good at compartmentalising," I explain. "Focusing. Filtering everything else out. I'd go mad otherwise, everything I can hear and smell and see."

He spills a cold, stinging liquid over my cuts. It's like sticking your hands in fire. "Ow, ow, ouchie!"

Nick splutters with laughter. "I'm sorry, did the big, tough, badass superhero just say *ouchie?*"

"I wasn't expecting that!"

"Just... filter it out!"

I stretch my hand out in front of me, and fix my thoughts on the skyline instead. I think about other parts of my body; my ears, my toes, the tip of my nose. I draw the focus away, and the pain dissipates. Nick starts on the other hand and I feel almost nothing.

"What's it like, feeling as much as you do?" he asks, as he slowly cleans away the dirt and grime.

No one has ever asked me that, not unless it was part of some experiment.

"It's... overwhelming," I tell Nick quietly. "Or it can be, if I don't keep a lid on it. It was awful when I was little. At times..." At times, it got so bad that I wanted to claw it out of my brain, or crawl out of my body. I didn't want to be me any more. I didn't know what I was, or what I was supposed to be, but I didn't want to be either. I wanted to slither away, slide out my skin. Stop seeing, hearing, feeling, thinking.

"But would you trade it?" he asks.

"For what?"

"For a chance to be ordinary?"

No. Of course not. Not here. I need my abilities. They're my armour. "Here?" I ask.

"Anywhere. If you could trade your abilities and live in

Luca, and never have to worry about anything ever again...
would you?"

But I wouldn't be me, and that's not what I want any more.

"No."

"No? Just like that?"

"I can't imagine me in any other shape but this," I explain.
"However easy it might be to be otherwise."

Nick finishes with the gauze. "Strange, isn't it, how we
cling to our troubles?"

"Maybe we just like the fight."

He reaches down for some bandages.

"You won't need those," I tell him. "It's a waste. I heal too
quickly."

"Won't it hurt, to have them exposed?"

"I'll manage."

His hands are still cupping mine. "Ashe?"

"Yes?"

He coughs suddenly. "Never mind," he says, straightening
up. "It's pretty much dark now. We should head home for the
night."

"Need me to walk you back to your car?"

He smiles wryly. "I'll manage."

CHAPTER 16

Ben sleeps with me that night, bunched under the covers, smaller than he has looked in a long time. Usually I quite like a snuggle with my boy, but the whole night is a struggle. I wake several times with his elbow in my eye.

Morning comes creeping in like a fog. We are all up the moment the sun slithers over the slums, none of us having slept well. We eat in almost silence. It goes without saying that there's no school today, but plenty to be done.

"I want to go the Phoenix headquarters," says Abi. "I want to see what I can do to help."

"Me too!" Ben chimes.

I nod solemnly. I may want to keep them out of there, I may want to keep them safe, locked up here in our crumbling concrete tower, but if yesterday showed me anything, it was that no where is safe. They will feel safer helping. Like I did.

Mi clears his throat. "Well, you know where I stand on the subject."

"I know. Let's clean up and head out."

The walk towards the market place takes forever. People are already back out, continuing with the work we started yesterday. The devastation spread far. Half of the school is little more than a blackened hull, the building next to it a pile of rubble. The school will be rebuilt, eventually. The building will be used for parts, or left to crumble into nothing.

I'm not entirely sure how to get back to Phoenix HQ. The back entrance is a bit far away for everyone else, so I'm thinking of the secret entrance, although my level one clearance is unlikely to get me very far. Luckily –or unluckily– I see Pilot assisting with the erection of a rebuilt stall.

"Hey," I say.

Pilot groans. "Oh, it's you."

It's a step up from 'super-freak.'

"My family wants to sign up."

"Your family?" His brow crinkles as he takes us all in. We couldn't be less alike. "Right. Your fellow... um..."

"You can call us chimeras, if it helps," says Abi pointedly.

"Yeah, sure. Well, Nick isn't here–"

"But I am!"

Scarlet appears, lugging a tool kit. She smiles at us, with far more cheer than a morning like this should really warrant. Her short hair sticks out like the petals of a daisy.

"Your family, huh?" she grins. "Nice to meet y'all. You lookin' to sign up?"

"Who's speaking?" Mi whispers to me, not particularly quietly, "She sounds pretty. Is she pretty?"

"Too pretty for you."

Scarlet laughs. "Name's Scarlet, and I'm sure if Ashe and I had talked a little more, she'd have told me a lot about you."

Names and pleasantries are exchanged, and she agrees to take us to HQ. We walk down to the secret entrance together.

"Fascinating," Abi comments. "These tunnels must be part of an old railway line. You added the entrances yourself?"

Scarlet nods. "In days gone by, they led all the way to Luca, but they're fully blocked up now. Believe me, we tried. We do not have the resources to dig through them again."

I know that the whole aim of the Phoenix Project is to make the world better, but I can't help but wonder how they hope to achieve that in the long run. What would they do, if they could tunnel into Luca? Would they burn the place down, like I said I would the Institute? Or are there things in the city worth saving?

Abi asks lots of questions as we walk, mostly about the construction and maintenance of the tunnels, how they've been lit, how long they've been using them etc. Ben holds my hand and asks if we're there yet. He's not too keen on the dark. Before long, we arrive at the main door; Scarlet swipes her wrist under a scanner, which leads to another slew of questions from Abi. Ben gasps when we enter the main arena.

"It's so *big*!"

"Hmm, bit bright for my tastes," Mi says.

Abi elbows him in the side.

Scarlet leads us into the mess hall, where she locates Rudy and introduces us.

"Ah, your family came around to your outlook, then?" Rudy raises an eyebrow. "How fortunate."

"Yesterday put a lot of things in perspective," I say stonily. "And believe me, they have things to offer."

He glances at Mi. "I heard about you from Dr Thorne. She seemed quite impressed with you yesterday."

"I was glad to be able to help," Mi responds, holding out his hand, "and I am keen to do so again."

"Is that so?" Rudy takes his hand, the cold metal fingers gripping Mi's thin fleshy ones.

"Nice prosthetic," Mi says. "Whole arm?"

"You can tell?"

"I can hear it. It goes all the way up to your shoulder?"

Rudy's is wearing a jacket; it is impossible to tell from looking alone. Sometimes, I will close my eyes and try to imagine what it's like, to live with Mi's senses. My hearing is exceptional, but even I couldn't make that out.

"Impressive," Rudy says, with a fraction of genuine admiration. "Well, you better get down to Harris, and then run along to Dr Thorne's. She is a very willing teacher."

"I'd like to help too," Abi says.

Rudy did not second-guess Mi when he saw that he was blind, but he does a slight double-take with Abi. I'm not sure if it's her age, her paint-splattered dress, or her wild curls stuck with a pencil.

"Oh? And what's your particular skill set?"

"I have a computer for a brain."

He raises his eyebrow further. "1422 divided by 73?"

"19.4794–"

"OK, we'll assume that's right. Probability of it raining tomorrow?"

"Forty-three percent."

"Time it will take to get the market square back to normal?"

"Ten-point-four working hours until normal function can resume, based on past data and current manpower. I would need more information as the definition of 'normal' in order to–"

"All right, final question. What's the likelihood of one of you being some kind of spy?"

Abi blinks at him. I keep expecting her to answer –I would just say zero percent– but she's too stunned. Scarlet looks at Rudy, aghast.

"Scarlet, could you take everyone to Harris, please?" I ask, as calmly as I can. Scarlet nods, looking happy to be free of the situation. I wait until they've disappeared down the hall.

"What the hell do you have against me and my family?" I spit.

"I don't know you, or them."

"So where do you get off on–"

"I've heard rumours about the place you came from. I think that sort of place could do things to a person. And I think it's strange you've been here so long and have only just decided to join, and that, one day later, there's a raid."

"If you think we had anything to do with that–"

"I don't know what to think."

"There's no way I would be in league with the Lucans. *No way.* They're as bad as the Institute. They'd rather people like Mi were dead. They attacked my family, and they are going to pay."

"Tough words for a rookie."

"I think it's pretty well established that I've always been tough," I hiss. "You better pray you don't get in my way."

CHAPTER 17

By the time I get to Harris, Abi and Mi have already been given their passes, thankfully with more warning than I got. Harris declines, sensibly, to give Ben one, especially since he won't be staying at the base and shouldn't need access. The engineer is incredibly fascinated by Abi, and is asking her more questions than she did in the tunnel. She is equally curious about what he does. I can sense they're going to get along.

Scarlet takes Mi to the clinic, and Ben goes with them. I ask him to get Julia to give him a check-up. He seems fine, just a little bruised, but I don't want to take chances. I wander back to the mess hall, searching for something to do. The place is largely empty except for the younger members. I guess most people are still out searching for the missing pax victim or cleaning up the city. I find someone with access and head to the garage to help with loading up vans and sorting out supplies. I wish Nick were here.

Things get a little busier around lunchtime, when people trickle into the mess hall for food, and my family materialises again. Ben has apparently been helping Julia organise her lab and has received an apple for his efforts. Abi has been assisting Harris with certain 'algorithms' and other words I don't know. Mi is so enamoured with Julia already, I half expect him to declare he's moving in. Julia smiles as she thanks her, assuring him that she's grateful to have such an obliging pupil.

When the others move away to clear their plates, she turns to me. There are dark circles under her eyes, and a weight to the sallowness of her skin.

"I hope they've not been a handful," I say.

"Not at all," she replies. "I meant what I said; Mi is an excellent pupil. I think he'll be a great asset."

"But Ben?"

She chuckles. "He is a little enthusiastic."

"Sorry about that."

"Don't be. He's sweet. You've done so well with him."

Before I can ask what she means, the others return, but quickly depart. Scarlet is going to give them a tour. I already have my bearings and decline to join. Julia asks to run a few more non-invasive tests. She wants to measure my speed, strength, accuracy. These are the kind of tests I actually enjoy. It's like a competition, one I know I'll win. We head to the gym rather than her lab.

There were a few places in the Institute I actually had fond memories of. One of them was the gym. I loved training. I loved testing myself. I loved fighting. And unlike when they'd let us lose in the woods surrounding the compound, things were controlled there. No one ever made me kill anything in the gym.

Julia measures numerous things, and I surpass her expectations in each. I even surpass my own. I remember every one of my personal bests from my time in the Institute, and I've gotten better since then. After about an hour of running, jumping, punching and climbing, I sit down and Julia hands me a glass of water while she ticks off things on her clipboard.

"Does it bother him?" she asks suddenly.

"Bother who?"

"Michael. Mi. Does it bother him, being... you know?"

I swallow, remember Mi's words. *I was expendable.* "More than he will admit," I tell her.

"I'm surprised they couldn't fix him."

"They tried. At first, they hoped that time would heal him. Most of us heal super quickly as it is. When it didn't, they tried other things–"

"A transplant?"

I shook my head. "They considered it, but they couldn't

get a precise match. We're too unique. His body would have rejected it."

I leave out the part of this story when Gabe begged them to take one of his eyes. I can still remember the exact sound of his fists hammering against the door. Mi was crying in the corner of the room in Abi and Ben's arms, and I stood between him and his brother, wondering who I should go to, and why they wouldn't consider it. One eye is a lot easier to adapt to than none.

"We escaped because they wanted to shred him," I tell Julia, instead of telling her about Gabe. The entire story rushes out of me. "They kept him around for weeks at first, despite their creed that only the strong survive. I don't think they expected us to protect him. What the Institute failed to understand was that we were only following what we had been told: only the *strong* survive. Mi was strong. Perhaps the strongest of us all, because he got up every day when someone told him not to bother. It never occurred to us –not for a moment– that there was anything defective about him. He helped us realise who the defective ones were."

My fists have coiled into tight circles, my short nails digging into my palms. I hate them with renewed vigour, and I hate the Lucans for echoing their sentiments.

Julia slides down beside me and places a hand on my shoulder. She gulps audibly, and then opens her mouth as if to speak. She doesn't. She cannot find the words.

Luckily, the door opens. Nick enters, breathless and dishevelled. He smiles when he spots me, and I feel hot.

"Ah, Jules," he says. "You've got a patient. Nothing too serious, but–"

Julia bolts upwards. "I'm on my way. Would you mind–" she gestures to her equipment.

Nick nods, and she sweeps out of the room with nothing but her clipboard. He diligently begins to tidy everything away.

"How are you?" he asks.

"Fitter than ever, according to Julia."

"I meant, how are you... after yesterday?"

I hold up my hands. They're still a little pink, but the wounds are closed and barely visible. Nick seizes one. I generally don't like people touching me without warning, but there's something about his fascination with me that excites me.

"That's amazing," he says, turning it over. "You can barely tell–" He lies out his own in comparison, and then becomes conscious of what he's doing, of my skin on his. He drops his hands away and mutters an apology.

"It's all right. For some reason, I don't seem to mind when it's you." The hotness in my cheeks ripens. "Are there any showers here?" I ask, suddenly aware of the sweat I've worked up.

"Y-yes. Of course. The dorms. This way."

He leads me off down a narrow corridor. We pass a series of rooms, made up for sleeping. I expected something cold and clinical like the Institute, but the resemblance is minimal. The beds are mismatched and the sheets are an explosion of colour. There's clothes strewn about the floor, over chairs and headboards and chests. The rooms are packed with gear, books and *stuff.* Some even have drawings pinned to the walls.

"Which one's yours?" I ask Nick.

He smiles. "I've got my own. I've been here a long time."

"How old are you?"

"Nineteen. You?"

"Eighteen, I think."

He cringes slightly at *I think.* I remember being told I was thirteen before I escaped the Institute, but I have no notion of when my birthday might be.

"How long have you been here?" I ask, to save him from any awkwardness. "Doesn't seem like it can be too long, if you're only nineteen."

"I was ten, when I came here."

"*Ten?* That's young. You got any family?"

Nick smiles, jerking his head towards the mess hall. "Sure. Out there."

"C'mon. I shared my story with you," *most of it.* "'Fess up. What's the tragic backstory?"

"I lived the first ten years of my life in Luca," he explains. "Middle ring. My mother was a doctor. From what I remember, she was a good person. I remember her arguing with dad once, about them needing to do more. Said it wasn't enough to hide the suffering."

"Why would he argue with that?"

"Because she kept going to visit the slums. He said it was dangerous. Turns out that they were both right; she bought the pax home with her. Truck picked us up at the first sign of a rash and ditched us here. They were dead within weeks."

"But not you?"

"No, not me."

It's unusual, someone surviving the pax in a family. They must have been extremely careful not to touch him during their infection. It must have been a lonely time for him. Lonely, and terrifying.

"How... how did you wind up here?"

"Julia. She was the doctor –the only doctor– that would come anywhere near us. She did everything she could to help them, and me. Afterwards, she brought me here with her. I couldn't do much as first –I was a soft ten-year-old who'd grown up in luxury– but I trained. Learned how to fight, how to help. There were worse ways to grow up."

So Nick is from Luca. I would never have guessed. I know I hate Lucans, but he isn't one of them. He's like me, a person without a home or a family, carving one out of a world that doesn't want us, or wants us to be something we're not.

Nick directs me to the shower block and goes to find me some new clothes. It's only when he's gone and I've stepped under the steaming water, that I realise how strange that this. *He is like me.* My entire life, I've only counted a handful of others to be like me in any way shape or form, and now, within a matter of days, I'm letting someone else into that same space.

What is happening to me?

I let the water flow over my skin, washing away the dirt and grime of days of toil. I can almost feel my body shifting, like the shape of my shell reflects a change inside. My thoughts spiral, turning like the liquid against a drain. I think I am becoming something better, but I am not sure that I like it. Empathy is harder than carelessness.

I do like a challenge, though…

I turn off the water and stand there in the steam, blissfully clean. The experience is almost enough to make me want to move in. I wonder if they could hook us up with hot water once I've won them over?

"Ashe?" Nick's voice calls from outside the cubicle. "I've found some clean clothes for you."

"Thanks."

I step out, clutching a towel to my face, and find him only a few feet away. His face shoots to red.

"I, er, um–" He turns sharply on his heels.

"Calm down," I say, whipping the clothes from his arms, "It's only skin. You've got communal showers. You never seen a naked woman before?"

"Not so… unexpectedly."

I gather that a lot of people are not so free with their bodies, but I grew up in fairly tight quarters and it's never been an issue for me.

Nick gulps loudly. "So, perfect body, huh?"

"That's what it says on the tin."

I pull on the clean clothes and towel down my hair. "You can turn around now."

"Oh good." Nick stares at me, and I feel the flicker of a blush rise in my cheeks, too.

Here's one of the other weird things about being a genetically-engineered superhuman who grew up in an isolated lab to be turned into a human weapon; you don't understand dating rituals. I've never read about them, I've never observed them up close. I've never even had a conversation with someone about their relationship. All of this is very new, very uncharted waters. What am supposed to say? What I supposed to *do?*

Nick is still staring at me. His gaze his intense, curious. I wonder what he thinks of my strange eyes. I wonder if he thinks I'm attractive. The signs seem to point to the affirmative. I think about asking him outright, but what good would that do?

"You all right?" he asks. "You spaced out a bit there."

"Do my eyes freak you out?"

Nick frowns, and then chuckles. "I'm sorry, I just saw you naked, and you're asking about your eyes?"

"Yes."

He stops smiling. "No, I think they're interesting," he replies. "Like the rest of you."

"Are... you talking about the naked thing again?"

"No," he says, "I'm really not."

There's a buzzing on his belt. An old-fashioned pager. "Ah, looks like Harris has got something for me," he says. "I should... I should get that. Will... will you be here tomorrow?"

"I hope so."

"Then... I'll see you then."

"If you're lucky."

"If I'm *very* lucky," he says, halfway down the corridor. He turns around briefly to smile at me.

I think, for once, I've actually said the right thing.

CHAPTER 18

Abi's prediction is right about the market soon returning to function, but the scars still haunt the city. I never noticed the wounds before, so used the general state of disrepair and decay, but I see them now. They crawl out of the rubble, white as bones.

We spend the next few days making what remains of the school safe and habitable. Harris comes out of his lab to visit the site, with plans to rebuild it. Everyone is keen for it to be done as quickly as possible. I have never seen so many people united in a single endeavour. What else have I not seen?

Nick is busy with another project, and I don't see much of him. Mi spends every waking moment with Julia. Baz gives him time off in light of the incident. Abi is all but strapped to Harris' side. On the rare morning I find myself with nothing to do, only Ben is my companion. I decide to take him into the wilds to learn how to hunt; it is about time I taught him. He is excellent with the bow, but tracking game is another matter. We come home with a couple of plump birds though, one of which I donate straight to Phoenix. We can get by with just one.

That night, after the carcass is picked clean, Abi makes an announcement.

"I'm not going back to school, when it's rebuilt," she says. "I'm going to help out at Phoenix HQ."

This shocks me, at first, but the next feeling is one of relief. Abi has been too old for school for some time, and there's nothing the local place can teach her. Even before it went up in smoke, it was just a collection of run-down rooms where local volunteers ran a few classes every day. Most of the teachers are either very old, or very young. Kids are taught the basics: reading, writing, maths... maybe some science if they're lucky. It sounds super boring but both Abi and Ben seem to love it. I think Abi went for something to do, and because it stopped her having to think of what to do when she really was too old for classes.

Good, steady, legal jobs are hard to come by... hence why I don't have one. Abi can do almost everything I can do. She could easily be a hunter, a thief, a fencer, a runner. But she doesn't want to be any of those things, and I don't want her to have to be. The only thing she truly loves to do is paint, but there's not much of a market for artwork in the slums.

I thought the last thing she would want to do would be to head back to the world of technology and be the machine she was built to be. But it occurs to me, this still is a revolt against her programming. She might be using her abilities, but she's using them to help people. She's doing it because she wants to.

I nod my head. "Sounds like a good plan, Abs. Just stay out of the field, 'kay?"

"Yes, mum."

She says it sarcastically, but it warms me nonetheless. I ruffle her hair affectionately.

The school soon re-opens, Mi goes back to work, and Abi and I head into Phoenix HQ together. She wants to show me something she's been working on, so we head to the lab, only to find Rudy booming at Harris.

"No, absolutely not!" he seethes.

Harris throws up his hands. "I've run the numbers. It's our best shot."

"You've run the numbers using *another* one of them! You

think that's a coincidence?"

"I've double-checked myself–"

"It's too risky–"

"*Not* using her is far riskier–"

It's at this point I realise they're probably talking about me and knock loudly on the glass. "Hey boys. What's up?"

Rudy's temple swells. "Nothing."

"We've got an important mission for you," Harris says instead. "Rudy isn't sure you're ready."

Rudy glares at him. "We'll send Scarlet," he decides. "She's done espionage before. She's our fastest runner. If anyone can do it, she can."

"She *was* our fastest runner. Ashe is faster by far. You'll risk Scarlet's life because you're not willing to trust someone new?"

Rudy's eyes narrow even further. "Not *someone*," he says. "My decision is final. Prep Scarlet."

He sweeps out of the room, casting a final sour look in our direction as he goes.

In a completely deadpan, matter-of-fact voice, Abi calls after him. "You'll regret this."

He does not stop.

Harris sighs, running his head through his hands, and smashes his fists against the table. He swears loudly. "That stupid – stubborn – idiotic – jackass!"

"He's going to get someone killed," Abi adds.

"I know," Harris swings his chair around to face us. "The thing is, he wouldn't even usually think of doing something this risky. He'd listen to my numbers. But he's so determined to prove he can do this without you–"

"What even is the mission?" I ask.

Harris gestures to a nearby monitor and punches something into the keyboard. We all move closer. A glamorous white building springs onto the screen; a fancy hotel in Luca.

"There's an important conference being held tomorrow night in the upper ring," he explains. "Lots of important politicians and diplomats. The event is being broadcast live, maximum coverage. We want to sneak in, and replace the mayor's speech with footage of what his soldiers did to the marketplace."

"You... you filmed that?"

"We've had cameras in place for months, hoping to catch something."

"But... but *why?* What good will it do, showing it to the world?"

"Luca isn't completely full of asshats and idiots. Neither is the whole world. We want to show them the truth about what is happening on their doorstep, weaken their faith in their leaders."

"So... what's the plan?"

"Get two people in under fake IDs. When the broadcast begins, one of them needs to be in the control room, switching out videos. The issue lies with timing; I can hack into the security cameras and loop the feeds for approximately five minutes. After that, they will pick up an intruder and the building will go into lock down. Abi and I have calculated all of the variables. You are the only person fast enough to get in and out within a safe window."

I pause for a moment to take this all in. "I see," I say eventually.

It's at this point that Nick arrives, a little breathless. He looks at Harris. "I've just seen Rudy," he rushes. "Did he–"

"Flat out refused. Said we should take Scarlet."

"She'll never get out in time."

"I told him that."

"So... what do we do?"

Abi raises a hand tentatively. "I may have an idea..." she says.

CHAPTER 19

The plan relies on a lie. Namely, that everyone involved promises to do exactly what Rudy has told them to, and at the last moment... we don't do that. Harris will be technical support. Nick will be the second person going into the hotel. Scarlet still gets into the van. The only problem is the driver. Pilot is currently down for this, and we all know there's no way he'd be OK with me substituting at the last minute. He has to be taken out of action. This is where Mi comes in. His job is to spike Pilot's evening drink with a powerful laxative that will put him out of action for at least twelve hours. Another driver will be assigned, hopefully one who won't question my appearance in the van.

We spend the rest of the day preparing in secret. Scarlet has to look like she's training, so we all head to the gym and book it out. Abi and Harris set up an obstacle course designed to mimic the length between the hotel control room and the exit, complete with a computer mock-up where I practise loading up the video. Even with my speed, it's tight, especially while wearing a pair of heels that Scarlet assures me are "the least offensive in your size." I have very little margin for error.

"We'll be right beside you the whole time," Harris assures me. "Communicating through these virtually invisible ear-pieces."

He hands one to me. It's a tiny, transparent little bud. I place it to my ear, and experience an unpleasant, sucking sensation. It's a bit like having a screw inserted in the side of your head.

"You can press it on and off, but it's best to keep it on as much as possible in case we need to contact you."

I'm talked through the cover story, time and time again. Nick is the grandson of some rich politician. I'm his escort. I only met him that night. I'm assured that no one will be talking to me, but if anyone does, just smile and nod. They seem to think I'll struggle with this.

"I'm a trained assassin!" I insist. "I can smile and nod while I *murder you*."

Scarlet and Nick chuckle at this, but Harris looks mildly horrified. I unscrew the earpiece and hand it back.

Finally, eventually, the gruelling training is over, although there will be more to come tomorrow when I'm squeezed into some tight little dress and made up to look like some harlot. I can't even remember the last time I wore a dress; probably when I ran out of clean laundry and had to borrow one of Abi's.

Nick and Scarlet start stacking away the obstacle course. Harris packs away his technical gear and wheels it back to the lab with Abi. Mi then arrives with the leaves for Pilot's tea, and Scarlet sneaks off with him to go and spike it. She seems a little bit too cheerful about the notion of drugging her friend.

When it's just the two of us, Nick turns to me.

"Would you like to get a drink?" he asks.

I blink at him. "Are you flirting with me?"

"Only if you want me to."

He pulls out a small crate that must have been left by the others, and gestures to a couple of bottles. It's been a long time since I've had a drink. There are only a few bars in the slums, and despite the general low quality of their clientele, it's still a luxury that most can't afford. I've occasionally been given a bottle of something as a bonus on the job. We mostly use it in cooking. I quite like the taste of wine, but due to our fast metabolisms, I'm not sure that any of us can get drunk and I've never tested our limits.

I shrug. What harm can it do? "Sure, I'll have a drink."

He chucks a bottle in my direction. I catch it neatly and open it with my teeth, much to his amusement.

"I've never had a drink with a guy before," I tell him.

"You've... never been for a drink before?"

"I'm a genetically engineered superhuman who doesn't like people. You work it out."

"You like people."

"Most people are idiots." I take a long swig. It's a bitter, lukewarm, mostly flat beer. I can't compare it to much, but I don't rate its quality.

"Some, but not all. And you do like some of us."

"Some, I admit, I'm starting to warm up to."

Nick grins at me slyly. "Any ones in particular?"

"Well, Scarlet's a babe, and Pilot's really not that bad when you get to know him."

Nick elbows me in the side. I like that, the strange easiness between us. I'm not used to feeling this way with regular folk. What it is about him that I find so comfortable?

"You're not that bad either," I say quietly.

Nick drinks. "You may just be my favourite genetically engineered superhuman," he says.

"You need to spend more time with my family."

"Something tells me I'd still prefer you."

I try to ignore the seriousness of his compliment. "You should spend more time with Mi," I advise. "He's much nicer."

"I'm not," Nick says, stepping closer to me, "particularly interested in *nice.*"

All the blood in my body suddenly rushes to my face. My heartbeat pummels in my eardrums. I should ask him what he's interested in. Or... or I should take a step back. I should make a decision, one way or another–

Abi crashes back into the gym, and I almost drop my beer.

"Long day tomorrow," she says. "Should we head home?"

CHAPTER 20

We're advised to be back at base bright and early the next day, ready for departure at ten.

"Why so early?" I ask.

"We've got someone on the gates into Luca who'll let us through," Nick explains, "but his shift ends at eleven."

"Do you bribe him?" It seems odd to me that any Lucan would just let us through.

"No. He does it because he believes in our cause."

I raise a sceptical eyebrow.

"He has family here," is all Nick confirms. There's obviously more to the story, but perhaps it's not his to tell.

"Do... do you have any family, still in Luca?" I ask gingerly. Life expectancy on the other side of the gate is pretty high. It seems unlikely that Nick doesn't have grandparents or aunts or uncles or something.

"A few," he admits. "I wouldn't call any of *them* allies, however."

Harris has to inject another ID chip into my arm, taken from a recently-deceased Lucan. He can alter the details from that in case anyone double-checks. Tonight, I am not Ashe, but Selene Bellecour, high-class escort. Lucan names are *so fancy*.

I'm expecting a few more hours of going over the plan, but what happens is infinitely worse. Scarlet whisks me off to a private room and presents me with a slinky dress, make-up, and a razor. I pick up the latter tentatively.

"What am I supposed to do with this?" I ask. "I don't have a beard."

"It's for legs and underarms."

"People shave those in Luca?"

Scarlet sighs, as if she's as disgusted as I am. "*Girls* do," she says exasperatedly. "Well, most of them use other methods of permanent hair removal, actually–"

"What? Why?"

"Beats me. Guess they have to invent things to worry about when they're not starving to death."

She hands me the razor and a bar of soap. "Are you going to need help with this?"

I stubbornly refuse the offer and end up shredding my legs as a result. Good thing I heal quickly. I concede and allow her to smear on the make-up. It feels awful against my skin; thick and cloying. My skin tightens like I'm wearing a mask.

She attacks my hair next, smothering it in sickly-sweet cream and pulling it back into an updo, mostly to hide the abysmal uneven mess it usually is. Then I'm presented with underwear.

"What even is this?" I shriek, confronted with an under-wired monstrosity.

"It's a bra."

"I know what a bra is! This... this is some kind of archaic torture device!"

Scarlet laughs. "Did you just use the word *archaic?*"

"No," I say quickly. "I don't use fancy words. I'm not smart. Shuddup!"

I force myself into the twisted garments, pull on the slinky dress, and climb into the ridiculous shoes. I feel myself slipping away. It's even worse when Scarlet hands me a box of coloured contacts. I've never particularly liked my eyes, but it feels wrong hiding them, even when they would look too out of place in perfect Luca.

Nick knocks on the door. "Van's ready to go. Are we done?"

"We're good!"

He enters the room, and stops abruptly when he sees me. "You look–"

"If you say 'hot' I will take off one of these shoes and stab you with it."

"I was going to say 'uncomfortable', but duly noted."

He picks up a long coat and throws it at me. "Best cover up. You'll turn a few heads leaving looking like that."

He heads on out into the corridor. We haven't gone far before I hear someone coming down the other end. A large, heavy-footed person, carrying something... metallic?

"Shoot," I hiss, "Rudy's coming."

"What?" Scarlet looks panicked.

Nick wrenches open a nearby door. "Quick, in here!"

I leap into it without a second thought. Moments later Rudy's footsteps stop.

"There you both are," he says roughly. "The van's waiting. Are you ready to move out?"

"Er–" Nick starts, not particularly confidently.

"Why aren't you dressed?" he barks at Scarlet.

She, thankfully, is quicker. "What, you think I'm going to sit in those clothes for the next eight hours? No thank you! I'll get ready at the safe house."

He makes a noise of protest.

"Don't say another word. You've never put on a pair of heels in your life. You have no idea of the sacrifices I've made for this–"

Rudy growls, cutting her off. "I hear Pilot's... out of action. Jameson has been assigned instead. He's an experienced driver. He shouldn't let you down."

"I'm sure he won't, Captain," says Nick. "But we should really get going–"

"Quite right. I'll see you to the vehicle."

"That's really not–"

"Oh, but I insist."

Does... does he know that I'm hiding here? Is... is he suspicious that we have something planned? The hardness in his voice is as sharp as the sudden intake of Nick's breath; he does not know what to do.

"Come," says Rudy, closing the gap for him, "We've got a

short window."

Their footsteps trail off down the corridor.

What am I going to do? Abandon the mission? Leave Scarlet to her probable death? Follow behind them and take Rudy out?

The last option does have its upsides, but it is extreme... and others are likely to intervene if they see me do it. No, that won't work either. I'm going to have to get off base and try and intercept them...

If I'm going to do that, I need to act fast.

I dash back to the dressing room and grab my old shoes, tying the heels together and strapping them to my back. I must look quite the picture, rushing towards the exit, but I don't stop to examine any gaping faces. If Nick and Scarlet have any sense, they'll try to delay leaving, either hoping I'll turn up or anticipating my next actions.

I drop into the tunnels and sprint along in the dark. Even at my speed, it takes a good ten minutes. The van will be moving through the slums now.

I scramble on top of a building, but it's not tall enough to see the road they should be taking. There's nothing for it but to head towards the gate. I'm hesitant to get too close; the gate is heavily guarded and ally or not, someone is bound to react to a girl leaping several stories onto a moving vehicle. But what other choice do I have? Someone else is driving. It is out of anyone's control now.

I leap onto the next low roof, slide myself onto the fire escape of the block next to it, and hurtle to the top. I still can't see the road, but I have a clear view of the gate now. I launch myself across the city rooftops, wishing it were dark; I am not sure how many cameras line Luca's walls, or how accurate they are. Can they see me from this distance, hopping from building to building like a flea?

At last, I see the checkpoint. There are only two vehicles at present; there is never much traffic in or out of the city, or certainly not by this entrance. Neither one looks like those I saw in the hanger at Phoenix HQ. Which either means I'm early, or far, far too late.

My eyes aren't helping me much here. I close them, trying to filter out everything else around me. I can hear the muted conversations of the checkpoint guards, a few kids playing with a ball in an alley not far away, a woman screaming at her husband for forgetting the bread. I imagine the line of the road, focusing on the tyres creeping over the tarmac, and try to trace sound along it. Back, back, far back.

A few blocks away, a van is moving at speed. It is still invisible from my spot, but I can feel it rumbling along as keenly as if it were right next to me.

I bolt from my position, hurling myself onto the rooftop behind me, and fly towards it.

Finally, thankfully, the van turns the corner and swings into sight. It's shinier than most of the ones I remember, but for a mission into Luca, it makes sense. It's certainly the right size. I have no other options; I wait for it to get closer, judge the distance, and drop down onto the roof.

I hear a screech from inside, and the van jerks to a skidding halt.

"What was *that*?" someone hisses. Jameson, was it?

I hear a familiar chuckle, and the side door slides open. I roll off the roof and swing inside.

Jameson wheels around in the driver's seat.

"Who's this?" he flusters.

"Last member of our team," Nick explains, directing me into a seat. "Did no one warn you?"

"No!"

"Who briefed you for the mission?" Scarlet asks innocently, "They really should have–"

"But where did she come from?"

"You missed the rendezvous," I explain, trying to mimic Scarlet's face. "I didn't see I had another option."

"Who the hell are you?"

"Jameson," says Harris warningly, "we're running out of

time here. We need to get to the doors ASAP."

Jameson looks at Harris, who's the oldest and possibly most senior person here, and decides to trust his judgement. He nods, Nick closes the door, and the engine starts up again.

Scarlet pulls a leaf from my hair. "You messed up your 'do," she tuts. "*And* your make-up. Good thing I'm here, right?"

She leans into one of the supply bags and begins to 'fix' my face, with yet more sour-smelling creams and pastes.

Nick grins at me. "We weren't sure you would make it."

"What, me miss a big party in the city? Never!"

We slow down as we reach the checkpoint beside the gate. Jameson rolls up the partition between us as a couple of guards saunter over. One checks our credentials, the other says he'll check the back.

I freeze, but Nick's hand goes to my arm. "It's all right," he promises.

The door slides open again, and a young man of twenty-something in a guard's uniform peers at us intently. He has white-blonde hair and pale eyes, and looks familiar. His gaze settles on Harris and he swallows, as if he hadn't expected to see him there. The two of them nod curtly.

"Nothing here," he calls to his colleague. "Wave them through."

The van jolts into life again, and the enormous black doors into Luca City slide open. There is little I can see through the divider, but it feels like passing through a shadow.

CHAPTER 21

It's a lot noisier in the city, but the noises are denser and sharper, pressed cleanly together. Even I struggle to make out one voice from the next, and the sounds all slide together in an endless layered cacophony. There is a constant low whirring of a thousand different machines, all playing along to the same perfect harmony. My skin prickles.

Everyone is very quiet, as if afraid the city has ears that can pierce through metal. Their breath is measured, but their heartbeats all thump wildly. I do not know how long our journey takes. It could be twenty minutes or two hours. Years have passed by the time Jameson slows to a stop and turns off the engine.

"Base camp," he announces.

Everyone nods and springs into action. When I emerge from the vehicle, I find we're inside a garage of some kind. There's shelves of wires and supplies, a few bunks in the corner, desks of monitors and keyboards. A sleek, shiny car is parked beside the van.

"All right," says Harris, still inside, "we'll load up everything we need this end. Got your communication devices?"

"Er..."

"Here," Scarlet presses an earpiece into my hand and I diligently stuff it in my ear.

"We won't be manning them until 1800 hours," Harris explains, then winks at Nick. "Give you some privacy."

Nick hurls a dirty rag at his face, and Harris throws him the pen drive. Nick places it safely in the pocket of his blazer, then goes to the swish car and pops the trunk. There's a suitcase in the back, which he examines carefully, making sure every-thing is in order. He looks back at the rest of his team.

"Are we good to go?"

Jameson frowns. "Scarlet's not dressed yet."

"That's because she's not going."

Jameson looks at the rest of us, waiting for someone to explain.

"There's been a change of plans, Jameson," Scarlet starts. "Ashe is going instead. She's way faster than I am."

"Why... why wasn't I told?"

"It was last minute. I'm going to stick with you and Harris and run support. A second pair of hands is never a bad idea."

Jameson looks very sceptical about this, but there's not much he can do at the moment. There's a quick round of "good luck" and then we slip silently into the car.

It is the most pristine thing I have ever been in. I didn't know anything could be this *clean.* It's all smooth edges, black and silver, soft and sleek as a puma. Where did they get it from? Another gift from an ally? It seems excessive.

It purrs into life, quiet as a ripple, and we slide out of the garage and onto the streets of Luca.

It is a towering metropolis of glass and steel. Every curve looks sharp, and every colour muted. It is a land of silver, grey, blue, black. There are no bright awnings here, no mar-ket folk peddling their wares, and people walk by robotically, as if moving along a conveyor belt. I stare transfixed, my face pressed against the glass, gawking at their strange fashions and heavily-made up faces.

We glide along the streets, but each one looks very much like the next. The city is a symmetrical beast.

"The guard who let us through," I start quietly, "was he Harris' brother?"

Nick nods, his eyes still tight on the road. "Half-brother," he admits, looking guilty. "Same father."

I am already understanding where the story is going. "Har-ris' mother–"

"Came with him to Terminal City when he was just a few weeks old. He... he was born too early. The government said he had little chance of survival, and even less chance of being a 'contributor'. They recommended 'letting nature take its course'. His father thought that would be best, but Diana refused."

"You knew her?"

"For a time, she was like another mother. She died only two years ago. A raid."

"I'm sorry," I say, both for Harris and for Nick. "His father?"

"He... he came to the slums a few times, begging her to return, offering to send Harris every convenience he could afford. She wouldn't go."

"Of course she wouldn't."

"He eventually moved on, married someone else, and had Henson. I don't know when he found out he had a brother, but I know he got the job as a guard just so they could meet."

"He's brave."

"He is. One of the few allies we can definitely trust."

A glistening building of white stone and glass towers over the others. The hotel. I recognise it from the briefing. Nick glides down the parking ramp and skids to a halt.

"Ready to play the part?" He smirks.

I obediently push my feet into the heels and abandon my boots in the back.

"Just hold onto my arm and say nothing."

"Not my usual style."

"Not my usual demand."

We both slide out. Nick tosses his keys to a valet nearby. "Room 207, boy," he says shortly. "Have the bags brought up promptly."

He doesn't even look him in the eye. He's already marching for the exit, and I have to run to catch up with him. He grabs me around the waist.

"Sorry," he mutters, virtually inaudibly. "Keep walking."

We enter the hotel foyer. It is a glimmering white and gold

palace, all fountains, marble and pillars. It is difficult not to stare. I repeat the name of my character, and remind myself she sees this all the time. I look at the expressions of the other women, whose noses are all turned up in indifference. I force myself to mimic them as Nick drags me towards the desk.

He holds out his wrist for them to scan.

"Nicholas Lilywhite," he announces, in the way I imagine ancient royalty might. "My usual room."

"Of course, Mr Lilywhite," says the receptionist, reading something from her screen. "And your guest?"

I soundlessly lift my own arm and hold it out in her direction.

"Just the one night?"

He nods.

"Are you here for the mayor's broadcast?"

"Indeed."

"The drinks reception begins at seven. Is there anything I can help you with in the meantime?"

"Send up something from the kitchen. Myself and my companion are famished."

"Very well, sir." She bobs and hands over a key card. "We'll have your luggage with you shortly."

A well-dressed porter in a blue suit escorts us up in a great glass elevator, and for the first time, I see the city fully. Great expanses of green pool out between the mechanical jungle. Pure blue lakes glitter under the sunlight. For a moment, all of Luca's harshness fades away. Yes, there is a beauty to this place, posed and manufactured though it is.

The elevator slows to a stop. The porter hops along and opens a door ahead of us. I find myself in a luxurious suite, all sleek surfaces and decadent furnishings. The bed is the size of what passes for Ben's room.

I wonder how he's doing.

I didn't tell him where I was going, other than I'd be back very late and he shouldn't wait up for me. As far as he knows, it's just another one of my jobs. Mi and Abi will wait up tonight though, desperate for word.

Nick tips the porter and the door closes with a soft thud. Without wasting another second, he races towards the bed and dives face down into the pillows.

"Oh my, this is so *good...*" comes his muffled voice. He rolls his face to one side. "Lucans may be terrible people, but their beds..."

Curious, I come towards him and sit down on the mattress. It's like a hot bath, like honey and cream, like warm summer days and fires on cold winter nights. It's all I can do to stop myself crawling into it right now.

Nick smiles. "It's good, right?"

"It's divine."

I kick off my shoes and we lie there together in absolute bliss for several moments, until there's a knock on the door and our luggage, as well as a tray of food, is rolled in. Nick shoots me a glance as if to say *you ain't seen nothing yet,* and then puts on his snooty demeanour again to converse with the staff. It disappears the moment they are gone and he tears into their offerings with vigour. It does not take long for me to join him.

The tray houses a myriad of cheeses, smokey, spiced and sweetened, with tiny jars of chutneys and dozens of little breads. There's fruit I don't know the name of, delicate savoury pastries, miniature bowls of steaming soup. I've never tasted anything like it.

"New plan," I announce, my mouth half-full, "I'm abandoning the mission and staying in Luca forever."

"I may have to join you. The cost of my soul is worth these rolls!"

"Who pays for all of this?" I ask.

"Allies, sponsors... a little bit of thievery," Nick says, a little more seriously. "From those that won't miss it, of course."

This makes sense, and a part of me wants to ask how much this all costs... but I feel it would sour the experience. "The name you gave at the desk," I start, a little cautiously, "that's actually your name, isn't it?"

Nick nods, looking mildly ashamed. "Nick Lilywhite may have been thrown out of the city with his parents, but he never died. Makes things easier. He's my own alias."

This is the reason he was picked for the mission, not just because he's calm and a good pretender. He fits the part so well because he's been playing it for years. I wonder what he's been forced to use it for.

Nick pours me a cup of coffee, and we go back to the bed. We lie there against feather pillows, inhaling the intense aroma.

"Good job we're not staying the night," Nick murmurs. "I'd hate having to fight you for this bed."

"And I would hate beating you."

Nick chuckles. "I think you'd get over it."

I squirm down further in the nest of wonder. "You know, I think I probably would."

He turns to face me, and I realise how close we are. I can smell the coffee on his breath, and it smells so much headier than mine. He does not seem startled by this closeness, although I'm suddenly conscious of a very rapid heartbeat. Mine and... his.

"Do you like me?" I ask.

Nick blinks for a second, caught off-guard my question, but then he grins sheepishly. "Have I not made that abundantly clear by now?"

"The clearest way to say it would be, 'I like you.'"

"Fine," he says, "I like you, Ashe."

"But... *why?*" It seems ludicrous to me that anyone other than three *–four–* people will ever like me at all. I've done nothing to endear myself to humanity. Nothing at all. "Why do you like me?"

"I find you fascinating."

"Because of the superhuman thing?"

"A little, yes. I find myself constantly amazed by everything you can do. Is it... is that wrong?"

"Maybe. I don't know. It's just... I want there to be more to me than that, even though for so many years that's all I ever really was."

"What do you mean?"

"After I escaped. I should have blossomed into something else, like the others did. I should have been and artist or a doctor or... whatever wonderful thing Ben will be. But I'm not. I wasn't. I was just... Ashe. Secret superhuman. Thief for hire. There really wasn't anything more to me."

"That's really how you see yourself?" Nick shifts upwards onto his elbows.

"Why?" I ask. "What do you see?"

"I see a person who's been through hell, who's experienced things I don't even want to imagine, who's protected her family against everything she possibly could, even at the cost of her own happiness, and despite everything, is still funny and smart and *cares* about people, even when no one could blame her if she hated the whole world."

Nick's confession shocks me. My first instinct is to protest, to fight against his convictions, but there is nothing I can argue against. I have done all of those things, although–

"I don't care about people." I say in retaliation.

"Then what are you doing here?"

"I mean... I didn't care about people until I met *you*."

We both fall very quiet for a moment.

"You cared about people before you met me." Nick's gaze is unwavering. I can count every fleck of brown in his otherwise vivid blue eyes, which I'm thinking about doing as it stops me from having to turn my thoughts to other things. *One, two, three...* "You saved me and Pilot the day we met. You didn't kill those guards."

"That's because I didn't want to feel bad for killing them!"

"You... you know that makes you a good person, right? Feeling bad about violence?"

"Does it? I think it's just more selfishness. I think that even when we do a good thing for someone else, it's to make ourselves feel better. When I spare someone, or save them, it's because I don't want the weight of their death on me."

"By that logic, no one is truly selfless."

"You are."

"How so? Every time I do something for someone else, it's because it makes me feel good."

"But you could have had *this*," I gesture all around me. "You could have had everything, but you gave it up. You sacrificed your own comfort for a cause I spent years viewing as lost."

Nick is quiet for a long moment.

"Ashe," he says softly, "do you like me?"

It's unfair of me to ask him to be upfront about his feelings, and not explain my own. But mine are a little more complicated.

"Yes," I say, almost inaudibly. "But I'm not completely sure why yet, or even if I'm OK with feeling anything for anyone, and I need to figure that all out before... before this goes anywhere."

"That's OK," Nick leans across and gently tugs one of my hands from my side. He kisses the inside of my wrist, and a rough sparkle of fire ripples through me. "I'll wait."

CHAPTER 22

We spend the next few hours going over the plans, double-checking every final detail. Now that we're in the building, Nick shows me every exit and entrance point in person. He points out the control room where the videos will be broadcast from. It's heavily guarded, and the guards look at us at we creep about, so Nick shoves me up against the wall and covers my body with his. The guards look down awkwardly.

"Sorry to be so rough," he whispers.

My mouth twist into a smile. "This isn't rough."

Nick bites his lip, a spot of colour rising in his cheeks. He raises an eyebrow quizzically, no doubt wondering how rough he'd have to be for me to feel it. He leans down until his lips are almost against my neck. He's quite tall, I realise. I'm hardly short myself. I'm not used to men being much taller than me.

"All part of the act," he assures me, "just trying to keep them off our tail."

"It's very convincing."

Then I feel awkard, because I know I could be more convincing, but I don't want to do that with him now, like this. If I do decide I want to move things forward, I want to do that as myself.

I shove Nick off me –attempting to look playful– and then grab his hand and pull him back to our room.

Shortly after, our earpieces activate.

"Well, hi there partners, this is your friendly neighbourhood Scarlet speaking."

"Roger that," Nick responds, while I cringe at the feeling of somebody else's voice inside my ear. "Everything OK your end?"

"All fine here. We're en route. How was the food?"

"Do you really want to know?"

"Talk dirty to me, Lilywhite."

"It was divine."

"I hate you."

Nick grins, and I slide myself into a seat by the window. The sun is setting over the nearby park, and the sleek city is finally awash with colour. Scarlet goes quiet for a moment.

"It's beautiful, isn't it?" Nick whispers.

"Like something out of a dream," I respond. "The view from our rooftop is pretty special, but this..."

"Otherworldly, I know." He sits down opposite me. "There are moments when you get why they're so obsessed with keeping things so... perfect."

"But then...?"

"The sun sets, and you realise a few moments of prettiness aren't worth the darkness that follows."

Hardly a statement I can disagree with.

Harris' voice sounds in our ears. He performs a few checks, grills us a little more. He and the others are parked nearby. When the time comes to make an exit, I will be heading out in the van, while Nick remains in the hotel to preserve his alibi. The rest of us will hunker down at the garage until morning, when Nick will join us. I don't like the idea of leaving him behind, but he's clearly way more at ease here than I am, and I'm anxious not to stay any longer in this place than I have to. It's comfortable, but I'm still in a nest of vipers.

We gear up and head for the reception, Nick flashing his fancy invitation. We're checked for weapons upon arrival, and my tiny clutch is searched. The pen drive gets through, as Harris assured us it would. They don't know yet how dangerous our information will be, or how my entire body was built to be a weapon in itself.

We're right on time, but already the room is awash with people. They are all ridiculously, unbelievably beautiful... but in a bizarre, crystallised, *pristine* way. They are all so polished and perfected that they barely seem human at all. Their blood must look more like oil, cogs and gears replacing the muscle underneath their skin.

We are shown to a table –thankfully one made up just for the two of us– and given glasses of bubbling gold liquid. It's as heavenly as everything else I've tasted so far. Nick sips carefully at his.

"Have to look the part and keep my wits about me," he explains.

"I think I'll be fine."

I want to neck it back and have another, put that doesn't seem to be how most people are drinking theirs, and I know all about blending in. It's difficult once they start coming around with trays of tiny finger foods. I could eat my weight in them. Maybe Selene's a starving escort who hasn't seen a decent meal in days?

The mayor arrives at seven-thirty. I've seen her before on the big screen in the market place, but never really given her much note. She is a tiny, silver-haired woman with flawless skin and eyes of pure crystal blue. She is swamped with people the minute she arrives. The guards by her side go no where.

Security isn't too tight, but I take a moment to count the number of staff, the number of guards, the unconcealed weapons, the exits. I wish our table were closer to one of them. I don't fancy my odds of fighting my way out of here, a feeling I'm not often confronted with.

I have another drink.

Eventually, someone gets up on the stage at the far end of the room, and a hush falls over the crowd. They introduce the mayor and she takes to the podium.

"Citizens of Luca, honourable ambassadors, esteemed guests," she begins, "Welcome! It is my pleasure to have you all here tonight, on the 47th anniversary of Luca's founding."

A small cheer goes out, a round of applause.

"We have done so much in that time..."

My eyes trail off to a man seated not far from the stage. He doesn't look as perfect as most of the party-goers. There are some signs of ageing around his eyes, a greyness in his temples. He's nodding up at the mayor in agreement... but there's something in his face that irks me. Have... have I seen him somewhere else?

It doesn't seem likely. The logical, rational part of my brain tells me I cannot have seen this person before. He is too well-dressed to be from the slums, and if by whatever chance he ever frequented the market, it was unlikely that I would forget him so easily. I am usually uncommonly good with faces.

So why do I have this terrible feeling?

You forget faces you don't see often. Your brain changes them in your memory, fades the impression like ink in the sun. Sometimes I think I only remember Gabe's because of Mi.

If I can't place him... and yet I know him... it only stands to reason we did meet, long ago. A scar from my past that never quite healed.

"Ashe?" Nick touches my hand lightly. "Where have you gone?"

"That man..." I point carefully towards him. "Do you know him?"

"I've seen him before, at these events," Nick replies. "His name escapes me."

"Who is he?"

"Head of some organisation, I think. A sponsor of the mayor's?"

Head of some organisation. My initial thought –hope, even– was that maybe he was just one of the scientists. There were so many, coming and going all of the time. It stands to reason their faces would slip from me.

Only he wasn't a scientist.

I only saw him a few times, staring at me from the corner of the arena, overseeing my 'progress.' If he ever spoke, it was to someone else. "How is Eve progressing?" over and over again.

Not a scientist. The Director.

My skin freezes. My heart races. I shouldn't be here. What if he recognises me? I have changed a great deal in five years, and my make-up makes me virtually unidentifiable as it is, but that doesn't mean it's impossible. He has stared at my face a great deal more than I have stared at his...

"Ashe?" Nick's voice tightens. "You know him?"

My maker. My captor. My torturer. He is the one who pulled every string, the one who ordered me to kill those I'd beaten... the one who wanted to scrap Mi.

I need to get out of here.

Nick's fingers slip into mine and pull me back into the room. His eyes pour into me, and somehow I am anchored. He mouths, "breathe," and I do. I concentrate on that, and pray the Director doesn't turn around.

I have completely stopped listening to the mayor's speech, but suddenly there is a round of applause, and my old tormentor is taking to the stage.

If there was any part of me hoping I was somehow mistaken, that hope is quashed as soon as he takes to the podium. A shiver spikes through me and I remember, with perfect clarity, watching him watch me. He would stand up on the walkway and observe us, like a king might his peasants in the field.

Don't look at me, don't look at me...

"Dear citizens, it is a great honour to be invited here to speak to you today. I am the director of the Chimera Institute, an organisation that seeks to build a better tomorrow, by researching into genetic disorders that disrupt our ease of life."

Nick swallows, his grip on my hand tightening. Now he knows who the man is too.

"The Institute has been running for over twenty years now, and we have made fantastic progress towards eradicating..."

How can he stand up there so calmly, smiling about his research, as if unaware that it sanctifies the killing of *children?*

And for what... their 'ease of life'? I no longer want to flee. I want to bolt up there and choke the life out of him. It's tempting; I could certainly reach him before any one could stop me, and once I had him in a hold I could probably break his neck before anyone shot me. I wouldn't be getting out of this room alive though. A part of me thinks it would be worth it, if I saved any future children from his clutches, but I imagine someone else would rise up to head the Institute in no time. I would be saving no one. A pointless sacrifice.

He witters on for some time, talking about all the advances they've created, their progress towards creating a vaccine for the pax. They ought to have done that by now, given how many of us they must have bred. Or maybe they should just genetically engineer all new children, and forget about natural conception entirely. Clearly no one in this room has a problem with a few modifications... so long as they're pretty ones.

There's a voice in my ear.

"It's time," says Harris.

I nod across at Nick and grab my clutch. A woman leaving in the middle of a speech to go the bathroom is, I'm told, no cause for alarm. The guards let me out with barely a second glance and I head to the first floor bathroom, as instructed. Harris is going to loop the feed between there and the control room. I have five minutes to get up, take out the guards, load the video, and get back down again, at which point the cameras will resume their usual feed and show nothing but a woman leaving the bathroom. If I manage to do it in that time, I'm to slip out into the street and head straight to the van. Even though the cameras should offer me an alibi, Harris doesn't want to risk the guards coming to and identifying me. It's safer to get clear out of the place.

If I don't make it back in five minutes... well, that doesn't bear thinking about.

I follow my first instruction, and check that the room is clear. "I'm in position," I tell Harris, readying the small timer on my watch.

"Roger. Standby."

I stand poised by the door, hand on the timer, desperately praying no one else comes in in the meantime.

"Go!"

I slip silently outside. There are still too many people about for me to risk running, but I walk briskly towards the stairs and bolt up them, straight to the third floor.

Thirty seconds.

There's no one in the corridor, so I race down it, slowing just before I reach the bend. There are two guards stationed outside the control room door. I smile at them. "Excuse me, gentlemen, I seem to have completely lost my way! Could you please tell me where–"

"Ma'am, we're afraid we can't help you," one replies. "We've got strict instructions to–"

I snatch the gun from his belt and smash it into the other one's face. His nose breaks loudly, and blood splatters the carpet. The first one tries to grab me, but I duck out of his way and he hits the wall instead. Grabbing the fire extinguisher from the nearby wall, I crash it against the back of his skull. He goes down, and while the other chap tries to stem his bleeding nose, I do the same to him.

One-and-a-half minutes.

I take the gun and step into the control room. Two horrified technicians look up at me. I point the muzzle at one of them and hand her the pen drive. She trembles. Pity surges inside; she's just doing her job, after all. Is she even employed by the corrupt mayor? She could be just hotel staff...

Toughen up, Ashe, no time to be timid.

"Broadcast this," I instruct.

I was trained to load it myself, in case they refused, but this way is quicker and less bloody. It takes perhaps thirty seconds to download. The entire thing is only a minute long, and I have to stay to watch all of it, to ensure they won't stop it the second I leave. I am forced to re-watch the entire bloody incident, with Rudy's voiceover booming in my ear.

"This is your doorstop, Luca... this is your doing."

The image focuses on the body of a small child. A slightly older one is wailing beside him. One of the technicians gasps. She looks at me, the guilt on her face palpable.

"I... we didn't know..." Her voice sounds like she's swallowed glass.

My throat tightens. "Because you didn't want to," I say shortly.

The timer on my wrist buzzes. I have ninety seconds left.

"You've seen it now," I tell them. "Do something about it."

I turn to leave the room, but someone is blocking my path. A young man, the same age as me, with dark hair and eyes of azure. Handsome, clean-shaven, and unlike the Director, instantly recognisable. It may have been five years since I last saw him, but I never quite forgot his face. Neither, apparently, did he forget mine.

"Eve," he smiles.

I swallow. "Adam."

CHAPTER 23

"You know, I always hoped I'd run into you again," Adam continues, as if utterly oblivious to the horror pulsing through me. "I thought maybe I'd be sent to track you down one day. But meeting like this? How… fortuitous."

"Ashe?" says the voice in my ear. *"Did you load the video?"*

"Yes," I say stonily, ignoring Adam's confusion. "But I've run into a snag. I'm not going to make it back on time. You need to get out. Get *everyone* out."

Even if by some miracle I manage to evade Adam, I now have five witnesses about to identify me from previous footage. They'll see me coming in with Nick. They'll interrogate him in my stead. His alias may be blown for good, but he'll be safer out. He'll be *alive* out. Who knows what the Institute will do to him if they suspect he knows me?

Harris goes very quiet. *"Roger that,"* he says. *"Try to get out when you can. We'll… we'll be in touch."*

"Thank you."

Adam's smile widens. "Not acting alone, I see. Has Eve fallen from paradise? Found a devil to take you in?"

"I escaped a devil," I hiss at him.

He scoffs. "And found paradise?" He gestures to the frozen image of the wrecked marketplace.

"Everywhere is paradise compared to the Institute."

Adam looks very amused by this. "If you say so."

"I take it you're here on business?"

"Accompanying our dear Director, yes. He thinks it's time we stepped out of the shadows a bit."

"He'll find that harder when I set his precious Institute on *fire.*"

Adam's smile wavers, just a little. His face becomes crueller. "That's what you tried to do last time, isn't it?" he sneers. "How'd it work out for you?"

Gabe. He knows about Gabe. They must have brought his body back. Oh God, what did they do to it, to him? What did they do to the shell that held one half of my soul?

My first rises up to punch him, but he is too quick for me and before I know it I am pressed against the back of the door. A chair goes flying. The two technicians shriek and scuttle to the corner.

It has been a long time since anyone has fought me like this, with strength that matches mine, with nothing held back. Mi and Abi have never been a true match for me. Adam is. He always was.

"You're out of practise, Eve," he hisses in my ear.

I drive my free elbow into his stomach and spring to the other side of the room. "Not quite."

I gesture for him to advance. His foot swings round and collides with my outstretched arm. Pain slides out along the bone. It is not broken, not fractured, but it came close. I had forgotten what this could feel like.

While I reel from the move, his fist comes crashing down. I roll out of the way. I'm closer to the door now, but I don't think I could outrun him. The alarm has gone off; back-up will be here at any minute. Soon it won't just be him I'm facing, and I can barely beat him alone. I am not prepared for this fight.

Adam comes crashing into my middle, trying to drive me towards the floor. I hit him squarely in the back of the neck and tumble over him, but he grabs my leg before I can right myself and yanks me to the ground. He goes for my face and narrowly misses. I catch his arm before it makes contact, but his weight crushes down on me. I press against him with all the force I can muster. Concrete would yield more easily.

"You should come back with me," he says, grinning. "I could do with the challenge."

I want to yell, *never* or *I'd sooner die,* but all I can manage is a feeble, "I can't."

But then I remember why I can't. I can't because Gabe died to get us out. I can't because Mi, Abi and Ben are here, my family is here, my *home* is here. I can't lose to him. I won't.

Something inside of me shifts, like a fire fuelled. My muscles pulse and tighten. I push back against him, until he is the one struggling against *me.* I rise over him, and my gaze glides to the gun lying nearby.

"You won't use it," Adam says, but his eyes flicker with doubt. He's seen me kill before. "You never did much care for the violence."

I snatch it up and cock it. "You don't know what I'll do to keep my family safe."

At this, he laughs. "No one's safe out here, Eve."

"And you think you are?"

"Yes," he says firmly, "I think I am."

He's wrong. Of course he's wrong. And I will shoot him. I have to. But... but as I look into his cold, unresponsive eyes, all I see is a mirror. How easily could our situations have been reversed, if he had escaped, and I had not? Someone will mourn him. He's sure to have his own Ben.

I can't kill him. I can't have him follow me, either.

Bang.

Adam howls in pain, clutching his shin. Blood pools around him. He won't die. He won't have any permanent damage. But he won't be getting up, either.

I toss the gun to the ground, out of reach. The weight of the shot vibrates against my hand.

I need to run. Out in the corridor, two guards are hurtling towards me. I race towards the fire escape, turning the corner after bolting through the door and waiting until they've ran several paces ahead. They barely realise what's happening before one of them is sailing down several flights and the other is knocked out cold. I don't stop to see the damage; I can't. I can hear others moving up the stairs.

I race back into the corridor, heading for the exit on the other side. The elevator dings open. More guards.

I'm running out of options. I could break down one of the doors to the rooms? They're solid, but I could manage it with a few well-placed kicks. What then? The windows are thick. I'd need something incredibly heavy to break through them...

Before I can come up with an option, a nearby door clicks open. I don't see another pathway. I rush inside, preparing to grab whoever is on the other side and stop them from screaming, but the room is dark and the door seemingly closes itself. No, not by itself. My eyes adjust quickly.

"Nick?"

He holds his fingers up to his lips. The guards hurtle past. He waits a few moments until he's sure they're gone.

"What are you still doing here?" I screech. "They've got footage of us entering together! They'll know that you–"

"I'm working it out–"

"How did you get in here?"

"I stole a keycard from a staff member."

"You stole–"

"Don't worry about it!"

He goes towards the window. There's a small panel that opens right at the top, presumably just for ventilation. He points. "Can you get through that?"

"Yes, but–"

Nick climbs up onto the nearby desk, opening up the window with his card. Electronic windows? Really? "Our room is exactly two stories above here. Can you climb it?"

"Probably–"

He leaps down. "I'm going to go ahead and open it at our end."

"The cameras!"

"Harris has temporarily disabled them."

Disabled. Not looped. I suppose there's no point trying to be secretive now.

Nick turns to go.

"Nick!"

"What?"

"Why... why didn't you leave?"

Nick swallows. "Even if I wasn't falling for you, I could never have just left you here."

The door opens, a sliver of light cuts into the room, and he is gone.

CHAPTER 24

I get up on the desk, take off my shoes, and toss them out of the window, praying that no cameras catch a random pair of shoes falling from the sky, or that Harris has disabled everything on this side of the street. There's no way I can climb a building in them, but if anyone sees just the shoes, they'll know I'm still in the building.

Even if I wasn't falling for you...

I have to trust that Nick knows what he's doing, even though it feels completely wrong to be climbing up the hotel rather than down it. It is no easy feat; most of the building is completely glass. I am clinging on the merest hint of window-ledge, balancing like a hot knife in butter. Thankfully, the window above me soon opens and Nick drops down a bedsheet for me to clamber up.

I fall into the room. Nick leaves the window open, and we wordlessly put the bed back together.

He can't really be falling for me, can he? He hardly knows me. Then again, despite what he said... he took one hell of a risk staying behind. What other reason could he have to be so reckless?

There's a knock on the door.

"That's sooner than expected," Nick says. "You'll need to–"

"On it."

I'm already slithering back out of the window, which Nick closes behind me. I hold onto the thin ledge for dear life, glad that the mask of night will make me less visible to the human eye. Nick yells, "I'm coming!" as he slides the key card into the hem of one of the curtains. He grabs an open bottle of champagne from the table and splashes it over himself, then wrenches the door open.

Two security guards stand behind it.

"Oh," drawls Nick, "you're not room service. Where's dinner? After that complete fiasco at the broadcast party, a complimentary meal is the least we should be getting!"

The guards do not sound impressed by this. "Sir, cameras show that you entered the hotel with a guest tonight. Do you have any idea where she is now?"

"Beats me." Nick takes a swig of the champagne. "Little tart ran off before she could do what she was employed for."

"I see. And where did you, um, employ the young woman, sir?"

"Met her on the way here. Didn't stop to exchange much in the way of pleasantries, if you get my meaning."

"Quite. Am I to understand then, that the woman in question approached *you?*"

"Yes... look... you don't think *she* had anything to do with this, do you?"

"We are looking into all unaccounted guests, sir."

"Well, if that's the case, do you mind waiting until morning? I have a terrible headache coming on." He takes another long, hard slug.

The guard clearly decides he's not going to get much more out of him tonight and mumbles a half-hearted thanks. He tells him not to check out early and closes the door. Nick grabs the hidden card, races to the window, and hauls me back into the warmth.

"I thought they'd check the room," he rushes. "I never would have made you hang out here otherwise–"

"They *should* have checked the room," I say. "I guess you're just a very convincing liar."

"One of my secret talents."

He tosses the key card out of the window, and pulls it shut. It locks automatically after it.

"Hopefully somebody finds that and thinks you're in the

wind," he says. "We should be safe for the night."

"And then?"

"We'll work it out."

Before I can think of anything else to say, a voice buzzes in both our ears. *"Ashe? Nick? All you all right?"* It's Harris, although I can hear Scarlet in the background, asking the same questions.

"We're safe," Nick assures them, "but we're going to have to stay put for now."

"Understood. We'll speak tomorrow."

"We'll meet you back at the garage in the morning."

"See you both then, and... well done. The video is already online. It's going viral."

The line goes blank, and Nick removes his earpiece. I do the same with mine, placing it on the desk beside his.

Well done. This doesn't feel like a success. It feels like a failure. All that work to get me here, and I messed things up in a way Scarlet never could have. She wouldn't have been recognised by Adam. She wouldn't have put her family's safety at risk. I don't care about Abi's stupid calculations; I failed, and who knows what the consequences of that failure will be?

Stillness and silence settles on the room, and I realise what has just transpired. The Institute is working with the government. Adam was here. Adam knows where I am. He might even still be in the building–

Nick takes my hands and guides me towards the bed. "What happened?" he asks, his voice as soft as water. "Who did you have to fight?"

His fingers trail along the bruises on my arms.

"Adam," I whisper, "Adam was here."

"Who's–"

"The second," I rush. "He was the second, and I was the first, and ever since we were children they used to make us compete against one another. He knew me. He... he wanted to take me back–" I am trembling, trembling and breathless and... oh no, are those *tears?*

Nick clings to my hands.

"Ashe, no one is going to make you go back."

"I can't go back there! I *won't!*"

"And I won't let them take you." Now Nick sounds just as desperate as I feel, and his voice breaks the sobs I'm holding back. I shatter into his arms, tears pouring out of me with the same ferocity of the blood from Adam's leg.

Nick reaches up, and starts pulling the pins from my hair. "That day when I bandaged your hands," he tells me, "I wanted to tell you that you didn't always have to be brave. That I understand you don't want to worry your family, but you don't have to be all strong and stoic for me. You don't need to put on a face for me."

He inches me back, and reaches into his blazer pocket for a handkerchief. He starts wiping my cheeks, and at first I think he's just dabbing at my tears, but then I see the swathes of make-up against the cotton. He's taking it off, rubbing away the disguise. Making me more me.

"You'll need to take your contacts out," he advises.

I nod. He goes to get something to put them in, and offers me a long shirt from his suitcase. "You probably won't want to sleep in the dress."

"I want to burn it."

Nick chuckles. "We'll do it together once we're free of this place, but for now, let's just try and get some sleep."

It doesn't feel like I can ever sleep. Adam is still out there, the Director is still out there. I am still lying in the jaws of my enemy. But I shred my trappings anyway, crawl into Nick's shirt, and then into his arms.

In the end, there is no need to fight over who gets the bed. We fall back against the pillows together, and I fall asleep with my head pressed against his chest.

CHAPTER 25

The night after Mi's accident, none of us slept well. Ben gave way first, being so little, and Abi not long after him. Gabe was turned on his side, pretending to be asleep, while the tears trembled silently down his cheeks. I could feel what I could not see.

I crept out of my own bunk, tucking the covers around Ben, and crawled into Gabe's. I put my arms around him and leaned into his back.

"He'll be OK," I whispered.

Gabe's voice was little more than a ghost's. "And if he isn't?"

"I won't let them do anything to him. *We* won't let them do anything to him."

"Oh Eve," Gabe cried, "you don't know what they're really like!"

I didn't know what he meant by that, but this didn't seem to be the moment to contradict him. "I know what *we're* like," I insisted, my fingers curling into his nightclothes. "I know we're stronger when we're together."

"But not unstoppable."

My hand reached round and pressed against his heart. "Unstoppable," I whispered, "together."

I did not know then, how soon his heart would cease, how quickly we'd be torn apart. All I knew was that when we were together in the quiet and the dark, when the noise of everything else had shuffled away, I felt invincible. I felt akin to safe. We were conquerors, although of what I never found out.

In and out of consciousness I flutter, no longer entangled in

Nick's arms. I watch him sleep, soundlessly and peacefully, untroubled by dreams of old ghosts I both long for and despise. I haven't spent a great deal of my nights on this world alone; I am used to watching others slumber. I haven't passed many of the past eight years without checking in on Ben while he slept. I always found it calming.

Watching Nick is different. There is a new kind of warmth I feel in watching him, a new kind of longing. I want to reach out, to touch that smooth cheek, to run my fingers over his features. I want him to do the same to me.

It is difficult to sleep. The inches between us are like miles. Do I want to move closer, or scuttle away to safety? Are his arms a trap or a lifeboat?

I want to cling to him like I cling to my memories of Gabe. I want to hold him close, to stop him slipping away, but I feel all the powerlessness of a kite in a storm, untethered and lost at sea. It's a little like drowning.

Nick gets up early in the morning, thinking me still asleep. He dresses quickly and slips out into the hall. Exhaustion still stirs in every corner of my body, but I know sleep will evade me now. Old memories, faded scars and pressing dread rattle around my mind. I shut my eyes, but the thoughts roar like the wind.

When Nick returns, he's sourced another pair of shoes from somewhere, some dark glasses, and a long coat. There's the smell of freshly baked bread. He shakes me gently. I pretend to just be rousing.

"I got you breakfast," he says. "Wake up."

He presses a hot roll into my hand, filled with butter and

jam. It should be as fantastic as the food we inhaled yesterday, but it tastes like paste in my mouth. It is a struggle to swallow.

"You're going to walk straight out the front," he tells me. "I've checked security; it's pretty light. I think they've assumed you've left the building."

"And you?"

"I've got to get the car. Harris is waiting for you at the old rendezvous. We'll meet back at the garage."

I nod, then slither out of the bed, grabbing the dress from yesterday and heading to the bathroom. I remove the chalky residue from my face and dab it with some of the complementary creams, hoping it will hide the dark circles under my eyes. It doesn't. I tidy myself up as best I can, pull on my old clothes, and head back into the bedroom. Nick hands me my new disguise.

"I'll be right behind you."

I nod. It seems silly, as well as foolish, but I wish we were walking out together, and not because I don't like the thought of leaving him behind. I just don't want to be alone myself. This isn't like me. This is weak. Nick told me I didn't have to be brave in front of him, but I must, because the alternative is not being brave at all.

The corridors are grave-like this morning, despite how long it's been light now. There are very few people in the foyer, and even with the glasses and the coat, I feel exposed. Guards still hover around, although they look tired and preoccupied. I keep expecting them to pounce at any moment. The walk towards the doors feels like an age.

The sun strikes my skin like a pane of glass. I stand stunned for a split second, utterly baffled to be free of that place. My heart skips and sinks in the same beat. I am not out of the woods yet. I pick up the pace and head for the alley where I know the others are waiting.

I tap on the side of the van door. It slides open and I crawl inside. Harris turns in his chair, grinning at me wearily. Jameson nods from the driver's seat. Scarlet looks like she wants to hug me, but thinks the better of it.

"Morning, supergirl. You all right?" Her cheer is forced.

I nod my head.

"Nick?"

"He's fine." *Better than me.* "He shouldn't have stayed."

"'Course he was going to stay. He likes you, and he's, y'know, *Nick.* Big hero complex. Besides, if he didn't, you'd probably be dead... or running wild in Luca, which is as good as."

Maybe that's what I deserve.

"We managed to get a message to Mi last night," Scarlet continues. "Just to let them know the operation was successful, and that you were more or less safe. He made it quite clear he'd be very upset if something happened to you."

I can't think of anything to say to this, because sometimes, *sometimes,* I really don't like knowing how cut up they'd be if something happened to me. It's just one more thing I have to be responsible for.

The van jerks, and we start to pull away.

"I still couldn't have done it," Scarlet tells me. "Harris must've ran those numbers a hundred times. I could never have gotten in and out in that time. So if you're feeling bad about that–"

"It's not that," I say shortly. "I just... I'm tired. I'd like to get out of here."

"Of course."

I can tell she doesn't fully believe me, but she doesn't press it. We drive on in silence. It seems to take an age for Nick to join us once we reach the garage, but he eventually glides in, muttering something about giving a final interview and an address for where he picked me up.

"It's an area well-known for its ladies of the night, badly patrolled and practically off the grid. They'll hopefully deduce I was nothing to do with it."

I feel uneasy still, and while everyone sets about packing and unpacking equipment, I sit on a bunk sipping lukewarm tea. Nobody speaks to me or asks me to help out. I wouldn't know what to do anyway.

"Ashe, we're ready to go now."

I close my eyes for the journey home, and half-sleep. Someone –Nick, I think– drapes a blanket around me. I don't even open my eyes when we pass through the border. I don't know how we've gotten away with it.

There's nothing I want more than to go straight home, but of course we have to go back to HQ first to be debriefed. I don't give much of a thought as to what that means. Finally, we arrive at the hanger, and I'm met with the sound of several voices, all speaking very loudly at once.

"Ashe! Ashe, where are you?"

Mi's face rises out of the others, Abi and Ben beside him.

"She's there!"

"Ashe!"

I barely have time to open my arms before Ben launches into them, and Mi and Abi sprint over to join us. They murmur something about how scared they all were and it's all I can do to stop myself from sobbing once more. There's no way I can put them through this again.

Mi squeezes my shoulder. "Are you all right?"

"I'll tell you later."

I'll have to tell him and Abi about Adam sooner or later. They need to know that we could be in danger, but right now, there's no time for this. There's another person waiting. Rudy. To say he looks angry is an understatement. His glare is explosive.

"You five," he booms, "my study. *Now.*"

I shuffle off the hands still clinging me and dutifully follow Nick and Scarlet from the hanger. Jameson hangs back briefly, attaching a ramp to the side of the van to let Harris out. We all slow our gait a little to allow them to catch up.

The other members let us pass like coffins at a funeral. They are utterly mute, and when the door closed behind us, it is with a resolute thud.

"How dare you," he seethes, not looking at any of us. "This mission was of utmost importance. You risked everything – *everything*– by sending out this complete rookie! The entirety of Luca was in uproar–"

"They were going to be in uproar anyway, after seeing that video," offers Nick. "Don't try to–"

"Don't you dare make excuses–"

"The mission would have been a complete failure if we hadn't switched in Ashe–"

"It was barely a success as it was! And don't think I don't know that you stayed behind against warnings. You put your own life on the line–"

"I would have done the same if–"

"Don't be a liar as well as a fool. You would have followed orders, but for some inexplicable reason you seem to–"

"Stop," I say. "You don't need to yell at them."

"Are you taking the blame?"

"No, I think you're a giant ass, but on this point, I happen to agree with you. I shouldn't have gone. I failed."

"Is this... an apology?"

"No, it's a resignation." I announce, avoiding Nick's eyes.

"You won't need to worry about me not following your orders any more, or anyone risking their lives for me. Because I'm done."

I turn to leave the room, but I've barely crossed the threshold before Nick's arm reaches out to stop me. "Ashe–"

"I'm sorry. I know you think I'm some great saviour or superhero, but I'm not. I'm really not. I'm just a girl trying to get by. I'm not cut out for this. I'm not made for this–"

"Says who?"

"Me. And since I'm the one making the decisions in that regard, I get to choose. I choose a quiet uncomplicated life, just the five of us!"

Nick frowns. "Five?"

Gabe. It's been half a decade, and still –*still*– I sometimes forget to say four. He creeps back in before I can stop myself.

Gabe would never have been this foolish. Gabe would never had put our safety at risk.

"Please," Nick pleads, "just... think it over. Don't... don't make any decisions now. Go home, rest–"

"I don't need to sleep to know I can't do this!"

Rudy comes up behind him. "Let her go, boy, it's clear she's not cut out for this." His eyes bore into me. "So much for making them pay."

"You got your video out," I spit. "I'm not willing to pay any more."

I turn on my heels and march down the corridor. Somewhere along the line, the others start to follow me, asking questions I cannot answer. We walk silently all the way home, right up to my door, which I slam behind me and then run straight under the covers. The others whisper outside –a pointless action when you consider how great our hearing is– until I bark at them to stop. I bury my face in my pillow, and pray for the sweet release of sleep.

CHAPTER 26

I do not come out of my room for over a day, spurning all offers of company. Occasionally, Mi brings me offerings of food, which I pick at a bit or toss out of the window, just to convince him I'm not starving. I try to sleep, but I mostly fail. Adam's form is pasted onto the back of my eyelids, and Gabe's disapproving face haunts every dream.

Do you know what Gabe's last words to me were? He said, *"Keep them safe. Keep yourself, safe."*

I failed him. I failed myself.

At one point, I get out everything that I own and pile it onto my bed. It doesn't take up a great deal of space. The half that isn't weapons is composed of a few changes of clothes, a couple of notebooks, three pens, a rather unused hairbrush, a few hair ties, a necklace Ben made me out of nutshells, a thick wad of his drawings and cards, some little sculpture things from Abi, emergency food rations, blankets...

I could pack up everything in a matter of minutes, and so much of what I own is to do with *surviving* that it barely counts as a personal item at all. I feel a strange sense of... sadness? Regret? Is this all there is to my life?

There's the furniture, too, I suppose, each item with a story of where it came from. Taken from other abandoned buildings, salvaged from the scrap heap... and almost every piece lovingly restored by Abi in some way. I may not care about them, but she does. She's poured a little piece of herself into every part of this place.

When I do come out of my room, it's only because I know I have to talk to Abi and Mi. I wait until long after Ben is in bed, before creeping out, depositing myself in the rickety chair opposite them, and announcing that I saw Adam at the hotel.

They both go very pale and silent for a while.

"Are you sure—" starts Mi.

"Positive. He recognised me, and we fought."

"What did he say?" asks Abi nervously.

"That I shouldn't have left and that he wanted to take me back."

"He's... he's still with the Institute then?"

"Yes," I reply stonily, "and proud of it."

They both fall mute in sickening silence, no doubt both thinking the same thing I was: who would we be if we hadn't escaped?

"It also looks like the Institute are working with the government," I continue. "The Director was there. He did a speech."

"What... what does that mean?"

"I don't know. But... it probably means we aren't safe here."

More silence follows.

"Do... do you think we should run?" I ask carefully. "Head to the woods, or the next big city? We could make it—"

"This is our home—" starts Mi.

"*We're* home," I insist. "Wherever you three are is where I belong. Cities and walls and *things* mean nothing to me."

"They mean something to *me*," insists Mi. "And you might not care about anyone but the three of us, but I do."

I swallow, the pain in his face palpable. "I know you're angry at me. This is my fault—"

"It's not that. It's not that simple. I just don't want to run—"

"And we don't have to," Abi interjects finally. "I've run the numbers. I calculate that we will be five percent safer running. I don't think we should abandon our home based on five percent."

"Five percent?" I query. "That seems very low."

"When you take into account natural disasters, wildlife, chance of injury, chance of the Institute having sway in another town, the upcoming winter season leading to frostbite and/or starvation..."

"You make a compelling argument."

I drop the idea, because the truth is, I want to believe her. I don't want to quit the city. The loft may be leaky, the windows may be more tape than glass at this point, but it's *ours*, and it means so much to the three of them. And it doesn't mean *nothing* to me, not really. It just means so much less to me than their lives.

There's also... there's also Nick to consider. He's crossed my thoughts many times since we abruptly parted ways. Is that the last memory of him I want? What *do* I want? Can I really conceive any future between us?

I think back to the night in the hotel, the warmth of his body pressing through the sheets between us. I want something, certainly.

"Um... is... is Ashe blushing?" Mi's brow wrinkles.

"You know? I do believe she is!"

"W-what?" I stammer. "You can't– *how can you tell?*"

"Increase in temperature, awkward silence, sudden increase in heart rate..."

"What did you and Nick do," Abi smirks, "alone in that hotel room for hours?"

My cheeks get even hotter. "We... talked."

"Oh," she says, a little disappointedly, "Is that all?"

There wasn't any 'is that all?' about it. It felt more intense, more intimate, than anything that had happened to me for a long, long time. I mean, I grew up with another boy's voice in my head, and yet sharing all that with Nick felt far more personal, far more freeing. Perhaps *because* I had to share it. It wasn't a thing accidentally given.

What is it about that boy, that makes me unravel? And why do I want to let him tug at those strings?

"It doesn't matter," I say shortly, standing up. "I'm not going back there."

I march to my room without another look at them, knowing they're not done talking about this. I close the door and block it out. I focus my ears on the engines roaring in the distance, and pretend it's something far more pleasant.

CHAPTER 27

The next morning, I go hunting, more for the silence than any need or desire. I head deep into the wilderness, until all traces of road or path have long since faded, and bush and bough grow so thick and fast that only the merest trickles of sunlight can reach me. I lie down in the damp earth and fixate on any fragment of sound I find appealing. I am miles away from anyone. No residue of the city can taint me here. I span my senses out over hillocks and trees, the grassy knolls and winding streams. I focus on tiny things: the trickle of water, the smell of leaves and chestnuts, a rabbit digging beneath the earth.

I wish I could be a rabbit, stowed safely under the earth with the rest of my little colony. But then, a rabbit is not safe outside the warren, and it must eat. Perhaps I better be an eagle, majestic lord of the skies, feared by all, food to none. The world must be very different from way up there.

Eagles must be very lonely though, and I would not call their nests a home.

I catch a couple of wild birds and head back to the loft. I'm in no mood for the market, so I string them up and leave them for Mi to deal with, whenever he gets back. I didn't speak to him and Abi about whether or not they were continuing at Phoenix HQ without me. It's no business of mine, but I probably haven't made things easy for them if they are.

Ben comes back mid-afternoon, but I'm in no mood for

chatter. I hear him racing up the stairs, stopping shortly outside my room. He raps on the door excitedly.

"Ashe, I made you a card! It's not a 'get well' card, since you're not sick. It's a 'get happy' card! Are you awake?"

I do not reply.

"I'll just post it under your door. Hope you get happy again soon!" He skips off to his alcove.

I should go out and speak to him, or hug him, or do anything with him, but every time I see his little face I am reminded of what I risked to pull that stupid stunt. What I still risk, just by sticking in this place.

I can't let him suffer for my mistakes. I can't. But what if I don't have the power to protect him?

For two more days, I am a ghost. I barely speak, I barely eat, I flitter from room to room and place to place with the energy and volume of a whisper. It gets to the point where I wonder if I'll just remain this way forever, living between life and death until the Institute finds me and my choice on the matter is surrendered.

I mull on my options. I rarely doubt Abi's guidance, but we did not consider every possibility. It would, I'm sure, be safer to move to Phoenix HQ. I will not go, but if our enemies come knocking, they will find only me. They have no reason to suspect the others have remained with me. They taught us to scatter in enemy territory to stand a better chance of escape. I would die before telling them otherwise.

Of course, they could ask the locals. Or torture me. Everyone talks eventually. I might not have the option of death.

Maybe these are things Abi has taken into account. Perhaps it would be better to listen to her and move on.

Only... only move on to what? I cut my ties to Phoenix. What am I planning on doing next? Can you move on if you go backwards?

Tired of my thoughts, I head up to the roof and let loose on the punch bag. I feel a little better for the exercise, productive, like the day hasn't been a complete waste. I'm so focused on my punches it takes me much longer to register a presence coming up the fire escape, footsteps that don't belong to any one in my family. I tighten my senses on their other sounds; the beat of their heart, their breathing–

Nick.

He emerges, nipped from the cold and slightly out of breath.

"Hey," he says.

"What are you doing here?"

"I wanted to see you. Not... not to convince you to come back, I promise. Just... just to see how you are."

"How did you... how did you know where I lived?"

"I'm not stalking you, I promise. Your... Ben told me. He's been hanging about the base *a lot.* He's worried about you. He showed me a picture he's drawn of 'sad Ashe'. It was the saddest, most pathetic thing I've ever seen. I had to do something. He had these enormous, puppy-dog eyes–"

"Yeah, that'll get you every time."

"He seems like a really sweet kid."

"He is. Doesn't get it from me. Or the Institute."

"Who, then?"

"Mi, probably."

Nick goes quiet for a moment. "I know... I know most of your life really quite sucks," he says eventually, "but you're lucky to have them."

"I know."

"I'd love to have a family. I've got Scarlet and Harris and Julia, and maybe a few others, but... it's not quite the same as *always* having someone, you know?"

I nod, because I know even more than he is suggesting. Now would be the perfect time to tell him about Gabe. My other person, my other half. The other hand in the dark.

"How... how are you?" Nick continues, before I can say anything. "I'm really happy every time I see one of your family at the base, because that means you're probably still here. I was worried you were going to run away."

"I've thought about it."

"Why didn't you?"

"Abi said not to."

"Oh."

"Were you hoping there was another reason?"

"Yes," says Nick, unashamedly.

"You're hoping I'll come back."

"Of course I'm hoping that."

"You said you just came to see how I was."

"I did. I meant it. I wasn't going to say anything–"

"But you did."

"Does it occur to you that I might have entirely selfish reasons for wanting you to return?" He pauses. "I miss seeing you every day."

"You don't know me enough to miss me."

"But I want to. I really, really want to. And don't ask me again to tell you what I like about you, because I don't fully understand it yet myself, but you told me you felt the same."

"Feelings can change."

"So soon?"

I have never changed my feelings on anything, not once. There is a permanence to every emotion, every person I've ever known. If I let Nick in, he won't be able to get out, and I like it and hate it at the same time. I want him here, I want him gone. His weight is a crutch, his weight is a burden.

"If... if that's truly how you feel, of course I'll leave you alone." He swallows, turning back towards the fire escape. His movements are minute; he wants me to stop him. I want to stop him, but surely it's safer this way?

"I'm sorry I couldn't be your superhero," I mumble instead of goodbye.

"I'm really not sure that's what I was looking for," he answers, not looking at me. "But whatever I was waiting for... you were it. The answer to the question I hadn't even asked."

I listen to every one of his footsteps as he heads back down the fire escape, and watch him until he fades completely out of my sight.

CHAPTER 28

The following night, Mi does not return. Abi tells me he went out with Julia in the afternoon, to visit the infirmary where the pax patients go. We're not worried about him catching anything, but we worry nonetheless. It is a long walk back, and even though Mi knows the streets better than our faces, there are those that would take advantage of his blindness. He can handle himself in a scrap, but in a large group... and there are other dangers, dangers we would all struggle to fight against.

We eat a sombre meal, just the three of us, and Ben goes off to bed with a little grumbling. Abi and I go to sit on the roof, to see if we can spot him. We're just debating going to the infirmary directly when his form wanders into dim lamp light. We head back inside to wait for him. He comes in slowly, immediately taking off his shirt. There's blood on the cuffs. I can just make out the larger droplets in the darkness, but I can also smell it on him. The heavy, metallic odour clings to his skin. It must be even worse to his attuned senses.

"Mi?" I whisper hesitantly.

"Doctor Herb is dead," he says shortly, dumping his shirt in a bucket and heading for the sink. "It... it wasn't an easy end."

"Oh Mi," I exhale. I cannot imagine what that must be like, watching someone you care for die. Sometimes I am grateful for how quickly Gabe was lynched from me. Other times... other times I would give anything to have had a goodbye.

But what would Mi have said to the Doc?

"I thought about offering Julia some of my blood. It's supposed to be effective, right? At helping ease the symptoms? But... if I gave some to Doc, I'd have to help everyone. And there were so many... so I couldn't. I didn't."

"You couldn't have helped them all."

"I could have tried to." He drops to the floor, in front of the counter, his forehead pressed against the cupboard door. "What use are we? What's the use of being this way if we can't help people?"

My answer to this is not the one he wants to hear, because we shouldn't *have* to help people, especially at the cost of our own well-being. Why can't we just forget about the rest of the world? What do we owe it, anyway? It's never exactly been kind to us.

But Mi and Abi don't see the world like that. They see a broken world and want to fix it, although I've never seen that desire bring them any real happiness.

Am I happy though? What good has come from me blocking it out?

Do I even believe in good and bad?

A bang reverberates through my memory. The feeling of my heart torn in two, while I held a shaking toddler in my arms. An image of Moona, one of ours, bleeding. Forrest's body being carted off like luggage. The cold voice, *"We'll have him scrapped."*

Yes. I believe in good and bad. I may even believe in fighting. I just don't have the strength that they do.

Abi and I sit wordlessly beside him. "What can I do?" asks Abi.

"What you're already doing," Mi replies. "Working against this mess. Find out what we need. Find out where to get it."

I want to yell at them, because they're doing what Nick did; trying to force me into being something I'm not. I'm not a good person. I'm not made for sacrifice. I could never give up myself for a stranger.

But I'm not going to scream at them, not right now. That

would not be fair to Mi. I may not be a brilliant person, but every time I wonder if I'm an awful one, I realise that I'm not because of them. How could two such wonderful people love me if I was? How can I be evil if I love them back?

"I'm sorry, Mi," is all I say instead, and then the three of us link arms and sit there in the dark.

◆ ◆ ◆

We help Mi clean himself up, boiling water to soak his clothes in, pulling out our meagre supply of soap, and scrubbing every inch of him he's content to let us. He is a strange, solid kind of limp while we do this, numb and cold and far away. We even have to dress him for bed, and we're both relieved when he comes round at that point and shuffles off of his own accord. Abi makes him some chamomile tea. He sinks into an uneasy slumber.

After I'm sure he's asleep, I turn my attention to her.

"I'm sure I don't want to ask this question, but... how bad are things right now?"

"Pax is on the rise, supplies are low. The escaped patient is still at large. They can't have much longer left, but they can infect a lot of people in that time if they're not careful. A lot of people are going to die, and painfully, and there's very little we can do that isn't already being done."

That makes me feel a little better, at least. There's nothing I could do anyway.

"Stay out of trouble," I tell her.

"I invariably do."

She's right, of course. I'm the one that's always taken the large bulk of the risks. But not any more. Not again.

CHAPTER 29

Abi's predictions rattle me, and her words cling to me for several days after. I cannot shake them. They rub against my skin like burrs, and every time I think myself free of them, I find another in a crevice I didn't know I possessed.

I finally emerge from my slump. I take another job from Abe, although I'm conscious this time of not stealing anything too precious that could be better put to use. It's stealing some artefact from one warehouse to another, presumably to be fenced in another city for a much higher price. I don't have much appreciation for art, and if people with far too much money want to fight over it, they are more than welcome to.

Mi is busy at the infirmary most days, occasionally punctuating it with shifts as the butcher's. Baz is very accommodating, but we need the work and Baz can't do it all by himself. One night, Mi comes back so late that he's still spark out by the time his shift starts. I walk to the butcher's to explain what's happened, offering a free bird as a peace offering. Baz is out back. His adopted son –a mute boy named Wart– is manning the counter. I've always thought him something of a simpleton, but he seems to understand me just fine. I know he's developed a way of communicating with Mi, so he can't be too dumb, even though his clickings and tappings mean nothing to me. How does Mi have this kind of patience?

Eventually, he gets too frustrated and goes out back to find one of his little sisters to translate. She's a tiny thing, a dwarf next to her giant of a father. I think her name is Sally, but I have no concept of her age and she's virtually indistinguishable from her sister.

"I will tell Papa," she promises, taking the bird from me. "Bye-bye, Ashe-Ashe."

This is a pet name Ben used to use when he was little. Are the two of them friends? Did she pick it up from him? I have no idea.

The marketplace is back to full swing now. With Mi so busy both at the butcher's and at the infirmary, I've taken over the role of cooking. I'm not nearly as skilled as he is in this department, but there are no complaints and I can tell that he is grateful for the slack. I take Ben on another hunting expedition and the two of us cook our catch together. A rabbit and mushroom stew is served that evening, with wild garlic and only slightly-stale bread.

As much as I usually like the silence of the wilderness, I enjoy spending this time with him, and organising our stocks is much more fun with him by my side. It's far easier to see what we have and not what we don't, although that might just be the infectious side of his optimism.

"Ben," I ask him carefully one day, "what do you want to be when you grow up?"

The last time I asked him this, he said a truck. I'm hoping for a better answer now.

"I don't know," he says. "Happy, I guess."

It's such a good answer, but it makes me worry. I worry I'll never be able to give him this, that I can't protect him from the world and all its ills. Sooner or later, he'll see the truth of our lives. Then he'll never be happy again.

"Are you not happy now?"

"Yeah, mostly, but it looks harder to be happy when you're older."

Too damn right. Not that I got to be happy when I was younger, either.

"What do you want to be?" he asks.

What future did I have in mind for all of us, if I ever allowed myself to think so far ahead? I'm not sure I ever had. I'd always seen it as just being the four of us, pretty much forever. Ben was the most normal. Maybe one day he'd leave and start a new family. But he was just a child, that was so far ahead, and I didn't want to imagine my baby ever going. It seems strange that I never contemplated the rest of us getting involved with someone. Did I think we were all too badly damaged? Mi is so likeable; why had I never thought that he would find someone to share his life with? And though Abi has never expressed any such desires, is it really completely implausible that she'd *never* fall in love? She's only fourteen.

The truth is, I just never imagine the future beyond the next day. I was never brave enough to. But I can't explain this to Ben.

"What do you think I'd be good at?"

"Saving people!" he says quickly, making my insides twinge. "Ooh, maybe you should be a helicopter!"

I splutter with laughter at this, and chase him around the room making silly noises.

CHAPTER 30

By the end of the day, neither Mi nor Abi has returned. It is not like them to be quite so late. I surrendered my communication device to one of them to take back some time ago, so there's no way to get in contact. Ben can sense my unease and fights sleep, but eventually gives over. I sit on the roof for several hours, awaiting their return. Nothing.

It grows so cold even I begin to feel it, and finally head back inside. I sit on the couch, wrapped up in a blanket, my ears pricked for any whisper of movement on the stairs.

Mi must be at the infirmary, I reason. That's the sort of work that sucks you in, that doesn't stop when the sun goes down. As for Abi... she must be working on some project with Harris, or perhaps she's running technical support for a mission of some kind. She wouldn't mention that to me because... because I made it very clear I wanted no part of it.

Somehow, sleep creeps upon me.

It is Ben that wakes me, the room awash with bluish light.

"Mi and Abi aren't here," he says, his bottom lip trembling. "Did they come home last night?"

"It's OK, bud," I sit up and take his hands. "They were just working late."

"So, you spoke to them?"

"I'm sure they're fine."

"Can we go check on them?"

I hesitate. I'm in no mood to go back to Phoenix HQ, but

I'm just as keen as Ben is to work out what's going on.

"Shall we walk down to the marketplace entrance? You can pop in to see them, and I'll get some supplies for today?"

I try to keep my words light and breezy, to mask the dread scuttling away inside. Nothing can actually be wrong, surely? Someone would have told us. Nick would have let me know. I can fold away my feelings, I can tell myself that we do not know each other, but I know enough of him to know that. He would never let me languish in fear, even if it meant giving way to grief.

Ben nods, and goes back to his space to dress. I take a moment to clean myself up a bit, splashing water on my face and dragging a hair brush through my shoulder-length tangles. It doesn't help very much. Just before we leave, I grab a hunk of bread and a piece of cheese; Ben should eat something on the way.

A silent mist has slithered in this morning. The buildings loom like monsters, the clouds pressing down on all of us forced to get up on such a morning as this. Everyone we pass is secretive and slow.

Things pick up a bit around the market. This is nothing unusual. There's only so quiet you can be when you're haggling over the price of pungent vegetables, after all. But as we get closer... the noise doesn't quite match up. There's less shouting, more... murmuring, and the sound of the screen overhanging the square is louder than the people. What can they be watching so intently?

Ben and I press forward. Images swirl out of the mist. A news reporter, running footage of some kind of raid. Police pulling people into a van. I recognise some of them– Phoenix members?

There's no need to get much closer; Ben and I can see and hear it perfectly with our senses. I almost wish we couldn't.

"Six members of the terrorist organisation known as 'the Phoenix Project' were apprehended last night, while attempting to steal medical supplies from one of Luca's busiest hospitals. An anonymous tip led to their arrest before the theft could take place. In the ensuing struggle, one member was killed and another wounded."

A chill sweeps through me. Oh, oh no...

"The survivors have now been taken into custody, to await justice."

There's some booing in the background, but for a minute, I think it comes from our crowd. Only it hasn't; there are protestors on the streets of Luca, holding up signs. Just a few. A precious, tiny few. "HELP OUR BRETHREN" "LOVE THY NEIGHBOUR" "WHAT IF THEY WERE YOUR CHILDREN?"

"Ashe," Ben trembles at my side, "I know some of those people."

Of course he does. I bet he learned all of their names, sitting in the mess hall while we were training. He's been back since I left. I bet he saw some of them yesterday, happy and alive. Now one of them is gone forever, and the others...

I didn't see all six faces.

"Come on." I grab his hand. "Let's go find Mi and Abs."

Neither of them would have gone on that mission, right? They promised to stay out of the field. Unless... unless they went to support. How useful would Abi be, in Harris' van, running off numbers? The newsreader didn't say where they were intercepted–

I am racing down the tunnel before I can stop myself, dragging Ben behind me. The long run is both endless and over in no time at all. I hammer against the door, yelling at it to open. It's an age before it does.

The corridors are empty, but noise is spilling out of the mess hall. The huge overhead screen is still showing footage from Luca's streets. The protest has been garnering some attention. Officers have arrived to "calm the crowd" but they are armed and do not look peaceful.

"Ashe! Ben!" Abi is making her way through the swathes of people towards us. She almost crashes into our outstretched arms, using them to steady herself.

"Mi–"

"He's safe. He's with Julia."

"What's going on?"

"We had a tip about some supplies. Too good to pass up. I ran the numbers myself–"

"Bad tip?"

"It was a set-up."

My jaw tightens. "I see."

"Ashe... Nick was with them."

My stomach twists into some dark, powerful knot. Somewhere between my head and my heart, a voice roars. *No, please, not him...*

"Is he... do you know if he..."

Abi shakes her head. "We don't know who survived."

There's a great roaring within the room, a hundred voices, young and old, all yelling at once. It feels like we're the only ones who are quiet. It's at this point that Rudy barrels into the room and steps up the platform underneath the screen.

"Everyone, quiet!" he booms.

The volume quickly dies. The screen above him is muted.

"As you will all have seen, last night an attempt was made to liberate supplies in Luca. That attempt has failed, and as a result, six of our members are currently being held captive. One is reportedly to have died, another has been injured, and I'm afraid we do not know at this time who is still alive. The people who went on the mission were as follows: Amy Arbor, Derek Moon, Clara Dawn, River Stone, Izzy Severin and Nick Lilywhite."

A wail, a sob, or a gasp goes up for every name, but the

noise made for Nick is loudest. He is clearly popular. The three of us are the only silent part of the crowd. Perhaps it is this that draws Rudy's eyes to us, how still we are compared to everyone else. His eyes settle on me, just for a split second, but his stony gaze is difficult to decipher.

"All six of these noble souls knew the risk they took in undertaking such a mission, but each believed it to be in the best interests of our community. They marched into Luca with little thought for themselves, true warriors of the people. It is likely our brothers and sisters are being held in a maximum security facility, but rest assured, a rescue attempt will be made. I cannot promise anything other than we will try our utmost to ensure they are returned to us. I ask you to be brave in the meantime, to not lose hope, and to endeavour to hold true to the values that they have all fought for."

There is no clapping, only a whispered silence, as Rudy steps down from the platform. He points to the three of us, and nods towards his study. We follow without another word. Harris is already there, pouring over hologram. Mi is there too, looking completely lost.

"Tell me you have some good news," Rudy snaps at Harris.

"Negative. We've narrowed their location to three likely points, each one virtually impenetrable."

"Narrow it down to one," I rush, "and we'll test that theory."

Rudy spins round to face me, as if he'd completely forgotten he invited me here.

"You think you can get in?"

"Nothing is impenetrable," I say solidly. "Not with me."

"Not with *us*," Abi insists.

I look at her in shock.

"What? I'm not quite as tough as you, but you *know* I can handle myself in a fight."

"And me," says Mi.

Even Harris looks a little baffled at this, which Mi must sense.

"Me at my worst is still better than everyone else here at their best," he insists. "Julia's already tested me; my scores are almost equal to Ashe's. Plus, there's at least one wounded. You need someone with medical training."

"Julia's no field agent," Harris adds hurriedly, "and she'd be reluctant to leave her current patients, even for Nick."

Nick. I have to get to him. He has to be OK.

"Well, Mr Boss-man," I say, as flippantly as I can manage, "you have three superhumans on your side. What do you say?"

"I want to go too!" says Ben, before he can answer.

"No!" rush Abi, Mi and myself, in one hurried breath.

"You're too young," I continue, "and I'd like to give you the best chance of being older."

"You did dangerous stuff when you were my age," he says, pouting.

"I did, because I didn't have a choice. You do. We do."

"But–"

"Not now, Ben!" I snap, because I don't have time for this. *You are my world, and I will not risk you. You do not know how insane with worry I will go, having you out there.* If I had my way, I'd wrap Ben up in bubble-wrap and keep him home forever, foolish and silly though that would be. I know he needs space to grow up, that one day I'll have to let him make his own decisions, but not today.

There's a sudden knock on the door, and a rather rushed young man stands there. "We've got a visitor at the tunnel entrance," he says breathlessly.

"Well? Let them in."

"Um... he's wearing a Lucan guard uniform, sir."

Rudy's jaw tightens. "How would a Lucan guard know where–"

"Does he look like me?" Harris asks.

"He... well, yeah, actually, he does."

"Bring him in."

Rudy looks at Harris, his glare livid. An argument will happen between them later, I'm certain, but not right now.

Within a couple of minutes, Henson arrives, beet red and panting hard. Mi rushes to get him a glass of water.

"I'm so sorry," he pants, "I had no idea–"

"You said the tip was from a trustworthy source," Rudy fumes. "You said she was a friend."

"She is. She was. I had no idea–"

"Are you in danger?" Harris interjects. "Does she know you're helping us?"

"I think she might have been the one set-up," Henson continues. "I think... I think after the stunt at the hotel, the Government have been laying a few false trails, planning a number of traps. I don't think she had any idea."

"Where is she now?"

"I... I don't know." Henson swallows. "I'm hoping she realised what had happened and got out of the city. She's got family in Solis, I know–"

"Do you know where our people are being held?"

Henson nods solemnly. "Birchwood Holding Facility," he says. By the looks on the faces of Harris and Rudy, this is the worst place they could be.

"Are you sure?"

"I checked myself. I didn't want to be wrong again."

Rudy nods tersely. "Very well."

"There's something else. I was talking to some of the other guards at the facility. It's all just rumour, of course, but–"

"Spit it out."

"Due to the rising sympathy for Phoenix, they suspect the captives are likely to be quietly executed or infected and released... into the outskirts, this time. They don't want a big show."

A collective breath is sucked from the room. My head spins with a vision of Nick, covered in purple splotches, standing in another ruined street while panic fires around him.

"I see. Thank you for the intel, Henson, you may leave now." Rudy gestures to sentry to escort him out.

"Wait–" Harris wheels forward and grabs his arm. "You

shouldn't go back to the city. It could be dangerous–"

"The longer I stay, the more danger I'm in," he says, "but I have to go back. My life is there."

"You could have a life here."

Henson stares at him, the ghost of a smile flickering in the corner of his lips. "Someday, brother, I sincerely hope I can. But not now. I can still do some good for you yet."

He pulls away his hand, and disappears down the corridor.

Rudy turns back to Harris and Abi. "Well?" he says "You've got the location. How soon can you get me some numbers?"

"We can have a plan formulated within a couple of hours."

"Anything you know you'll need for certain?"

"Two vans," says Harris quickly. "And as much firepower as you can spare."

Rudy turns to Ben. "Do you know Jenn, from the armoury?"

"Uh-huh."

"Go and find her. Bring her. Quick as you can."

"OK!" Ben speeds off, glad to finally have something to do. Harris and Abi move off next.

Rudy next looks to Mi. "Go to Julia. Tell her what's going on. Get some supplies ready. Be back here in two hours."

Mi rushes off without another word, leaving me alone with Rudy.

"So... you're going to trust me now?" I ask hesitantly.

"I figured you must be back for a reason."

I swallow. "Nick," I say quietly.

Rudy rolls his eyes. "Figures. Boy's besotted with you as well. I've known him for close on ten years now; he's a good judge of character. Sees things in people they don't see themselves..." His eyes glaze, just for a moment, and I realise he's not just talking about me. "Besides which, I'm not entirely sure I have another choice right now. It's trust you or let them die."

He loves them, I realise suddenly. Whatever his misgivings are against me, he loves his people. A part of me thinks he's foolish for letting so many people in, but another part of me admires him. I would do no less for Mi, Abi and Ben. Can I blame him for caring for a family larger than mine?

"Go and find Scarlet," he orders. "She'll want to be in on this. Tell her to round up our best fighters. I'm not sure how many we'll need, but I want as much time as possible to prepare. I'll see you in two hours."

CHAPTER 31

I go immediately to the gym. There is nowhere else I am needed at present, and I absolutely must do something. I set up an insane obstacle course and run it as fast as I can, ending it with a vicious assault on the trio of dummies stacked by the side. Then I do it again in record time. The monumental clock on the wall is soundless, but I hear it ticking nonetheless. How many hours away is this facility? How long have our people been there already?

Our people. I told myself I came here for Nick, but I don't want the rest of them suffering either. I remember the sniffling, the wailing, as Rudy announced each name. They're all somebody's Nick. They all don't deserve to die like that man in the market place.

And one already has.

Twenty minutes after I've set up, Scarlet comes to join me with a handful of other people. She introduces them briefly. "Chuck, Blue, Jack, Odine, Thor," she says, each bobbing their head or raising a hand in turn. "They'll be assisting us in the mission. They're our best fighters."

I try not to judge by appearances, but it's easy to believe this about Chuck and Jack. Chuck looks like a baby giant. He has a big, round face with massive eyes, but is nearly seven feet tall and has muscles the size of hams. Jack is shorter and leaner, but strong as an ox. Blue is small, but has a lot of muscle packed into an otherwise willowy frame. She looks flexible, swift. The only two it's hard to see this in is Thor and Odine. They're young –perhaps fourteen or so– with the same beetle-dark eyes and pitch-black hair. Twins, I assume. They remind me of a pair of birds, and look like they could give flight at any moment.

"Ashe?" Scarlet asks, cutting short my appraisal. "What would you like us to do?"

If I'm surprised to be deferred to, I do not show it. I jab my thumb towards the obstacle course. "Start running it."

None of them match my speed, but the twins make a very good go of it. The older boys are slower, but make quick work of the dummies. Blue is probably the best overall. I spar with each of them in turn, testing their strengths. They're all capable, hopefully better than the average Lucan guard. Hopefully as good as their soldiers. The twins take me on together, and I realise this is their style. One distracts while the other attacks. They're very efficient, each reading the other's move before it happens.

Gabe and I used to fight like that. Mi and Gabe, too. No matter how much I've trained with the others, it's never matched the symmetry I shared with him. It never will.

Eventually, we head back to the study.

Harris, Rudy and Abi are already there, pouring over the blueprints of what must be the facility. Mi arrives not long after we do. He makes his way towards my side and whispers in my ear.

"Are the building plans as scary as the silence in the room would suggest?"

"It's a fortress."

"Great. Glad I didn't volunteer to storm it. Oh, wait..."

Rudy glares at him, and then realises how ineffective this tactic is likely to be and hisses at him instead. Mi has already fallen silent. He can feel Rudy's eyes.

"As most of you can tell, Birchwood is highly secure building. It is well-guarded and tightly patrolled. They may well be expecting us."

"Can we be sure this isn't another trap?" Blue pipes up.

"No," says Rudy stonily. "But I am uncomfortable with the alternative. You are our finest, but everything you do here is purely voluntary. If you do not wish to go, please say so now."

His gaze lingers a little longer on the twins, and I know he's unhappy with the thought of ones so young placed in such a situation. The twins seem to register this.

"No way, we volunteered!" says Odine.

Her brother finishes. "Those are our people, man!"

"Very well. Harris?"

Harris comes forward. "This is not going to be a stealth mission," he explains. "But timing is of the utmost importance. If we don't get everyone out quickly, the building will be flooded with every guard in the city and escape will be impossible."

"So we have to storm it carefully," Abi takes over. "One van will be disguised as government issue. It will go straight to the front gate and cause a distraction. The second van will be positioned at this corner–" she points to a nearby street– "Mi and Ashe will be in this one. They will scale the wall, then the tower. There is an access point on the roof."

"Guarded?"

"No. But it's a reinforced steel door."

"I hate to sound like a weak little kitty-cat," I interject, "but the last time I checked, I couldn't *quite* break one of those down." I could barely dent it, truth be told.

"Which is why you'll be blowing it up."

"Sweet!" says Thor, and then looks down abashedly.

Scarlet raises a hand. "Won't that bring everybody a-running?"

"Hopefully they'll be distracted by the ruckus at the gate.

It will be a controlled explosion. Ashe and Mi will slip inside, everyone else will pool into the yard. I will take down the sentries on the wall. Guards will be drawn into the fray outside, hopefully partially clearing the way for Mi and Ashe to locate the captives and bust them out."

"I'm understanding it so far," says Jack, "but how do we avoid and all-out bloodbath in the yard?"

"With a lot of smoke grenades, stun guns, a heavily armoured vehicle, not acting like an idiot, and luck."

"Well, I'm a big fan of not being an idiot..." Jack agrees.

I don't like it. I'm OK with my role, I'm used to fighting in tight corners and if Abi's plan works, we shouldn't encounter a huge amount of resistance. But I don't like so many people being outside, exposed in the open. It seems too risky... and what if the guards don't abandon their posts? What if plenty stay inside? What if Mi gets hurt and I have to get him out? What if the opposite happens, and he's there practically defenceless?

"Can I have one more with me?" I ask Abi.

Abi quickly runs some calculations in her head. "It makes little difference to the chances of success," she says. "Who can scale a wall quickly?"

The twins, Scarlet and Blue raise their hands.

"Take Scarlet," Rudy orders. I can tell he wants, if at all possible, to keep the twins in the van the entire time. He'll probably ask whoever's in charge of the vehicle to try and make sure that happens. I know I would, if it were Ben in there. I know I'm not happy with Abi being on the walls, taking out the guards. Stun guns or bullets? One is a lot more efficient, a lot quicker. She'll know this.

"Are there any further questions?" Harris asks. "I'll brief the gate team on the way."

No one says anything more; I think we are all keen to

move. Rudy gives the order, and we go down to the hanger. Two vans are waiting, already being stocked by a burly-looking woman with dark silver hair. Jenn, I assume, the armoury master. Ben is her ever-willing assistant. He grins when he sees us come in, but his face drops when it settles on mine. He must still be mad at me for snapping at him.

There are a few words and then everyone starts piling into the vans. I hang back a bit to ask Jenn to watch over Ben for me. She assures me she'll find him something to do. I try to talk to him, but he doesn't want to talk, so I just tell him to be good and we'll be back as quick as we can. I don't think he believes me. I think about talking Mi or Abi into staying with him, but it's too last minute. They're as committed as I am. It feels all kinds of wrong though, leaving him behind.

Scarlet, Harris, Abi and Mi pour into one of the vans, the non-government issue. A driver is already stationed in the front, but not one I recognise. The other five climb into theirs. Twelve people, all in all. Is Rudy right to send so many on a mission to rescue so few? Or is this the smallest number that offers us a decent chance of success?

Trust in Abi's numbers, a voice reminds me.

We close the doors and drive off.

CHAPTER 32

Henson lets us in through the gates again. I wonder what he risks, every time he does this. Someone must know what he's doing, or they'll figure it out soon. Does he rely on bribery to keep him safe, or are there others that share his views? Does he know he's living on borrowed time?

We enter the city without much trouble, and are a good few minutes in before Mi tries to lighten the mood.

"I can't see anything– are we there yet?"

Abi punches him in the arm.

"Yeah, I deserved that."

"We could play a game of I-spy, if you're bored?" Scarlet offers.

"I like you. You're funny."

"I spy with my little eye, something beginning with S–"

"Spanner," Mi says, not missing a beat.

Scarlet blinks. "How–? How did you–?"

"There's a tool box banging about in the corner, it was a good guess."

"I could actually have fun with this..."

Incredibly, Mi and Scarlet do actually partake in a game of I-spy as we crawl through the city, while Abi and I stare at each other, somewhere between incredulous and delighted. Scarlet initially comes off worse in this, giving him far too easy subjects while his are often out of sight. She complains this isn't fair.

"I'm sorry, are your two good eyes inconveniencing you?"

"In this case, yes!"

"Try closing your eyes."

"You have super-hearing!" She pouts. "You still have a clear advantage!"

She ups her game, and I do manage to find a little amusement in this. Perhaps they're forcing it a little, not just for their benefit, but for ours. We need a little lightness, however fleeting, however brief.

A horrible thought coils inside me. I have a sudden feeling, like this moment is dissolving before my eyes, and it will be a long time before any one of us knows such brevity again.

Nevertheless, there are things to be done. I set to work memorising the layout of the compound, at one point pulling Scarlet over to do the same. We check through our equipment, choosing our weapons. Scarlet slides a pair of goggles onto her head and then packs a small armoury onto her lean body: handgun, throwing knives, dagger, baton, knuckles, grenades. I don't really need or want any of those things. Blunt weapons can't add much to my current repertoire, and sharp ones are likely to lead to fatalities. I take a small knife, more a tool than a weapon, and refuse everything else. Scarlet looks baffled when Mi does the same.

"This may shock you, but I am not a terrific shot," Mi explains. "I'll take a quarterstaff, if you have one?"

Scarlet raises an eyebrow. "I'll go find a time machine and order you one in the Middle Ages," she says. "For now, we have batons?"

"That'll do."

Mi does not need help as a general rule with anything but reading, but he does not complain when Scarlet helps him strap on a couple of batons. She helps me with mine too, and it is a little easier with her assistance to get kitted up.

All too soon, the van is coming to a stop. I spent so long wanting to get here, but now I don't want to leave. I don't want to plummet in the belly of this concrete monster and know, for certain, whether or not Nick is waiting there. But he could be, and so I must go.

I tap the driver on the shoulder.

"What's your name?" I ask.

"Er, Dave."

"I'm Ashe."

He smiles at this. "Yeah, we all know *your* name!"

I wonder how much everyone at Phoenix knows about us now. We've not been very secretive these past few weeks. Is this what Mi and Abi like about being there? Not having to hide any more?

The feeling isn't as terrifying as I thought it was.

Harris hands us all earpieces. "Keep in contact," he insists.

One of the monitors suddenly starts beeping. He picks up his headphones and plugs himself in. "Harris," he says, then looks back at us. "Get ready."

We push the earpieces in, do a final equipment check, and slide the door open. The great wall rises ahead of us. Abi points to the precise spot we must climb up to avoid detection.

"I need to wait until the distraction to take out the guards," she announces. "Falling bodies will present just as much as a risk."

"When you say 'take out'–"

Abi pats a stun gun at her side, but she has another, much more lethal option, hidden beneath her jacket. Does she think I don't notice it? I hope she doesn't have to use it. I know too well the weight of another's death on your soul. I'd shoulder it again before having her relive that pain.

We move swiftly towards our mark, listening to Abi, who times everything perfectly to avoid any gaze.

Scarlet hands me a pair of wire cutters. I tuck them into my belt. Abi and Mi ready a boost. I take a short running jump, they thrust me into the air, and I catch the top ledge.

It is difficult, even for me, to hang on with one hand and cut the wire with another, and it takes me longer than I would like. Eventually, though, there is enough of a gap for a human to squeeze through. I loop a rope around one of the posts and drop it down for Abi to follow, then tell Harris we're in position.

Within seconds, the van bursts through the gate. Every sentry on the wall springs immediately to life. Bullets are blazing. Armoured guards run out. There are a dozen in total, all firing. A smoke bomb is released –one of ours– and everything is lost in a haze.

There is no time to waste. I drop into the yard and spring towards the tower, Mi and Scarlet quick at my heels. Abi is already on the walls, one guard down. Unfortunately, the other notices his comrade fall. He turns, but Abi is quicker. The strap of his rifle now wrestles against his throat.

"Ashe!"

Scarlet is by the foot of the tower, standing beneath a grapple. Time is of the essence. Without another word, I seize the cable and crawl up the wall, leaning back down to help the others up. Scarlet lays the explosives at the hatch, and we scurry as far away as possible for the detonation.

It is strangely quiet, and I creep back towards it expecting it still to be welded shut, but the hinges are blown clean off. I go to lift it–

"Look out!"

Mi launches himself forward, just as a hail of bullets shoot up into the air. One skims straight by my cheek. Red droplets dust the floor beside me.

Mi glares. "You have super hearing too!" he hisses. "Use it!"

All three of us remain flat against the floor, waiting for the shots to cease. I can hear Mi counting.

"How many?"

"Three."

"Don't suppose you know how many bullets–"

"No," says Mi. "But they're reloading. Quick!"

I throw myself into the hatch, landing squarely on one of their shoulders. I hang on fast as he flails, knocking into the other two. One has almost finished re-loading when Mi soars down, yanking the rifle from his grip and smashing it into his face. Scarlet wrestles with the third, but it is no easy task. She is no match for his sheer strength and it's all she can do to stop him from firing as we struggle with taking out ours.

"Mi!" I hiss, tightening my hold around the guard's neck dangerously, "Help Scarlet!"

Mi immediately leaves his own opponent, elbowing Scarlet's in the back and sending him crumpling to the floor. Scarlet whips out a baton and smacks him in the base of his skull with it. The remaining soldier recovers, moves for Mi, but he senses him coming and ducks out of the way. His bullets hit his fallen comrade instead and he freezes with shock and terror. Scarlet takes advantage of this and knocks him out. Finally, I let go of my own.

Two unconscious, one dead. Not by our hand, but by our presence. We will all carry a little piece of this.

Not losing another moment, Scarlet removes all the rounds from their weapons, just in case they come to, and we move for the stairs.

"They knew we would come," Scarlet pants as we run, "They were guarding that entrance– who knows how many more there are?"

We'll find out. The holding cells are eight floors down.

The tower quickly branches into a corridor, and voices rise from the other end.

"Five," says Mi, swallowing.

There is no cover. In a matter of seconds, they will appear, and fire will rain down upon us. We are completely exposed. We need to get out of this corridor. I turn to the nearest door. It's locked, but it's only wood. A swift kick quickly fixes that.

"Wait," says Scarlet, "do the next one– hurry!"

I don't argue with her. I don't have time to. Two doors are now knocked down, both revealing classrooms of some kind, used for military training. They're stuffed with books and boards and paper.

Scarlet pulls down her goggles and wrenches something from her belt. "Tear gas," she says. "Lure them into one, get out, and we'll let this baby do the work."

It's a decent plan. Taking on five heavily-armed guards in close quarters and trying not to kill them is no simple task.

Mi and I nod, rushing into the first room. We each grab a desk and flatten ourselves against the internal wall. The guards stream into the room and we crash into their backs before they can turn, leaping back out into the corridor as Scarlet breaks from her hiding spot and chucks the grenade into the room. Gas explodes. The place is thick with it.

Not even we are fully immune to the effects of tear gas, so we sprint away as it spills out into the corridor, leaving the guards coughing and choking in the haze.

We hit the main stairs. All the way down now till the bottom.

A voice buzzes in our ears.

"Alpha team! Have you found them yet?"

"Not yet," Scarlet replies. "We're experiencing more resistance than expected. How's the other team?"

"Holding strong, but they're heavily outnumbered."

"Can they escape?"

A short pause. *"Yes,"* he replies.

Scarlet and I both look at one another.

"Are you safe, still?" I ask.

"We remain undetected."

"Then get the other team out," I decide. "We'll find the captives and get them to your location."

"Roger," replies Harris stonily. *"Hurry."*

More voices from the bottom of the stairs, a readying of weapons.

"Three," Mi tells us.

I launch myself over the railings and down several flights at once, crashing clean into one of them and rendering him instantly unconscious. My hands on the bannister, I deliver a kick to another and send him flying into the last. All three are out cold by the time Mi and Scarlet arrive, panting and out of breath. We disarm them and fling their weapons to the bottom floor. We're close now, so close–

The door at the end of the final floor is barred, but we've anticipated this. Scarlet brings out the remainder of our explosives and attaches them to the locks and hinges. The door blows over with ease. There are two more guards stationed inside. Bullets immediately begin firing. Mi seizes Scarlet and yanks her to the ground, but she's up again in an instant, readying a smoke bomb.

The room explodes into thick, palpable smog, but this means nothing to me or Mi. We slide into the room, listening for the wheezing of guards, making quick work of them together.

"Here!" Mi says, pressing something into my hands. A key card. I fumble along the corridor, calling out, searching for a cell. Muffled cries –calls from behind several sheets of glass– finally reach me. I find the keypad and slide the card against it. The smoke begins to clear.

"Hello?"

Four faces swim into view, frightened, hopeful. But not one of them is Nick's.

No.

"The other two," I swallow, "where are they?"

"They killed Amy," one of them, a lean, muscular man says.

"And... and Nick?"

A small girl in the corner sobs. "They... they said they were going to... to do something to us." She swallows, as if whatever they threatened them with is too horrible to be repeated. "And Nick... he volunteered to be first. They... they took him... just a few hours ago."

"Is he still here?"

"I don't know."

I wheel round to Abi and Mi. "Get these people out. I'm going to find Nick."

"Ashe–" Mi starts.

"Get them out. Do not wait for us."

One of them shouts at me to stop and Mi calls my name, but I filter everything out.

CHAPTER 33

I race to the next level and find myself somewhere quieter. I need to find another guard, another person. I need to find out where they've taken him. All of these men are out cold, but there will be someone left in the building–

I think back to what Mi said earlier. *You have super hearing too. Use it!*

When I think, when I *really* think, and stop, and listen, I can hear everything. The steady heartbeats of the fallen guards. The distant rumble of machinery. The footsteps of the others making their way to the exit, the scraping of a door opening, two stories above me–

Two stories above. There's a person moving about freely.

Not for much longer.

I bolt up the stairs, two at a time, plunging into the next corridor. No guard. I'm not thinking clearly any more, I'm not being careful. I try to still my breathing and span out my senses, but my moment of foolishness costs me. An iron hand grips the back of my neck and sends me flying into the wall. I am knocked senseless. My eyes feel like they're pouring out of my skull. My ears ring. One side of my head throbs dizzily; I've lost my earpiece.

A blow that hard could have killed an ordinary person, or should have at least disabled them. My opponent clearly thinks it was enough; he makes no further moves. I even think I hear him laugh. I focus on a spot of dirt on the floor, waiting for my sight to return to normal, and count each breath.

I just need to listen.

He is about four feet behind me, holding a handgun, just in case I turn. But I can tell he does not expect me to, nor does he expect me to be so fast.

In a few movements, his weapon is in my hand, and he is pressed against the floor.

"You won't shoot," he says, his words a lot surer than his expression.

I don't know who this person is that he thinks I won't shoot, but I quickly correct him. I aim my weapon at his arm and pull the trigger. He seethes in pain as the flesh rips open.

"That's a flesh wound. The next bullet goes in your knee-cap. People tend to be *very* attached to those. Pun intended." I take aim again. "Now tell me... where is the last prisoner being held?"

"He's... he's in the infirmary."

"Is he hurt?"

The guard grins. "Not too badly. I'm sure he'll walk out just fine."

I'm not sure what's so amusing about this and my mind immediately jumps to all the *other* places that they could have hurt him, all the other body parts that would leave the legs completely intact. I swear, I will return every injury on this guard if they even dared–

"Take me to him," I order, trying to refocus.

"I'm not going–"

"Kneecaps. How many would you like to have by the end of the day?"

The guard glares, clutching his arm, and shuffles out of the room with my gun pointed squarely at his head.

"Walk faster–"

"Or kneecaps. Yes, I know."

It would be counter-productive to shoot him in the legs now, but I don't tell him this; he picks up the pace. We go up two more flights of stairs, along a corridor, turn a corner and–

"There." The guard points to a room at the end of the hall-way.

"Thank you, henchman, you have been most obliging."

I gesture to a nearby glass pod. The entire floor is com-posed of them; cells lined with medical beds, equipment.

"Go on." I nudge his back with the muzzle and he grudg-ingly slips inside. I run my key card over the panel. It slides shut. I give my prisoner a wave and blow him a kiss.

Nick.

Not wasting another fraction of time, I sprint towards the last cell. A figure is strapped to the bed, his dark-blond head turned away from me. It's him. *It's him.* My eyes hover his inert form, checking him for any damage. There's a few cuts and bruises, but nothing that looks particularly deliberate. Fin-gers, hands, arms, all intact.

I unlock the door. His face turns towards me and breaks into a wondrous, rapturous, bewildered half-smile.

"Ashe," he breathes, "You– you're... what are you doing here?"

I cross the room and start unbuckling, pulling him out of the bed with a frantic, desperate energy. I almost want to cry as I pat him down and double-check for any injuries.

"Even if I wasn't falling for you, I never would have left you here," I rush. "Come on, we need to move."

"Ashe–"

A crash sounds not far off. Reinforcements.

If I hoped that our way out would be easy because I must have dispatched most of the guards, I am sorely disappointed. We've barely got up half a flight before I hear the sounds of people moving beneath us, many of them, dozens, perhaps more. There is no way I can take them on, and Nick is much slower than I'd like. We belt up the stairs, towards the tower, the hatch that was our entry, now our only way out.

I could outrun them, but Nick is struggling. By the end, I'm almost carrying him, pushing him up the ladder onto the roof. I slam it shut behind us, but it does little good; we damaged it too much getting in.

The yard is swarming with guards. A helicopter swarms above us.

Is this it?

"What's that?"

Nick points to a cable, tied to a flagpole. A thick, heavy cable, that goes straight over the wall and finishes above the window of a nearby abandoned building.

A zip line. It's from Abi. I know it is.

I unbuckle my belt.

"Grab onto me," I instruct.

Nick only makes one slightly flustered sound before following my advice. We launch ourselves off the roof, the window of the next building rushing up to greet us.

We catapult through the window in a shower of glass and dust, hitting the concrete floor in a sprawling mass of limbs. I roll to my feet immediately, but Nick staggers and I have to reach out to catch him.

"Look, I know I'm quite the heroic rescuer, but there's no need to swoon!"

I laugh, but Nick doesn't laugh back. They've done something to him, something he doesn't want to mention yet, because we don't have the time and I need to focus.

I shake him, even though what I really want to do is touch his cheek, ask if he's all right, and *help him.* "Hey," I say, "Stay with me."

Nick breathes deeply and blinks several times. "If you insist."

I cut the cable with my dagger before the guards can follow us. We have a few minutes with which to make our escape. Even if guards on the ground saw us crash into the building, they would still need to exit the compound, locate the entrance, and race up the stairs. Five minutes minimum; longer if they came from inside.

We are still far from safe.

"Come on," I urge Nick, "We need to move."

I haul him towards a window. It affords me a better view of the area. We are next to a stream that gives way to a lake; the same lake I must have been able to see from the hotel. It could offer me a good means of escape. My underwater vision is excellent and I can hold my breath for five minutes, and no way are any heavily-armed soldiers following me, but Nick won't be able to last that long. I need to stay land bound–

Or do I?

Nick needs to stay land bound, but if I can convince everyone we've both plunged into the waters–

The helicopter whirs overhead. I scan the floor for cover. There are empty crates, broken pieces of furniture, ripped tarpaulin. I grab Nick's arm and pull him over to the corner, practically stuffing him inside one of the boxes.

"Um, what are you–"

"I'm distracting them," I rush. "Don't worry, I'll come back for you."

Nick looks like he wants to say something else –or do something else– but I don't give him the chance. I'm already back on my feet, streaming towards the door. Several stories below, footsteps are approaching. I look around for something to grab their attention, to make them focus on me, ignoring the other floors.

I spot an empty fire extinguisher, wrench it off the wall and lob it over the side. It's hard to ignore, but I don't wait for any confirmation. I need to get to the roof.

A few seconds later, I've reached the top, but I pause, waiting for the helicopter to pass over. I need to be sure they aren't going to realise I'm alone. I focus on the sound of the propellers cutting through the air, the whir of the engine. I wait until it's tilted away from me and the soldiers are much closer, then pick up the remains of a chair and bolt out into the open, straight for the edge.

I toss the chair into the water. It makes a resounding splash and I draw attention to it, yelling and screaming at the ripples to dive, pretending it's Nick that's just gone over. The helicopter spots me and turns around, and I wait just long enough for it to register a disturbance in the water before I plummet over the edge.

Bullets spear the water after me, but their speed is slowed once they strike the surface. I crawl through the murk, skimming the top just enough for them to think I'm going further out, and then I dive down deeper, double-back, and wait.

One minute. Two.

The guards stand at the edge of the dock, waiting for me to resurface. One of them starts to count how long I've been down.

Three minutes.

By four, they are giving up. My lungs burning, I slide under one of the docks, surfacing carefully, breathing inaudibly.

"She's dead," says one of them. "No one can stay under that long."

"And the boy?"

"Must have gone in first."

"Boss'll want the bodies."

"Then he can get some divers in. Come on, we're done here."

I wait until all footsteps have died away. The helicopter is hovering far out over the lake, still searching, but it would be almost impossible to notice me at this distance. I crawl out of the waters and back inside the building. My energy is low, but I'm keen to get back to Nick and get out of here as quickly as we can.

He meets me halfway down the stairs, gripping the banister as though in pain. His face is incredibly grey.

"I saw you go into the water," he breathes. "I was sure... you were down so long... can you breathe underwater?"

Somehow, I manage to laugh. "No, just great at holding my breath!"

He knows this. He was there when I told Julia. Has he forgotten in the heat of the moment?

"Right..." He stumbles forwards and I rush up to catch him.

What's wrong with him?

"Can you... can you hot wire a car?" he asks.

"Yes."

"Can... can you drive one?"

"I can do that too."

"Great... because I think I'm going to pass out."

His face goes even greyer, his body loses all energy and he goes completely limp. His eyes roll back in their sockets.

"Nick!"

"Don't worry," he whispers, "I won't die. I never do."

CHAPTER 34

Nick stays conscious just long enough for me to locate a car, hotwire it, and thrust him inside. He programs the controls to direct me towards the garage safe house and then passes out in his seat.

It is at this point, in the quiet, that the terror truly sets in. I have no idea what is wrong with him and I am utterly alone in this strange land. With my earpiece missing, there is no way for me to contact Harris and the others. I do not know if they escaped, and I do not know if they will come back for us.

Going to the safe house is definitely our best bet, but crawling through the city is no easy task. I wasn't lying when I said I could drive, in that I can steer and use the peddles and such, but the slums aren't exactly big on rules and road signs. I have no idea what all these lines and lights mean, and rely on copying others a great deal of the time. I do not think I do a very good job, and I'm conscious of all the cameras. I'll need to ditch this vehicle as soon as I can.

Finally, blissfully, we arrive at the garage. It's locked, but Nick's ID chip opens it up. I haul him out and place him in one of the bunks. I've no idea what to do next. I'm at a complete loss. I need Mi. I need someone, *anyone* here to tell me what to do. I'm OK with blood and broken bones and injuries, I've had enough of them myself, but this... this is out of my comfort zone.

I watch Nick on the bunk, his cheeks flushed, his breathing restless, and every organ twists inside. *Way* out of my comfort zone.

All I can do for him is to take off his boots and cover him with a blanket. I don't know much else about medical care, and nothing appears wrong with him externally.

I need to ditch the car. A lot of the fancy models have tracking chips and I can't afford anyone discovering us before... before whatever happens next. Ditching a car I can do. I drive it a few blocks away until I find a street that looks free from cameras, and walk back swiftly. I can't risk taking it any further away, as I've left the garage door ajar and Nick defenceless. Thankfully nothing looks out of place when I return.

My own clothes are still soaking. I locate the warmest part of the garage and strip, hanging them up to dry. There's a pile of mostly clean hoodies in the corner, which do for now. I go through the rest of the supplies; basic medical kit, food rations, a stack of credits, lots of tech I can't name. I try turning on one of the computers, but it needs a password. I'm no hacker. I'm locked out.

How am I to get word to the others? Surely Rudy won't just leave us here? He might not be my biggest fan, but he cares about Nick.

Except... no one knows he's alive. The other captives certainly thought he was a goner. And when I lost my earpiece...

Will they think we're dead?

Oh God, Mi, Abi... *Ben*. Had they reached base by now?

Please, I pray to whatever force might be listening, don't let them think I'm dead. Don't put my family through that.

Nick stirs on the bunk and I fly immediately to his side.

"Oh good," he murmurs groggily, "I didn't imagine you coming to my rescue."

Despite everything, I manage to smile. "No, you didn't imagine that."

He puts a hand up to my cheek, a gesture I first take to be affectionate, but then I realise he's inspecting the graze from the bullet. "You look awful," he says.

I hadn't given much thought to it, but cheek aside, one of my ears is covered in dried blood, my hands are ripped to shreds, and I'm covered in dirt and lake gunk.

"You don't exactly look like a picture of health yourself."

Nick doesn't smile. He props himself up on his elbows and starts to cough wildly.

"Nick..." I whisper, "What did they do to you?"

Nick exhales slowly. "I need you to stay calm, while I explain a few things."

"All... all right."

He lifts a hand to run it through his hair, and that's when I see it; the beginnings of a purplish rash sprouting at his wrists.

No.

What had Henson said? That he suspected the government would infect them and turf them back out?

No, no, no!

Something in my face must register, because Nick's eyes widen. "Ashe, don't–"

"No, Nick, *no!*"

"It's all right–"

"How can you say that–"

Nick tries to climb out of the bunk, but he stumbles and crashes onto the floor. I stay where I am, breathing heavily, my mind spiralling. This can't be happening. Not again, not now. Don't let me lose someone else. Don't make me *watch.*

He crawls towards me, grabbing my trembling arms. "Listen," he says, "Yes, they infected me with the pax –and a very fast-acting strain at that– but I won't die. I don't think."

"Why... why would you think that?"

"Because I've had it before."

"W-what?"

No one catches the pax and survives. No one. But then... it's miraculous he survived when his parents didn't. That alone is virtually unheard of.

"I've had it four times, since it killed my parents," he explains, "but it's never killed me. Somehow, every time, I recover. Julia's at a loss to explain it. She's ran every test she can think of, trying to create a cure. Nothing. I'm not immune, but I won't die. I will be infectious though, to everyone but chimeras apparently. So it's rather lucky that you're the one that came!"

I pause for a moment to process all of this.

"Who... who else knows? Apart from Julia?"

"Rudy, Harris and Scarlet. We've managed to keep it secret from everyone else. We didn't want a panic."

"So... what happens every time you get it?"

"As soon as the first symptoms appear, I'd go to the infirmary. Rudy would say I was on a mission. Harris would have to be in on the cover too, and Scarlet—"

"She figured it out?"

"Yeah, she's pretty smart. And unflappable."

She's more than his friend, I realise. She's his Mi. His person. Someone he can rely on for anything, tell anything to. She must be going crazy with worry. They all will be. I can see them now, back at the base. Ben will be curled up in Abi's arms, and Mi... he's either sitting with his head in his hands, listening to Scarlet pace, or... or they're sitting together with their fingers entwined. I hope it's the latter. I hope they find some comfort in each other.

"Aren't... aren't there any others you want to tell?" I ask.

He's been with the Phoenix crew half of his life. They're his family.

"Yes," he says slowly, "but I wouldn't want to worry them, or..."

"Or have them be afraid of you?"

He nods. "I... I wanted to tell *you,* but..."

"I didn't give you much of an opportunity."

At this, he manages a small laugh. "Can... can I hug you now?" he asks. "It's something I've been wanting to do since you appeared in my cell."

I don't waste time teasing him about jumping off a building together, or me carrying him to the car; I close the gap between us with far more force than I intended. It feels both awful and wonderful to cling to someone like this.

"You're hot," I whisper.

"Sorry."

"You should get back into bed."

"Would you... would you lie down with me?"

I can't imagine sleeping, and I should probably clean myself up and try to force something down me, but I consent anyway. We squeeze onto the narrow bunk together. Nick wraps his arm around my middle. His hot, slightly laboured breath brushes against my neck.

"The hotel bed was better," I mutter.

Nick murmurs something, but I don't quite catch it, or perhaps he never used words at all.

Somehow, mercifully, sleep comes.

CHAPTER 35

The following morning, Nick is worse. I manage to get a bit of soup in him, but he balks at the offer of crackers. He's hot and shivery and there's nothing I can do.

"If I get you to a hospital, won't they just dump you outside the gate anyway–"

"No hospital," Nick insists. "The rash is spreading; I don't want to infect anyone. Or risk a scene like the one at the market."

I ask him how to contact the others, but he informs me that Harris changes the password for the computer every new mission, just in case the location is ever compromised.

"Henson, then," I try, "how do I contact him?"

Nick doesn't know, and doesn't seem to want to talk.

"Let me help you," I plead, "tell me what I can do."

"There's... there's nothing..." he says. "It'll pass."

I've never seen the pax up close in full swing. I've heard Mi's horror stories. It'll pass, he assures me, but it'll get worse first.

When he's coherent enough, he tells me not to worry. Someone is bound to make contact at some point, but I'm no good at sitting by. It's not my style and I'm going crazy without daylight. The walls seem to shrink.

Nick spends a lot of time sleeping. Stir-crazy as I get, I prefer this, because when he's awake, it's worse. He's shivering one minute, burning the next, coughing and wheezing and hacking. He turns restlessly in his sheets, biting his lips, trying not to moan. His skin feels like fire whenever I'm brave enough to touch him.

I try to distract him by talking, although he often isn't in the mood.

"One of the other captives said you volunteered to be taken," I ask at one point. "Why'd you volunteer?"

"Figured I was less likely to die than the others, and it might buy them more time to be rescued."

"So not a stupid, self-sacrificing thing because I'd left Phoenix and life without me wasn't worth living?" I jest, poking him softly in the ribs.

Nick laughs weakly. "I like you, Firebird, but that's just ridiculous."

"Firebird?"

"Oh, yeah, sorry, it's just this nickname I had in my head, you know, because your name's Ashe... If you don't like it–"

"No, I like it, more than 'Supergirl', I think. If I ever get a call sign, that's what I want."

"I'll bear that in mind."

"What's your call sign?"

"White Knight."

"Of course it is."

Nick closes his eyes, but he's still conscious.

"Do you know where I got my name from?" I ask.

He shakes his head, too uncomfortable to speak, and I turn away to avoid having to watch. I stay close, my back pressing against his bunk.

"The day we arrived in the city, I stood before the Phoenix mural, and read what it said there. *We will rise from the ashes.* That's the moment I choose it."

Nick smiles. "I designed that mural."

"You did?"

"I was just a kid at the time. I didn't paint it by myself. But it was my idea."

"So, you're an artist, like Abi."

"Not quite..."

Not for the first time, I wish I had some special talent, something *pretty* or helpful or nice.

"You have a thing too," says Nick, apparently reading my mind. He smiles a little.

"Why are you smiling?"

"It's just that you're the most amazing person I've ever met, and it amuses me that you think you're lacking in any way."

"You only think that because you like me."

"I'm besotted with you, actually. Perhaps irreversibly." He lifts a finger to circle against the exposed skin on the back of my neck. "I'm still waiting on that conclusion."

I turn to face him. Our eyes meet, and I worry he's going to press me about my announcement that I was falling for him when I rescued him, but then he starts coughing again, and very quickly the conversation is over.

CHAPTER 36

At dusk, while Nick is sleeping, I head into the city. I'd stick out like a sore thumb in the day with my black, tight-fitting clothes, but I steal a pair of dark glasses to hide my eyes and lack of face paint and keep to the shadows.

Luca doesn't have a slum, but it has a down town like any other city, no doubt the address Nick gave for picking up his fictional escort. It's easy enough to find for someone like me... it's practically got a homing beacon. It's shiny, awash with bright, neon light, and filled with music and whispers.

I speak to a few people about passage out of the city, but no one has anything to offer there. The next thing I ask for is drugs.

"What you after, cherie?" asks a voluptuous woman in a red dress.

A list of the symptoms I expect Nick to start exhibiting is sure to raise alarm, so I just tell her I want something for pain.

"Want to heal your broken heart?" she says sympathetic-ally. "If you want to get back at him, I know someone who can track him down–"

"Can you help me or not?"

"How much do you have?"

I flash her a handful of the credits.

She pouts greedily. "Give me half an hour. Meet me back here. I'll have something for you."

I don't like leaving Nick for so long, but I don't see what

choice I have. I grab something hot to eat while I wait. It's easily the best thing I've had in days, but it still falls flat in my mouth. Eventually, the woman returns, with three small vials and a syringe.

"Nemean," she says. "Will that do?"

Nemean is a hard-core medical drug, expensive and highly effective. It's typically used post-surgery. I can't remember the side effects, but the fact that it's legit eases my concerns. I pay up promptly.

"Not too much, ma cherie," the woman warns. "One vial at a time, never more than one in a day."

I'm glad for the advice, as I have no idea about dosages, but I do not thank her. I disappear back into the shadows.

Mission accomplished, I head back to the garage. Nick is awake, looking thoroughly relieved to see me.

"Where did you go?"

"I had to get out–"

"It's not safe out there–"

"I think I've demonstrated quite aptly that I can take care of myself."

"I didn't mean like that," says Nick, "but I think we both know this city isn't exactly your comfort zone."

Neither is this.

"I got you something," I say, to avoid confessing just how awkward I am here. I dig my hands in my pockets and bring out the vials of clear, colourless liquid.

"Nemean?" Nick guesses.

I nod. "It should help, if–when– things get worse."

Nick shakes his head. "I... I can't take it."

"Why... why not?"

"You know how addictive that stuff is?"

"I've only got three vials, it's not that easy to come by. You can't become addicted to it if–"

"I have pretty easy access to the city, I'd find a way."

At this point, he starts to cough, great hacking, lung-crunching coughs. His entire body spasms.

"But you're in pain–"

He clears his throat. "Do you know what the side effects are?"

"No–"

"It can make you completely impervious to pain, amongst other things."

"That doesn't sound too bad."

"Says the girl who can barely feel pain anyway," he snaps, far more harshly than I have ever heard him.

I know that our pain threshold is much higher than normal people's, but that doesn't mean I don't understand it. That doesn't make this any easier to watch.

"I know pain," I whisper.

Nick hangs his head. "Just... don't make me take it. Don't *let* me take it. Even if I beg."

I'm not sure I'll have the willpower to refuse him if he asks for it.

"I'm going out again," I say shortly.

"Ashe–"

"We're running low on food."

A complete lie; there must be a week's worth, but Nick is unlikely to check, and I have to, *have to* get out of here. I can't sit in this place and look at him and listen to him and do *nothing* to help.

This is probably why I avoid caring about people, and definitely why I avoid caring about society, because it can destroy you to watch them suffer.

CHAPTER 37

I climb the nearest building I can find. It feels better to be up here, above the whir of the traffic, the noises merging together into one. Less cameras this high up, too. Less things to hide from. I can see Luca's great wall. Behind that, home. There are one or two high rises tall enough to see over it. I could probably see my own apartment on the outskirts. If only the Institute had thought to make me part bird, I could be home in thirty minutes. Less, possibly. I do not know how fast I can hypothetically fly.

Pretending, just for a moment, that I can, I do a running jump and leap onto the next building. The feeling of being unattached to anything is exhilarating. I pick up the pace, running up the next one, launching and vaulting from one rooftop to the next.

Eventually, I reach the gate. I did not notice coming in, but this part of the city is almost as grim as the slums. It's cleaner, there's less graffiti, but it's still coated with the same dark grime. The few shops nearby look a little worn, and everything sits in the huge shadow of the wall.

I turn my attention to the guards at the gate. None of them are Henson. He could be on the other side, of course. Or it might just not be his shift. Or... or something could have happened to him. His superiors could finally have clocked onto the fact he's always on duty when someone gets into the city that isn't suppose to. One of his colleagues could have turned him in–

I'm so fixated on that thought, that I don't notice the gun until after it's fired. The world shifts into slow motion. I drop to the floor just as it passes over my head.

"She's there!" I hear someone cry.

Suddenly, the guards are everywhere, filling the streets like ants. They're lined up on the wall, taking aim–

They've been waiting for me.

I need cover. I bolt for the door to the building, break it open and stream inside before another bullet can catch me. I'm in the hall of some apartment block. The guards will be in the building at any moment. The stairs might be too risky–

I knock frantically on one of the doors. A short, rotund man answers. "Can I–" he starts.

I barge past him into the room. He stands there flabbergasted as I hurtle towards the window. There's a small balcony. I jump down to the next one, briefly hoping to stay there until the guards have cleared the building.

"Up there!" some helpful civilian yells, and a second later a guard is taking aim.

I roll into the apartment –helpfully the door is already ajar– and a stream of bullets enters after me. Someone starts to scream, multiple people. I wheel around and see a woman crouched in the corner, desperately shielding two small children from the chaos.

"I won't hurt you!" I assure her, holding up my hands. A lot of good that will do when her own goddamn people are firing on her.

I glance around the apartment, searching for cover, ideas, anything. It's really little better off than the slums. I'm sure they have hot running water, but they've got a super-old gas hob. Luca is virtually all hydro and solar– clean, renewable stuff. We don't always have access to that; we use what we can get. Clearly they do too.

There's noises in the hall. No time to run.

"Get down!" I shout at the mother.

A heavily-armed guard bursts into the room, his rifle raised. He freezes momentarily when he spots the cowering occupants behind me, giving me just enough time to disarm him and empty the weapon of its rounds.

"Are you guys crazy? There are kids in here!"

I slam the weapon into his head and race out into the hall. I try to span out my senses, but there's too much going on. Too many people are running about, up and down stairs, inside of apartments. I kick open another door. This one's empty, used for storage. There's boxes and crates, broken furniture, rolls of supplies and spare gas canisters.

I make a beeline for the window, but voices fill the space outside the door. I grab one of the cannisters instead and hurl it towards the entrance. It collides with a weapon and bounces off into the corner, hissing.

Shots are fired. I dive behind the kitchen island, searching for something to use as a weapon.

A sulphuric smell uncurls in my nostrils. The gas cannister! One of the guards shouts to stop firing, and then goes silent. They're doubtless planning to surround me, but at least they can't fire with the room filling with gas, and I've just found an old frying pan in one of the cupboards.

They emerge either side of the island as I spring on top of it, kicking one of them in the face and cracking the frying pan over the other's head. It's not strong enough to render him unconscious, only dazed. I wrap my legs around his neck and slam him into the counter, rolling away as he falls and going for his partner. I kick her legs out from underneath her and punch her squarely in the face.

A gun cocks near the door.

"Wait–" I shout.

I hold out my hand to stop him, and for a moment, time seems to slow. My fingers reach out as if to stop the bullet, but they seem to shake uncontrollably.

I do not hear the bullet. I do not remember much of the next few seconds. Everything is lost under the roar of the flames. The room erupts. Heat blisters into being. I am thrown back against the wall, dropping behind the counter, and blackness spreads across my vision.

CHAPTER 38

My ears ring. Something is crackling. Fire dances around the room. Still spinning, I force myself onto my knees.

What just happened?

I don't think I was out long. A few seconds at most. How can there be so much fire already? Why am I uninjured?

A bookcase topples over. A scream is cut horribly short, only to be replaced by several others, out in the hallway.

I emerge from behind the counter. The guard under the bookcase, who was standing right next to other cannisters, is very clearly dead. His colleague is still breathing, although she won't be if she stays in this room much longer.

I should leave her. She wouldn't save me, if the positions were reversed, and the fire will probably make it easier to escape. I have a family to get back to. I have *Nick* to get back to. I'm not being completely selfish if I leave her here. But... she might have people to go back to as well, and I won't sleep easy knowing I left her.   "Oh, fine," I say to no one in particular, and pull her over my shoulders.

The hallway is awash flames. Part of the wall to the apartment has been blown away, fire spills out into the space, licks the ceiling. I do not feel heat as keenly as others –my skin is almost impervious to it– but I can feel this blaze and the smoke as it winds its way through the air.

People have flooded the corridors, but only a few are brave

enough to attempt running through the flames towards the stair door. The three that have cannot open it; the handle has been welded shut.

Barely protecting my unconscious passenger, I stream through the flaming arch, kicking the door down at the other end and giving way to those waiting. I turn back to the nervous ones and gesture for them to follow.

"Quickly!"

The fire is getting worse.

They come, reluctantly, one after the other, only picking up the pace once they are clear of the heat. I rearrange the guard on my shoulders and hurtle after them, breaking out into the street.

In the chaos, the enforcement seems to have abandoned its search for me, perhaps assuming that I escaped in the confusion or perished in the blaze. Why would I stick around, after all? The few that remain unhurt are assisting with the evacuation or trying to put out the blaze. I deposit the guard in a waiting ambulance, turn to run–

The glare of a dozen small recording devices light up the street like fireflies. Of course people are recording the carnage. Why else would you watch? I should get out before anyone gets a good shot of my face, although at this point I'm close to abandoning the whole facade of anonymity entirely. Let them know it was me at the hotel, me who pulled a guard out the wreckage. I'll be Nick's stupid *Firebird*.

There's a cry from one of the floors, followed by frantic whispering, screaming. "Up there!"

The woman from earlier, the one with the two children, is standing on her balcony, trying to flag someone's attention. The little girl clings to her legs, the little boy... he's no where to be seen.

Someone goes to alert the guards, but I saw the inferno the

stairs were becoming. There's no getting out that way, and the smoke–

Another siren howls in the distance.

Leave it alone, Ashe. It's not your problem. Let someone else save them. They'll be fine–

And if they're not?

Within seconds, I am running, not caring that a dozen eyes and screens are suddenly fixed on me. I leap into the air, flinging myself straight onto the first balcony and crawling up the building until I reach my mark. I drop straight in front of the mother and her child, holding out my arms to the girl.

"Come on," I urge, as softly as I can manage.

The little girl buries herself further into her mother's legs.

"It's OK, sweetheart, I'm going to help you. I'm going to get you out of here and come back for your mother and brother. All right?"

The little face looks up at her mother, who nods desperately. The girl reaches out and wraps her arms around my neck.

"I'm going to need my hands. Can you hold on tightly enough?"

She whispers an affirmative in my ear. I lift her up, her tiny legs swinging around my waist.

I leap off the balcony, the mother screaming as I vanish, not expecting me to jump straight from the fifth floor directly onto the concrete below with her baby in my arms. But we land as safely as cats and within seconds I am springing back up the building, trying to gather her up.

"No!" she hisses. "Jase– my boy!"

In the panic, I had almost forgotten about him, but she leads me inside, into the bedroom, and points to the bed. "He won't get out!"

I have no patience for this. I lift the bed clean off the floor and drag the child out from under it, shouldering him despite his protests and leaping off the balcony a second time. He stops screaming shortly after we land.

I'm just about to return for the mother when another explosion tears through the building. The entire floor seems to sag, and before I've even moved from the boy's side, the woman is blown into the air and plummeting towards the floor–

Faster than the air, I follow the direction of her fall, leaping out and grabbing her before she can land. She utters a sound – a shocked kind of thanks– and then she is tumbling out of my grip towards her children.

It is then I notice all the cameras trained on me.

"What *are* you?" asks one bystander. "Are you... are you here to hurt us?"

I could sneer at her and point out I just rescued four people from a burning building–one of which had tried to kill me moments before– but maybe all my aggression is spent.

"I'm not here to hurt anyone," I tell her. "I'd actually rather like to help, and if people could *just stop shooting at me,* that'd be great!"

"Why are they shooting at you?"

"Ask your government."

"Wait, but... who are you?"

"My name is Ashe," I declare.

Please, please... let this get back to Harris. Let him send someone for us!

More people are amassing, more cars, more guards and police. I need to get out now, before I can't get out at all. I give the girl a mock salute, and then stream off down an alleyway, up a fire escape, and away into the night.

CHAPTER 39

Back at the garage, Nick is still asleep. I clean myself up as best I can, scrubbing smoky residue from every inch and crevice. I look down at my hands; they tingle slightly, in a way I don't remember before. Did... did I start that fire?

I don't see how it's possible. Abilities were not unheard of at the Institute, and there was always the inexplicable connection between myself and Gabe, but I've never shown any kind of pyrotechnic abilities before. If I was capable of it, they surely would have known. How many tests had they run on me at that awful place?

But then... I don't remember the guard firing.

I push the thought away, scrubbing my hands clean, and make myself something to eat. For the first time in days, I'm famished. After I've mopped up the remains of my powdered soup and crackers, I crash on the spare bunk, so exhausted that even Nick's coughing doesn't wake me up.

I don't know what time I wake. With no natural light, time has little meaning here. Nick is awake, looking worse than ever and trembling in his skin. He still tries to smile when his eyes meet mine.

"Hey," he whispers hoarsely, "Where'd you go yesterday?"

"Oh, you know, out and about."

"You smell of smoke."

"Well, I am a *firebird*."

His laugh turns into a hacking cough, which I try to ignore

as I slip off my bunk and make him something to eat. His limbs are shaking so terribly that I have to hold the spoon to his lips, and he curls back up after managing only a few mouthfuls, seizing in his sheets.

I touch his arm. It's like burning iron.

"There must be something I can do..."

"Honestly... just... having you... here is... pretty good. Don't normally... get that."

"Me?"

"Anyone."

It must be very lonely, shivering on a bed, with only a few volunteers in hazmats around, if you're lucky.

"I can try to get hold of a transfusion kit. Our blood can ease the symptoms–"

"You hate needles."

I hate this more.

"Small price to pay," I say swiftly.

"Do you... do you even know how to use a transfusion kit?"

"I'm pretty handy. I could work it out."

The truth is, I *don't* know. It can't be as simple as stabbing each of us with a needle and pressing a button. They'll be plenty of ways to do it wrong, and with my aversion to needles... oh god, what if I pass out in front of him?

Nick pulls on my jacket cuff. "What are you thinking about?"

"How mortifying it would be if I passed out in front of you from a *needle*."

Nick chuckles feebly. "Because you're so tough and it's a tiny needle?"

"Because I am so tough, and it is a tiny needle."

I inspect his rashes. They're starting to blister. This, at

least, is something I can ease, cleaning them with hot water and bandaging the worse ones. Wounds I can do.

"Lucky you're immune, eh?" Nick coughs.

"If I wasn't, I'd probably still be here."

"That's a dumb thing to say... dumb thing to do."

"You make me dumb, but I don't mind as much as I should."

"I knew you liked me."

"I do," I whisper, my voice almost as hoarse as his. "I do like you." *A lot, too much, enough to break me.*

I tell him another story, about finding the loft and making it our home. It's one of the few nice stories I can think of. I try a few more, like making a birthday cake for Ben when he complained that all the other children had birthdays. It must have taken me a week to secure all the right ingredients, so much bartering and trading, all of it worth it to see the little look on his face. We played old-fashioned party games for hours after, and when he finally fell asleep, we three went up the roof and asked ourselves if we wanted birthdays. I said it was too much trouble. Mi could not have a birthday without thinking of the real, unknown one he shared with Gabe, and Abi said she thought she would like a date, to feel more normal, but not a party.

Nick does not talk much, but whenever I stop, he requests some other tale.

I am running out of happy ones.

I tell him about the first time we took Ben out on "a mission" –how we strapped him to our backs and shielded him from harm. It was a test, of course, everything was. We just didn't always know how we were being tested. Some things were obvious. "How fast can Eve run?" "Is she stronger than Adam?" "How quickly can she work out x?" "How fast does she heal?"

Others were stranger. We were given philosophy books as

we got older. They would present us with scenarios. "Who should you sacrifice to save the rest?"

Questions that had no right answer, something I angrily spat at them once.

I remember the Director was there for that one. He found something amusing about my reaction. The others didn't, and Abi's wails as they hauled me off for punishment still crawl around my insides.

I spoke my mind less, after that. Gave them any answer that would do. I didn't want her –or any of the others– to cry over me.

"Strange questions, for a soldier," Nick wheezes.

"Strange questions for anyone."

"Are you sure... are you sure that... that's what they wanted you to be?"

"Pretty sure," I whisper. "Why else would they make me kill?"

Nick goes very quiet for a moment. "I'm sorry. That they made you do that."

"Have you ever taken a life?" It's a silly question, of course. I've seen him holding a weapon before. He fired on those guards at the warehouse. It seems unlikely he's survived this long if he keeps missing.

"Yes... when it was absolutely necessary."

"It wasn't always necessary, for me."

The first time I killed someone I knew was human, I was ten years old. He was Adam's second, Beta-2. We just called him Beta. We were not friends. He did not like me. He hated that I was better than him and I disliked him because he wouldn't accept that. One day, during a match, he just kept going. Every time I knocked him down, he got back up. Every time I disarmed him, he kept punching. Eventually I realised he wasn't going to stop until I made him. I got him in a head-lock, trying to choke him out. He did not go down easily.

"Stop struggling," I told him, "just drop down. Let's finish this."

Only he wouldn't.

I do not know his last words. He couldn't say anything, his throat was being crushed by my arms. He just flailed, making choking, guttural sounds. Time and time again, I replay that moment in my head, trying to remember if he said anything during the match at all, if I overheard him talking to his com-rades beforehand. I cannot recall.

"Finish the match, Eve," the Director called.

I tightened my grip. He still didn't stop.

"Finish *him*," was my next instruction.

I knew what was expected of me. Perhaps they had de-cided that Beta wasn't strong enough, or smart enough. Per-haps they didn't like that he couldn't follow orders. But I sus-pect differently. I suspect they just wanted to know if I'd do it.

And I did.

I wanted the match over. I was tired, I was bored. I was angry at him for not listening, for being silly. So I snapped his neck.

For one fraction of an awful, blissful second. I enjoyed it. The power, the control. The *winning*.

But then his body hit the floor. One of his comrades – Beta-4– started to scream, and Adam looked at me in a way he never had before. In that moment, I was no longer his com-petition, his rival. I was the monster who had taken away his friend.

Afterwards, they interviewed me. They asked me how I felt. I told them nothing. I was just following orders. I seemed callous, cold, unfeeling.

When night came around, I screamed soundlessly into my pillow and wept as quietly as I could. That morning, when I woke, I had been ordinary, as far as I knew. Now something inside of me was different. My soul was damaged, stained, fettered. I was not the same. That act had twisted me into something awful and ugly.

What had I done?

Gabe crawled into my bed. He held my shaking hands.

"You had to do it," he whispered.

But I didn't. They would not have killed me, *me,* their golden girl, if I had refused. They might have beat me, but I could handle a beating. If I had refused, a life would have been spared. I would not be a monster.

Eventually, I learned to recognise the real monsters from the victims, to place the true blame of his death on those that ordered it and manipulated a small child to carry it out. If there was a monster in me, it was one of their making, and I didn't have to let it loose.

But I have never forgotten the feeling of his life in my hands, the scream that cut into my flesh, and the look of horror on Adam's face.

Never again would I be a monster.

"Tell me something else," Nick asks quietly.

"About what?"

"Anything. When are you happiest?"

"When I'm in the wilderness," I say quickly. "Or... or when I'm with Ben."

"He really is your baby, isn't he?"

I nod. "Which is just as well, 'cause–"

I stop abruptly. This is something personal, something I've not discussed with anyone else, apart from Abi, just the once, because it applied to her too.

"Because what?"

"We can't have children," I say shortly. "At least, Abi and I can't. I don't know about the boys."

"How... how would you know that?"

"When I was about eleven, they did something to me. I didn't know what, at the time. I was used to experiments. This one was different. I woke up from surgery with cuts across my hips. It was only when we escaped I realised what that probably meant."

"They... they did the same to Abi?"

"She doesn't remember any surgery, but neither of us have ever had periods and we've *clearly* hit puberty–"

"Clearly," Nick agrees.

I go quiet for a moment. "I've never told anyone else that." I look back at him. "Does... does that bother you?"

"Am I bothered you shared a secret with me? Quite the opposite!"

"I mean... does it bother you, that I can't have kids?"

Now it is Nick's turn for silence. "Does it bother you?"

"No, no really. I've got Ben still. I think he could be enough for me."

"Then it doesn't bother me."

I wonder if he's lying, lying to be kind. *I'd love to have a family,* he'd said. Maybe he'd envisioned settling down one day and having a couple of sproglets, and now has to come to terms with the fact that if he wants me, that won't be a part of a future we share.

Of course, we could get together, have fun while it lasts, and go our separate ways. But somehow, that seems an unlikely end. If I thought this could be a fling, I wouldn't be so hesitant to start it.

Nick sinks into another fit, filled with violent coughing

and painful thrashing. The sheer terror of being with him is eclipsed only by the fear of being without him. Oh Ashe, what have you done, falling for a boy more perishable than the last that stole a little part of your soul? But another part of me trembles at another thought; that whatever Gabe and I were to each other, this is something else. Some other frightening, wordless feeling, rapturous and shapeless and utterly terrifying.

And I can't watch him suffer like this. I need to get him to Julia. I need to get him home, by whatever means necessary.

I reach over and touch his cheek. "Don't hate me for this," I whisper.

CHAPTER 40

I head back to the downtown area, searching for the curvy women who secured me the drugs. She's no where to be found, but I do find someone to swap the Nemean with for some morphine. It's a terrible bargain and he comes off much better for it, but anything is worth it for a few days of easing Nick's pain, and mine. I can't take much more of this.

Which is why I have to get him out of here, back to someone who knows what the hell they're doing.

I stick around the square for hours, hoping to catch her, mostly trying to stay in the shadows and out of sight. There's a huge screen attached to the side of one of the buildings, playing adverts and newsreels and the occasional cartoon. I don't often have much time for watching frivolous things, but I'd probably enjoy it more if I wasn't so jumpy.

It's news that plays most often though. Rousing speeches from the mayor about how great the city is. Crime reports – *an all time low!*– and food production is higher than ever. Great research being done at the Institute in regards to the pax. It'll soon be "a thing of the past"– a statement we've all heard too many times to believe.

I should have shouted that at the cameras last night. I should have told them what the Institute really does.

I'm so preoccupied with that bitter thought that I barely notice when the screen switches to an image of a burning building, until I'm watching a dark shape shooting up it.

Hmm, good moves, is my first thought, before realising that of course they are– those are *my* moves. A giant Ashe is lighting up the square. People are noticing now, eyes fixed on my image, my superhuman agility, the way I leap out of a fifth-story window without a scratch. They are muttering, muttering among themselves.

"Did you ever see such a thing?"

"What is she?"

"Is she dangerous?'

"She said she was here to help–"

I pull up my hood, mess up my hair, and sink further into the shadows. I can't risk being spotted now.

Some dim hope remains that the report will reach the base and Harris will send someone to fetch me, but I can't rely on that. I have to use my own resources.

Finally, I spot my mark.

"Ah, bonjour cherie!" she says as I approach her. "Back for more so soon? I told you not to exceed the dose–"

"I need something else, now," I say quickly. "You said before that you could track someone down?"

"I know a person. What's the name?"

"I don't have a name."

"Then I can't help you." She turns to leave.

"I need you to find the relatives of Nicholas Lilywhite," I tell her. "His closest ones, preferably."

I do not know if they will help us. Nick himself had said he wouldn't consider them *allies*. He clearly doesn't hold them in much high affection, but still... would they let him die?

The woman narrows her eyes at me. "Why are you after his family, ma chere? Some twisted revenge?"

"I'm trying to save a life."

"There's no sympathy discount. It'll cost you."

I reveal my remaining credits. "This is all I have."

She sniffs at my offering. "It'll do. I'll meet you back here in an hour."

"An hour?"

"Too long?"

In truth, I am surprised that such a thing can be accomplished so quickly, but I don't want to seem clueless. I tell her that's fine. I go back to the garage briefly to check on Nick – he's no better, no worse– and then head back to meet her. She hands me a little slip of paper.

"You could almost have worked that out yourself, cherie. Nicholas Lilywhite, born to Daniel Lily and Dr Eveline White, daughter of Edward Peregrine White."

This name should clearly mean something to me, but it doesn't.

"The governor?" she continues.

"I'm not very political."

She scoffs. "Evidently. Anyway, here is his address. Do as you will with it."

No wonder Nick said he wouldn't call his family allies. His grandfather is part of the very government he's trying to overthrow. That complicates things. Is it even worth going to him, especially with my face being plastered on screens across the city? He'll know I'm part of the resistance.

But then I think about going back to the garage, of trying to pass another night listening to him cough and moan, and wonder if, maybe, this time will be it. Suddenly, it doesn't seem like I have a choice.

It takes some time, even with the address, to locate his

apartment, as I need to be careful who I ask for directions and travelling incognito isn't precisely easy. Then, once I finally locate the place, I'm presented with another problem. It's a swish, expensive building, with a doorman and receptionist. No one I couldn't take out, but not without alerting others, which probably wouldn't give me enough time to locate this guy and convince him to help me before the place is swarming with enforcement. No, it's going to have to be stealth.

If I was more appropriately dressed, I could try and sweet talk the doorman a bit, at least learn which side of the building the apartment was on, but such questions in my current attire are bound to cause suspicion. Oh well, the hard way it is.

I climb onto one of the neighbouring buildings and fix my gaze on the windows. I spot two kitchens per row, which likely means two apartments per row, four per floor. Edward White lives in apartment twenty-two. Fifth floor.

I scan both options. One has young children in –unlikely– and the second a middle-aged couple, too young to realistically be grandparents. I hop onto the next building, and the one after that, trying to glimpse the remaining two. A young woman in one, and the fourth... no one visible.

It has to be it.

I leap across to the private terrace and peer inside. It is a smart, elegantly furnished residence, all smooth lines and sleek curves, largely colourless apart from the occasional splash of paint on a canvas. There's a desk by the door covered with pictures of grandkids. None look like Nick, but a few look enough like him to be cousins.

I try the door. It's open. I guess when you live high up in a fancy city with a low crime rate, you probably think you're safe.

By the door, I find a package with the right name and address. This is the place.

I scan my senses about, listening for life. It's a little tricky in a building like this –it's not always clear to me who is in the next room, or the next apartment, or the next floor– but I think I'm alone. I do a quick search for weapons. I don't get very far before I hear someone coming along the corridor and dash into the kitchen. A few moments later, a man enters the apartment. He is tall and grey, somewhere in his sixties, clean-shaven, polished. Handsome, really, in a mature kind of way. He has high, defined cheekbones... like Nick's. Little else about him, though. He is too sharp and manicured.

I wait until he moves away from the door. It wouldn't do to have him startle and run for the corridor before we've had a chance to talk.

I slip into view. "Edward White?"

His hands fly immediately inside his coat, and he whips out a pistol. He barely has time to aim before I've flown across the room, wrenched it from his grasp, and pushed him up against a wall. I clench my hand over his mouth.

"I'm not here to hurt you!" I say shortly, "I'm here on behalf of your grandson."

White's saucer eyes shrink just a little, and I let him slide to the floor, taking a step back and unloading the weapon.

"He needs your help," I add.

"Oh yes? Which one?"

"Nick."

"Nicholas?" he looks baffled. "What on Earth... is it money? Does he need money?"

"Has he asked you for money before?"

"Well, no, but... what else could he want from me?"

At least it looks like they've spoken some time in the years since Nick left the city. At least they have some kind of relationship.

"Well, you can tell him to forget it," the old man continues, "I'm not giving him anything. He'd just squander it on some other lost cause."

So he knows something about what Nick does, and yet... he's a governor. If he truly knew what Nick was doing, he could report him. Have him properly exiled or... executed. Either he doesn't know the whole truth, or he cares. *Tread carefully, Ashe.*

"He doesn't want your money," I say, "although... although what I need might cost you."

"Then you can forget it too. What's the meaning of this anyway, breaking into my home?"

"I didn't break in. You left your terrace unlocked."

"I– it's five stories up!"

"I'm a good climber."

His gaze intensifies as he searches my face. "You... you're her, aren't you? The girl from the news?"

I do a mock bow. "In the flesh."

"You're from the Chimera Institute. One of their little escaped projects."

I freeze. He must be very high up indeed, to know the truth of the place, or else the whispers of what I am have grown far more dangerous indeed.

"What... what do you know of the Institute?"

"Just what it does. It's not really my area. I heard rumours a few of them escaped a few years back. Most of them fly under the raider, but you... my grandson must have gotten to you, hmm?"

I swallow, narrowing my eyes, hoping they don't betray the extent of quite how much Nick has *gotten to me.*

"Yes."

"With just two calls, I could have you on your way back to

that place."

"They wouldn't catch me."

"Then why aren't you leaving now?"

I inhale sharply. "Because I need your help."

"I won't give it."

"It's for Nick." The lump in my throat grows harder. "I think he's dying."

"What?"

"I need to get him out of the city–"

"Get him to a hospital–"

"They won't be able to help him."

"What do you mean?" His eyes widen, and his voice falls quiet. "Oh, I see."

"If I can get him out of the city–"

"He'll die anyway!"

"I don't think so." I don't want to reveal Nick's immunity, because I'm not sure what he would do with that. I don't want to risk him being hauled off to some secret facility and poked and prodded like a lab rat… Nick can't run anywhere at the moment, so I put myself on the line instead. "There's… there's something I might be able to do, but there's equipment that I need to have, *people* I need to help me. But they're on the other side of the gate and I can't get a message to them."

"You… you truly think you can save him?"

I nod.

The old man crosses the room to the bureau, his gaze drawn to a photograph right at the back. Smaller than the others. Secretive. A fair-haired woman holding a grinning four-year-old. Nick.

White's fingers twitch, as if he wants to reach out and touch him. "I might disapprove of my grandson's life choices," he says quietly, "but I don't want him to die. If only he'd listen to reason–"

"I imagine he feels the same way about you."

The old man scoffs. "A child's answer."

"Will you help us?"

"Yes. You just need passage out of the city?"

"Safe passage. And... and no one can see Nick. Do you understand?"

"I think I can arrange something. Give me two hours. Where shall I meet you?"

I can't let him come to the garage. I can't compromise the safe house. But transporting Nick anywhere will be difficult right now.

"Do you have a map?"

White draws out a handheld device and clicks on a little icon. I carefully scroll to Nick's current hiding spot, looking for a place nearby that's covered, far from crowds. It's a fairly industrial area, and I notice a parking structure close by. It'll do.

"There," I point. "Two hours, right? Don't be late."

CHAPTER 41

I head straight back to the garage and dose Nick with the morphine. He's in a terrible state, seizing and trembling and conscious, horribly conscious. He's crying when I return, but he can't speak, and I feel awful for leaving him for so long like this, for leaving him at all.

"Not much longer now," I tell him, stroking his matted hair. "I'm getting you home. You'll be home soon, I promise…"

I do not know if he can hear me, and time seems to slow down to an agonizing rate.

Eventually, the time comes. I load Nick into the car, wrapping him in a blanket inside a tarpaulin. I take very little else with me.

The drive does not take long. I am the first to arrive, and as the minutes tick by, I am convinced it's a trap. White doesn't care about Nick, or else he's decided to right him off anyway. He's just using his grandson to get me to the proper authorities. I'm going to get hauled back to the Institute and Nick…

Well, perhaps they will just throw him back into the slums. Perhaps he'll be OK after all. Maybe something good will come of such a thing–

I'm just about to impart some last words onto Nick when a sleek silver vehicle pools up alongside me. White gets out. There's no one else with him.

"Did you get what we need?" I ask, climbing out.

He holds up a blue jacket and cap, similar to the style worn by the hotel staff. "Put these on."

"What are they?"

"A chauffeur's uniform. You'll be driving us out of the city."

It seems incredibly bold and daring, but I don't argue. "Pop the trunk," is all I tell him. "Nick can't be seen."

He does as instructed, and hovers curiously close as I lift Nick out. Most people give pax patients a wide berth.

"Don't get too close."

"You're immune?"

"Lucky me, eh?"

I fold Nick carefully into the trunk, wrapping the blanket around him. He does not seem to know I'm there.

"Are you sure... are you sure you can save him?"

"I know I'm going to damn well try."

I close the lid, and climb into the driver's seat. White slides nervously into the passenger's side. "Are you... his girlfriend, or something?"

I'd like to say, 'he wishes!' but instead, all that comes out is a trembling, "Or something."

Girlfriend doesn't come close. It won't ever be close enough. Which is, of course, what scares me. If it were that simple I would have given in long ago.

White taps an address into the console. "I take it you don't know where you're going?"

"Not by car."

He laughs a little at this. His laugh sounds like Nick's and I hate it.

We drive on into the city, me clunkily stopping and starting at every traffic light and junction.

"You... are not a good driver," White says eventually.

"Well, you're not a good person," I respond, stopping narrowly short of a 'so there.'

"Do you really think all Lucans are bad?"

No, clearly not, because I'm falling in love with the one I've got stashed in the trunk, idiot.

"Not all," I whisper, "but I've seen the cost of living as you do. I've seen the consequences of your great city. Also, not a big fan of you supporting the Institute. Just... putting that out there."

"The Institute was designed to help people."

"Well, it didn't help *me*," I hiss. "It didn't help Forrest or Moona or Archer or Beta or Gabe–"

"Friends of yours?"

"Most of them. All of them victims of the Institute."

"But without that place... you wouldn't exist."

"Great, then I wouldn't be alive to be so miserable."

"You wish you were dead?"

"I wish sometimes I hadn't been born," I admit, "and I'll always wish I hadn't been born *there*."

This is a hard thing for most people to understand. I don't object to being alive. I don't want to die. I more or less like who I am. But I wish I could be me with a different background. I wish I could be who I am, with Ben and Abi and Mi, and not have to be their sister because we were cooked up together in a lab.

White can't think of anything to say to that, so we carry on in silence.Eventually, we reach the checkpoint. I'm still hoping to see Henson, but no such luck. Another guard, one with narrow, suspicious eyes, knocks on the door. I roll down the window, avoiding his gaze, certain I'll be recognized.

It's a trap, it's a trap, cries the frightened bird inside me.

But the guard doesn't look at me. He looks straight across at my passenger. "G-governor White," he stammers, "I–"

He stops there. It can't be good to question why a politician might be heading outside the city walls. There are two gates into Luca. This one leads to the slums, the other to the high road– the main route to the next city. Anyone going this way... it is likely for some nefarious purpose. Suddenly, I understand a little of what Nick's grandfather is risking.

White says nothing. He hands the guard something; documents, I think, and credits. *Keep your mouth shut. You saw nothing.*

The guard waves us through without another word, and moments later, we pass under the wall, through the checkpoint, and out the other side.

I'm free. *We're free.*

It is a short ride from there until I see the looming shape of the loft. I do not want to give my precise location to White, but I also don't want to risk infecting any civilians as I carry Nick into it. I stop on the outskirts.

"Won't it look suspicious, you returning without your chauffeur?"

"Possibly. But I usually find money very helpful in ridding suspicions."

I slide out of the car and click open the boot.

"What do you really want?" White asks, before I've fully emerged. "You said on the news you wanted to help people. Is that true?"

I think for a minute. "I used to think I just wanted to not live in a prison," I say eventually. "Now I realise I want the same for everyone else."

"Luca isn't a prison."

"I didn't say I was talking about Luca. But now that you

mention it... you're the one living inside of walls."

I pull up the lid and check on Nick. He's clammy and hard, shaking and shivering. The morphine is wearing off.

White climbs out of the car. "Tell him... when he comes round... that I helped get him out. Let him know, if he changes his mind–"

"He won't," I snap, "But... I'll tell him it was you."

"Thank you."

I lift Nick out and onto my shoulder, closing the lid behind him. White slides into the driver's seat, takes a final look at his grandson, and slowly drives away.

CHAPTER 42

Nick starts seizing as I am halfway up the stairs. He's jerking so much that I can barely carry him. He's struggling to breath, his chest is like iron. He gasps like he is drowning.

"Mi!" I scream. "Help me!"

It does not take long for him to hear me. Thankfully, mercifully, he's in.

"Ashe!" His voice sounds far above me. He starts pelting down the stairs. "Oh, thank God, we were so–" He stops. "What's... what's wrong? Is that... is that Nick with you?"

"Yes, it's Nick! He has the pax but he won't die–"

Mi's face pales. "Ashe, no one survives–"

"You don't understand!" I hiss. "Just– help me!"

Mi stops asking questions. He grabs Nick's legs, and together we manoeuvrer him upstairs and onto my bed. It's the closest space, and the one with the most room.

"Ashe!" Ben and Abi appear at my side. I want to hug them, but there's no time–

"I need you to get Julia," I rush, "tell her it's Nick. She needs... the usual stuff. She'll know what that means. And a transfusion kit!"

Both of them nod, saying nothing as they race away.

Mi is stripping Nick of his clothes, examining the blisters with his fingers.

"This is very advanced–"

"It won't kill him!" I insist. "He told me, he's survived it before."

Mi looks sceptical. "That doesn't mean–"

"*Please, Mi!*"

"All... all right. Get me my med kit and some damp towels. We need to cool him down."

I rush off to do as he instructed, while Mi rolls him onto his side. I am gone only a few seconds. The horrible gasps seem to increase in volume the further away I am.

Mi does not look hopeful when I return. "He's not breathing properly..."

"Then help him breathe properly!"

Mi riffles through his equipment while I cover Nick in damp towels, whatever good it does. He convulses underneath them. Desperately, I grab his face. His eyes are wide, but they don't seem to see me.

"Nick, Nick, it's going to be all right. You just need to breathe. You're home, now. Julia is coming. I'm here, I'm here, please... just breathe–"

Nothing. He cannot hear me, or see me, or feel me. He's going. He's slipping away–

Mi plunges something into Nick's chest. There's a sharp *pop* and Nick gasps. The convulsing slows, his breathing gets deeper. His face relaxes. His body is still burning like a twisted lump of iron, but it's better. When I take his hand, he squeezes back.

"I think I can brew up something for the pain," Mi says, exhaling very quickly. "Watch him."

I'm not going anywhere.

When Julia arrives, Nick is unconscious, breathing better but not easily. She's fully kitted out in a hazmat suit, and her visor starts to steam when she sees him. She barely says anything, only asking Mi what has been done already, and then sets to work.

"I was told to bring a transfusion kit?"

I nod. "You need to give him some of our blood. It's helped ease symptoms in the past. It won't cure it, but..."

"I'll do it," Mi volunteers. "I know how much you hate needles."

"And you don't?"

"I'm tougher than you, when it comes to them."

"That's true, but you need to keep your strength up if you're to look after him. Let it be me, Julia."

"If you're sure..."

She sets it up and I lie down on the bed next to him, wincing as she slides the needle into my arm. I can't look. I bite my lip and try to focus on something –anything– else.

Julia holds my hand. "It's all right. It's in now."

"Is he going to be OK?"

"Thanks to you, I think so, yes."

"OK. Good. I'm OK then." I feel like a pathetic child, whimpering over a scraped knee. I want the needle out.

Julia strokes my hand, a feeling, an action, that soothes me down to the bone. Her voice is feather-soft. "Nick really cares for you, you know."

"I do know. I believe he used the word 'besotted'."

Julia smiles.

"I like him too, for the record," I tell her. "I just... I'm just careful."

She nods knowingly. "You've lost someone already."

I nod. "And I haven't quite been able to explain this to Nick. It's... it's complicated."

"Don't... don't hurt him," she says very quietly. "He has endured enough over the years. As I know you have. I know that can sometimes make it... difficult... to let people in."

She's lost someone, I realise. She knows about hurting. She's been through something too. Nick's never mentioned her family. She's alone, apart from the Phoenix crew.

"Julia?"

"Yes?"

"Why are you here?"

"What do you mean?"

"You've not from the slums, are you?"

"What makes you think that?"

"Your accent, partly. It's too soft, too proper. Everyone here speaks roughly, briskly. And you're way too clean."

She laughs at this. "You're quite right."

"But you're not from Luca, either, are you?"

"No. No, I'm not. I grew up in Gardia, to the east."

"Then... what are you doing here?"

Julia swallows. "My penance," is all she says.

CHAPTER 43

Once I'm freed from the needles, I get up and go to sit with Abi and Ben. I fill them in on everything that's happened, apologise for worrying them, and curl up with Ben on the sofa. Mi brings me something to drink. I can hear Nick stirring, talking to Julia, sounding more coherent than he has in days. Suddenly, I feel a bit nervous. It was one thing to be with him in the garage when we were trapped together. This... this feels new.

Abi hands me a hot cloth to clean myself up with, and gives me a thumbs up when I look presentable. Julia passes me at the door and pats my shoulder.

Nick grins at me weakly from the bed.

"Hey," he says. "Hey. How do you feel?"

"Like I got stabbed in the chest. Otherwise... a bit better. Julia says you gave me some of your blood?"

"I did."

"But you hate needles."

"I *detest* needles," I correct him. "Luckily for you, my hatred of needles is just about outweighed by my affection for you. So... so there."

I hang there in the doorway, letting the words sink in. Nick looks up at me, slightly baffled.

"Did you mean what you said? When you rescued me?"

My cheeks suddenly feel very hot. "What part exactly–"

"When you said you were falling for me."

"Oh. Er. Yes. That part."

"Did you think I'd forgotten–"

"It was a while ago–"

"Did you *hope* I'd forgotten?"

"No... yes. A little."

"Did you mean it?"

"Yes."

"Do you still mean it?"

I swallow. "Now more than ever." I turn towards the window, because I can't quite look him in the face right now. "Your grandfather was the one who got us out," I say quietly. "Don't hate me for going to him. I was desperate–"

"I don't think I could ever hate you."

"You don't know the things I've done."

"If you ever want to tell me, I will listen," he says. "And I don't think I'll be as shocked as you think I'll be."

I cannot think of anything to say to this, so I trace lines on the window instead, looking out at the dusky city.

"Why does it matter to you anyway?" Nick asks. "Why are you so concerned with why you're liked?"

"I don't know. I guess part of me is a little baffled that anyone does."

Nick chuckles at this, but registers something in my voice. "Oh wait, you're serious."

"I've never tried hard to get people to like me. In fact, I've done the reverse. Why would anyone like me after that?"

"I've got my reasons."

"But–"

"I know, I know, I don't know you. But I'm enjoying getting to know you. No one knows anyone when they first meet."

Except when you've known that other person your whole life, when you can't remember meeting that other person because they were in every memory you've ever had, when they were in every thought and every moment.

How many years have I wasted on this dream, convincing myself that no one can know me in the way that Gabe did, and so there is no point in letting myself get close to anyone? Or was it a lie I told myself, to protect against the pain of intimacy?

No one will know me in the way that Gabe did, but that doesn't mean I can't show them. That doesn't mean I shouldn't let anyone know me, ever. It is unfair for the shadow of his soul to haunt my future. I knew him, I loved him, and he is gone.

"Ashe?" Nick's brow furrows. "Where did you go?"

I turn back towards him and take a few steps forward. "I... I have to tell you something."

"All... all right."

"Well... I don't have to tell you. I *want* to tell you. I mean, I think I do... I just... I don't know how to..."

"It can't be any more shocking than 'I'm a genetically engineered human being who escaped from a secret government lab.'"

It isn't. It shouldn't be. I don't know why this is so shocking.

"There were five of us," I say quickly, before I lose my nerve. "Five of us in that room. Five of us that escaped. The fifth was Mi's brother, Gabriel. Gabe." I stop briefly, gathering my nerve. "He and I... in the early days, it was just the three of us. I was the eldest, but my earliest memories are of holding his hand in the dark. We didn't quite understand the concept of family or blood then, but we knew we belonged together. Gabe and I... we shared a connection. It was somewhere between telepathy and empathy. We could read each other's emotions like words. It made us a formidable force on the battlefield. No test they could run could explain it, but it felt completely normal to us. I grew up with his voice inside of me, and it was only when he died I knew what it was to be alone. I felt that connection between us snap as keenly as bone."

I look up at him, trying to gauge his thoughts, but his face is unreadable. Instead, he holds out his hand. When I reach out to take it, he pulls me onto the bed and into his arms. It is a warm, beautiful place, difficult to describe. It's hot soup on a cold day, but it smells of summer rain. I am so safe here, even though it is utterly unfamiliar territory.

"He died saving us. He died so that we could escape. I thought a part of me died with him. It felt that way. I thought I would never be happy again." I curl my fingers in Nick's shirt. My hands are trembling with warmth. "I thought *that's it, I will carry this hole inside me until I die.* Nothing could plug it up. I got better, of course. And I never stopped loving the others. I learned not to feel so alone, to know I had them. But it was just them. It was only ever going to be the three of them. Until... until I met you. Nick, I'm..." But then my words fail me again. "I'm... I'm really struggling here."

Nick's fingers interlace with mine. He brings them up to his lips and kisses them. "We can go as slowly as you like," he says softly.

A part of me, in that moment, wants to say *and what if I don't want to go slow?* But I cannot be this bold, not when I'm twitching with such nervous energy. The fox has become the rabbit.

There's also a limit to what Nick can do in his current condition. He probably can't manage more than a kiss and... and I'm still saving that. I burrow down further into his chest.

"Nick?"

"Yes?"

"Please don't die. Like, ever, if you can help it."

I feel his cheeks twitch into a smile. "For you," he whispers, "I will do my very best."

CHAPTER 44

Julia departs back to Phoenix Headquarters to give everyone a watered-down version of the truth, and to let Rudy know that his base is missing a car and all of its emergency credits. The car can probably be recovered. The credits are gone for good. I'm hopeful that he'll understand my need and not judge me, just this once.

It is decided that Nick will stay here with us until he recuperates. He'll be more comfortable at the loft than at the infirmary, and will have superhuman healing blood on tap. Mi, Julia assures us, is more than capable of looking after him. Now that he appears to be out of danger, I am no longer keen to have him removed from my sight, although I put my foot down when Nick slyly asks where I'll be sleeping.

"I'll bunk with Abi!" I say quickly, and fling a towel in Mi's face when he grins.

I set up a bed on the floor, strip down to everything but my underwear, and dump my clothes to soak in a bucket in the kitchen. If I didn't need them, I'd set them on fire. I'd been wearing them for so long they could practically stand on their own. Exhausted, I fall into my makeshift bed. Abi comes in not long after and climbs into her own.

"I'm glad you're home. We were worried there, for a bit."

"I tried to get your attention."

"It worked. Harris and I were already working on how to get you out."

"Henson?"

"He's OK. Doing shifts at the West Gate for a bit. We need to be careful about using him for a while."

I breathe deeply, glad of another weight lifted. "I'm falling for Nick," I say abruptly.

The smallest, slightest laugh slips out of Abi. "And you're worried about this?"

"Terrified. I'm not... I'm not used to letting people in. And I've not felt like this before."

"Not since... Gabe?"

I swallow. "Not since... ever."

"Oh," says Abi slowly, "Well, that does sound scary."

"Yeah."

"It's kinda funny that you can leap off buildings but a little thing like falling in love scares you."

"I know I'll survive leaping off a building... and it's not a little thing."

"Have you told him?"

"Yes. About falling for him... and about Gabe."

Abi nods. "I'm a little jealous of you, you know."

"Of me? Why?"

"Of what you and Nick share."

"You could have that too, one day, Abs. You're still young. If you want it–"

"That's the thing," Abi explains, "I don't want it."

"But, you just said–"

"I want to want it, but I just... I don't. I've never even felt a twinge like that, not for anyone. And I don't think I'm going to."

"Abi–"

"I thought at first that maybe... maybe they made us all that way. It would be convenient, after all, if we weren't going to be distracted by hormonal imbalances etc... but then I remembered the way Gabe used to look at you. And Mi very clearly liked girls. And now you..."

Perhaps she thought that it wouldn't affect us girls, that we'd lost such desire when... when they did that thing to us. I struggle to find the right words to say.

"It's all right," she continues. "It hardly matters. Such a little thing, after all. Still. I should have liked to have known what all the fuss was about. You'll have to tell me."

I smile weakly at her in the dark. "I'll try my best."

◆ ◆ ◆

I sleep in the next morning, somehow shutting out the sounds of everything in my body's stubborn desire to finally have a full night's rest. I'm thankful for it, although I miss Ben going to school. I vow to pick him up later and spend some time with him, just the two of us.

I borrow a top from Abi, who is already gone. It's too small for me but everything else I own is soggy or trapped in my room with Nick, and I remember his reaction to seeing me naked before. He probably couldn't handle such... excitement right now.

Nick is awake; Mi is checking him over. He seems happy with his progress. I poke my head around the door, cradling a bowl of porridge in one hand.

"Mornin'," I say, my mouth filled with oats.

Nick's eyes go as wide as saucers. "Nice outfit."

I shrug. "All my clothes are in here." I tiptoe into the room, put my bowl on top of the dresser, and riffle through my drawers. There's not much to choose from, but they're mine, and they're *clean.*

"You... you're not going to change here, are you?"

"Well, it is my room..."

Nick gulps and turns to Mi, who is checking his pulse. "Are you OK with this?"

Do not ask me how a blind guy and can look at you derisively, but Mi somehow manages it. "She is my sister, this is her room, and I *can't see anything.*"

"Right, yes, forgot. Sorry."

I wink at Nick. "Don't worry, I'll get changed in the bathroom. Could do with a proper soak anyway."

"No, it's fine, you can get changed here–"

"I'm good."

Approximately twenty pans of boiling water and half a bar of soap later, I emerge from the bathroom, scrubbed clean and fresh as a daisy. I attack my hair with a comb, dress in my old clothes, and feel, just for a second, like the goddess of hygiene.

"You're in a good mood," Mi remarks, as I prance into the room. He passes me the porridge I forgot to finish.

"I am clean again!"

"Nothing to do with the strapping young gentleman we've got stashed in your bed?"

"How's Scarlet, Mi?"

"Quite well, thank you."

I was hoping to get a rise out of him, but he doesn't even blush. I pout at him instead.

"How do you know he's strapping?"

"I've felt his arms."

"So have I," I say coyly. "And yes, I'm very happy he's not dying."

"That must have been scary for you."

"Just a bit," I whisper. "I had no idea what I was doing, and I wanted you *so badly...* but I'm home now, and now, at least, everything is fine. It may not last, but..."

"Now is good," Mi finishes.

I nod. This is one of our things. It was awful after Gabe's death, especially for the two of us. It was so hard to be happy. Eventually, we came up with this little saying, whenever we had just a moment of goodness, of not hurting. *Now is good.* The past was awful, the future uncertain, but just for a few moments – when we were all sitting around the table together, or playing some silly game, or watching Abi and Ben draw– life could be worth living.

I feel like I may have a few more of these moments coming, but I don't want to curse them by believing in them too fiercely.

Mi takes my finished bowl from me and washes it up. I go back to Nick's room. He's sitting up in bed, looking quite bright. Someone –Abi, I assume– has found him a book to read.

He smiles at me. "So... this is your bed, huh?"

"That it is."

"I really thought there would be an easier way of getting into it..."

I fight the rising blush and smirk.

"When I go back," he continues, "can I tell all my friends how you dragged me in here and threw me down on the bed?"

"No, you may not," I tell him. "And Mi helped."

"I might leave that part out." He shivers, hugging the blankets closer to him.

"Are you cold?"

"Your place is a little on the chilly side for us mere mortals."

"Huh? Oh yeah, guess it is. We don't tend to feel the cold so much as others... uh, Mi? Nick's cold. How do I warm him up?"

"Crawl into bed with him!" he shouts from the main room.

"I–! You crawl into bed with him!"

"I'm not sure I'm his preferred option."

"For the record," says Nick, "he is not my preferred option."

"Why do you delight in torturing me?" I holler back to Mi.

There is a distinct grin in his voice when he replies. "I've just never seen you so flustered, it's adorable."

"I'm not sure I like being adorable."

"I like you being adorable," says Nick.

"Oh, *fine!*" I drop down on the bed, squirm under the covers, and wrap my arms around him. "Better?"

"*So* much better..."

I smile, burying my face in his back. Nick runs his fingertips across my hands. We stay there for a few moments in complete and perfect silence. It feels like I could press my body into his a little more, and fold into him entirely.

"If you only had five minutes left to live," he asks quietly, "what would you do?"

"Not thinking of shuffling off your mortal coil just yet, are you, Lilywhite?"

"Not presently, no. I'm just curious."

"Grab Ben," I tell him, "and try to make sure he wasn't scared. You?"

"Kiss you, obviously."

At this, I blush furiously, and pull away from him.

"I'm sorry," Nick, flusters, "I didn't mean to–"

"No, no, it's all right, I just wasn't expecting... that."

"I'll put a warning on my flirting, in future."

My lips burn. I am painfully, agonisingly aware of how much I want to kiss him. It seems ridiculous that we haven't yet. But I don't want to kiss him like this, when he's trapped here and a little bit helpless. I want to kiss him when he's fully him and I'm fully me.

I want to know what it feels like.

Right before we put our escape plan in motion, Gabe grabbed me. He placed a hand on my cheek. There was almost nowhere on my body that Gabe had not touched at some point in our lives together, but there was something different about this touch, this look.

"In case we don't make it..." he said softly, and then he placed his lips on mine.

I didn't know what to do. I'd never even *seen* a kiss before. Looking back, I'm surprised that he had any inclination.

It was the most gentle of things, soft as a butterfly, but I stood there as if I'd been hit with a hammer. I was utterly confused.

"I've always wanted to do that," Gabe said.

Then we had to move.

It was the one and only kiss of my entire life. I'd never been curious enough to try it with anyone else, or been willing to risk getting that close to anyone else before. I wonder how many people Nick has kissed...

"How many women have you kissed before?" I ask him.

Nick, who has apparently grown used to my bouts of blunt questioning, barely blinks before replying. "A few," he says, "Never had this much build-up up with the rest of them, though."

"I see," I say tartly. "And... how many women have you been with?"

"Two. One woman on a mission, one girlfriend of about six months. Her name was Allie. It didn't work out, but we're still on friendly terms. No need to be jealous."

"I wasn't... I'm not... I just like knowing–"

"It's all right," he says. "Can I then deduce that you..."

"Am a little inexperienced in that department? Yes. Although..." This next part is difficult. "Gabe kissed me. Once. Right before we escaped. That's all."

I've never told anyone that. The other three were there. Ben was too little to remember, Mi was only just blinded and likely not paying any attention. Abi must remember. But someone seeing a thing is not the same as telling them.

Mi knocks on the door.

"While I'm hesitant to interrupt Ashe actually bonding with another human being for the first time ever," he starts, "our food supplies have been running a little low in your absence..."

Of course they have been. With him taking less shifts at Baz's, me not bringing in any work from Abe, and no hunting, there's precious little to put on the table. I hadn't even thought of that while I was trapped in the city. Foolish, selfish Ashe.

I leap straight up, grabbing my jacket and bow.

"You're going hunting?" Nick frowns.

"No time like the present!"

If I don't go now, I won't be back in time to collect Ben from school, and finding food is always a priority, especially as I daresay I won't be getting any more jobs from Abe again. If he hasn't seen the footage of me in the fire, he will soon. He'll know where my allegiances lie.

I buckle my quiver to my hip, zip up my jacket, and pull on my boots.

Nick turns to Mi. "Is she always like this?"

"Sudden and changeable and dedicated to the well-being of her family? Yes."

"I'll be at least three hours," I say, tumbling out of the door. "Take care, bye!"

Out in the corridor, I hear Nick turn to Mi. "So... are you climbing into my bed now, or..."

"I'll get you a hot water bottle."

CHAPTER 45

It feels good to be out in the wilderness again. The weather is colder now; a crisp air fills my lungs. It's like drinking after being stranded in the desert. I'd wander in further, away from the noise of the city, but I'm conscious of keeping to my time-scale. Instead, I stay closer to the gate, soaking up whatever autumnal rays of sun I can. I'm in the mood to be still, which suits my agenda, so I climb to the top of a rock, ready my bow, and wait for whatever game comes my way. I'm rewarded for my patience with a couple of fat birds and a rabbit. Enough food for a couple of days, with one to use for bartering.

Mission accomplished, I head back to the market and sell the fattest bird. I get a decent price for it, so I purchase some grains. With the winter coming, we need to make sure our stores will last. I've seen many a person starve in winter for lack of preparation. I'm done in just enough time to pick Ben up from school. He's delighted to see me, wrapping his arms around me in a tight squeeze.

"I made Nick a card!" he announces, proudly holding out a flimsy drawing of a clumsy man covered in purple splotches. I really hope his teacher doesn't realise we're harbouring a pax fugitive in our home and has just taken this as the over-active imagination of a child.

"It's very... detailed!" I say. "I'm sure he'll love it."

Nick actually does a very good job of pretending to be delighted by this rather unflattering depiction, and even consents when Ben offers to teach him how to play chess as I pluck the bird for dinner.

Abi comes back late afternoon, with some of Nick's things

from the base. Mi takes over with dinner duties shortly after and tells me to go and sit down with them. They are all piled on the bed, which is covered with brightly-coloured images and panels.

"What are these?" I say, reaching down to grab one.

Nick hastily stuffs a couple of them under the covers. "Uh, nothing!"

"They're Nick's!" Ben declares, brandishing one in my face. "He draws comic books, look!"

The style is very different to Abi's, more block colour and less fine lines, but they're very good. I just can't quite find the words to say so.

"I thought he might appreciate something to do," Abi explains. "Wouldn't want him to get bored."

"I wouldn't get bored," says Nick, glancing at me. He starts coughing suddenly, and I learn forward to steady him. Abi steers Ben out of the room.

"Are you all right?" I ask, "Do you need another transfusion–"

"Mi hooked me up with his when you were out."

"Oh," I say. "I'm sorry, I should have thought before I–"

"It doesn't have to be your blood–"

"I know, I just..." *it kind of feels like it should be.*

"I know how much you hate needles." His hand curls around mine, which is still fixed on his chest. "I don't ever want to make you uncomfortable."

"I don't mind being a bit uncomfortable, if it makes you a bit better."

It would be so easy now, to reach across and close the gap between us. I can almost see it unfolding, feel the steady droop of my eyelids and the pull of his face towards mine. I tingle in anticipation of the warmth–

"Dinner!" says Ben proudly, appearing in the doorway with a tray. "Mi says you can eat in bed, but I'm not allowed to."

"That's because you are messy, and not sick."

"If I ever get sick, can I–"

"Sure, but for now– table."

Ben sighs, and sets the tray down. There are two bowls. "Mi says that you're allowed to eat in here too."

"Fancy that."

"Why are you allowed to–"

"Ben, your dinner will be getting cold."

"M'kay," he says. He glares at me and shuffles off.

I hand Nick a bowl and take another for myself.

"Not quite how I imagined our first date..." Nick admits.

"This is our first? We spent the night in a hotel together!"

A bit of colour rises in Nick's cheeks. "Yeah... that we did. If my cover's not completely blown, I should take you to another, less scary hotel, one day."

"I think I'd like that." I pause. "Is there any chance your cover *isn't* blown?"

Nick shrugs. "Harris could find out for sure. They never properly processed us. I suppose they figured we probably wouldn't have proper ID chips anyway and when they decided what they were going to do with us... what would have been the point?"

My fingers crunch against something underneath the bed sheets. Without even thinking, I pull them out. They're a couple of Nick's drawings, sketches of a girl robed in flame, with gold-green cat eyes. I stare at the image, at this striking, imposing, beautiful *me.*

"They're not my best–" Nick tries to cover them, "I haven't quite got the–"

"The cat eyes don't match the fire bird theme."

"The eyes," Nick says resolutely, "are perfect."

"I'm... I'm not this pretty."

"You are to me."

It sounds stupid and foolish and not at all like me, but I almost feel like crying. I don't care about being beautiful. I've *never* cared how I looked. People did reckless things in pursuit of beauty, and the idea of it always seemed like much more trouble than it was worth.

And yet... and yet I like Nick seeing me this way. I like him thinking I'm beautiful.

Slowly, ever-so-carefully, I lean across and kiss his hot cheek. I am incredibly close to his lips, so near I almost brush them.

"I'd kiss you properly," I say, "but I'm not sure I'd be able to stop."

"What if I don't want you to stop?"

I smirk at you. "You can't handle me right now, *trust me.* Just... eat. Rest. We've got time."

CHAPTER 46

I wake in a bed that's not my own. It's moving. Not a bed, a gurney. I'm belted in and it's moving at speed down a concrete corridor. I want to scream, but I don't. There's no point in struggling. I learned that lesson young.

The gurney slides into a surgical suite. Needles appear in my arms. A mask covers my face.

The Director appears in the observation deck. He smiles at me. "It's for the good of the world, Eve," he says. "Bear it. We are making you stronger. We are making you the best."

What does that even mean?

The lights flicker. Thunder rumbles outside. The scientists pause in their experiments. For a moment, there is blackness.

When the lights come up, Archer, Forrest and Moona are standing beside me, bearing the wounds that killed them.

"We weren't strong enough," they say in unison. "Are you, Ashe? Are you strong enough to free us?"

I am on the floor in my own room, breathing rapidly, half-asleep. The air is sucked from my lungs. I can't breathe.

"Ashe!" Nick appears above me. What's he doing here? Why's he in my bed? "Are you OK?"

I'm not there. I'm here. I'm not there anymore.

My body doesn't seem to understand that, though.

Nick's hand reaches down and strokes my hair. "You're dreaming," he says gently. "You're safe now."

Slowly, my breathing shifts back to normal. "What... what am I doing here?"

Nick's brow wrinkles in confusion. "You... you live here?"

"I meant... what am I doing... in bed with you?"

I assume I was in bed with him, before I fell out of it.

Nick smiles. "You gave me another transfusion and you fell asleep. None of us had the heart to move you."

"Oh."

I stand up, checking myself for any injuries. I've been known to scratch and cut myself during particularly violent nightmares. I appear to be fine in this instance, though.

"I... I didn't hurt you, did I?" I ask Nick. "Sometimes I... lash out a bit."

"No, you just suddenly jerked yourself off the bed..." he pauses. "Does this happen often?"

"Less often than it used to."

It used to be endless. Every night when I slept, I was back at the Institute, fighting to get out. Every night, I heard the bullet that ended the other half of my life. Every night my former comrades, friends, victims haunted me, offering their advice.

Then it was every other night, every few days, once a week.

I've never gone a month without them.

"You could talk to Julia," Nick suggests. "She's really good with things like that."

"I thought doctors just fixed bodies?"

"Good doctors can fix minds. And Julia's the best."

"She's helped you."

"Well, my parents did die in a somewhat traumatic fashion when I was a kid. Not a thing easily brushed off."

I tried not to think too much, what that must have been like for him. To watch your parents die... I had nothing to truly compare it to, but it must have been awful. It would be perfectly right, perfectly normal, not to be either of those things after. But Nick *is* right, he *is* normal. Could Julia really help me achieve something of the same inner peace?

I sit back down on the bed, turning to face him. He brings the blanket up to my shoulders.

"What were your parents like?" I ask.

"You really want to know?"

"I really want to know."

"Well, I told you mum was a doctor. She cared just as much about her patients as Julia, but she was... a lot louder. A lot more blunt. Forceful. She didn't... what was it dad used to say? She didn't 'suffer fools gladly'."

"I like the sound of her."

"She had an immaculate desk but was otherwise incredibly messy, and a terrible singer. Dad used to tease her about it a lot."

"What was he like?"

"Calmer. Quieter. He was a professor of Classics at the university. He spent a lot of time reading to me."

I remember the picture of his mother, but I imagine her animated now, singing around the kitchen as she left a trial of chaos in her wake. Nick's dad would be sitting quietly in the corner, shaking his head and silently smiling. It feels like a nice way to grow up.

"Tell me a story," I ask Nick. "One of your father's."

Nick grins, as if he would like nothing more in the world, and starts to speak.

CHAPTER 47

Nick is bed-bound for almost a week, but improves rapidly under Mi's constant care and the daily transfusions. Within days, his rash is going down, the colour fading from purple to pink. Julia comes in a few days later to swab the scabs to test for infection. He can return to base as soon as he isn't a risk to anyone and looks normal enough not to arouse suspicion.

The day after, Julia returns with the test results and no suit. "You're all clear," she announces. "You can come home as soon as you're ready. I bought a car; I wasn't sure if you'd be up for the walk."

Nick grumbles something about being fighting fit, but he knows after so long in bed, it will take him a while to regain his strength. I elect to go back with them, just to check he gets in safely.

"Is that the only reason?" he asks, while Julia and Abi set about packing up his things.

"Maybe I'm just not ready to see the back of you yet."

"I don't know why. I've got quite the fine backside."

I poke him lightly in the ribs, and help him climb to his feet. He is very unsteady.

"What did you tell the others?" he asks Julia, as we head for the stairs.

"That you were injured in Luca and it was best not to move you."

"Do they know I've been here?"

"Yes. Pilot is particularly distressed."

I sigh. "Is he still sore about that one time I knocked him

unconscious? I could have killed him instead. He knows that right?"

"He knows..."

It would be way easier for me to carry Nick down to the bottom floor, but he's determined to do it with as little help as possible, holding onto the banister. Towards the end, he almost loses his footing, but he reaches out to grab me instead, and I support him all the way to the car. We slide into the back together and he holds my hand tightly.

All too soon, we reach the base.

A small party is waiting in the hanger. Rudy, Harris, Scarlet, Pilot, most of the rest of our team from the rescue mission, and a few more I don't recognise. Nick barely has time to climb out of the car before Scarlet shoots across the room and tackles him into a fierce hug.

"Jeez, Lilywhite, you know how to scare us."

"I know. Sorry. I missed you too."

Pilot nods at him from behind her. "'Sup, asshole?"

"'Sup."

He glares at me, although his glare is overshadowed by Rudy's. The leader crosses the room to shake Nick's hand and welcome him back, but then he turns his attention to me.

"My study, if you please."

I nod curtly, and follow him out.

I had been expecting something from Rudy about my little stunt in the city. If anything, I was surprised he hadn't ordered me back to base earlier. Once in his study, he clicks something on his computer, and a large screen starts playing my newsreel.

"You've made the news again," he says.

"It really was an accident–"

"Those do tend to happen a lot around you."

"Only twice..." *that you know of.*

"I'm not sure you're cut out for stealth."

That's putting it lightly.

"And honestly, I still have my doubts about whether or not

you're cut out for *this*," he gestures wildly, "but Nick trusts you. And you saved him, at great personal risk to yourself."

There is a tightness in my throat that wasn't there a few moments ago. "I couldn't let him die."

"I believe you. I also believe what you told those people: you want to help."

"Yes."

"More importantly," he clicks something else, and other images flash up on screen. Protesters outside of city hall, clamouring for aid to be sent to the slums. Footage of shipments being sent over. Banners of my face. "So does everyone else."

"Oh," is all I can say.

"You've made quite the impression in Luca. Mostly among the people of the lower rings. The government is yet to be swayed. But it's a step forward. A good one."

"So... what would you like me to do next?"

Rudy rubs his chin. "I'm working on an idea," he says cryptically. "Something public. Something that will send a message. I will let you know."

"All right."

He dismisses me with a wave of his hand.

I go to find Nick, but he's currently swamped by friends and it seems rude to interrupt when I've pretty much had him to myself for so long and there's plenty to be getting on with elsewhere. I walk home slowly, wondering what Rudy has in store.

CHAPTER 48

I return to the base the next day, telling anyone who asks it's to see if Rudy has come up with an idea yet, but knowing in my heart it is to see Nick again. Mi and Abi accompany me, although both peel off the moment we arrive.

It doesn't take me long to locate Nick. He's in the mess hall, surrounded by friends, but he gets up as soon as he sees me and follows me into a corner.

"You didn't say goodbye yesterday."

"You looked busy. I didn't want to interrupt."

"Could you just assume next time that I *always* want you to interrupt?"

"Your friends not good company?"

"My friends are excellent company," he says. "I just prefer yours."

"I'm not much of a conversationalist."

"Who says I want your conversation?"

My cheeks prickle, but I take a step forward until we're only a few inches away. Nick backs away, ever so slightly.

"What do you want, then?"

I can see him fighting the urge to swallow. He opens and closes his mouth several times, before finding any words at all. "You," he says. "I just want you."

A group of kids rush out of a room two doors down, pushing through the corridor towards the mess hall. I pull away from Nick to give them enough space to get by. Another moment is lost to us.

"All right..." I sigh, pushing back my hair behind my ear. "How are you feeling?"

"Better. Julia's sorted me out an exercise regime to get me back to fighting fit. I thought I might head there now, actually. Would you come with me?"

I nod. I quite relish the chance of a workout myself, and it probably won't be busy so soon after breakfast. We move briskly, our hands almost touching. I'm just about to push open the door when I register two people in there already, conversing in low voices.

"What is it?" asks Nick.

"There's someone in there."

He checks the board beside the door. "It's not booked out–"

"It's Mi and Scarlet."

Nick grins. "Oh, I see. We probably shouldn't disturb them then."

"Probably not."

"Want to spy on them?"

Spying on Mi is pretty difficult, as he always seems to register your presence. No doubt he already heard us pushing open the door and scuttling away again. If his focus is solely on Scarlet, though...

I nod, and Nick leads me up a narrow set of stairs to a platform above the gym. It's far enough away from the two of them that I can be reasonably assured that Mi won't overhear, as long as we're quiet.

Scarlet hands Mi a long wooden staff. It's not as simple and blockish as some of the practice ones at the side. This is a real weapon, something someone has taken hours to construct. A quarterstaff, like the one he jokingly requested during our last mission.

"I had our carpenter knock it up," she says. "Is it OK?"

Mi runs his hands over the engravings, his face rapturous. "These markings..."

"Feathers, for phoenixes, but also..."

"Wings," Mi finds them. "For the angel Michael."

"Two wings," Scarlet adds, and I realise, in that moment,

he has told her about Gabe. She knows about his brother, and has honoured him in this gift.

"Thank you," whispers Mi, his words far weightier than they should be. He looks like he wants to hug her, but before he plucks up the courage, his thumb falls across a red band at the top of the staff. "Red paint?" he frowns.

Scarlet blushes. "Er, yes, I, um... wait... how do you know it's red?"

"It's called synaesthesia. I feel in colour. It's not necessarily a blind person, or a super-freak person thing."

"I don't think you're a super-freak," Scarlet whispers. "I actually think you're pretty cool. I mean, all of you are amazing, but you..." She bites her lip. "How much... how much can you see?" She arches her neck forward inquisitively, staring into Mi's eyes as if they offer her the answers she seeks.

Mi sighs. "Nothing. I can't see anything– it's all dark."

"I mean, what can you... sense, I guess? I close my eyes and I'm lost. I wouldn't know how to get out of this room. But you... you never seem to bump into anything, not even in the middle of a fight. What do you... experience, instead?"

Mi chews his lip for a minute. "It's a bit hard to describe," he says. "I can't see where anything is; but I can feel it. Like... how you always seem to know where the end of the bed is."

"And what... what can you tell about... me?"

Mi smiles. "I can tell you're really close to me. I know that you're looking at me right now. I know that you're tall, though not as tall as I am, that you're slim, light on your feet. I think you've got short hair, because I never hear it swish when you move."

Slowly, Scarlet reaches out and takes Mi's hand, and drops it at the back of her hair.

"Short," she confirms.

"Soft, fair, almost white." He strokes it between his fingers. "Scarlet?"

"Yes?"

"Can I... touch your face?"

"Yes. Yes of course."

Mi's fingers reach out to touch every one of her features; her eyes, her nose, lips, cheeks, brows. Every curve and line of her. His mouth twitches into a smile. Hers does too.

"Nice to see you, Scarlet."

Scarlet looks like she wants to say something else, but at that moment, she looks up and spots the two of us on the platform. I'd been so concerned with staying quiet, I hadn't thought to hide my visibility. She looks mildly amused to see the two of us.

"Shall we try it out?" she suggests, turning back to Mi.

"What?"

"The staff– want to fight with it?"

"Oh, yes. Sure."

She grabs one of the practice weapons and heads back to join him, both of them getting a lot closer than you need to to fight with quarterstaffs. Nick turns to me, grinning from ear to ear.

"Well, that was adorable. Hope she doesn't kick my butt later for spying on her."

"You're probably safe due to the whole nearly-dying thing."

"You're right. Wonder what else I can get away with..."

We watch the two of them fighting together. They're a good match.

"I want to spar with you." Nick says.

"You serious?"

"Very."

"You are aware that there exists no scenario in which you would beat me, right?"

"I don't know. I'm sure you have an Achilles heel some-where. I'll find your Kryptonite."

I blink at him.

"You've never read a comic book, have you?"

"I know what superheroes are," I reply, "But no."

There's not much of a market for comic books –or any kind of literature– in the slums, although I have fenced a few volumes before. They're a luxury, one most people can't afford.

"I have *got* to show you some."

"So... this is what you do, in your spare time? Read comic books?"

"Mostly. Don't sound so judgemental. You might like them."

"I know I'm going to like beating you."

"I might enjoy that too."

"You want me to beat you up?"

"I want to learn how to fight with you," he explains. "Partly because it'll make me better, but also because I want to learn how to help you. I want to be your ally in a fight, and not have to have you worry about covering me. I want to be an asset."

"You *are* an asset."

"Are you sure? Because you end up coming to my aid, *a lot.*"

"You pulled me out of the warehouse," I insist, "and you stayed for me at the hotel. So I'd say we're about even."

"Does that mean you won't spar with me?"

I chew my lip for a moment. It's not that I don't want to spar with him. It's not that.

"I... I don't fight very well with others," I tell him. "I mean, I taught Ben, and I fought a lot with Abi and Mi growing up, and we're not a bad team, but... but..."

"It's all right."

"Gabe and I were the perfect team. Partly because, you know, we could kind of read each other's minds. I don't want... I don't want to learn how to fight with you, and be always comparing it to *that.* I don't want you to feel inferior because you're not a mind-reading chimera."

Nick smiles. He reaches out and touches my arm. "Ashe, I'm not a mind-reading chimera. And fighting with you isn't going to be like fighting with Gabe. It won't be. It'll be different. I still think we should do it, though. I think we should try."

I swallow. "If you're sure–"

"If you're comfortable, then yes. My manly pride will not be damaged by how soul-crushingly awesome you are. I've kind of come to terms with that."

An echo of a blush rises to my cheeks.

"All right," I say. "Shall we go down and join them?"

CHAPTER 49

Nick is not yet in the best of shape to be sparring with me, but he sets to work on Julia's assignments while I tackle the climbing wall and then spot for Mi. I even have a bit of a spar with Scarlet. She's a good partner. What she lacks in strength, she makes up for in speed and agility. She's no where near our level, but she's impressive. I wouldn't mind having her watch my back in a fight even if it were just the two of us.

I spend most of the day at the Institute. We have lunch in the mess hall, welcomed by the other members. Nick departs for Rudy's office and I converse with Jack, Thor and Odine. I learn a little about their backgrounds. They're all orphans, like so many here, but the twins initially joined with their Dad until he was killed on a mission two years ago. Jack doesn't remember his parents. The base is the only home he knows. His first memory is of one of the older members finding him on the streets and bringing him in for a hot meal. He never left.

A part of me is concerned with the ethics of this –taking in young kids and basically indoctrinating them to the cause– but Jack doesn't seem to mind. "A just cause is a just cause. Not starving to death is an added bonus."

I'm just about to head home –I don't like Ben being alone for too long– when Harris appears at my elbow.

"Rudy wants to see you," he announces.

I nod and follow him into the study. Nick is there, smiling awkwardly. Rudy looks down at me.

"You figured out what you want me to do yet?" I ask.

Rudy nods. "We want you to be the face of Phoenix."

I stand in stunned silence for a moment, sure that I heard him wrong. "What?"

"We want you to do another video, proclaiming who you are –who *we* are– and release it into the city. Luca is close to rioting. We need those fans flamed."

"And you... want me to fan them?"

"The people already know your face. Let them know your story."

"Whatever you're comfortable with," Nick adds.

"It... it isn't safe." I manage. It was dangerous enough saving those people from the fire. This would be like setting a beacon above my roof. *Come and find me, do your worst.*

"It is risky," Harris admits. "Abi has run the numbers. The Institute will realise you're in the slums, if they haven't already. They're likely to try and take you back."

"You can move in here, if you're concerned for your safety," offers Rudy, "but know that you will have our protection anyway."

"There is also a chance, Abi assures me," Harris continues, "that they will decide not to retaliate. That attacking you will just make you a martyr."

"What kind of chance?"

"Sizeable but slim."

"I see."

"You don't have to do anything," Nick assures me. "I know you know that, I just..."

"It's all right. Can I... can I have some time to think? To talk it over with the others?"

Rudy nods solemnly. "I would advise thinking quickly, however. There's no point fanning where there is no flame."

There is not much more I can say to that, so I go to find the others and walk home in contemplative silence. I wait until after dinner to tell them Rudy's idea.

"It's more risky than anything I've done so far," I tell them. "It could have massive implications for all of us."

"Yet... you want to do it?" Mi guesses.

"I... I think I'm tired of living in fear, waiting for them to come and grab us. I want to take a stand. And... and what if this works? What if this is the spark that starts the explosion that brings down Luca's walls? What if no one starves this winter because there's enough food for everyone, and access to medicine? What if this could bring the Institute to its knees?"

"So do it," says Abi.

"Are you sure? The chances are–"

"The chances are that something will change. I think anything's worth that, don't you?"

I lean across the table and tug one of her curls. "I know you were born smarter than me, but would it kill you to pretend you're not, every now and again?"

She smiles, shrugging.

Ben taps my shoulder. "What if they come for us?"

"Then we fight them."

"All of us?"

"All of us. Phoenix has our back."

"I like having a big family," says Ben. He pushes out his chair and comes to sit on my lap. I kiss the top of his head. I know I'm not going to sleep for days after we release this video. I'm going to be far too scared that someone is coming for him.

But I still need to do it.

CHAPTER 50

I do not write the speech alone. Rudy has several things he wants me to include, and Abi and Mi help with the rest. They are largely left out of what we construct, but it is still our story. It would not be right to do it without them.

Once it's written, it takes several days to film. Rudy wants to use footage from the slums behind my words, and then it's up to Harris to painstakingly pull it all together.

"How are we going to release it?" I ask. Harris can probably do it from here, but much like our previous video, it needs to be somewhere public. It won't float around long on the internet otherwise. The Government have ways of getting things like that shut down fast.

"We have an ally in the city now, who is going to help us," Harris explains.

"Can we trust them?"

"I hope so. You met her, actually. She was one of the technicians from the hotel."

I remember her face, barely. She seemed so shocked when she saw the video. Can something so small change a person so much?

But then I think about how much I've changed, and decide to trust her.

A runner is given the video when we're done and takes it the gate to give to Henson, now back on duty there. This is a low-risk exchange.

All the rest of us can do is wait.

"Shall we go for a walk?" I ask Nick.

"What?"

"A walk. I'm no good at waiting."

"Sure."

We head out of the base together from the hanger entrance, along the old road that skirts the wilderness. It's the closest I can get to a semblance of calm.

"How are you feeling?" Nick asks. "Dumb question, I know."

"Nervous," I respond. "I'm not sure what the repercussions will be. I'm... I'm frightened."

"I won't let them take you away."

"Don't."

"I'm sorry?"

"Don't make promises you can't keep. And don't put your life on the line for me. Not ever. You won't be doing me any favours–"

"Ashe–"

"If they ever find me and I wind back in that miserable place, the only thing that will give me any solace is knowing that you and the others are alive and safe somewhere. So if they ever come for me, you keep *them* safe, do you understand?"

"But what about me?"

"What do you mean?"

"What do you think will happen to me if something happens to you?"

"I–"

"Because I will go out of my *freaking mind,* Ashe. You have no idea–"

"Yes," I say quietly, "I do. And I'm sorry if I ever have to put you through that. But please, *please,* protect my family. Protect yourself. I can't survive another loss of this magnitude. I can't–"

"Don't make *me* survive another loss!" Nick yells. "I won't pretend to know that I understand what you and Gabe were to each other, but I've lost people too! I know, *I know,* that your death is the one I will not recover from. You don't think I'm terrified about what will happen next? I wish I was strong enough to protect you. I wish I could convince you to stay here, because every single time you leave the base I wonder if that's the last time I'll ever see you, and it *kills* me. You have no idea–"

"I have no idea? I nearly watched you die! You don't think I know exactly how you feel?"

"Then why won't you–"

"Because I am so, so scared of losing you, that a part of me thinks it would be easier not to let you in any more. But... but it's too late. Don't you see? It's too late!"

Nick stares at me, but I don't have any more words. Instead, I lean forwards and eclipse the gap between us, seizing his face and pulling it down to mine. Our lips collide, and I hang there for several minutes, waiting for the earth to shift apart. But everything is still and impossibly quiet, except for the sound of our hearts, frantically beating against one another like one indivisible creature.

I draw back. My face feels like it's on fire. "Oh," I say breathlessly, "that wasn't... I shouldn't have... I had all these plans! It was supposed to be a happy, cheerful moment, that's why I didn't–"

I am so flustered that I barely feel Nick grab my wrist, barely notice him at all until his face is right next to mine, and he is kissing me again.

"I have no idea what you're talking about," he says when we eventually part.

My whole body is trapped by some strange, warm sensation. I cannot tell my toes from my torso. "I've... I've been thinking about kissing you for a *very* long time, only it never seemed right when you were sick, but at least then we weren't getting angry with one another–"

Nick holds a finger up to my mobile mouth. "Any moment would have been perfect," he insists. "Are you still angry with me?"

"No."

"Me neither." His mouth twists into a smile, and drops to cover mine. His hands glide along my back and I melt into him, drawing my arms around his neck. My flesh is on fire, and I am soaring and falling in the same breathless moment.

I never knew I could feel like this.

We stand there on the old road, underneath the shadows of the trees, until time loses meaning. We could be there for a minute or an hour; I do not know. Seconds, minutes, hours blur into one indivisible unit.

It is Nick that parts first, breathing rapidly. His heart hammers underneath my hand, in my eardrums, under my very skin. *Ba-dum, ba-dum, ba-bum.*

"Worth waiting for?" I ask, as boldly as I can manage.

"Hmm, on a scale of one-to-ten–"

"Are you honestly rating our first kiss? Because I can and will murder you. We're all alone out here. They'd never even hear you scream."

"You are *insane*," Nick laughs, "and incredible, and I think I've spent my entire life missing you."

I hold his hands and lean my head against his, because I know exactly what he means.

CHAPTER 51

We stay outside for some time, saying very little, kissing a lot. There has not yet been a resolution to the don't-put-your-life-on-the-line-for-me request, but I know I cannot ask him again. This is a price we both have to pay.

We walk back to the base hand in hand, only dropping them when we step back into Rudy's study.

"You were gone a while," says Harris slyly. "Also, Nick, there's leaves in your hair."

Nick frantically pats it down.

"And dirt on your butt."

I brush this off, which makes his cheeks redden.

He swallows. "Any news?"

"The package has been received. It's ready to be released on the morning news."

I do not fancy walking through the marketplace when it plays and everyone knows, once and for all, what I am, so I ask Rudy if we can stay for a few days while we analyse the damage. He agrees, and I set off to find the others. Abi elects to go back to grab a few things.

Mi sniffs me as I walk past. "You smell of the outdoors."

"I went for a walk."

"Alone?"

"Not alone, no."

"Are you smiling?"

"Yes, quite a lot, actually."

He grins. "So, that finally happened then."

"Yup."

"I'm happy for you."

"Thanks." I nudge his side. "You next!"

Somebody finds us some spare bunks and bedrolls. We're not together –no one has four spares– and there's a split between boys and girls. There are some exceptions with sibling groups, but Ben decides he's happy to be with Mi and doesn't fight this.

Despite the nervousness of tomorrow hanging over us, it's not an unpleasant evening. After dinner, people play games with one another. Some of the adults and the older ones share a quiet drink. I'm not interested in any of this though, not at the moment. Nick and I sneak off and go to his room.

It's about a quarter of the size of mine and has about four times as much in it. Clothes, bedsheets, boots, weapons, books and comics, pens and paints, great big stacks of paper and crates of slightly-broken equipment, waiting to be fixed. A dresser in the corner is heaped with toiletries, probably from Luca, souvenirs of his missions there. It's tidy but cluttered, with a warmth to it despite the harsh glare of the overhead lights.

"It's not much," Nick says, "but it's home."

"It's certainly cosier than mine," I agree, sitting down on the bed.

"Yeah... how long have you lived there?"

"Five years."

"Wow. Because–"

"It looks like I just moved in. Yes, I know."

"Any reason–"

"Well, I spent the first three years expecting to leave it at any moment."

Nick's face pales.

"Don't worry," I assure him, taking his hand and pulling him down next to me, "I'm a lot less flighty than I used to be."

"No plans to skip town at present?"

"I'm unfortunately becoming rather attached to it."

Nick smiles then, because he knows exactly what I mean by that, and kisses me because of it.

We stay there in his room for a few hours, alternating between talking and kissing. Nick shows me his comic books collections and some of the designs he's drawn for new phoenix graffiti that he hopes to install in Luca once my video goes viral. They're very good.

Eventually, we realise it's getting late. People are sloping along the corridor, back to their dorms.

"I suppose you ought to go," says Nick regretfully. "Wouldn't want the others to notice you're missing. Ben will want you–"

"He's bunking with Mi," I assure him, "but yes, I suppose you're right. Wouldn't want the endless teasing."

Except... I'm not sure I would mind, any more. They're going to have to get used to us... being an us.

"Quite."

I take a reluctant step towards the door, but don't even have time to grasp the handle before Nick strides across the room, wheels me around on the spot and presses me against the door. His mouth comes crashing down on mine with a warmth that ignites a fire in my blood. When a breath escapes me, it comes out as a moan.

"You're making it very difficult to leave."

"That's the point."

I kiss him again, lightly this time, afraid of getting carried away. Somehow, I disentangle myself, whisper goodbye, and slip out into the corridor. It takes me a while to catch my breath. I can still hear Nick on the other side of the room, this warmth spreading through the space between us. His heartbeat pumps in my ears. I have never felt another person's presence so keenly before, not like this. Nick has not just invaded my mind, but poured into my heart and soul and body.

Abi is already installed in her bed for the night when I slip into the dormitory. She smiles knowingly at me when I enter, but says nothing. I lie down in the bunk beside her as others trickle in, too dazed to sleep or even undress. My heart is racing, my mind whirring.

Sleep descends on the room, soft and steady as the stream. A dozen heartbeats throb quietly under their coverlets, a dozen breaths inhale, exhale. The bedsheets rustle. Pipes hum. People still awake move up and down the corridors. The noise amplifies the longer I fixate on it.

I can't sleep. I'm too hot, too full of thoughts. Nick's phantom weight presses against me still. It's seeped into my skin.

Eventually, I give up. I kick back the covers and creep out of the room, back along the corridors to Nick's door. I hover outside, trying to gauge whether or not he's awake. I can make out the sound of pencil on paper; someone is scribbling away.

Nervously, I rap at the door. There's shuffling, and then Nick appears at the threshold, dishevelled and half-dressed in the dim lamplight.

"Ashe," he breathes, "what are you–"

I brush past him into the room. "Can I stay here tonight?"

"Are the dorms not quite to your liking?"

"Hmm, let me think. Shall I spend the night in a room full of strangers with super hearing bound to keep me awake, or shall I bunk with my boyfriend in his private room?"

"Boyfriend?"

"Yeah, you got a problem with that?"

"I have the opposite of a problem with that. It's just going to take some time to adjust. Let's try it. Ahem," he clears his throat. "Hey everyone, this is my amazing superpowered girlfriend Ashe–"

"You don't need to tell everyone I've got superpowers."

"Ok, this is my amazing girlfriend Ashe. She can murder you with her pinky, but that is a totally normal thing to be able to do–"

"Shut up," I say, and kiss him.

"Oh, what do you know, I'm used to it. My girlfriend," he places a hand against my cheek, "Ashe..."

Instead of saying anything more, and before I lose all my nerve altogether, I lean up, take Nick's face in my hands, and pull it towards mine. I am very slow, very gentle, waiting for him to join me. I might be shaking. I'm nervous, terribly nervous.

Then Nick's lips collide with mine and a warmth unlike anything I have ever known spreads through me like wildfire. I am unravelling and wound up all at once.

"Ashe," Nick whispers.

"Don't stop."

CHAPTER 52

I do not know what time it is when we eventually fall asleep. I do not know what time it is when we wake. Time has become a shapeless, liquid thing, that only exists outside of this room.

Nick is stroking the bare skin of my arm, his touch feather-light. Warmth ripples through me. My eyelids open.

"Morning." He grins. His smile reaches the pit of my stomach.

"Morning."

"How do you feel?"

"Different," I admit. "A *good* different, but different nonetheless. How do *you* feel?"

"Like it's just as well you aren't the first woman I've been with, because I needed the warm-up, shall we say."

"So... OK then?"

Nick slips his arm around my waist. "OK is not quite the word I would use," he whispers, grinning at me madly. He reaches across and kisses me.

"What? What is it?"

"I just can't believe that in this awful, crazy, messed up world, I met the one person who made me feel like all of that was worthwhile."

"Nick..."

"I mean it. I'd take a week with you over a lifetime of luxury. You're wonderful and amazing and I never want to be without you."

I cannot find a way to match the weight of his words, so I kiss him instead, as hard and as deeply as I possibly can. I feel like I'm unravelling again, but this time each little thread of me is tightly weaving itself onto Nick. Soon we'll be utterly and irreparably indivisible.

There's a knock on the door.

"Nick?" says Julia. "It's getting a bit late. You've missed breakfast. Are you OK?"

"Uh... yeah! I'm fine—"

"You sound strange—"

"Morning, Julia," I call back shamelessly.

"Oh, Ashe!" Her voice goes very high. A long pause follows. "Would you like breakfast?"

"I'm OK, I'm pretty stuffed already..."

"Uh, oh, well. Quite. Um... have fun. I mean, um, bye!"

Nick is as red as a beetroot when I turn back to him. "You can't say stuff like that to Julia! She's like my... designated adult!"

"You know you're an adult too, right?"

"Yeah but she's... a proper adult! She practically raised me! Would you have said that to my *mum?*"

I have very little clue how regular families interact, so I just shrug. "She seemed cool with it."

"Julia is always cool," he says defensively. "Oh, I'm getting the talk again tonight...""It's nice that you're the embarrassed one for a change."

"I regret ever teasing you." He sighs, sitting up. "We should probably go and... face the music."

I had almost forgotten. The video. It should be live by now.

"Of course." I shuffle out of bed and scurry about, fetching my clothes. Nick stops suddenly. "What?"

"Nothing, there's just a naked Ashe in my room."

"Going to take some getting used to?"

"It will be a steep learning curve, but one I hope to tackle."

I plant a quick kiss on his lips and get dressed hurriedly. We step out into the corridor together and totter along to the mess hall. It's a hive of activity, and the minute we enter, people rush up to greet me. I recognise some —Blue, Chuck, the woman from the armoury– but others are a blur. They all know me.

"Excellent, excellent–"

"Very moving–"

"People are already stirring in the city–"

"This is going to be it, I can tell!"

A shadow falls across us. The crowds close to a murmur. "Good morning," Rudy quietly booms. "Come to the study."

Harris is already there. A screen shows news clips from across the city. There's a whispery energy to every crowd. Something is happening.

"It's already going viral," Harris declares.

"We should send in a few small teams to help in case anything gets violent," Rudy says. "We want to be seen as heroes here, not instigators. We don't want revenge, only equality."

Abi appears in the study. She's dressed for the outside and smells of cold. She's already been out.

"What's it like out there, Abi?"

"Uh, a little chaotic. Some people look a little wary of us. Others have a lot of questions. Ran into Abe. He looks ready to murder. We may have to neutralise him."

I cannot tell if she is joking or not.

Rudy shrugs. "We'll pay him off. Men like him are weasels. Easily bought."

I'm touched Rudy is willing to spend money on our behalf, but Abe makes me uneasy. He *is* easily bought. He probably knows where we live. Anyone with cash could get him to spill, not to mention the other ways of making people talk..

Rudy turns to Nick. "Are your designs ready? I want one in every ring by tonight."

"You're going to the city?" I pipe up before he has the chance to reply.

He nods.

"I should go too–"

Rudy shakes his head. "You'll draw too much attention right now. We want a presence, not a panic."

I don't like the thought of Nick going anywhere without me –is he even recovered enough yet?– but I'm not sure I can dissuade him. It's his own choice, after all.

"I'll be all right," Nick assures me. "Try not to worry–"

"I'm not–" I start, "all right, maybe I am a little bit, but..."

Nick kisses my head, which startles me in full view of Rudy. "It's all right, I'd feel the same if you were going and I don't have superpowers to protect me. But I'll be as careful as I can."

I nod, because I can't think of anything else to say.

"I want you in the first van," Rudy continues. "We're going to have to stagger people going in. Luckily, it looks like we have a few more allies in the city than before... but be careful who you trust."

"Always am."

Rudy squeezes him on the shoulder. "Quickly then!"

I help stack the vans with some of the others, feeling exceptionally useless. Abi is staying behind to monitor things with Harris, but even Mi is going to the city to act as a medic in case things get ugly. He and Nick are on the same team.

"Hey," says Scarlet, appearing beside me, "don't worry, I'll keep an eye on him."

"Nick or Mi?"

"Both," she grins. She looks over at Mi, who is double-checking the medical supplies in the corner.

"You like him, don't you?"

Scarlet's gaze does not waver. "He is rather exceptionally likeable. And stupidly cute."

"I'm glad you like him." I'm glad when anyone likes Mi. And they all usually do. But not like this though. This is new for him. "You should tell him."

"I'd rather like him to get the hint himself..."

Pilot leans out of the driver's seat and hisses something about hurrying up. Before I can even think why, I yank Scarlet into a quick hug. Great, somebody else I care for. Nick, Scarlet... what's next, Pilot?

And it's not just them, is it? I like Julia too. I respect Harris. I grudgingly even respect Rudy. I'm getting to know some of the others here. I'm letting them in, so many of them, and I can't keep them all safe. Some of them are going to hurt me.

But maybe... maybe most of them are worth hurting for.

Nick climbs in last.

"Stay safe," I tell him, and squeeze his hand. If I kiss him now, I'll never let him go.

His eyes stay on me until the door shuts.

CHAPTER 53

I am not good at waiting. I pace restlessly around the facility, exploring rooms I didn't notice before. There's a games room off the mess hall where a lot of others are trying to while away the time. The twins challenge me to a game of what they call "foozball". I cannot tell you who won. Ben enjoys it in here, so I leave him playing with others and go for a walk along the road. I don't have my bow with me, so I can't hunt. I consider going back to the loft to get it, but I don't want to stray too far away from the base in case there's news.

Training in the gym offers some distraction. Other people have had the same idea, and all of them are keen to learn from me and listen to my instruction. Their stamina is much lower than mine though, and within a couple of hours they're all gasping for a break. We hit the showers and then I visit Harris and Abi, hoping for news. Nothing yet.

Eventually, I wander over to Julia's. She has no patients at present and is busying herself re-stocking supplies.

"Need any help with anything, Doc?"

Julia looks up, perhaps hoping I was the one in need of assistance, but says she'd be grateful for the help nonetheless. She summons a huge list of chores that simply must be done, and by the time we've finished I feel like we've re-arranged the entire surgery.

We sit down and she hands me a cup of tea.

"How do you do it?" I ask.

She glances at me over the rim of her cup. "Do what?"

"Stay here and wait, all the time?"

She shrugs. "You get used to it."

"I don't mean to be rude, Doc–"

"Julia," she insists.

"Julia, then. I don't mean to be rude, but you look as anxious as I feel. How can you ever get used to that?"

"I don't have a choice. I can't stop myself from caring about them. And if I could... I wouldn't. Would you?"

I swallow, shaking my head. Life would be easier if I cared less. It would not be better.

My gaze falls on Julia's shelves. They are stuffed with medical textbooks; volumes of anatomy, infectious diseases, medicinal plants, DNA splicing, surgical procedures, physiology, microbiology... there must be hundreds, all well-thumbed and stuffed with post-it notes.

"Quite the collection you've got there."

"Hmm? This is nothing."

"You should lend some to Mi. We don't mind reading for him."

"He's a very keen learner. I think he'll be an excellent doctor one day."

There's such a sincerity to Julia's words, that I can tell she truly believes it. The idea warms me. Mi as a doctor.

A slight creaking of wheels down the corridor. "Harris," I say, just before he appears. He knocks on the already-open door.

"A couple of reports," he says briefly. "Some rioting has occurred. A few civilians injured, none of ours that we know of. No dead. Nick has got his first image up; it's getting a lot of attention."

"Good," I say. "That's... that's good, right?"

Harris nods. "We might not get much more from them. As soon as the images are up and things are calmer, they'll be out." He slides in closer, and pats Julia on the arm. "Try not to worry," he says softly.

He swivels around and moves out.

"Hey, where's my arm pat?" I call out after him. I see him grinning, but he doesn't reply.

I turn back to Julia. "It was nice of him to come and tell us."

She smiles sadly into her cup. "He's always nice."

CHAPTER 54

Somehow, I get through the day. There aren't many other reports. Nothing has gotten too wild, and our teams seem to be controlling the crowds pretty well. This is not reported in the main news, but word is still getting out. Good word.

Night comes, but no one has returned. Rudy has been anticipating this, as the gate is likely to be more tightly controlled, and the riots might flair up again. He urges us all to try and sleep. I tuck Ben into bed, and Abi joins him not long after, citing low-risk numbers and a human need for sleep to function at maximum effectiveness.

I stalk the corridors. Older members sit silently in the mess hall or games room. Julia, Harris and Rudy sit down in engineering, watching the monitors. I could join them, but I don't think I could handle scanning all the images for Mi, Scarlet and Nick, waiting to see them, panicking when I didn't.

I head to Nick's room instead and lie down on the bed. It smells of him. I cannot for the life of you explain *what* he smells of, only that his scent fills the sheets and slides into my bones. It makes me feel safe and warm in a way I'm not sure anything else ever has. I have no intention of sleeping, but I hold the pillow close to me, and somehow, eventually, my eyes begin to droop...

I drift somewhere between waking and sleeping, in some voluminous cavern of distorted, shapeless thoughts and visions. There's a feeling of missing something, of a voice inside a void. The images grow stronger, more solid. I am running through a concrete maze. Someone is calling to me, but I don't want to follow. The light lies behind–

Light cuts into the room and I bolt out of bed, my fists raised for a fight.

"Ashe?" Nick asks groggily, "What are you doing here?"

I stop in my tracks, slowing my breathing. "I, er…" There isn't really any way to put this that isn't super embarrassing. "I kinda… came in here… to, you know… be close to you."

Nick grins, and closes the door. He fumbles for my hand in the dark. I'm glad he doesn't turn on the lights; my cheeks must be glowing something fierce.

"You don't have to be embarrassed about that," he says, kissing my fingers. "Sorry if I woke you. I wasn't expecting you here, is all."

"Don't worry, I'm not about to move in or anything."

"I'm not entirely sure that's the bad thing you're implying it is…"

"Nick," I say softly, "it's too soon for any of that."

"I know," he says, "and let's face it, I'd have to move in with you. You've got far more space and a whole family to think about–"

"You mean that? You'd move in with me?"

"Of course."

"But… you have a family too."

"You kind of have a kid and that takes precedent. Plus there's *more* than enough space for my things. And natural light. And you know… *you*."

I slide my arms around him and pull him to the bed. "Let's have this conversation again in a few months. You might have changed your mind when you realise how messy I am."

"I can cope with mess."

"There will be mud on your bedsheets."

"As long as there's Ashe *in* my bedsheets, I will deal." He kisses my neck, and the kisses quickly descend. We fall together against the mattress, and very quickly I cannot tell where I stop and he begins.

We stay at the base for a few more days while things fan up and sizzle down. The rioting draws to a close, but there's an air of things being different now. Every day, a news story pops up about a new government bill, or a story about a missing family member exiled to the slums, or someone who narrowly escaped being labelled a "non-contributor" and how the boundaries need to change. People are hungry for it.

I quickly give up pretending I'm still sleeping in the dorms and spend every spare moment with Nick. We eat together, spar together, walk together, work together, sleep together and, in one highly amusing incident, even shower together. At some point Ben asks if he's coming back home with us.

"Not yet," Nick's reply is lightning-fast. I kick him under the table. "Hey! Careful! Not all of us are made of diamonds and rubber."

Finally, we decide it's safe enough to go home. If they haven't retaliated by now, they likely aren't planning on it. Perhaps they've decided it isn't worth the potentially bad publicity. I'm nervous still, but I hide it from the others. They're anxious to get back to normal. The definition of normal though, has shifted for me. Normal is being with Nick.

"I'll come to yours tomorrow morning," he assures me, "You can finally take me into the wilderness."

Parting from him is not easy, especially since we are surrounded by others at this point, and even though they all know about us, kissing him in front of everyone else seems...

awkward. Nick has no such qualms, but can clearly see mine. He hugs me instead, and plants a kiss on my forehead.

"Tomorrow," I nod. I take Ben's hand and begin the walk home.

CHAPTER 55

I do not keenly feel the cold, but my bed seems arctic without him, the extra space voluminous and unnecessary. I don't like this, the pang of separation, the feeling of being lost without another person. It's terrifying, it's dangerous. I do not want to be reliant on him. But what other choice do I have?

Morning seems to take forever to come, and I'm jittery all through breakfast. Mi and Abi smile secretly to themselves as Ben makes himself "a bread sandwich" utterly unaware.

Finally, blissfully, I hear footsteps in the corridor. I leap up, grabbing my quiver and bow, and rush out into the corridor, meeting Nick on the stairs. I crush him into the wall and stand there for some time.

"Uh, good morning!" Nick says, when we finally part. He grins sheepishly. "Nice to see you."

"I guess I should have started with that, huh?"

"I have literally zero issues with your current method of greeting," he assures me. "Although, sadly, I once more have to remind you... I'm not unbreakable."

Only now do I realise how roughly I smashed him against the wall. I drop away from him, looking at the ground. "I'm sorry, I didn't think–"

"Hey, it's OK. I'm fine. I'd rather be crushed by you than not be with you at all. Way worse." He comes forward and takes my hand. "There's only one way you could truly break me," he says quietly, "and it's not like that."

I know what he means, but I'm grateful he doesn't spell it out.

◆ ◆ ◆

The first real frost of the year dusts the woodlands. Every surface glitters. There is a strange, quiet beauty to the morning, that each spent breath seems endless. Time stops, expands, grows meaningless. Nick's hand glows warmly in mine, his warmth spilling into me. There is not one bad thing in the world, in this moment. Every dark thing, every worry or concern, every residue of misery... all is swept away. The haunting shadows of my memories are eclipsed by his presence.

"What a strange feeling," I mutter under my breath.

"I'm sorry?"

"I was just... admiring the frost. It's like I'm seeing it for the first time."

Nick smiles, detaching his hand from mine and walking on a little further. "I've never been out here before, you know. This is my first time!"

He does not get very far ahead before I'm beside him again, tugging on his scarf. "Glad I could be *one* of your firsts," I tease.

"Oh, you're first in a lot of ways."

"Go on."

He swings me around in a circle. "Hmm, let's see... first girl I've been with who could crush me between her thighs. Or arms. Or fingers."

"Flatterer."

"First girl who's ever saved my life."

"I do not believe that Scarlet has not saved your life at some point. Or, you know, Julia?"

"Ah, yes, good point, but I have never *been* with them–" he pulls a face at the very thought– "so it does not count."

"What other things I am your first for?"

Nick chews his lip. "So, OK, I'm a bit stumped, but the point is, you are *going* to be my first for a lot of things, so even doing stuff I've done before feels brand new. You know?"

"You're quite literally the first human being I've connected with, so everything's new for me."

"Do you honestly not see yourself and the others as human?"

"Hmm... I'm not really sure."

"Do you think yourself better or worse than us mere mortals?"

"Both. Neither. I don't know. We're just... different." I swallow, sliding my hand over his chest. His heart beats against my palm. "The same in the ways that matter, though."

Nick kisses me. "On that, I think we can agree."

We spend a few more hours in the woods before heading back. I don't catch anything, but I'm not really trying to. This was not the point of today. Today was about showing Nick a piece of my world, so we wander aimlessly about the woodlands, largely hand in hand, with me pointing out areas of interest and Nick being suitably intrigued. We take a break around midday, eat a lunch he's packed for us and drink from a stream. The water is crystal clear and glorious. Everything is glorious today.

I have no desire to return to the slums. It seems infinitely more desirable to stay here with Nick forever, but it is cold and the nights are coming sooner. I can almost see in the dark, but Nick cannot, and the creatures grow more deadly at night.

We arrive back well before evening and decide to stroll into the market to see what's available. It sounds so silly, but even the thought of going to the market with Nick sounds like a lovely idea. A giddiness rises inside me at the very thought of inspecting the wares with his hand in mine. I really am a sap.

The old me would have hated the new me. I don't care.

Screw old Ashe. She's as dead to me as Eve is. New Ashe is where it's at.

"I love your smile," says Nick. "I may not know exactly what's going on inside your head, but it must be a nice thought."

"Wouldn't you like to know?"

"Always."

I link arms with him and stop just short of placing my head against his shoulder. I can hear something. Something... bad.

"Ashe?"

"Something's coming."

Vehicles, several of them, are speeding from the direction of the gate. I tear myself from Nick's side and hurtle up the closest building to get a look. Half a dozen heavily armoured vans are screaming along the tarmac. They'll be hitting the centre in minutes.

CHAPTER 56

The roads scream under the speed of the vehicles.

What can I do? At the very least, I need to delay them– but how to detain six vans at once? If I leap in front of them, one or two will brake... the rest will swerve straight round and continue their assault. Can I knock something across their path? The roads are wide here, no trees. Unless I can topple a building...

But all I have on me is my bow and arrows. Nothing explosive, but the car is speeding so quickly an arrow to the tyre could prove disastrous. Whether or not I can hit it, whether or not the arrow tip can penetrate rubber... that remains to be seen.

I ready my bow.

Before the vehicles have even entered my range, a dozen more come racing into view. Other cars, vans, trucks appear out of nowhere. A dozen snipers spring to life. A small army crawls out of the abandoned buildings on the outskirts.

Phoenix.

The firing starts immediately. One of the vans brakes, skids, and flips onto its side. Soldiers start crawling out, but bullets hail down on them. Another of the vehicles careens into its side, accidentally taking out one of its own. The remaining four split off, two in each direction, but another two are quickly halted and the third slides into my range. A few well-aimed arrows slow it right down, and Phoenix foot-soldiers descend on it. The last vehicle manages to avoid everything and is still tearing towards the centre of the slums.

I jump off the building and straight onto its roof, race towards the passenger window and smash into the seat. I jab the driver in the eyes and seize the steering wheel while he howls in pain, slamming on the handbrake as soon as we're clear and turning it on its side. Not even pausing to catch my breath, I scramble out the window as the soldiers climb out of the back. I reach for my arrows... only to find all of them gone. They must have slipped away from me as I was leaping.

I still have my bow. I smash it into the nearest one's face, then loop it over his head, pulling it against his throat, swinging round him like a pole and kicking the other three. He falls away, but I keep my grip tight on my bow. Two are already back on their feet, winded but wild. Luckily, they're unarmed, or have lost their weapons in the confusion. I stab at them with the end of my bow, then fling it up and deliver a flurry of punches to the gut.

Just as they drop to the floor, something comes flying out of nowhere and knocks me to the ground. A fist comes sailing towards my face. I roll clear of it just in time and twist to my feet.

A girl looks at me. She's my age, perhaps a little younger, almost impossibly fast and strangely familiar. She's dressed in the same combat gear as the rest, but she carries herself differently. A soldier, yes, but stronger than the others. Her movements are perfect.

Her leg swings into a kick. I meet it with the back of my arm, but the hit reverberates through me. I know this pain. I know this strength.

"You're from the Institute," I say. "You don't have to fight me. You can run away. You can be free."

She gives no notion of having heard me and lashes out again, her strikes even more precise and vicious than before. I don't want to fight her, because she knows how to resist my moves. I don't know how to stop her without killing her.

"Don't do this," I ask. "It will not end well for either of us."

She takes no heed.

I let her push me back a few times, getting a sense of her speed, her timings. Her moves are almost robotic. I can count them. I've seen them before. Letting her get a few punches in makes her overconfident. She's sure she's winning. I wait until she's surer, and then dart away from one of her swings at the last minute and somersault over her, twisting mid-air and delivering a punch to the back of her spine.

She topples over with a cry and a sharp crack. Her spine is broken. She lies on the ground like a dying fish, her arms flailing while the rest of her is horribly, horribly still.

We can probably recover from a broken back, but I am not certain.

Blue, and two other people I don't know, appear out of nowhere. They leap onto the semi-conscious soldiers and force them into handcuffs, while I deal with the remaining one. He does not put up much of a fight. Swarms of Phoenix members have flooded the roads. They drag people out of flaming vans, strip them of equipment, detain those still struggling. There are a few dead, many alive. The panic quickly quells.

I see Rudy standing over a row of captured guards, looking very smug.

"What... what's going on here?" I ask.

Rudy's grin widens. "A victory, that's what!" he says, practically cackling.

"But... how?"

"I knew they were bound to retaliate sooner or later. I did think it would be sooner. I've had these vans stationed here for days– there's no other way for them to get into the centre. We've been taking it in shifts."

This explains, at least, why the base seemed so quiet the last few days.

"Sir!" A young scout appears at his side. "We've captured eighteen soldiers alive, sir. Four dead. Three are wounded."

"Have Julia see to the wounded," he instructs. "Do what you can for them in the meantime."

"Very well, sir!" He scurries away.

My eyes turn back to the soldiers before us. "What will you do with these ones?" I ask.

"Take them prisoner, for now. Negotiate their return."

"Useful bargaining chips," I say. "Luca wouldn't do as much. They *didn't* do as much."

"True. Which is why we must. Peace cannot be delivered through violence, after all. Only understanding."

I know that from somewhere. "Emerson?" I hazard a guess.

Rudy looks surprised. "You know it?"

"They had us read it at the Institute. Part of our varied curriculum on the culture of violence."

Rudy scoffs. "Are you sure they were raising you to be a soldier?"

"Believe me," I say, remembering the feeling of Beta's neck snapping underneath my hands, "I'm sure."

Nick arrives at my side, breathless. "We all OK?"

I nod, and he turns to Rudy. "Sorry I missed out on the action, Captain. What can I do now?"

Rudy barks a series of instructions, and we all begin to follow them. The uninjured guards are taken away in trucks. Not, I note, to the base, but some other location that's less important if it becomes compromised. Mi arrives to help the wounded, having heard the chaos from the loft. He is tending to the girl from the Institute. She does not seem to be in any pain, but she's staring at her shoulder with frightening intensity. I wonder if she can move at all.

I crouch down by Mi's side. "Will she live?"

He nods. "She might not walk again."

"She's a chimera."

There is a slight pause. "Then she probably will."

The girl is on her side. At the base of her spine is a horrible, black burn. Where did that come from? Either way, it doesn't seem to be bothering her. Her eyes are glazed and empty.

"Why are you fighting for them?" I ask her. "Why not use this opportunity to escape?"

Her blank eyes briefly circle to me. "Escape from what, to where?"

"Anywhere! Anywhere you could be *free.*"

"Freedom is a lie," she tells me. "Long live the Director, long live the dream!"

Her mouth opens in a wide, almost snake-like fashion, and reaches for her shoulder as if she intends to bite it off. I realise what it happening seconds before it does.

My hand reaches out to stop her, closing around the fabric of her shoulder. I feel the cyanide capsule underneath my palm as her teeth dig into my flesh. I hiss, and a second later she is howling. At first, I think, because I've foiled her plans. Then I see the smoke rising against her skin. The smell of sizzling flesh pervades the air.

"What... what just happened?" Mi blinks, his nostrils flaring. "What's on fire?"

There are plenty of small fires around to blame it on. Maybe a stray spark...

But then why is her mouth and shoulder burned, and my hand fine? And the mark on her back, and the fire in that block...

"I... I think I just burned her..."

"You what?"

I stumble upwards, clutching my hand to my chest. It's burning hot.

"I... I need to get out of here."

"Wait, Ashe–"

But I don't wait. I run away from the others, away from everyone, and try to ignore the fact my fingers are shooting sparks.

CHAPTER 57

I find an abandoned building, far away from people, to shelter in while I calm down. My hand has stopped smoking, stopped sparking. It's still very warm, but that could just be because I'm nervous.

So... I can create fire. With my hands. This is quite possibly the worst ability for me to suddenly develop. Am I to go up in flames every time I lose my temper? What if it's just completely random, and I set fire to my sheets while I sleep?

Inhale, exhale.

I have learnt to control my strength. I have learnt to rein in my senses. I have learnt not to kill people even when they are really, really pissing me off. I can do this. *I can do it.*

Preferably before I actually hurt someone.

I can't hide for too long. People will be worried. I crawl back out of my hiding place and head back. Clean-up is still in effect, even though night has fallen. The prisoners have been shipped off, the vans stripped. Only a few people still remain, clearing the debris off the road.

One of them is Nick.

"Hey," I say, hovering beside him.

He turns to face me, half-relief and half-fear. "Hey... where did you go? Mi said you just ran off–"

"I can set fire to things with my hands."

Nick blinks. "I'm sorry, what?"

"I accidentally burned one of my opponents and... and I think I set fire to that building in Luca. Accidentally."

"You set a building on fire?"

"Accidentally."

"Right." He nods his head, as if this is a perfectly normal piece of information. "Have you ever... heard of this sort of thing before?"

"Back at the Institute, there were a few with... extra abilities. I don't mean like Abi's. I mean genuine, inexplicable... gifts. They usually present themselves a lot earlier than this, though."

They were also often out of control and rarely survived into adulthood. I don't tell him this. Partly because I don't want to worry him, but also partly because I know I am stronger than that.

"What's the trigger?" Nick asks.

"What?"

"What made you set it off? Fear, anger–"

"I wasn't angry," I snap, "and I don't think I was particularly afraid, either. It just... happened."

"And... you're scared it could happen again. And you could hurt people."

I pause. "Yes," I say. "Wouldn't you be?"

"Yes. I would." He thinks for a moment. "What... what do you need me to do?"

"I'm... I'm not sure. Maybe... not be afraid of me?"

Nick takes a step closer. "I think I can say with some certainty, that I will never be afraid of you." He reaches out and touches my arm, only briefly. "What else do you need?"

I need answers, a solution, a safe space, a way of magically gathering up all of my fears and squeezing them into a box, at least for a moment. But most of all, I just need sleep.

"I... I'm tired," I say eventually. "I just want rest."

Nick puts his arm around me, and I have to force myself not to shirk away.

"That I can help with."

We climb into one of the cars and drive to the other side of the slums. Nick radios the base or wherever Mi is, and lets him know I'm safe. He's looking after the injured hostages, including my own victim. I'm too scared to ask about her, and he says nothing about the burns.

Nick takes me to the most fireproof place he can think of at short notice; a deserted swimming pool. It's lain dormant for so long that a tree has started crawling into the building. It has been decades since the pool was used.

I climb down into the empty crater while Nick fetches something from the car. There's not much in the way of combustibles; some leaves, a broken bench, a couple of boxes. There's no way for a fire to spread if I should accidentally set off a spark.

I try to push that thought aside and pull off my jacket. My flesh trembles, and I wait for it to betray me.

Nick returns from the car with an emergency pack of rations and a couple of sleeping bags. I'm still paranoid I'm going to burst into flames at any moment, so he runs around the building, filling every receptacle he can find with water. He places them in a circle around my makeshift bed.

"I'll sleep on the bench up there," he suggests.

"Thank you."

I want him down here with me, and my skin now burns for a very different reason, but I also don't want to set him alight.

What if I never get to touch him again? What if I never stop worrying that I'll lose control and hurt him?

Nick unrolls his own sleeping bag and shuffles into it.

"It'll be OK, Ashe."

Sometimes, when he says it, I believe him.

CHAPTER 58

The next morning, I feel better. Not quite ready to take on the world, but ready at least to tackle this problem. We formulate a plan of action. It would be sensible, of course, to go to Julia. She could run some tests. I reason, however, that she's already performed dozens of them and nothing has suggested I've ever had powers before. Plus, although she could explain them, could she help me control them? No, I want to have a go at figuring this out for myself. I need to go somewhere far away from people, somewhere near water.

"We could try to refill the pool?" Nick suggests.

I shake my head. I'm no Abi, but I theorise a pool this size would probably take days to fill. It would need to be deep enough for me plunge into if I couldn't control the fire. Plus, although this building is deserted, ones nearby aren't. I don't want another incident like at the apartment block. It may have been exacerbated by the gas, but I don't want to risk any lives on the assumption that I can't summon more than a few sparks.

"There's a river, out in the wilderness," I tell him. "It's far out though. We'd be gone all day."

"We've got supplies. We'll take the car as far as we can."

I like that there's no debate as to whether or not he's coming with me, and mere moments later we load ourselves into the vehicle and head towards the old wire gate. We don't get very far on the road before it forks off in the wrong direction, and we abandon it and continue on foot.

It's a good trek towards the stream. The lake might be better, but that's even further in and Nick doesn't move as quickly as I do through rough terrain. Once more, I am conscious of time, how easily the daylight could slip away through our fingers.

We break for lunch after a few hours, but don't rest long. It's a cold day and even I can feel a slight sting in the air. Nick rubs his hands to keep them warm.

"Want to borrow my scarf?"

Nick shakes his head. "Why do you even wear a scarf, if you don't feel the cold?"

I shrug. "Mi made it. He said I should keep warm even if I couldn't feel it. He made them for all of us."

"He's quite the caretaker."

"Hey, what can I say? I'm high maintenance."

Nick smiles at this, and jogs up to my side. He slips his hand into mine. I freeze, but he squeezes my fingers re-assuringly.

"I promise to pull away if you start to spark up, but at the moment, I quite fancy a bit of heat…"

"I wouldn't have to set you on fire for that."

"No," he whispers, "you wouldn't."

He stops in his tracks and pulls me into his arms. His mouth surrounds mine. Warmth spreads through me, a warmth that quickly climbs, dives, soars. His lips explore every inch of mine, and I feel I will explode with sensation. My knees turn to putty. My back crushes against a tree, and I arch against it, feeling like I could fall away to nothingness without it.

Our kisses permeate the air. When we finally part, I can barely breathe.

"Warmer?" I ask him, trying not to look too smug.

"Yes," he grins back. "Happier you're not about to burst into flames if we touch?"

"I could use a little more reassurance…"

Nick is only too happy to oblige, but eventually it's time to move on. We reach the spot not long afterwards.

It's a wide stream, waist-height at the deepest point, next

to a small waterfall. It might be beautiful on another day, but there's a bitter sting in the air that even I register as I take off my boots and extra layers.

Nick tries not to look, but does not do a very good job.

"You really don't feel the cold, huh?"

"Not like regular people."

I wade in half-way, and flex my fingers. Right now, I couldn't feel any *less* like summoning fire. I may not feel the full effects of the cold, but my body reacts nonetheless. My skin shudders and my breath ekes out in icy spurts.

"Is there anything you want me to do?" Nick calls from the bank. "Apart from stand a safe distance away?"

"I don't know," I say, "You could try getting me angry? See if that triggers anything?"

"How would I do that, exactly? Pull your pigtails?"

"You could try being mean to me."

"I'm not that good a liar."

"Really? You can't think of one single thing to rile me up?"

"Your scarf doesn't go with your outfit."

"Outstanding insulting there, Lilywhite."

"Your left buttock is less exquisite than your right."

"Oh, how ever will I contain my anger?"

Funny as the fake insults are, they can't help me. I try to think of other things that make me angry. The Institute, pulling us apart at night, making us fight one another, making me kill Beta... but every angry thought just gives way to fear. It's not fear that triggers it, and it's not quite anger. What's the connection?

I remember feeling... threatened?

"Shoot at me."

Nick blinks at me. "I'm sorry, what?"

"Did you bring a gun?"

"Of *course* I brought a gun–"

"Shoot in my general direction. I want to see if it triggers something."

"But... what if I hit you?"

I raise an incredulous eyebrow.

"You're right, I'm far too good a shot, of course I'll shoot at you."

He takes his weapon out of his backpack, loads it, cocks it, and shoots it. The bullet hits the water several feet away.

"Come on, like that's going to work."

"You're not bulletproof!"

"Don't be a wimp. Closer."

His next shot –his next three– are much closer, but he might as well be firing daisies. I don't feel remotely threatened.

I think about all of the other times it would have been useful to have fire powers, how I could have used it to fight back against my captors. Almost every memory comes spilling back at that single thought. All the times they told me to fight, to kill. Every time they pushed me into another experiment when I was already weak with exhaustion. Every time they dragged Ben away to do something similar, only to throw him back into our room a few hours later, bloody and whimpering.

I could have used it the day we escaped. I could have stopped Gabe from going back. I could have saved him, saved my family from years of heartbreak–

My breath starts to increase. My fists start to shake.

"Ashe–"

But there's more than that, so much more. I am overwhelmed. The memories, the feelings, the confusion... all rushes back with startling clarity. I am there, useless again.

The cold weight of the stream intensifies, the sounds of the wilderness expand. My heart races in my chest. I can hear everything, smell everything, see everything, feel *everything.* This has happened before, lots in my youth, before I learned how to control it. Your already heightened senses inflame; you feel like you are drowning. But it has been years, so many years...

"Ashe!" Nick's voice blazes in my ears.

Flames erupt from the tips of my fingers and spread towards my elbows. My flesh feels like it's being peeled away. I start to scream, and the flames grow further and wilder. I can smell my own flesh singeing–

Nick bolts from the bank and slams me under the water. The pain dissipates immediately. The choking fear remains, even as Nick pulls me back up and into his arms. He whispers soft words that don't quite reach me, and holds me there in the freezing cold while the world slides back to normal.

CHAPTER 59

We walk briskly back to the car, Nick a lot slower than I would like. He is soaked through, and a lot less adapted to the cold than I am. I had some extra layers to pull back on, but he is walking around in ice cold clothes.

I insist on driving us back. Nick is shivering a great deal by this point. He removes his boots in the car, pulls out one of the sleeping bags from the back, and I whack the heating on full.

We race back towards the base.

"You are not a great driver," Nick observes, as I clunkily switch gears.

I snort.

"What?"

"Your grandfather said something similar."

"Finally, something we can agree on."

He leans forward to fiddle with the heating dial, and I see red marks on his wrists.

"I burned you."

Nick shakes his head between shivers. "You burned yourself. I wasn't going to let you burn to death. You'd have done the same for me."

He's right, of course, but that does not make it any easier.

He's still shivering when we arrive back at base, but is reluctant to go to Julia's.

"I'm fine, I just need rest."

"*I* just need rest. The less superhuman amongst us need to see a goddamn doctor."

He sighs. "All right."

I march him down to Julia's, whose eyes widen the minute

she lays eyes on us.

"What on earth happened to you two?"

"We er, went for a walk in the woods," offers Nick, "and er, I fell in a puddle."

"You're both soaked through."

"It was a large puddle."

Julia narrows her eyes. "Clothes off," she insists, drawing a curtain around us. "Both of you. I'll fetch you something warm."

I do as I'm told and strip immediately. Nick is reluctant to do so at first, so I turn my back to give him a medium of privacy. We've barely removed our trappings before Julia returns with fresh clothes.

"Nick, your chest!"

I spin around, and see immediately what Nick was trying to hide; the burns on his arms and torso. They're worse than mine, of course they are, even though he only touched me for a few seconds.

"It's fine," he says quickly, "they're just surface burns. My jacket took most of it."

"But– what happened?" asks Julia.

"It... it was me," I mumble, "I... I did that."

"It wasn't your–"

"No, no, *no*..."

I back out of the curtains, tripping over something, crawling over the floor. I can't believe what I've done. This is worse than the building. He was trying to help me, and I hurt him.

"She can do *what?*" Julia asks incredulously, emerging from behind the curtain. Nick is talking to her, explaining what has happened, but their voices reach me as though through a fog. I feel like I'm losing myself again. I'm dribbling away, unravelling. I'm being torn apart, blown away. This can't be happening again. What's wrong with me?

"She's smoking again," says Nick.

"I'll get a bucket–"

"No, it's fine, she can do this."

Nick is on all floors, the damage covered by a fresh t-shirt. He does not reach out to me, but crouches close by. "Ashe, you're all right."

"But I... I..."

"Just breathe. We're here with you."

I can't. I can't be here with you.

"Don't be afraid–"

I am always afraid.

"I'm not afraid of you. I'm not going anywhere."

Maybe you should.

"Focus. Think of something good."

But there's so little good, anywhere.

I try, anyway. I think of Ben, holding my hand, running in the woods, grinning, laughing. I think of Abi's art, of her sitting cross-legged in the sitting room, lost in some beautiful creation. I think of Mi, singing as he cooks in the kitchen, folding the clothes I could never be bothered to fold myself. I think of all of us, together.

The way Nick smiles at me burns through these other memories. They flitter up and away, like feathers in the wind. Only he remains, the weight of his arms unfurling around me. I am untied from the world, drifting above its cares, but at the same time anchored and immovable.

My breathing returns to normal.

"She's all right," Nick says. "I told you she could do it."

To say Julia looks shocked is an understatement. "Your arms look a bit burned," she says instead. "And... I may have a few questions."

I swallow. "I will answer as best I can."

I tell Julia all I know, which isn't much. Yes, I've only been able to do this recently. No, the Institute has no idea. Yes, I *think* I know what triggers it. No, I don't think I can control it, very much.

I'm worried she'll want to lock me away, that she'll deem me unsafe to be around, but she seems confident that I'm calm enough now. She says that she'd like us both to stay tonight, just for observation, as it's getting late and she still needs to see to Nick's burns and check him over. We both consent, and before long are both safely installed in two of her beds. She sends a runner to let someone know I won't be home again but not to worry.

I didn't even think about how long I'd be gone. What must the others be thinking?

Nick turns over on his side and pretends to fall asleep. His breathing is far too regular for sleep, but I let him pretend. Julia has bandaged him up, but I can still see the gauze bulging under his clothes. It has been a long, long time since I have hurt someone accidentally, and longer still since it was some-one I cared about. Not since I was a child, learning the limits of my strength.

Julia slips back inside our cubicle. "Do you need some-thing for your burns?"

"I'll be healed by morning."

"Do they hurt?"

"I barely feel them."

Julia says nothing, but unwinds a small tub sitting beside Nick and applies a colourless ointment to my exposed skin. "You don't have to suffer, you know."

"Yes, I do," I say, squeezing my eyes tightly shut. "You don't know the things I've done—"

"I have an inkling," Julia whispers, "and regardless, I know that you were made to. That there was no real choice."

"But what about the things I *could* do?" I open my eyes, just briefly, to stare at Nick's back. Is he asleep now? It's difficult to tell. Please, please be asleep. Don't let him hear this.

"Ashe, you're not going to hurt anyone."

"How do you know?"

"I'm hopeful. I saw you today, calming yourself. I know the sort of person you are. *Nick* knows the sort of person you are."

"I'm not sure I do."

The tears start flowing thick and fast down my cheeks, and sobs rise from inside me. Julia sets aside her tub, and levers me into her arms. I am stung by a strange feeling, like a sliver of memory, but at the same time I am almost certain I have never been held this way before. This is the way I hold Ben, almost like... almost like a mother.

I fall asleep in her arms, with her slowly stroking my hair.

CHAPTER 60

It comes as no surprise, I'm sure, that I hate infirmaries almost as much as I hate needles. I'm usually OK with Julia's clinic, with its old books and potted plants and silly drawings, but the smell of antiseptic and the starch white quality of the sheets fool me into thinking I'm somewhere else.

I'm back at the Institute infirmary, undergoing some procedure. There's a small child in the next bed, different from me, but in a way that a nine-year-old can't fully comprehend. His face is partly covered in fur and he has a tail. All the other details are lost to me. He is nothing but another sick child.

The Director comes in and looks at his chart. He sighs and clicks at the nice scientist to join him.

"The odds aren't in this one's favour, alas," he says.

The nice scientist, who had been reading quietly in the corner, gets up. She looks appalled. "He's primed to make a full recovery!"

"We don't have any room for imperfects right now, and the budget needs redistributing. See it done, Dr Rose."

He sweeps out of the room without another look at the child whose death he's just ordered.

Here is what I remember:

The boy looked at me, and in that single glance, I knew he understood what had just been said. I knew he didn't want to die.

He wasn't in the bed in the morning.

The nice doctor was gone a few days later, and none of them were ever kind to us again.

❖ ❖ ❖

When I wake, Mi is standing over me, his arms folded. "Where on earth have you two been and why do you both smell of smoke?" he demands.

"I can set myself on fire. Please don't tell anyone."

"Oh, of course! What a simple explanation! Why didn't I think of it?"

"Mi," says Nick groggily, "has anyone ever told you, you're rather funny?"

"Thanks, it hides the trauma." He turns back to me. "Are you serious? You can set yourself on fire? Because this seems like something I might have noticed before now."

"I'm a late bloomer."

Mi is quiet for a moment. "You burned the chimera girl."

"Is she OK?"

"Burns are looking better, or so I'm told. Julia's not sure about her back. There's not much she can do for her here but it could heal itself."

I chew my lip.

"How... how are you controlling the fire?" he asks.

"I think I just need to stay calm."

"But you're so very bad at that."

I narrow my eyes at him.

"I can feel you glaring at me. Am I about to be set on fire?"

"Don't tempt me."

I am so distracted that I don't register the presence of someone else enter the room until the curtain is wrenched back. Harris is behind it, staring at me with gleeful intensity.

"So," he says, clapping his hands, "Julia tells me you can set yourself on fire?"

CHAPTER 61

"Don't be mad at Julia for telling me," Harris says, as he rolls down an unknown corridor. "She knows I can help."

"To be fair, we didn't tell her *not* to say anything," Nick adds, as I scowl at him. He's right, of course, but that doesn't mean I have to like it.

"Um... where are we going?"

Harris stops in front of a panel in the wall and runs his wrist under a partially obscured ID reader. Something hums into life, and the panel slides back to reveal a small lift. We all cram inside.

Nick looks just as confused as I do when, a few seconds later, we appear on another floor.

"I had no idea another level existed..." he says, as Harris slides out. The corridor is dark and dimly lit. There's a steady drip coming from the end, a smell of rust and metal.

"Rudy and I had this place set up when we first formed the Project," Harris says, rolling down a flimsy ramp. Another door creeps into view, opened by another ID lock. Harris wheels inside. It's a bright, white chamber, harshly lit and divided into two. The second half stands behind a wall of thick glass. There's a sink, toilet and bunk installed. A prison cell.

"We built it to house our enemies, before realising it was too risky to have them on site. I can't guarantee that it's completely fireproof, but we've got sprinklers if you set yourself alight, so Nick won't have to dive heroically into the water."

Nick scratches the back of his neck.

I'm struggling to look Harris in the eyes, but I manage a quiet thank you.

"No problem. Come to us in future, you hear? Don't go off doing risky things by yourself, it makes Julia worry."

Nick looks down at his feet, shame spreading across his cheeks. I suppose I should bear the brunt of that guilt too, as it was my idea. It seems odd though, to have a proper adult worry over me. The thought had never crossed my mind.

Harris heads to a desk in the corner of the room and starts fiddling with some of the equipment there. He hands me something, a small round device.

"No needles this time, promise. It will monitor your vitals. Press it onto your chest."

Nick is all too happy to help me do this.

"You're not going to refuse to master your powers because of one little slight singeing incident, are you?" he asks, his hand still pressed against my chest.

"No, I'm going to train even harder, and show those powers who's boss."

"That's my girl. Wait... can I say that?"

"You may." I kiss him briefly, and my palm slides to his neck, touching the top of the bandages covering his shoulder. My throat tightens. "I'm only going to say it once more, and then I promise I'll stop with the self-punishing... I'm sorry I burned you."

"Oddly enough, you are forgiven. Or should I trade forgiveness for kisses?"

"You drive a hard bargain, Lilywhite." I press my lips against his, hanging there for a little longer than planned.

Harris coughs.

I murmur a quick apology and step into the chamber. I make a big show of it, skipping in there without a whisper of fear. "How incredible would it be to shoot fireballs? Or use them as jets and fly about everywhere?"

"Super-incredible," says Nick without skipping a beat. "You've been reading my comics again, haven't you?"

"Would you still like me if I wasn't a super-powered bad-ass?"

"That depends. Are you still a whip-smart badass with a secret heart of gold?"

"Uh... I'm still whip-smart?"

"Then yes."

"Er, whenever you're ready, Ashe..." Harris taps the dashboard impatiently.

"Right!"

I don't want to concentrate on things that make me angry. I don't want to think about the Institute. I don't want to lose control this time. Instead, I focus my thoughts on battle. I think back to my fight with the girl, the skirmish in the building. It was not anger. It was not even really fear. It was more *you will not hurt me.*

It's a defence mechanism. Of course it would bubble up when I was lost in thoughts, fighting against myself. They're like a hedgehog's spines... like an ostrich, burying its head in the sand to escape.

But I am not prey.

My fingers start to prickle. Heat stretches from the tips. I look down. Both of my hands are twitching, pinpricks of light spark from my flesh.

Harris' voice sounds around me. "Heart rate increasing..."

Smoke begins to rise. I focus on the heat bubbling under my palm. I breathe in and out, slowly, carefully.

A flame darts into life. It looks oddly beautiful, dancing in my palm. I clench my other one tightly shut and focus purely on this light burst, unfurling like a flower in bloom.

I hold it up for the others to see. I'm a child, showing off my latest creation. The flame grows brighter.

"Can you feel anything?" Nick's voice asks.

"Yes, but... it doesn't hurt."

The flame spreads until it covers my whole hand. My flesh begins to tighten.

"OK, it stings a little now..."

"Let us know when you want to stop."

I flex my fingers, trying to will away the pain. Each movement of muscle affects the flames, making them smaller, larger, brighter. Only I can't quite figure out which does which.

The flames leap to my elbow. My shirt catches fire.

"Ah, ah, OK, stop!"

I pat the flames furiously with my free hand, only somehow I seem to draw the fire from my clothes into my palm, and now both hands are alight and my clothes are smoking and—

The sprinklers go off. Nick storms into the room with a bucket, which I plunge both hands into gratefully. We stand there in the shower, me steaming slightly, giggling with nervous energy.

"You all right?" he asks.

"I did it. I turned it on. By myself. Without freaking out."

"Bravo, Ashe," Harris sounds. "Shall we go again? I think I speak for everyone when I say I'm more keen on finding your off button…"

CHAPTER 62

I spend the better part of three days in the basement of Phoenix HQ, learning how to control my powers at a very basic level. I burn through a lot of clothes. I get doused in a lot of water. I use up half of Julia's supply of burn cream, on her insistence.

I only go home twice, mostly for Ben's sake. I spend two nights in Nick's arms, where we conclude that I will not burst into flames in the heat of passion. We keep a bucket by his bedside just in case.

Our beside.

I eventually master turning it on and off. I gain a little headway in learning to control the intensity. Turning it off is the challenge, and I usually find myself making it worse, flapping about like a headless chicken. The training is gruelling, and although there are some moments where I just want to persevere, Harris always forces me to take a break when my heart rate spikes too much.

On the afternoon of the third day, I get so frustrated with my inability to turn it off that I start lashing out. Nick vanishes, presumably finally having found my temper too much for him. This, of course, only makes me angrier. My fists start to burn so wildly that I set off the sprinklers, but I still don't stop. I fill the room with steam, hissing and cussing and sending out sparks, the closest I have been able to come to some kind of fireball.

Nick storms into the chamber, swinging a sword at my head. Without thinking, my hands catch the blade. I hold it fast between my flat palms, which begin to grow hotter and redder. The heat spreads up towards the hilt, until Nick drops it with a clatter. He grins at me.

"You just threw a sword at me!" I seethe.

Nick doesn't stop smiling. "Look at your hands."

I look down. They are completely normal.

"I... I turned it off."

"You did."

"How... how did you know that would work?"

"It's instinctual. You turned it off before, in the building, and when you were fighting that other chimera. When the threat was neutralised, you stopped. You're using the wrong muscles. You have to *think* it away, not feel it."

I pull a face. "Ugh, thinking? Must I?"

Nick picks up the sword. "Admit it, you're slightly impressed."

"Congratulations, Nicholas, you attacked your girlfriend with a sword."

"I helped my super-powered girlfriend unlock her potential. It's OK. You can thank me later."

"I think I preferred you when you were less confident."

"Really?"

"No."

Harris coughs uncomfortably in the corner. "I think that's enough for today," he declares. "Would you mind cleaning up the mess? I'm going to analyse this data upstairs..."

We do as instructed and head up ourselves shortly after. I go to change my clothes, which are less singed than usual, and head to Julia's where I left my jacket. Mi is there, roped in conversation about the lone chimera. Physically, she's showing signs of improvement, but she's barely uttered a word since she was brought in.

"Knock-knock," I say, announcing my presence. "Guess

what? I can now turn my flame *off*! Well, sort of. I'll refrain from giving any demonstrations just yet–"

"Smart," says Mi tartly.

"But it's coming along." I swallow, my mood dropping as it fixes on their faces. "What are we going to do with her?"

Julia shrugs. "Rudy's in talks with the government about returning the guards, but no one's even acknowledging she exists."

I think about her attempts to swallow that pill. "She's supposed to be dead."

"Julia wants to see if... deprogramming is possible."

"It's a lengthy process."

I sigh. I can't get a handle on that girl. There was a nothingness to her eyes, an unfathomable emptiness. She might as well have been a robot. A robot would be easier to crack. What did they do to her in that place, to carve out her soul? Would they have done the same to us?

I hoped, once she got better, once she was treated to a bit of human kindness, she might start to... see things differently. Understand the monsters who made her.

Give us their location.

I don't know where they are. I have a rough idea, a direction, an estimate... but it was five years ago and we were trying to evade. We zigzagged all over the wilderness before making it to Luca.

But now, with my fire powers improving day by day... I want to start formulating a plan for taking it down. I want to stop them before they hollow out any more children and turn them into weapons.

"I want to speak to her," I decide. "As soon as possible."

CHAPTER 63

The hostages are being held in a refurbished building on the edge of the slums. I don't know what it used to be, but it's a blockish, square building, with very few exits and several internal rooms. There's a lot of glass and steel and concrete. Nowhere to hide. Even I would have difficulty escaping some of these rooms. The glass is about eight layers thick, the doors are incredibly solid, and the walls look made of sheer stone. The ceilings look flimsy though; little more than cardboard in places. An old ventilation system? A possible route out.

The chimera girl isn't going anywhere, though. She's strapped to a gurney in re-purposed medical suite, hooked up to a machine. An armed guard is stationed outside the room at all times, just in case she makes a miraculous recovery. She does not look at me when I enter.

I sit down beside her, playing the part of a concerned friend. Would she even know what that looked like, I wonder? If the rest of her unit are like her...

"I'm Ashe," I tell her. "You... you might remember me as Eve, though. You look a little familiar."

"I know who you are," she says, still facing away from me.

"What's your unit?"

"My designation is Foxtrot-5."

"Do you have a name?"

She says nothing.

"I'm going to call you Vixen. If you want to change it at any time, let me know."

I don't expect a response to this, and I don't get one.

"Mi says you're healing nicely. We don't know how long

you'll be out of operation, but it looks like you'll recover. I'm glad. I... I didn't want to hurt you."

I wait for her to ask why I did then, or why I didn't want to.

"You're a great fighter. I'm glad I didn't have to face your leader. I'm not sure I would have won against them."

I don't remember Foxtrot-1. It could be someone else by now anyway.

"Your unit must be much tougher than I remember."

I'm not sure how much longer I can do on like this. Why am I even here? Mi's been treating her for days. He's not got anything from her, and he has the patience of a saint.

"You talked before, about a glorious dream. What dream is that?"

The flicker of a smile rises in the corner of her mouth. "He never told you, did he?" The smile widens. "Great, wonderful *special* Eve. The best of the best. But he never trusted *you* with the dream."

"Maybe I wasn't that special."

She sneers. "Clearly."

"Must be some dream."

"You wouldn't have left if you'd known."

I don't care what the Director's vision is. Whatever his end goal is, I want no part in it. I never did. I want to throttle his girl for even suggesting such a thing. "You've met Mi, right? The guy who's been tirelessly looking after you? Your great Director wanted him killed. I would have torn the world down to make sure that didn't happen. You wouldn't do the same for one of your unit? Mi wouldn't have been the first we lost. They killed our sister because she couldn't control her powers. They let others die because they didn't fit under their stupid made-up rules of strength. I don't care what your dream is. Nothing glorious can come out of such aberration. *Nothing.*"

Vixen fixes me with a look of pure satisfaction. I think I preferred the emptiness. I want to calm down, I want to tell her to spend some more time with Mi, to teach her that there's good here, but I can't. I have to leave the room.

Nick is waiting on the other side of the door.

"How did it–"

"It sucked."

"I just got a message from Harris. There's someone there to see you."

"To see me?" I frown.

"But... I don't know people."

"Trust me. You'll want to see this one."

CHAPTER 64

We speed back to base and straight to Rudy's study. Harris and Rudy are there, as well as Julia. She's conversing in a low voice with a young girl by the desk. She's about my age, blonde, straight and supple as a willow. She has an unearthly look to her eyes, the look of someone older than her years. I know the look. I know her.

"I know you," I say dumbly. "Delta... Delta-1?"

She nods solemnly. "Eve."

"I go by Ashe now."

"So I hear. I go by Sia."

"What... what are you doing here?"

"I want your help."

"Sia's been living in the North for... for some time," Julia explains. "In the woods not far from Auros."

"Not far from the Institute," Sia adds.

"But... but you escaped," I say. "Why... why would you stay anywhere *near* that place?"

"I escaped. My sisters did not."

I remember the Delta team. Three girls, three boys. "Your brothers–"

"Char died trying to get out. Tiny and Dor are back at the woods still."

I don't remember their faces. I couldn't tell you what Tiny or Char's numbers were. But to her, they are Mi, Abi, Ben. Maybe Char was her Gabe. I try to imagine, just for one moment, the awful reality of leaving them behind, and know in that instant what she has spent the last five years doing.

"You've been trying to get them out? All this time?"

She shakes her head sadly. "We gave up, for a while, thinking it hopeless. We tried to move on. We made a good go of it, but we couldn't. About a year ago, we went back, looking for ways to break in. It's a fortress, more so than before. I thought about coming back here and asking for help, but it seemed a big ask. Then I went into Auros' terminal city on a supply run. I saw your video. I hoped... I hoped you could help me."

I don't think of the risks. I don't worry about the odds. All I can think of is Ben, growing up in that dreadful place, all alone. One of the Delta girls was barely older than him. That much I remember.

This is my chance. To rescue the rest of them, and burn the place to the ground.

"I will help you," I tell her.

"We *all* will," adds Nick, not even looking at Rudy.

Harris and Julia both look to their leader. "Captain?"

He nods. "It's a big operation. There's a lot to consider. I may have some requests, ways you can pay us back–"

"Anything," says Sia, "anything at all."

"Go with Harris," he instructs, "tell him everything you know. Get some figures together."

I want to go with her, this girl I barely know. I never knew quite how our groups were assigned. Most of them had an Abi, some a member much younger than the first. Some groups were just hodgepodges, made up of other groups that had lost too many members. In another life, in another snap decision made by some faceless white coat, she could have been my sister.

She files out of the room after Harris, giving me a curt nod as she goes. Julia and Mi go too, leaving only Rudy, Nick and myself.

"Are you all right?" Nick asks.

"I'm... I'm not sure how to feel."

He touches my arm gently.

Rudy speaks up from behind his map table. "Anything you need, let us know."

"Why... why are you doing this? Why are you trusting us? You've never–"

"One of you has clearly won me over," he says shortly, "I'm not sure which. My money's on Mi. He is very useful and by far the best looking of all of you."

"Um..."

"He is way too young for you, dude," says Nick. "Also straight. Also *way* into Scarlet."

"Hmm. Pity."

Rudy sweeps off without another word, leaving Nick and I alone.

"That was... bizarre." I say, staring after him.

"That's Rudy. I told you he would grow on you."

"I am not sure that you did," I reply, "and I am not sure that he has."

Nick smiles. "He likes you. He likes you all, now, but he definitely likes you."

"Really? You're sure?"

"You're like him."

"Six foot six of pure black muscle?"

"A leader. Someone who looks out for others. Someone who *cares.*"

I would maybe admit to being one of those things, but I'm not exactly sure which one. I'm not sure I like the idea of being a leader. I remember learning about the great ones back at the Institute. At the end of one lesson, our instructor asked us to define what one was.

Gabe wrote, *a leader is someone who gets other people killed.*

He wasn't wrong.

"Ashe? Where'd you go there?"

"I... I don't think I want to go back there," I whisper. "I know that's stupid. I know I have to. I always said I'd burn it to the ground, and now I get the chance. But... I still don't want to go. I never, ever wanted to go back to that prison, and I don't want to lead others there."

Nick swallows.

"What? What is it?"

"It's... it's nothing." His gaze drops away, and he turns to Rudy's desk, desperately reshuffling the papers there. "You should go and... prepare. See what the others are doing. I'll come and find you if there are any updates."

"All... all right."

CHAPTER 65

It takes days to formulate any kind of plan. Sia works with Abi and Harris to recreate blue prints from memory and shares what she knows about the current guard rota. Due to several of them still being in our captivity, the number is as low as it has ever been, another reason she wants to strike now.

Despite this, it at first seems to be impenetrable without any actual army, despite Sia's steadfast belief that as soon as we free some of the other chimeras, that's exactly what we'll have. Then I tell her about Adam and Vixen, and *their* steadfast belief in whatever the Director's vision is. She is as shocked as I was.

"My sisters will fight," she says resolutely. "And... and there must be others. You've only seen the ones they *trusted* to let out, after all. If they were all like that, they'd all be government soldiers by now, right?"

I want to agree with her, but we can't leave anything to chance.

"Be that as it may," says Rudy, "we cannot rely on them as an option. Our main goal is to shut down the facility irreparably, and get as many people out as possible. We cannot trust that they will be our allies during an invasion."

Nonetheless, a plan begins to take place. We need to wait until the morning shift changes. That much is always a given. When the guards at the main entrance changeover, myself, Sia, Abi, Dor and Tiny will invade the compound. No one else is fast enough or familiar enough with the location to go with us, but they'll have reinforcements on the outside ready to knock down the fences as soon as there are people to let loose.

Once past the fence, we proceed towards the side entrance of the main building. It is built like a castle, thick, sheer stone walls, virtually impossible to climb and heavily patrolled. Hence the shift change. If we time it right, the doors will open for us. We'll take out the guards as silently as we can and enter the courtyard.

Abi predicts we have less than five minutes before someone notices the guards aren't at their posts, and the alarm is sounded. I groan.

"Why is it always five minutes?"

This receives a few much needed chuckles from the team, although Rudy seems unamused. I guess I haven't won him over as much as I hoped.

At this point, we split. There are two dormitory wings, all of which should be full if we strike when we do. Dor and Abi will go one way, Sia and Tiny the other. They will open the dormitories, take out anyone that tries to stop them, and try to convince as many as possible to come with us. If they go back out into the courtyard at this point, they're probably walking into a death trap. The guards will have undoubtedly been alerted to our presence and will all be up on the battlements, ready to open fire.

This is where I come in.

I will be making my way to the main server room, where all of their data is kept, and blowing it to kingdom come. This mission serves a dual purpose. I will be able to wipe out everything they've ever worked on, hopefully stopping them from ever recreating their hideous experiments ever again. It is also handily located beneath one of the walls of the compound. Blowing it up should bring it crumbling down, allowing everyone to escape to the vans Rudy has positioned at every corner, and cause enough of a disturbance that the guards are more likely to flee for their lives rather than try to attack.

Hopefully. Abi still predicts a high body count, but she also predicts that seventy-percent will make it out alive. A lot of people will be freed.

The morning after the plan is finalised, Sia leaves with Harris and Jameson, to inform Tiny and Dor of the plan and double-check the perimeter. The rest of us are left behind to organise the other vehicles, a task that doesn't take nearly as long as we would like. The rest of the day drags by.

Mi is convinced to stay behind. If anything goes wrong, we don't want to leave Ben completely on his own. Julia is key in convincing him; she's going along for support and doesn't want to leave her practice unmanned. He's to take over... again if anything happens. He tries not to look too pleased that she trusts him with this. Scarlet decides to stay too, which seems to solidify his decision to remain.

The hours tick slowly by.

The Base is oddly quiet. Only a select few know of the mission, but they must be able to sense something from the ones that do. Perhaps they've noticed the number of vans being signed out, or have seen how empty Jenn's armoury has become. Maybe they even spotted Sia, and recognised her from before. Something stirs in the air, thick and palpable. It itches under our collars.

Rudy provides a crate of non-alcoholic beer and sets up a party of sorts in the common room after hours. Everyone involved in the mission is there, all the drivers, all the support, all of us. Some twenty people, all in all. I can name almost everyone.

I wonder how many will be here tomorrow night.

Everyone is surprisingly chatty after a little while. A friendly game of cards is on the go. Someone sets up a couple of darts teams. Nick is very good at this, although Rudy gives him a run for his money.

Someone hands me another bottle. Mi.

"Thanks," I say, taking it to my lips.

"How are you feeling about tomorrow?"

"You already know."

"Perhaps you should say it anyway."

"I... I don't want to go back there," I admit. "I feel like I'm walking into my own tomb. How... how about you?" I will him not to say anything about his fear of being alone, or about how worried he is over our safety. Right now, I don't want to know how much he loves us.

"I feel like it's time to give everyone else the chance we had," he says. "Don't you?"

"Yes." Something almost like a smile rises from within me. "I do."

"Just focus on that. The rest will follow."

He wanders over to sit beside Scarlet, so close they're practically in each other's laps.

It's getting too stuffy in the room, too loud. I wander out of the room, through the mess hall, and into the hanger. I hadn't thought about it before, but my ID chip lets me go more places now. I don't remember it letting me open this door before. Rudy must have raised my level.

I find Abi at the entrance, sitting in the gravel, staring up at the skies. She was never one for big groups of people either.

"Can I join?"

"Stars are for sharing," she replies, immobile as I sit beside her. She picks at the label on her bottle.

"It's a pretty night."

"It will be frosty tomorrow," she says. "Might take us longer to travel, if the roads are slippery."

"Always best to be prepared."

A few more dark, star-filled moments tick by in silence.

"I lied," says Abi abruptly.

"About what?"

"When I said it was best for us to remain in the city. I knew it was dangerous, but I calculated that we could do a lot of good before we got caught. *A lot of good, Ashe.*"

This, I realise, is Abi's goodbye. No *'promise me you'll return'* because she knows the odds. She knows that a promise is a slippery thing, far too hard to hold onto. She just wants me to know that we've done the right thing, that I've done the right thing... even if it's the last thing I do know.

"Do you forgive me?"

I put my hand against her hair. "You are my sister," I tell her, "Nothing you do will ever be unforgivable to me."

"But... I *lied...* I put our family in danger, the one thing you would never do–"

"The world has enough people like me, Abs."

"No, it doesn't."

"Keeping you three safe has been the most important thing to me since we got out. The most important thing to *me*. Just me. But I was selfish, trying to keep you all to myself. I should have shared you with the world long ago."

"Statistically speaking, a similar course of events was likely to play out regardless of when you joined Phoenix–"

"The point is, you were right. We had to do it."

"All right," she says, sounding a little more sure of herself. "Good."

We sit there in the inky darkness for a little while longer, our heads pressed gently together.

CHAPTER 66

Finally, everybody heads to bed under the pretence of getting some sleep. I wonder how many actually will. I don't feel like I will sleep at all. If I do, my dreams will bring the Institute to life, and I'll be running through its corridors all night.

One more sleep, Ashe. One more sleep until it's gone for good.

Nick and I undress and climb under the covers. We huddle there like children, holding hands. "Are you afraid?" he asks.

"Yes." That part of the answer is easy. "But please don't ask me what of."

I am afraid of that place, of the shadows of my past. I am afraid that I've given my memories too much power, that they will swallow me whole.

I am afraid of death, but most of all I am afraid of being without you.

I swear I never used to be so scared, and I understand why the Institute used to encourage us to guard against our emotions. Loving someone is giving life the power to unravel you.

Let me unravel then, I dare it. *Tear me apart. Hollow me out. Only don't let me be without this.*

"All right," Nick whispers. He slides a hand around my back, and we trade a few kisses in the dark. Tears scratch at my eyes, but I refuse to let them fall.

"Ashe?"

"Why? Why did you have to be so perfect?"

Nick pauses. "I... I don't feel perfect. I just–"

"Try to do the right thing. I know. Every day you try to do the right thing. Every day you *succeed* at doing the goddamn right thing. I really wish I'd met you sooner. Then at least I'd have a hope of matching you on the good person front before I die a painful but hopefully not pointless death."

"Don't."

"I'm a realist."

"So am I." He rolls onto his elbows. "I chew food very loudly."

"What?"

"It's one of the things that makes me not a good person. It drives Scarlet mad. I will 100% use the last of something and forget to replace it. I'm not patient with idiots. I'm also a very good liar, which is not a good thing. And... I've killed before, and not regretted it. I've seen it as the right thing to do. You, I think, have regretted every single one."

I am quiet for a moment, remembering their faces. I have not forgotten.

"Don't think I'm perfect just because fate has been slightly kinder to me than you."

"Not much kinder."

Nick shrugs, as if the pain in his past pales compared to mine. Perhaps it does, but I am in no mood to compare. Pain is pain, and I feel his as keenly as I do my own.

"Do... do you believe in that? Fate, I mean?"

"I never used to. I believed your life was what you made it. That it was a fairy tale to believe that some things were just written."

"That's what I believe too. What changed?"

"You," Nick says simply. "I try to explain it, I try to rationalise it, and I come up wanting. It seems impossible that the way I feel for you isn't part of some great, cosmic plan. It's too large to be anything otherwise. I can't fit it into coincidental, fortunate, dumb luck. It won't go. You could tell me the universe had no other plan but you and I meeting, and I would believe it."

I swallow, his words trickling into me. "I don't believe in fate," I tell him. "In fact, I rally against it. I rally against everything that seeks to control me. But I do believe in you."

We slide together, and I kiss him until I feel light-headed, and this great cosmic universe slides into the abyss.

CHAPTER 67

We wake early, long before the others, and lie there in the silence. I try to memorise the sound of his heartbeat, the feeling of his breath against my ear. We do not speak.

Eventually, I hear quiet shuffling along the corridors, the pulling of people from beds, moving along to the mess hall. We join them all there a few minutes later. Mi and Scarlet are there as well, looking like they've barely slept either.

"Are we all ready?" Rudy booms quietly.

There is a silent chorus of nods.

"Then we'll head out."

Everyone shuffles to their feet and moves towards the hanger.

"Wait!" I say, grabbing Mi's arm, "Where's Ben?"

"Fast asleep. It's like four in the morning."

"I didn't say goodbye to him."

I tucked him up last night, of course I did. I let him know Abi and I were going on a mission first thing, and that we would be back late. I told him not to worry, and he didn't seem to.

I said goodnight, but not goodbye.

"Give me two minutes!" I ask, and race back to the dormitories.

Ben is sleeping soundly when I get there, wrapped up snug in his blankets like the baby I used to carry around. I miss him being that little, even though I love seeing him grow into the person he's going to be.

Please, let me see that person.

I don't have the heart to wake him. I lean over and kiss his forehead instead. "Sleep well, my baby."

He murmurs something softly in his sleep, and the words I wanted to say choke me. I brush back his hair and leave the room as silently as I entered.

Rudy glares at me when I arrive back at the hanger. "Are we ready now?"

"Perfectly."

People quickly begin climbing into their assigned vans. Each has at least two people in it, a driver and a support, either medical or technical. Abi, Nick and myself are all travelling in the main one. As we double-check all our equipment is in place, Julia pulls me to the side.

"Ashe?"

"Yeah?"

"Don't... don't try to use your new abilities in there. No matter how desperate you get."

"Don't worry, I'm not an idiot. Not going to risk burning my people down."

"When you get back, we'll find something to help you. I know it might be scary at the moment, but we'll turn it into a gift." She reaches out and touches my cheek. "You really are a firebird."

I blush slightly. "Nick told you about that?"

"He loves you, and he's not very good at hiding it."

Before I can think of anything to say in response to this, she throws her arms around me and pulls me into a brief hug. "Be safe," she whispers, but her words are tight with others.

I climb into the van and buckle myself in. It is only after we start to move that I realise I forgot to say goodbye to Mi.

CHAPTER 68

We hurtle through the slums, out onto the old road, through frost-covered wilderness and countryside. The partition at the front is down and I can see it all unfold as the sun slowly rises.

It is a very quiet journey.

Eventually, Pilot starts to slow. Nick crawls into the front with a paper map, helping him locate the spot they must have picked out with Sia. We crawl to a stop. The other vans pass us, towards their destinations.

A few rations are passed around while we wait for Sia and the others. No one is particularly hungry, but I chew on a couple of crackers just for something to do. I can't stop thinking about forgetting to say goodbye to Mi. We spoke so briefly last night, he was too wrapped up in pretending he could play darts and talking to Scarlet. What if the last thing I said to him was *where's Ben?*

It'll be oddly appropriate. He'll certainly know to look after him. But there were other things I would like to have said.

Goodbye. Take care. I love you.

He knows all of these things, I just wish I'd had the chance to repeat them.

Finally, Sia arrives with Dor and Tiny. Tiny is, of course, massive. He is probably only around fifteen, but he looks like a giant baby, with a large round face and the stature of a titan. Dor is smaller, maybe about thirteen. He looks too young to be doing what we are going to do.

We go through the plan once more and load up. We need to

make sure we're there for the shift changeover.

Nick packs my explosives himself, talking me through the detonation device, where everything needs to go, how far away I need to be.

"This might shock you," I tell him, "but this is not the first time I've blown something up."

"Right. Of course. I know. I'm just... really nervous. There's a lot riding on this."

"I know. Big mission. Lots of people to save."

"I don't... I don't mean like that."

"I think I know that, too."

He pulls the belt around my waist and clips it into place, his hands hanging there for a while longer than they should. Everybody else climbs out.

"I wish I was going with you," he says quietly, his eyes not meeting mine.

"I know," I tell him. "I'd want to go with you, too."

"I wanted to tell you, that day in Rudy's study, when you said... when you said you never wanted to come back here... I wanted to tell you not to. I wanted to say, 'don't go. Let's just... run away' or something. We could make it elsewhere."

"Not a terrible idea."

"It's silly," he continues, "I wanted you to join us because I knew the good you could do, the amazing potential you had. I was as bad as your creators."

"It never felt like that, to me."

"I'd do anything now, to keep you safe. I understand now why you didn't want to fight to begin with. Why risk it, right? No future could be worth it. There's no better world for me without you in it."

"I'm sorry," I whisper.

"For what?"

"For making you feel this way."

At this, Nick smiles weakly. "Somehow, it's still all worth it. I'd take our few weeks together over a lifetime of days without."

I reach out to take his hand, but Nick is already pulling me towards him and onto his mouth. I crawl into his kiss. Every cell of me vibrates, as if longing to rip free of this mortal coil and shackle itself to his. But time does not stop for us, not this time. The moment is slithering away faster than I can hold on.

Someone knocks on the side of the van. Sia.

"We need to move," she says shortly.

Nick and I part, our fingers taking a long time to untangle.

"Keep your comms on," he insists. "It'll be like I'm there with you."

You're always with me.

"And Ashe?"

"Yes?"

His eyes skim past me, as if examining our audience. "I'm really glad you stole those supplies that day."

I nod, trying to laugh. "Me too."

CHAPTER 69

We move swiftly to the spot that Abi has ear-marked, a spot virtually hidden from cameras and out of view from the only entrance. We wait for Abi's signal, and then leap over the wire fence, boosting each other up.

The wide stretch between the fence and the wall is carpeted by frost, but we make our way across it at record speed, stopping at the side entrance. Tiny presses his ear to the door; movement on the other side. We stand back and wait.

Three guards step out into the cold and are immediately dispatched. We pull their unconscious forms to the side, nab their key cards, and set our clocks. We need to move quickly before they are late reporting for duty at the main gate.

We slip into the compound. The main courtyard is deserted, but there are guards on the battlements above us and to the sides. We need to move carefully.

Abi signals for us to split. We nod.

Time to go.

She glances at me as we set off in different directions, and I can read her eyes as keenly as print. *Take care. Good luck. Farewell.*

I use one of the key cards to slide into the main building.

It is the one I know least well. We visited the laboratories a lot, but all I knew of this place was a dark corridor that connected it to the infirmary. It always had a strange quality to the air, a kind of palpable silence, that still reigns now. The quality of light reminds me of skies during a storm.

I always wondered what it held, why it was so large and visited so rarely. What could take up so much space?

I locate the stairs down to the server room, find the door, slide the key card against the pad and step inside.

Lights flicker on.

In the distance, I hear the sound of something brewing, and know that the others have reached the dormitories. But any feeling of relief, elation or excitement does not reach me.

The room is lined with hundreds of tanks, filled with greenish water, and bodies float in each and every one of them.

The attempt I made at breakfast crawls inside my stomach. It takes everything I have to keep it there.

I breathe sharply.

"Ashe? What's happening?" Nick's voice sounds in my ear.

"They... they kept them..."

I know some of these people, these *children.* I don't see any as old as me. I suppose it never takes that long to work out whether or not they were effective. There's Echo-5, killed in a training accident when I was eleven, Delta-3 who lost to Adam... and Beta-2, who lost to me. There's Charlie-6, who couldn't control his senses... and Moona right next to him, her silvery hair floating around her head like a halo, brushing against the puckered mark in her temple.

Even in death, they couldn't rest. Many are scarred, their bodies pulled apart and stapled back together. Still experiments, even now. No sleep for them, no rest.

"Kept who?"

"My friends... my... my siblings..."

Are you here, too? I call out in way I used to, half wanting a reply, half terrified by the thought. There is an answer, but it's not from Gabe.

"Eve."

It's Adam. I know the voice, but I cannot tear myself away from the tanks. I register his presence in the doorway, coming slowly towards me.

"What's going on?"

I ignore him.

"How could you support this place?" I ask my rival instead.

"How could you be *any* part of it?"

Adam just shrugs. "It's my home."

"Really? This place is your home? You don't know the meaning of the word."

Adam smirks.

"Something amusing?"

"I'm just thinking of all the things you don't know the meaning of."

I stare at him, at the same time thinking of Foxtrot-5, Vixen, and her absolute belief in her superiority. *I know something you don't know...*

Adam does not enlighten me further. "Are you here to destroy us?" he asks.

"I'm here to destroy *them.* The monsters who would do a thing like this. You I'm largely indifferent to."

"That hurts."

"We still don't have to do this."

"You're honestly going to try and convince me to run?"

"Just giving you a sporting chance."

"I won't need it."

Adam smiles, and then his fist comes sailing towards me. It hits Moona's tank and fractures the glass. A shudder jolts along my spine. *No, no, leave her be!* I don't know what I'd do if her body came spilling out of that container.

I take a few steps back and jump behind another tank. They're tightly packed, making for poor fighting quarters. There are so many, so many... all stacked like crates in a warehouse. No care, no reverence, no concern that these were once people... that they were once my friends.

I'm sorry, I'm sorry, you'll rest soon, I promise, trying not to look at their faces.

Nick's voice explodes inside my ear, a stream of thoughts and fears.

"Quiet! I need to focus!"

I dart back into the aisle, the one that leads directly to the server room. I could try and make a beeline for it, avoiding this conflict with Adam entirely. If I could just get in and lock the door... I could lay the explosives. I'd still have trouble getting out, but it would be quicker than this–

Adam cuts across my path. A leg swings towards my face, but I smack it away with my arm, holding my ground. Adam goes for another punch. I dart round him, ramming my elbow into his back, pinning his arm behind him and slamming his face against Beta's glass.

"Look at him!" I hiss. "Why would you side with people that would sanctify his murder?"

For a second, I think I've got to him. There's a sudden, sharp silence, but it's quickly followed by a back kick and a punch to the gut. I stumble backwards, Adam taking another swipe at me. He briefly grabs my belt but I scramble away, diving back into the maze of tanks.

"There's a plan, Eve," Adam says, "A purpose. It'll be worth it in the end."

"Don't you get it? Nothing could be worth this!"

I kick out, pushing him back against another tank. *Forrest.*

"What was his name?" I ask. "Beta-2's?"

"That was his name."

"You never gave him another?"

"Not all of us were as sentimental as you."

"Did you love him?"

Adam tilts his head, as if I've spoken in another language.

"I don't know what that word means."

"Then why are you fighting?"

"I don't understand."

"What are you trying to *defend?*"

Adam's confusion is tight in his brows.

"The world, Eve," he says in disbelief. "What else?"

Whatever answer I was expecting, this wasn't it. But I don't have time to question what he means.

"What good is the world without people in it?"

Adam pauses in thought, just long enough for me to emerge from behind a nearby tank and smash my palm against the bottom of his nose. There's a sharp crack. Blood splatters the floor. I do not stop. I twist his arm round his back and ram him against the hard, metallic base of Beta's tank, and keep ramming it until he stops struggling and slides to the floor.

"Ashe! Is everything OK?"

"It's fine. Adam was here. I've dealt with him."

"Things are getting pretty dicey outside. You need to set the explosives quickly."

"I'm on it."

My timer has long since gone off, but we can still win the day if I hurry. I try the key card on the server room door. Nothing. Honestly, I'm surprised it opened this door. I didn't think lowly guards would have that kind of clearance. Harris had equipped me with a device which would open most key card locks –it just took a while to activate– and some back up minor explosives just in case. I start to ready the device, but before I can, the door clicks open of its own accord.

Abi? Has she hacked into the mainframe from somewhere, trying to aid me or our escape? I don't question it. I don't have time to. I step inside the server room as the lights flicker on. Machinery hums all around, and there are no bodies in tanks. The only thing remotely out of place is a large screen at the far end, which starts up seconds after I enter.

"Hello, Eve," the Director's face stares down at me. "We've been expecting you."

Cold dread grips me. Nick somehow registers it too, because he launches into another barrage of questions. I have no choice but to mute him.

"How... how did you know I was coming?"

"You've not been precisely shy about your allegiances of late, Miss Media Sensation. We suspected you might try something like this. All we needed to do was wait."

"I do so hate to disappoint."

His smile widens. "Tell me, my dear... do you remember me?"

"You're the Director."

"Ah, you remember! I'm so pleased you do."

"It's difficult to forget the face of your torturer, but I did give it my best shot."

"Torturer?" he tuts, wagging his finger. "Oh, come now, Eve. I may have been a bit strict with you, but that's just the kind of guardian I am. It's a tough world. You needed to be prepared."

"Guardian?" I sneer.

"Yes, I won't say 'father'. That *is* too personal. I didn't see to any of the more day-to-day tasks of raising you. But I *did* guide you. Your education, your schooling, your training–"

"I killed because of you. You made me into a *killer.*"

"I made you strong. Even your years outside of this place haven't weakened you in any way. You've been strengthened by the fire, exceeding our every expectation, our every hope. Not everyone thought you would flourish, you know, in those early years, but I never lost hope. I knew you were the one. You have no idea, Eve, of your true potential. Your true purpose."

"Could you just shut up already, or do I have to make you?"

He laughs. "Were you always so... *snarky?*"

"Yeah, but now I get to say it all out loud without being *beaten.*"

"Aren't you even remotely curious? Don't you want to know what you were designed for?"

Cold hard rage bubbles inside me. "Let me make this clear: human beings are not designed. I don't care that you made us. I don't care what your plans are. *I* am the only one that gets to decide what my purpose is."

"Ah," says the Director calmly, "that, my dear, is where I'm afraid you're wrong."

I register a presence behind me, and turn just in time to see Adam by the door before it snaps shut. He was holding a detonator. My hands fly immediately to where mine should be, but it is not there. The fight... the fight was a ruse. It was there only to stop me. I am a rabbit in a snare.

No.

"I'm sorry, Eve, but we can't let you escape again. We have too much work to do together."

"No!"

"Don't be afraid. It's all for the greater good. You'll see that soon."

"The greater good?" I almost want to laugh. "Do you keep the bodies of my friends out there for *the greater good?*"

"They have proved most useful to our research–"

"Do you think I care if they were *useful* to you? They were my friends! They were invaluable to me!"

"They would have slowed you down."

"I would have carried them! I would have been happy to. I would have done anything for them and they would have done the same for me!"

The Director smiles. "You truly are remarkable, Eve. You have so much potential."

"Oh, shut up."

I need to think. I can't be trapped here. I can't let them take me back, or Abi, or Sia or any of the others. I can't let there be any more bodies in tanks.

But what can I do, without the detonator?

I bite my hand in frustration. The flesh is warm. My fingers tingle. When I pull them away, they're shaking slightly.

The explosives are still on my belt. I don't need a detonator.

The Director sees me staring.

"Eve?" he asks. "What are you doing?"

"Ending this."

I cross over to his screen and wrench it off the wall. His face will not be the last thing I see.

I lay the explosives, as quickly as I can, trying not to think about what comes next. How many will be spared if I do this? How many will be *saved?*

My choice. My decision. My destiny.

My death.

But maybe one of the people I save will return with the others. Maybe they'll join Phoenix, and be the hero I never could be.

Or maybe they won't, maybe all that will rise from these ashes is a few more scared kids, desperately trying to make their way in this broken world.

But a world a little freer for my sacrifice.

I close my eyes. I think of Mi, Abi, Ben... Nick. *Be safe. Be happy where you can. Be free always.*

There's one thing I must do first. I turn my comms back on.

"Ashe? Talk to me. What's happened?"

"Are the others still safe?"

"Hanging in there, yes."

"Good. That's good. I'm setting off the explosives."

"Is... is everything OK? You... you sound strange."

"I'm sorry, Nick," I whisper. "I have to do this."

"Do what?"

"Free them."

"Where are you?"

"Keep talking," I beg him, "when you speak, I'm home."

Just a few more seconds, just a few more moments, just a little longer with him.

"Ashe, what are you–"

"Thank you for making me join Phoenix," I swallow. "I don't regret it. Not a single thing. I hope I did good."

"You're... Ashe, please–"

"Tell the others I love them. They... should know by now, but it never hurts to say it again." The words catch in my throat. "And... and I love you," I manage. "More than I ever thought I could love anyone. You... you asked me once what I'd do if I had five minutes left to live. I'm not sure I have five more minutes... but if I did, they'd be yours. I would have shared my life with you. Goodbye, Nick."

I turn off the comm and sit down by one of the explosives. *Let it be quick. Let there be nothing left of me to mess with.*

I click my hands together, praying for the sparks to come. I think of everything that I will lose if I can't make this work. My family, my fellow captives, myself.

I will not be your weapon.

My hands begin to smoke.

In the end, I do not want my life to flash before my eyes. All I want is one final memory. I am in Nick's arms, the first night we were together. His heartbeat joins with mine.

"I love you," I whisper to myself, and then the room explodes into flames.

———————————

EPILOGUE

My name was Eve. It was the name that was assigned to me, the day I was born. I was the first "success". You can judge for yourselves what the ones that came before were like.

I was raised to be a soldier, a weapon. I was taught how to fight, how to hunt, how to kill. And I hated almost every moment. I only knew peace when I was alone with my comrades. My family.

When I was thirteen, my brother-in-arms was wounded in an accident. There was no room at the Institute for those considered burdens, much like in your "great" city. So, we escaped. We lost one of our own in the process. I lost a part of myself.

When I arrived in Luca, I gave myself a new name; Ashe. In my mind, it meant, 'she who rises' but for years, I didn't rise. I hid. I didn't want to fight. I wanted to be the opposite of what they made me, and I'm doing that now. I am still fighting, but for a different reason. I am fighting for others. I am fighting to save lives. I am fighting for a tomorrow that is perfect for everyone, a society where everyone can thrive and value isn't assigned.

I'm asking you to fight with me. I have been in the dark most of my life. Don't let others know what it's like to live in a prison. Look down at your feet– can you see shackles? I can hear everything. I can hear the rattling of the chains that contain us, and the chains that bind us all as one.

Break free. Fight with me. None of us were born to live in cages.

I flitter in and out of the light, treading water. I am weightless and heavy, made up and undone. I do not know where I am, but it is peaceful. My thoughts disturb me as little as tears in the rain. I am washing away.

In, out, darkness, light.

I drift in this void, far beyond the reach of senses. Time turns shapeless once more.

I must be dead. Somehow, I don't mind so much. It is a little lonely, though.

Eve.

Of course. Of course you're here. *Hello. I've missed you.*

I try to open my eyes. The light burns me. I jerk involuntarily, and my body collides against something cool and hard. Glass.

Something is fastened around my face. My throat is tight with it. Some kind of breathing machine? My chest feels like lead...

I'm... I'm not dead.

A face behind the glass. A hand reaching up to mine.

Mi? Oh no, they've found you. They've dragged you back–

But as the murky water clears, the face sharpens. Two perfect, gold-green eyes rise to lock with mine. It is not Mi. It is not possible.

I reach out to touch him nonetheless.

Gabe.

ACKNOWLEDGEMENTS

My first book, I did entirely by myself. The moral of this story is not to.

For this one, I owe thanks to so many people, namely to the delicious Writing Community of Twitter for their invaluable insights. Particular thanks go to Lou, Kira and A, for helping me with Abi's asexuality, and to Hunter, Zed and RL, for fielding my questions about what it was like to live with a disability. Your insight was invaluable and I hope I've done the characters affected justice.

As always, thanks has to go to my sister Kirsty, who remains an excellent person to bounce ideas off, and whose honesty and sensitivity constantly amazes me. Aren't you still, like, twelve? Also thanks to your other half Kieran, for suggesting "Nemean" as the title of the drug that plays a much more prominent role in book II.

Thank you to Alice Wicker, who reads as fast as Ashe runs, and convinced me this book was a lot better than I thought it was! You are a fantastic human being and I promise you first look at the sequel.

A group thank you to my fabulous friends, particularly the ones I bored with the tale during Fake Christmas. Special thanks to Abbie Jones, for watching my toddler when I was desperate to finish off the first draft. You are truly all spectacular human beings.

Thank you my father, a certifiable ex-military bad ass, who fielded a lot of questions about choke holds, smoke grenades and explosives. I have lived a very successful life thinking, "hmm, what would Dad do?" and then doing the exact opposite, but it was fun to write Ashe, who approaches things... differently.

Finally, to Demri, the most glorious stranger on the internet I have ever met. Your comments were absolute gems. I could have done it without you, but thank god I didn't. The book is so much better for it, and I cannot thank you enough.

ABOUT THE AUTHOR

Katherine Macdonald

Born and raised in Redditch, Worcester-shire, to a couple of kick-ass parents, Katherine "Kate" Macdonald often be-moaned the fact that she would never be a successful author as "the key to good writing is an unhappy childhood".

Since her youth, Macdonald has always been a storyteller, inventing fantastic-ally long and complicated tales to enter-tain her younger sister with on long drives. Some of these were written down, and others have been lost to the ethers of time somewhere along the A303.

With a degree in creative writing and six years of teaching English under her belt, Macdonald thinks there's a slight pos-sibility she might actually be able to write. She may be very wrong.

She lives in Kent with her manic little crotch goblin and two cats: Admiral Roe and Captain Haddock.

"The Phoenix Project" is her second novel. You can follow her at @KateMacAuthor or check out her website https://ka-temac89.wixsite.com/katemacauthor for updates on the se-quel and other projects.

BOOKS BY THIS AUTHOR

The Rose And The Thorn: A Beauty And The Beast Retelling

Taking shelter from a storm, Rose accidentally strays into a deserted fairy realm, and finds herself trapped there with only a mysterious talking beast for company. Although initially reluctant to befriend her strange companion, Rose quickly finds herself growing closer to him. She names him Thorn, and as the castle blossoms into a place of beauty, so too does their friendship. But something else lurks within the walls, a dark force that will stop at nothing to be free once more...

If Rose is to survive and lift the curse placed upon the castle, she will have to face her fears and conquer the nightmares that have haunted her since childhood, as well as confront the terrifying creature that stalks the shadows in the night.

KATHERINE MACDONALD

The
Rose
& THE
THORN

A classic tale of romance, adventure, mystery and magic.

A BEAUTY AND THE BEAST RETELLING

Printed in Poland
by Amazon Fulfillment
Poland Sp. z o.o., Wrocław